In a Thousand Years

In a Thousand Years

by
Emile Calvet

translated, annotated and introduced by
Brian Stableford

A Black Coat Press Book

ISBN 978-1-61227-192-7. First Printing. July 2013. Published by Black Coat Press, an imprint of Hollywood Comics.com, LLC, P.O. Box 17270, Encino, CA 91416. All rights reserved. Except for review purposes, no part of this book may be reproduced or transmitted in any form or by any means, electronic or mechanical, including photocopying, recording, or by any information storage and retrieval system, without permission in writing from the publisher. The stories and characters depicted in this novel are entirely fictional. Printed in the United States of America.

Introduction

Dans Mille Ans, signed E. Calvet, here translated as *In a Thousand Years*, was published in a handsome illustrated edition in Paris by Librairie Ch. Delagrave in 1884, having been serialized the previous year in the venerable *Musée des Familles*, where the author's name was given in full as Émile Calvet. That seems to be the sum of what is known of the author, who is highly unlikely, on chronological grounds, to have been responsible for any of the handful of other works signed "E. Calvet" or "Émile Calvet" listed in the catalogue of the Bibliothèque Nationale or recorded in Google Books. It is entirely possible that the signature is a pseudonym, but whether it was the author's real name or not, it seems not unlikely that *Dans mille ans* was his one and only publication, as the text exhibits numerous indications of inexperience.

Anything deduced about the author from the contents of the novel must, of course, remain purely conjectural, but the evidence strongly suggests that he was a Parisian schoolmaster specializing in the teaching of the physical sciences. Although *Dans mille ans* is set solidly in the tradition of "euchronian" fiction founded more than a hundred years earlier by Louis Sébastien Mercier's *L'An deux mille quatre cent quarante* (1771; tr. as *Memoirs of the Year Two Thousand Five Hundred*) it stands at the opposite end of a utopian spectrum that extends from works whose primary consideration is political reform to those whose primary concern is technological advancement. Like Mercier, Calvet agrees with the late 18th century philosophers of progress Ann-Robert-Jacques Turgot and the Marquis de Condorcet that the two kinds of progress go hand in hand—a supposition that had been treated with increasing skepticism during the long interim separating the works of the two novelists—but Calvet takes the view that if the technological problems restricting the adequate supply of

human needs can be solved, then political problems of distribution and social order will simply sort themselves out,
through the medium of efficient universal education.

The latter view probably seemed a trifle naïve even in
1883, and is bound to seem much more so now that so many
of the technological advances anticipated by Calvet have been
made without any conspicuous social development in the direction of consensual liberty, equality and fraternity, but that
does not detract from the fact that Calvet's work provides the
clearest and most extreme example of a particular train of
thought, developed with as much conscience as determination.
Indeed, seen from the viewpoint of the early 21st century,
Calvet's text is a truly remarkable combination of innocence
and ingenuity, unparalleled at the time and perhaps since.

It is important to remember, in reading the text today,
how closely the novel followed on the heels of the key inventions that it extrapolates. The telephone had been patented in
1876, the phonograph in 1877 and Joseph Swan's electric incandescent lamp—the first genuinely practical one—in 1880.
The first electric power network, producing 110 volts of direct
current, had been developed in 1882 to supply a mere 59 clients. The steam-turbine that would provide the basis for efficient electric power generation had not yet been invented. Hydrogen had not yet been liquefied, and experimentally useful
quantities of liquid oxygen were only produced for the first
time in 1883, the year of the novel's publication. The problem
of steering aerostats was still painfully unsolved, in spite of
long effort, as was the problem of heavier-than-air flight.
Heinrich Hertz had not yet demonstrated the existence of the
electromagnetic waves that would eventually give birth to
wireless telegraphy, and it would have been exceedingly remarkable had any such notion been on Calvet's "intellectual
radar."

Given that timetable, Calvet's notion of a world transformed by prolifically-distributed electric power and aerial
transportation is quite remarkable. His tongue-in-cheek repre-
sentation of the widespread uses of gold and platinum have

little technological basis, but his notion of the potential utility of aluminum—which was still more expensive than gold and platinum when a bar was exhibited as "the new precious metal" at the Paris Exhibition of 1855—proved much more prescient, although he could not have anticipated that significant new methods of production would make it available for widespread industrial use in the late 1880s. Although his slightly awestruck descriptions of an electric kettle and an electric grill with a rear reflector might seem a trifle quaint to readers perfectly familiar with such devices, whose actual design eventually followed exactly the same logic as his extrapolations, their envisioning really was a daring imaginative venture on his part, and exhibits an attention to utilitarian detail rare among constructors of utopias—and not, alas, reflected in others aspects of Calvet's somewhat tunnel-visioned description of life in the future.

Calvet was perhaps unfortunate in writing his futuristic vision only a few years before several crucial inventions were made that changed the technological prospectus dramatically. If his novel is compared with Albert Robida's *La Vie électrique*, published a decade later in 1893,[1] the difference in the anticipatable technological horizons in very striking—almost as striking, in fact, as the difference between Calvet's rose-tinted optimism and Robida's deep-seated cynicism. Calvet's novel is exactly contemporary with Robida's first satirical euchronia, *Le Vingtième siècle* (1883; tr. as *The 20th century*), which is considerably more similar in the spectrum of its anticipations, and not nearly as striking in the contrast of its attitude. If Calvet had written his serial as he went along, as most feuilletonists of the period did, he might have had a chance to read and react to Robida's work, but the evidence of the text suggests that *Dans mille ans* was written all of a piece, and was probably completed before its serialization began (perhaps as much as two years previously, given that the con-

---

[1] tr. as *Electric Life*, Black Coat Press, ISBN 978-1-61227-182-8.

temporary action is so specifically set in 1880), so the two novels were almost certainly produced entirely independently, and are all the more interesting in juxtaposition by virtue of that fact.

The fact that Calvet avoids any direct discussion of politically controversial issues, and makes no mention whatsoever of organized religion (although his characters are prone make to the occasional exclamation taking the Lord's name in vain), is presumably the result of rigorous self-censorship, but it must have helped considerably to obtain serialization in a self-declared "family magazine." Although the *Musée des Familles* had been a ground-breaking literary publication when it was founded by Émile de Girardin in 1833, playing a significant role in the popularization of Romanticism and the development of popular fiction, it had came to seem distinctly staid and conservative by the 1880s, and was far from being the kind of publication to court any kind of controversy. The particular complexion of the novel's optimism might be more accountable in terms of marketing strategy than the author's own interests and limitations, and it would be unfair to hold the author entirely accountable for his omissions. It is worth noting that the magazine had a long-running regular feature entitled *Science en famille* [Science in the Home] and frequently published articles glorifying the exploits of explorers in Africa.

Dans mille ans was written at a time when Mercier's method of "time travel"—the prophetic dream—was still standard, and it does not mark much of an advance in that regard, at least in comparison with Robida, who grasped the nettle of presenting an account of the future as if it had been written in the future, simply ignoring the question of how the account could possibly be made available in the present. It is, however, significant that Calvet's characters do not experience the vision of the future as if it were a vision, but have the subjective impression that they have been physically displaced by suspended animation. This has some odd effects on the plot of the novel, especially when one of the characters discovers his ashes and a record of his genealogy in the Necropolis of future Paris, without being able to jump to the conclusion that he must, therefore, be able somehow to return to his own time. Given the fact that dreamers are generally not aware of the fact that they are dreaming, however—and usually wake up fairly rapidly if they acquire that awareness—the narrative move is not unjustifiable, and might help to explain certain other eccentricities and curious instances of neglect regarding the characters' actions and thoughts a thousand years hence and subsequent to their return.

It has to be admitted that Calvet is no great literary stylist; his prose is often stilted, routinely prolix and annoyingly repetitive, but it is not devoid of a certain liveliness and quirky humor, and it is by no means merely insulting to say that he writes very much as a high school science teacher might be expected to write. It is true that his novel is now of primarily historical interest, but it is worth re-emphasizing that the historical interest in question is considerable, because rather than in spite of the fact that its anticipations went out of date in a matter of years. The "binocular vision" that allows 19th century utopias to be read now with one eye on the actual future that developed instead of the imagined future adds to the interest of the reading experience, and allows informed modern readers to appreciate fully what a narrow window of imaginative opportunity Calvet had available to him, and how ingenious he was in working around blind spots that confounded almost all his contemporaries.

Only a handful of Calvet's French contemporaries—among whom Robida far outshines the rest—had anything like his breadth of technological vision, and no one outside France could hold a candle to him in that regard; no one writing in English produced anything remotely similar to *Dans mille ans* in the early 1880s, and even the remarkable flood of euchronian fiction that followed the publication of Edward Bellamy's best-selling *Looking Backward, 2000-1887* in 1888, and the dramatic flowering of British scientific romance in the 1890s, failed to produce anything of similar breadth and detail with regard to the extrapolation of electrical technology. In spite of its limitations, *Dans mille ans* is a highly significant product of the scientific imagination, which ought not to be entirely overshadowed by Robida's work, and makes a fascinating comparison with it.

This translation has been taken from the version of the Delagrave edition reproduced on the Bibliothèque Nationale's *gallica* website.

Brian Stableford

Part One:
THE SECRET OF DOCTOR ANTIUS

I. A Scientist in Difficulties

On 13 June 1880, the physicist J. B. Terrier, whose works have cast so much light on the mechanical theory of heat, appeared to be prey to an agitation, betrayed by the disorder of his stride, which was normally calm, slow and measured.

The scientist was walking around his vast laboratory, sometimes stopping abruptly and darting long glances at a piece if paper he was holding in his hand.

"A singular message!" he said, suddenly, in a low voice. "It's only three words long—*Great discovery, come*—but it nevertheless constitutes an enigma for which I can provide no rational hypothesis. The discovery must be important, for Antius, who is as severe on himself as he is on others, only uses such epithets discerningly."

And the professor lost himself in conjectures once again.

"Rastoin," he said to his assistant, "What time is it?"

"Four-seventeen, Monsieur," the young man replied, after taking out his silver pocket-watch, as large as a pie-dish, and observing with alarm that the first hour of his free time had already been considerably eroded.

After a moment's hesitation, the professor headed for the door, picked up his hat, which was perched on a galvanometer and pulled it down over his ears. Rejecting his walking stick, and in spite of a clear sky and a temperature of thirty degrees, he picked up a vast umbrella worthy of service in a phalanstery. He stopped again, raising his eyes toward the ceiling, and then went down into the street.

He had not taken ten paces before Rastoin, the laboratory key in his pocket, launched himself briskly in the opposite

11

direction, exclaiming: "Thank God, I still have time to have a dip at the Henri IV baths."

In spite of the preoccupations agitating his mind, the physicist had adopted the calm and measured stride that is the most apparent indication of professorial dignity. Sagaciously, he walked on the side of the street that was not exposed to the ardent rays of the sun and emerged without hesitation from the labyrinth of bizarrely winding side-streets that furrow the area between the Quai des Grand-Augustins and the Boulevard Saint-Germain.

He went slowly up the Boulevard Saint-Michel and into the Jardin du Luxembourg, which he was proceeding to traverse in a straight line when, surprised by the outburst of a military band that was in the most direct path, he made an abrupt right-angled turn. That maneuver, provoked by the instinctive horror that the scientist had for any kind of noise, took him into the Allée de l'Observatoire, which he cut across obliquely in order to go through the deserted paths that, in that era, overlooked the pot-holes of the old botanical garden.

Five minutes later he went at a deliberate pace into the Rue Carnot. Having arrived at the end of that street, which has the deceptive appearance of a dead end, he turned right and followed the little used sidewalk of the Rue Notre-Dame-des-Champs for some distance. Finally, he stopped in front of a door that symmetrically divided an old wall, which was covered in moss and overhung by two vigorous poplars, planted behind it like sentinels.

The professor tugged energetically at a rusty copper bell-pull, which only quit its sheath with an angry grating sound.

Two minutes later, heavy and hasty footsteps caused the sand of the garden path to squeak, and the door opened slowly.

Terrier saw an old woman in front of him, who greeted him with a nod of the head and put her index finger over her mouth—a familiar sign that always announces a mystery. In addition, contrary to the convention practiced on the five continents of the world of letting a visitor in, the woman who was holding the door ajar slipped between the batten and the wall and came out into the street.

The old lady who had just performed that singular maneuver was known by the name of Madame Boquet; for twenty years she had been Dr. Antius' housekeeper, the glory and providence of the quarter. Within a radius of three hundred meters it was universally admitted as an undisputable verity that she possessed, to the highest degree, the knowledge, intelligence and organizational ability necessary for the provision of superior cuisine—qualities which, as all bachelors admit, constitute the three theological virtues of housekeeping.

On the day on which this story begins, the physicist was able to observe at the first glance that grave perturbations must have compromised the calm and tranquility of the doctor's house.

Indeed Madame Boquet, who seemed very animated, immediately launched into the following speech: "Thank heaven you're here, Monsieur le Professeur. Personally, I feel as if I'm losing my mind. I'm convinced, you see, that the devil is haunting the house. Can you imagine that Monsieur is no longer recognizable. For some time, he's been shutting himself away all day, and doesn't want to see anyone. At night, he gets up and goes down into the garden, where he wanders around slowly for two or three hours, talking out loud. He scarcely eats anything, and only distractedly. There's some great misfortune behind it, which is a threat to us, I can assure you..."

This exordium on the part of the housekeeper caused the physicist some anxiety.

"When, Madame Bosquet, did this trouble begin—which, in regard to the chronometric existence of my old friend, is as much of a surprise to me as it is to you?" he asked.

"It began last week, on Thursday evening. At two o'clock, Monsieur left for the Académie. At six o'clock, he still hadn't come back. For the first time in his life, he was late. I was beginning to get angry when Monsieur opened the door and came solely along the path, his eyes fixed on the ground. He went up to his room without saying a word and came back in an overcoat, with no cravat. He stated walking around the garden.

"I went to tell him that dinner was ready. 'Dinner doesn't matter,' he said, abruptly, and kept on walking. I never heard anything like it. I stopped stood in front of him and shouted that it was seven o'clock. He followed me, grumpily, and came to sit down at the table, but like someone whose mind is elsewhere.

"On Monday, his nephew, Monsieur Gédéon, came to see him. He tried to go into the study, but Monsieur flew into a temper and sent him away.

"I've tried everything to combat the mysterious illness. I've prepared the rarest dishes—a waste of effort. I've made all sorts of infusions; Monsieur hasn't touched them. Finally, the day before yesterday, I went to consult the old somnambulist in the Rue Stanislas, who's capable of divining anything."

"Well?" asked the scientist, curiously.

"She assured me that Monsieur was bewitched, and that as soon as the spell is lifted, he'll be much better."

"The diagnosis is more remarkable for its logic than its lucidity," said the professor.

"This morning," the housekeeper went on, "I had a ray of hope. As Monsieur got up from the table, he said: 'Madeleine, didn't Gédéon come here the other day?'

"'Yes, Monsieur,' I said, 'but you sent him away—the young man was furious.'

"'Good. Go to his house today and tell him to come to dinner. At the same time, take this telegram to the telegraph office—it's for my friend Monsieur Terrier; I have something important to tell him. The three of us will dine together. Put on a magnificent feast!'

"Imagine my astonishment—Monsieur was talking just like you and me. But it didn't last, alas. Scarcely had Monsieur finished giving his instructions than he went back into his laboratory, and hasn't come out again since."

II. Antius' Nephew

When this picturesque narration concluded, the two interlocutors went into the garden and advanced toward the
house. Suddenly, the bell at the entrance door started ringing a
formidable carillon.

"Who can be ringing in that savage manner?" exclaimed
the old lady, angrily.

The noise suddenly ceased and a hunting call, cleverly
imitated and uttered at full blast, resounded in the air.

"It's Monsieur Gédéon," said the housekeeper. As she
headed for the door, not without muttering some abusive re-
mark addressed to the facetious summoner, she added: "I
should have realized. That young man will take ten years off
my life."

But the latter abruptly appeared astride the wall, jumped
down into the flower-bed with the agility of a cat and ran toward the old woman, throwing his arms around her.

"Bonjour, Boquet," he said. "But what's changed my uncle's mind? The other day he kicked me out, very impolitely,
and today he's inviting me to dinner!"

Perceiving the immobile professor a few steps away, he
came to greet him respectfully, while the housekeeper returned
to her ovens. "You're doubtless here for the feast, my excellent Master," said the young man. "Your presence here doesn't
surprise me, for you're a regular guest at the house. As for me,
I'd gladly say what the Doge of Genoa said to Louis XIV:
'What astonishes me more is to see myself here.'[2]

---

[2] Louis XIV met the Doge of Genoa, Francesco Maria
Lercaro, in the Hall of Mirrors at Versailles on 15 May 1685,
when the latter came to confirm his capitulation after a French
fleet had bombarded the city for ten days in order to force the
abandonment of a commission to build warships for Spain.
The Doge was reported to be very impressed by Versailles, but

"Four days ago, in fact, I came to present my uncle with a perfectly legitimate request. He was in his study, the door of which was locked and bolted—a particularity that immediately gave me sinister presentiments. I knocked. 'Who's there?' he said.

"'Me.'

"'Who are you?'

"Stupefaction all along the line—he hadn't recognized me sonorous voice. *Has he gone mad?* I wondered, fearfully.

"I went on: 'I'm Achille-Gédéon Cahusac, your nephew, in person, legitimate son of the late Pierre-André Cahusac and the late Julie-Antoinette Antius, your sister. Possessed of a baccalaureate, vaccinated...'

"'Come back later.'

"'My dear uncle, it's a serious matter and I can't wait.'

"'Speak, but be brief.'

"'This is it, in brief. Can you imagine that I have a friend who's a medical student, named Jacques Collardon? Yesterday, we were walking along the quay when he perceived in a bouquiniste's box a superb edition of the works of Bichat, priced at thirty-five francs. *We can get it for thirty*, he said, and indeed, after a short debate, the merchant gave in. Collardon had the books wrapped up, dug in his pocket and exclaimed: *Damn—I forgot that I settled my tailor's bill this morning. Keep the packet for me till the end of the month and I'll come back with the cash*. The merchant protested. Always concerned with the interests of science, I took out my last thirty francs and lent them to my friend. You can imagine what embarrassment...'

"'Do you take me for an imbecile?' my uncle cried. 'Your tricks are becoming increasingly unsubtle, my lad.'

"The cat was out of the bag. It's true that I hadn't been very clever. Fiction having served me badly, I had recourse to sincerity. 'You're barbaric, Uncle,' I went on, 'but let's place

the irony of his widely-quoted remarks to that effect is understandable.

16

the question on its true ground. Do you believe, yes or no, that I need money?'

"'As to that, yes.'

"'Well, since you possess the two fine titles of guardian and banker, would you be so cruel as to refuse me a little advance of three louis on next month's allowance? I promise to tighten my belt.'

"'I know whose belt you'll be tightening—you won't get a penny. Anyway, I've been very kind to listen to you for so long.'

"'Come on,' I persisted, gently. "As good harmony results from reciprocal concessions, let's split the difference: thirty francs might save me from the gulf.'

"'Go to the devil!' the heartless fellow shouted.

"And he went away, just like that.

"Knowing that nothing would make him come out of his lair, I turned on my heel in my turn, my head prey to all the complex mathematical calculations capable of resolving the terrible problem against which I'd just broken my nose. Today, I was quite surprised by the arrival of Madame Boquet, who, without any preamble, brought me an invitation to dinner."

"For my part, my dear friend," said the professor, "I was invited by telegram. Antius tells me that he's made a great discovery—and it must be important, for his enthusiasm is rather measured. He doubtless wants to tell you about his invention, in your capacity as his ward and heir presumptive. It's quite probable that he'll be better disposed toward you today."

"Well, Master, you're opening welcome horizons to me—although not with regard to the direct cause of my invitation, if your anticipations are correct, for that leave me cold, scientific discoveries being of little interest to the profane. The important question for me is the probable softening of my uncle in my regard, and on that point, I share your opinion. The worthy fellow must have reflected, and, ashamed of the atrocity of his conduct toward me..."

The optimist's sentence was cut short by the housekeeper's summons. From the threshold, she called to the two interlocutors: "Monsieur has come out of the laboratory, and dinner's ready."

The professor and Gédéon headed toward the house, which was half-hidden by a luxuriant frame of flowers and climbing plants.

They had not taken twenty paces when a short man of about sixty came down the five steps of the perron ornamenting the front door at a rapid pace. His entire being appeared to be the seat of an intense activity. In four strides the doctor was with his guests, and he seized the physician's hand.

"Bonjour, Terrier," he said. "I'm very glad to see you, for I've decided, in view of our old friendship, and especially your great competence, that you shall be the first...but let's proceed in order. I must tell you, first of all, that I'm truly exhausted. For ten days, my brain has been prey to a continuous seething. I really should have exercised more moderation, for Aesop is right to say that the bow shouldn't always be kept taut—but the idea pursued me, fixedly, tenaciously, absolutely. Finally, yesterday, I was hopeful, and tonight I achieved certainty. But what day of the month is it?"

"Saturday the fourteenth of June, according to the calendar," Gédéon replied, having not yet said a word. Sententiously, he added: "It's true what they say: the calendar doesn't lie."[3]

"Ah! Very good. On seeing you just now I said to myself: *what particular cause might bring my nephew here, who only usually visits me on the last day of the month; is today the thirtieth?*"

"Come on, Uncle, I have neither the pretention, nor, above all, the desire to make scientific discoveries, but in spite of that, or perhaps because of it, as nothing troubles my head,

---

[3] Given that the narrative voice informed us in chapter one that today is the thirteenth, a smidgen of unreliability seems to have crept in somewhere.

it's in perfect equilibrium, and I recall perfectly that today, at one o'clock, Madame Boquet came to my lodgings on your behalf to bring me an invitation to dinner."

"I suppose that's quite possible," said Antius. "I was in such a good mood that I might have invited the entire universe."

"I thank you, then, for the preference."

"Oh, damn!" said the doctor. "Last Thursday I should have chaired the meeting of the Biological Society. Never mind—some other vice-president will have taken my place, and I must admit that they could all do it perfectly well—especially Mirbel, in spite of his absurd theory of neural polarity. But our cook seems to be getting angry, and she's about to head our way. To avoid the squall, let's go to the dining-room."

III. A Retrospective Glance at
the Three Heroes of the Story

The guests went into the house and into a rather large, comfortably furnished room. Long green velvet curtains, extending to the floor, regulated the entry of daylight. An assortment of pewter, crystal and polychromatic faience, skillfully grouped behind the glazed front of an immense dresser in carved oak, gave off a resplendent gleam. Four paintings, very honorably signed, representing the gastronomical treasures to which nature gives birth in the four seasons, decorated the walls. On the chimney-breast, mounted on a black marble pedestal, an enormous bust of Hippocrates in Florentine bronze appeared to have been set in that place of honor in order to watch over the scientific repasts that Antius hosted periodically. Finally, in the middle of the room, a stout oval table, supported by an enormous sculpted leg, presented an enchanting spectacle.

In front of each place-setting, a group of crystal glasses of various dimensions was arranged in battle order. At the sides, two large dusty bottles, corpulent and solidly coiffed in red, were reminiscent of two dragons set to mount guard on a magnificent silver soup tureen sitting in the center of the table—which, in spite of its thick lid, was emitting vigorous jets of odorant vapor.

The three men took their places.

We shall take advantage of the relative silence that reigns at the doctor's table to sketch rapid and faithful portraits of the three individuals who occupy the most important roles in this story.

Dr. Antius was a short man of sixty, plump, active and indefatigable; his face, always animated, always mobile, was illuminated by two bright eyes, keen and endowed with rare powers of penetration.

Scarcely had he emerged from the benches of the Faculty than his savant research on alkaloids had attracted attention. Four years later, after a brilliant competitive examination, he was counted among the graduates of the École and launched himself on a brilliant career in organic chemistry. Being rich, he had devoted himself entirely to pure science. Nevertheless, general rumor credited him with knowing the way to all the mansards in the neighborhood, frequently opening his purse beside sick-beds and leaving at the first word of gratitude. In consequence, the benevolent boor was the object of general sympathy. When he left the house, all hats within a radius of three hundred meters were raised to him.

The laboratory of chemistry and physiology that he had constructed, at great expense, in a separate building at the end of his garden, would have honored a Faculty, as much by the abundance as the choice of its materials and instruments. For a long time, he had devoted himself to the profound study of the nerve centers, and his remarkable work had won him a considerable reputation in the scientific world. No other anatomist had investigated the brain with as much skill, patience and interest.

Several times, his colleagues, in citing him in their reports, had not hesitated to add to his name the epithet "eminent," although some, it is true, disputed his theories passionately. It is necessary to add that few adversaries dared attack him directly with words, for contradiction caused him to lose his temper and provoked an explosion of comical sallies, some of which were legendary in the academic world.

The aphorism that claims that opposites attract seems particularly well-verified by the amity that had united the physician and Professor Terrier for thirty years. The latter, in fact, was essentially calm, grave, punctilious and measured. Possessed of an impassive temperament, he would not have been more emotional in the midst of a cataclysm than in the presence of a simple experiment in hydrostatics. His pupils were no less appreciative of the honorability of his character than the depth of his knowledge. More than one of them, without resources, had been able to pursue his transcendent studies thanks to the support of the master, who, in those circumstances, hollowed out formidable breaches in the modest edifice of his savings with an antique simplicity.

Gédéon Cahusac, the third guest, was a hearty fellow of twenty-four, with an alert appearance. He was able to live up to the title of "good companion" everywhere—and that, for the time being, was his sole worldly ambition. At the age of twenty, after three successive attempts, he had secured the palms of the baccalaureate in letters, and thought he had done sufficient merit to the fatherland. At fifteen, he had lost his father, a very honorable retired justice of the peace. When he had attained his majority, his mother had put him in possession of the paternal heritage, but the new capitalist found so many side-tracks along his path that after two years his notary had been obliged to warn him that henceforth, he would have to fight a rearguard action.

That day, Maître Desiflard had summoned his client and had delivered this sage speech: "My dear Gédéon, on examining your accounts, I have been horrified. I was your father's friend, as you know; I therefore owe you some advice. I will admit, first of all, that in your case I have been slightly at fault, for I should have kept a closer watch on you. But who could have imagined that you would conduct yourself in such a reckless fashion? Without either of us noticing it, you have arrived within two steps of ruination. Believe me, look after the remaining wreckage. Convert the five thousand francs that remains to you into an income, and go to live with your mother—who will, I'm sure, receive you with open arms."

Gédéon, who was not stupid, understood the wisdom of this advice, thanked the notary, and asked him to obtain an income of seven hundred francs for him. "So, on the brink of being ruined, I'm becoming a *rentier*," he said, simply. Resigned on that point, he said goodbye to his entresol, and, with his heart full of the most magnificent intentions, he also asked Maître Desiflard to go to his mother to ask her for bed and board for him.

The good lady wept with joy on learning that her son wanted to behave sensibly from now on, and prepared the best room in the house for him. She even increased the size of her apartment by renting a vast room that had previously served as a painter's studio; the prodigal son was therefore able to re-house his collection, which consisted of sabers, fencing foils, masks, gloves, canes, horns, rifles, daggers, knives, bows, arrows, clubs, nets, sculls, a hammock, pipes, etc.

Since then, Gédéon had lived a relatively tranquil existence. After a year, his imagination, his whims and his habits had seemed to be regularly channeled, when, in spite of his uncle's cares, assisted by his most illustrious colleagues, Madame Cahusac had been carried off by a sudden illness. The far-sighted mother, however, with the sureness and power of prescience that sometimes animates the dying, taking her son's hands in hers, had said to him in her brother's presence:

"My child, I'm doomed; they're hiding it from me, but I sense it. The moment has come; listen to me carefully. You've already spent a small fortune; I've mourned the fact, but I've never reproached you for it, and that was perhaps a mistake. You'll be in possession of what remains to us. Everything has been converted into an income from the State. Entrust your titles you your uncle, and he'll give you your pension regularly every month. It will be sufficient for you to live honorably, if you exercise a little order. In addition, my child, think about a profession for the future. Now I can die without regrets, if you promise to follow my advice."

Gédéon, with tears in his eyes, swore solemnly to his mother that he would obey her last wishes, and the doctor, no less emotional, had made a formal engagement to maintain his nephew on the right track. A few hours later, Madame Cahusac had rendered her last sigh.

A month later, Gédéon got rid of the apartment, only keeping the studio, to which he annexed two rooms in which he accommodated all the family furniture. The doctor, strictly preserving the cost of the rent, which had been considerably exposed, began to dole out a monthly pension of two hundred and fifty francs.

At first, the young man had had several fits of serious reflection and successively envisaged all the professions to which he might aspire, but all of them had presented him with inhibitory circumstances. *In fact, I have plenty of time*, he said to himself; *let's not rush into anything. A wise man assures us that, in serious matters, it's necessary to think long and hard. A classical author has formulated the* festina lente; *I therefore have the right to hide behind these authorities, if ever I'm taken to task on the matter. After all, I'm faithful enough to my oath not to remain inactive. Only yesterday, I took my canoe from Asnière to the Râpée, and I don't believe that there are many ditch-diggers who did as much work. The day before, I spent all afternoon fencing at Lecour's, and on emerging therefrom, I could certainly claim, like Titus, that I hadn't wasted my day.*

We ought to add that Gédéon had recently conceived a fine passion for painting, and had made several attempts to develop a talent still in its rudimentary state, but his art had only translated itself thus far in the composition of a whimsical fresco applied surreptitiously to a whitewashed wall, whose incendiary shades made all the art students in the neighborhood roar with laughter. In addition, he gladly sacrificed to Euterpe, by frequenting a horn class, which was held in the second basement of a café in the Boulevard Saint-Michel. Finally, thanks to a special disposition, he was able to imitate to perfection all the comedians in the capital.

This whimsical existence was not a veritable solution to living cheaply, so, by the middle of the month, Gédéon was generally harnessed, for a good fortnight, to Lucifer's tail. He had even got ahead of that fatal epoch, on the day when we saw him failing to make a breach in the doctor's inflexible blockade.

IV. Inter Pocula[4]

For the moment, Gédéon did not seem to be preoccupied either with his situation or his future; for five minutes, like a man who does not want to let anything go to waste, he had been battling against the calcareous part of a formidable lobster claw.

"I believe," he said, suddenly, raising his head, "that a man condemned to eat nothing but lobster claws would obtain scant benefit for his stomach, but would, on the other hand, exert terrible wear and tear on his jaws."

The doctor, who had just stuck a large silver-handled knife into a Nérac pâté, nodded silently. "Madeleine," he shouted, a moment later, "I can see the truffles but I don't see the Bordeaux."

Without saying a word, the servant seized a bottle with a fine label from the sideboard, extracted the cork with a twist of the wrist and filled the glasses of the second caliber.

The marvels engendered by Madame Boquet succeeded one another at a sagely leisurely pace before the guests, who continued to officiate actively for some time. The silence was only interrupted by the witty remarks of the young man. Contrary to his habit, the doctor remained mute, mechanically directing the feast. He was obviously thinking about something other than what was happening around him.

"Monsieur Terrier," said Gédéon, suddenly, whose face had taken on the color of a poppy, "you've been sent on a scientific mission to Oceania and have observed the mores of cannibals at close range, without having practiced them—at least, I hope so. Which of the two do you think the anthropophages would appreciate more: Madame Boquet or her cuisine?"

---

[4] "While drinking"—or, more familiarly, "while drunk."

"They would have the same success, I think," said the professor, gallantly.

The old lady crossed herself rapidly.

"It's said, however, that some voyagers have ventured among them, and even been resident there for some time while avoiding the spit. You are moreover, personally—and, permit me to and, fortunately—proof of that."

"Yes, certainly. The naturalist voyager du Chaillu, among others, hunted gorillas in equatorial Africa in the company of those gentlemen, and saw them eat the remains of those of their compatriots who died of disease—a procedure of which I don't approve, but which resolves a grave question of general hygiene. I would add that they are particularly fond of prisoners of war, which explains their perpetual conflict. I don't believe that their international questions have ever been regulated by peace conferences—an eminently moral spectacle that our descendants will surely enjoy."

"You believe, then, that battlefields will one day be definitively fixed on the green baize of conference-tables?"

"Undoubtedly."

"I hope so too. But what reasoning leads you to that humanitarian conclusion?"

"There are several. Consider, first of all, that people have successively fought individual against individual, family against family, village against village, tribe against tribe, province against province, nation against nation, and finally, allied nations against allied nations. Nothing any longer remains, therefore, but the possibility of fighting continent against continent, which seems to me to be impracticable. Now, as that tendency to agglomeration is undeniable, when all peoples are united, it will be necessary for them to remain tranquil."

"Very good. I understand."

"Furthermore, the innumerable quantity of combatants who enter the line, the precision, rapidity and power of weaponry, the facility and speed of transportation—conditions that develop increasingly with the progress of science—will make war an ever more terrible thing. Besides which, people are beginning to understand that they have an increasing need to become acquainted, to come together and to exchange their products."

"I'm convinced," said the young man. "It's now certain for me that in a thousand years, warriors will only be seen at the Opéra-Comique."

"In a thousand years," the professor added, pensively, "there are many things that will no longer be seen. On the other hand, many others will be seen of which we have no suspicion."

"I'm not curious," said Gédéon, "but I'd give a good quarter of my collection to be suddenly transported into the world as it will be ten centuries hence."

"And I half of my laboratory," declared the physicist.

The doctor straightened up suddenly, pale and tremulous. "You'd like to see what will happen in a thousand years?" he exclaimed, in a vibrant voice. "Well, Messieurs, you *shall* see it."

The professor and the young man, amazed by that unexpected explosion, looked at him without making any reply. The three men sat there in silence.

The meal was approaching its end. After having cleared the table, Madame Boquet brought in a silver-encrusted lemonwood tantalus of liqueurs. It contained four bottles filed with old liqueurs of esteemed origin. The guests took coffee with all the gratitude warranted by an operation whose importance has been remarked by the most eminent gastronomes. A few moments later, the doctor lit a cigar—an example immediately imitated by his guests. For a few minutes, blue spirals rose slowly toward the ceiling.

The professor broke the silence. "I confess, Antius," he said, "that your telegram surprised me greatly. I've had singular difficulty attributing a rational meaning to it. When your housekeeper opened the garden door to me, the good lady seemed so distressed, and testified to such alarm regarding the excess of your preoccupation, that I became seriously anxious myself."

"As for me," Gédéon remarked, "I'm convinced, in view of my incompetence, that this scientific secret will be almost as interesting to me as a problem in complex algebra—which is not saying much."

"Your suppositions are equally erroneous," said the doctor, in an inspired manner, "for my discovery is of interest to all humanity, and its consequences are incalculable."

"Well, Antius," added the professor, "the moment is very favorable to unveil the mystery for us. You've never had a more devout and attentive audience."

"First, I must rectify an error," the doctor declared. "When, just now, I said, *my* discovery, that was not entirely accurate. The initial elements, furnished by hazard, had been studied previously and had already yielded results worthy of attention. It is, moreover, for that reason that they were submitted to me. But I can affirm that, in a matter of days, from what was only a singular fact, I have extracted a prodigy. I ought to add that, throughout my research, my mind has been relentlessly subject to the intense concentration that caused the principle of universal gravitation to spring from the brain of Newton. I shall now begin at the beginning."

After collecting himself momentarily, the doctor looked hard at his guests and, in contrast to his habitual volubility, began to speak slowly and solemnly.

V. An Academic Incident

"On the fourth of June," he said, "there was an extraordinary meeting of the Académie. As I came into the hall, the president was just opening the session. Unusually, only half the members were there, for it was going to be a hot day. It was a matter of appointing an incumbent and two correspondent members. It was said that there was a cabal. During the reading of the minutes, a large party of latecomers came in, and when the opening of the correspondence began there were only a few empty seats.

"Things were going very smoothly when Rozier, one of the secretaries, took a little packed wrapped in cloth and carefully tied with string from the desk, which had escaped the attention of the audience until then. After having read what was written on it he opened his mouth very wide—a sign by which he habitually manifests his astonishment.

"Parading a significant gaze around the assembly, to demand attention, he handed the object to Barrière, who was in the chair. The latter, having read it himself, uttered the unsteady sequence of clucks that replaces laughter among hypochondriacs.

"That unusual occurrence produced its effect. All eyes were aimed at the desk, for the double manifestation presaged something extraordinary. In the midst of the most profound silence, the president spoke.

"'Messieurs,' he said, lifting up the package in his left hand, 'the object that I have the honor of presenting to you, the nature of which is unknown to me, has arrived from Indo-China. It has been sent by Père André, of the foreign Missions, to whom science owes very remarkable documents on the ethnography of the peoples who live on the shores of Cambodia.

"'The fact would not be astonishing in itself, if the card that is attached to the envelope did not mention a request contrary to all academic regulations. This is what it says, in its entirety: Sent by Père André, missionary in Ban Coksay, kingdom of Luang-Prabang, Siam. To Monsieur the Président de l'Académie de Médecine, to be confided to the examination of Dr. Antius, if he is still alive.'

"A general burst of laughter welcomed the prudent corrective that accompanied the respectable missionary's desire, and all gazes converged on me. I stood up. 'Père André,' I said, 'is an old friend, of whom I have not had news for ten years. I must confess that I had the same anxieties on his account that he has testified on mine. I observe gladly that we each have the right to be reassured.'

"A murmur of assent, which I believe to be sincere, welcomed my words.

"The president had an usher bring me the mysterious packet, and the assembly's attention was directed to the ballot that was about to held. For myself, I was agitated by a keen sentiment of curiosity. I did not suppose, in fact, that the missionary had sent me a mere stuffed lizard, or some analogous object, from four thousand leagues away.

"The appearance of the object was not at all extraordinary. It was cylindrical, no more than forty centimeters in length and about fifteen in diameter, but its actual dimensions had to be considerably less, for, on touching it, one sensed that it had been wrapped in several rather resistant envelopes. It was not very heavy. My mind embraced all the seemingly probable conjectures in turn, but in vain; each one ran into serious objections.

"Finally, no longer being able to remain in place, I meekly copied my neighbor's ballot paper, handed him my votes—or, rather, his in duplicate—asking him to throw them in the urn when it passed in front of our seats. I got up, gripping the Indo-Chinese packet, and retired to the most distant and quietest room in the building. I brought an armchair up to a little table by the window and, having sat down, set to work.

"A strong piece of oil-cloth, tightly sealed by very strong and skillfully-wound string, constituted the primary envelope of the mysterious object. The ends of the string were covered with red sealing-wax. With the aid of the blade of my pen-knife, I gradually disposed of the seal and found a very complicated knot. It seemed to me to be difficult to untie. As patience is not my dominant virtue, I proceeded like Alexander in confrontation with the Gordian knot; I cut through it. Beneath the initial cloth envelope I found another, in remarkably fine woven straw. The edges were joined by a suture, which I was obliged to slice along its entire length. I then encountered a thick bundle of rice-straw, doubtless intended to absorb shocks, and beneath that a sheath of sturdy cloth, which I was obliged to split from top to bottom. Finally, a tin-plate cylinder appeared, whose lid was firmly soldered.

"My curiosity was increasingly overexcited by all these precautions, but I was now forced to suspend the operation, for the only instrument I had at my disposal would not permit me to break through that final obstacle.

"I went to the laboratory, into which no one was supposed to come that day. I lit the oxy-hydrogen burner and brought the extremity of the poker to white heat. I passed the incandescent surface over the ring of solder; the lead gradually melted. When the entire circumference was reduced, I lifted the lid, which gave way easily.

"A gray paper bag, strung in a rectangular fashion, occupied almost all of the cavity of the container, only separated from the metallic envelope by a quadruple sheaf of white paper lining the interior of the cylinder.

"I lifted out the central bag and the paper, which I opened excitedly. It was a letter.

"The first three sheets were devoted to ethnographic notes and observations of general physics, destined for a forthcoming article, which will obtain a legitimate success. The last related an extraordinary fact.

"Having been struck down by an intense fever, accompanied by delirium, the missionary owed his instantaneous cure to an infinitesimal infusion of a plant that he was sending me. It had been brought to him by two of his neophytes, the fisherman Pha-Keo and his son Chang, who, confident in the virtue of the panacea in question, had gone to pick it from the sides of a frightful gulf.

"Under the action of the substance, Père André had experienced marvelous effects of lucidity and analytical power. Furthermore, his thoughts *and senses* crossing a distance of four thousand leagues, he had *witnessed*, in Paris, in the chapel of the Foreign Missions, the ordination of a young priest destined to support him in his apostolic labors.

"Five months later, on the threshold of his cabin, he gave the accolade to the young missionary, whom he recognized immediately."

VI. The First Experiment

"I must declare," the doctor continued, "that these confidences had made a deep impression on my mind, by virtue of their clarity and precision. The certainty of the phenomena, in spite of their excessive character, was guaranteed not only by the absolute honorability of my colleague but also by his real competence in the natural sciences.

"To begin with, I devoted myself to patient research on the rich and dazzling catalogue of tropical flora, in order to determine the particular characteristics of the precious plant. My efforts were in vain. Not only was it impossible for me to classify it rigorously, but I could not find enough analogous characteristics in any species to assign it a place in the botanical taxonomy.

"Abandoning that aspect of the question, which was only of secondary importance, I was no longer thinking of anything but experimenting with the properties of the marvelous herb. Considering that the substances that vegetal therapeutics furnish act specifically via their alkaloids, whose power is in direct proportion to their concentration, whether they affect the organs directly or their action takes effect on the nerve centers—and sometimes, in that case, on the thinking faculties—I resolved to obtain extracts.

"I set to work that same evening. Having detached a bundle of fibers charged with desiccated flowers, I treated it by alcoholic maceration. The operation was conducted with the greatest care.

"Success crowned my efforts. I obtained an initial solution, which I gradually brought to a syrupy consistency. I did not stop there. Mentally drawing a certain analogy between the principle of the Indian plant and opium, which one can still absorb in half-gram does, but which contains and alkaloid of far superior potency, morphine, which becomes poisonous at a dose of a few centigrams, the following day I divided the mass

33

obtained into two equal portions, one of which was set aside and carefully isolated from any contact with the air. With the second half I resolved to take the concentration to the maximum, convinced that the essential principle would gain in intensity in proportion to the diminution of its volume.

"My mind was in a state of extreme excitement throughout the duration of these operations, for I sensed that the solution to a strange problem was in my hands.

"For a week, I put the most patient and delicate procedures to work. Finally, I was able to collect a small amorphous, opaque brown mass weighing fourteen centigrams. It was perfectly odorless.

"I enclosed it carefully in a little bottle of thick crystal, whose emery-papered stopper was covered with a wax seal as a extra precaution. That was the ninth day. I had spent the whole night working; I was exhausted. In spite of everything, I resolved to begin the experiment that same evening.

"Two hours after dinner—or, rather, after a simulacrum of a meal, for my appetite had disappeared completely—I went back to my laboratory. I was prey to a secret emotion, the intensity of which I can't explain. I locked the door with the key, having sent Madeleine to bed.

"You can imagine the prudence that seemed compulsory, in the presence of that unknown substance whose effects were manifest with such extraordinary power. Reason advised me to experiment first with a very weak dose of the first extract obtained, the concentration of which had not been taken to the ultimate limit.

"With the aid of a precision balance, I weighted out half a milligram of the substance. I then measured five grams of distilled water in a graduated glass cylinder. Then I tipped the alkaloid into the water, and stirred the mixture for a minute with a glass rod.

"Without losing its transparency, the liquid had taken on a slightly iridescent tint and presented the uniformity of appearance that is one of the distinctive characteristics of perfect dilution. I sat down in my armchair, the beverage in my hand.

"Although, by temperament as much as by profession, I am not very accessible to ordinary emotions, I was prey to a keen anxiety. I experienced the sensation of indefinable anguish that takes possession of us in the presence of the unknown. Finally, I stiffened myself with a supreme effort, closed my eyes, and swallowed the mysterious liquor in a single gulp.

"For a few minutes, I did not experience anything extraordinary. Meanwhile, perhaps because the principle acts first on certain organs of vision, I felt my eyes gradually closing, in spite of the sum of the resistance that I had at my disposal at that moment. However, thanks to the energy I brought to bear, I was able to keep my eyelids partly raised for some time, and continued to see the objects in front of me.

"Then I experience all the fantastic aberrations that nightmares produce. Sometimes my lamp drew nearer to my eyes, rapidly taking on the dimensions of a barrel, sometimes it drew far away, diminishing in volume but without completely losing its brightness. The pendulum of the clock progressively took on formidable proportions, and then became gradually microscopic.

"Soon, all the objects in my laboratory seemed prey to a monstrous dilatation. While everything withdrew to the ultimate limits of the horizon, the walls, contrary to the laws of perspective, rose up all the way to the clouds.

"Then my eyes closed entirely. I did not take long to experience the singular sensation of annihilation that all eaters of hashish know well. That state of mind is particularly agreeable, and I now understand why many Orientals risk their heads by defying the law that, in some countries, punishes devotees of narcotics with death.

"That blissfulness, which has the primary characteristics of inertia and passivity, gave way to a sensation a hundred times more delightful. I was unable to compare it to any of the effects that the organism can experience. However, if the vaguest things can almost be translated by an image, I would willingly say that my entire being was gradually *melting*.

"When that crisis, the prolongation and frequency of which will not be without danger, eventually ceased, I had a few moment of absolute quietude. In spite of these purely physical impressions, my brain was subject to an intense activity, and my analytical and imaginative faculties had insensibly obtained a veritably prodigious power and conviction.

"In our scientific speculations—you must have experienced it, Terrier—we are sometimes in the presence of ideas whose assimilation is particularly difficult. We are only separated from certainty by a limit that is sometimes insensible but which often opposes a resistance, necessitating a forceful concentration of thought. In the state in which I found myself, all the clouds had disappeared, and the most transcendent abstractions penetrated me with an axiomatic evidence and clarity."

VII. A Case of Ubiquity

"I don't know what association of ideas led me to occupy myself with what was happening at the Académie that day, for I had not been present at the session, but, by a strange phenomenon, conjectures gave way to real vision. I found myself sitting motionless in my armchair, without my neighbors being able to perceive my presence.

"Mirbel went up to the podium and announced to the assembly that the president had gone home, having been taken ill after a great dinner given the day before by an opulent member of the Agricultural Society. The fact, I must admit, did not cause any anxiety and even provoked a few smiles.

"'Our honorable president,' he added, 'warned me this morning that he would be unable to chair the session and asked me to take his place.' After a few moments of silence he said: 'You will also notice, Messieurs, that our honorable colleague Dr. Antius is absent again today. Last Thursday he was supposed to take the chair, and did not put in an appearance. It is certain that only serious reasons could have impeded the exactitude of the most punctual member of our assembly.'

"While saying these words, Mirbel had looked at my seat two or three times. I was therefore invisible. I tried to get up in order to reply, but my entire nervous apparatus of voluntary movement was paralyzed. I tried to open my mouth to make my presence known; it was impossible. I realized that I was therefore forced to witness the session as an invisible and intangible witness. I say *intangible* because my two neighbors, Dulaurier and Thibault, exchanged a handshake through my stomach.

"Soon afterwards, I heard the reading of the minutes of the last session. There was nothing remarkable in hem, and I congratulated myself privately for having stayed at home. After two or three insignificant communications, the famous Poulard took the floor in order to refute a paper that I had read a month previously. His argument was even more wretched than usual. He had merely been boring until, having run out of resources, he suddenly became aggressive. At one time, he even permitted himself to call my thesis a collection of nonsense.

"I tried once again to get up, in order to reckon with the impertinent individual, but in vain. When he had finished, the venerable anthropologist Luberneau came up to the podium and opened a notebook, whose size and thickness provoked a general yawn. Shortly afterwards, all heads had slumped on to the backs of chairs. I even heard two or three sonorous and regular snores.

"Thibault and Dulaurier has escaped the universal torpor. The former was gravely sketching the orator's gigantic nose, which he had captured rather well; the latter was looking at the ceiling, searching for an elusive rhyme that would conclude a sonnet of the Anacreontic genre, whose termination seemed to be preoccupying him greatly.

"When the old doctor had concluded his sermon, which he had delivered in the desert, he took a Stone Age vertebra, jawbone and clavicle from his pocket. Lifting up the objects successively in his left hand, he rendered an account of each in turn with a prolixity of detail that would have rendered the Académie rabid if it had not been plunged into the profoundest and most legitimate slumber.

"The poor fellow, who—fortunately for him—is half-blind and three-quarters deaf, convinced that he had been listened to with religious attention, finally came down from the platform with a visible expression of satisfaction.

"The clock, which chimed five o'clock, woke up a few of the sleepers with a start, who shook the others, and the session was closed by Mirbel, who, retained by presidential propriety, had merely been dozing.

"In a few minutes, the hall was empty. I was not without anxiety, feeling that I was shackled to my armchair for a period whose duration it was impossible for me to anticipate.

"The usher suddenly came into the hemicycle, and, seeing that he was alone, proceeded to hum some baroque music-hall refrain. He headed for the rear door, opened it and disappeared down the staircase that leads to the interior courtyard.

"Suddenly, it seemed to me that I had entered into possession of the power of voluntary movement. I made an effort and stood up without difficulty. While applauding myself for having quit the state of a mummy, I hurried toward the main door and went rapidly down to the street. The noise of my footsteps reassured me. I was no longer a phantom. I went back into the house without being perceived by Madeleine, who was filling the feeding-trays in the aviary. I went to the laboratory and threw myself down in my armchair.

"I soon went to sleep. When I woke up, it was six o'clock in the morning. The action of the narcotic had, therefore, lasted for eight hours, during which I had lived partly in duplicate.

"I went up to bed. It was impossible for me to close my eyes, for my mind was suffering from an extraordinary over-stimulation. After an hour, I got up, but I was afflicted by vertigo and obliged to sit down. With great difficulty, I made my way down to the drawing room. I lay down on a divan. Suddenly, I was invaded by a profound terror. I could not succeed in stringing two ideas together; it seemed to me that I was going mad.

"All day I remained in the state of absolute idiocy. It was not until the following day—this morning, in fact—that I recovered possession of my faculties, after the most agitated slumber. Scarcely had I woken up than I leapt out of bed. I had to check the various phases that had marked the singular vision without delay.

"I ran to Dulaurier's house, which is a hundred meters away. He's a very early riser. When I went into his house he was just finishing grooming his beard.

"'Well, Colleague,' I said, going into his study, without any other preamble, I didn't know you were a poet.'

"'Oh!' he said, visibly embarrassed, 'if you've come so early, Antius, to compliment me on that subject, you've wasted your time, for I haven't tried to compel the muse in all my life.'

"'It seems to me, however, that the day before yesterday, while old Luberneau was delivering his soporific report, you were putting the final touches to a sonnet that seemed to me to be rather risqué. Shall I recite it for you?'

"'Don't you dare! All right, I admit my crime. But how the devil do you know about that bad habit, which I conceal with the greatest care, and to which I only abandon myself very rarely?'

"'I was beside you, and, not suspecting my presence, you didn't take any precaution. I will add that Thibault succeeded rather well in capturing the orator's obelisk-like nose.'

"Dulaurier looked at me suspiciously. 'All that's accurate,' he said, 'but I assure you that, if you were at the session, no one saw you.' He added: 'It's true that all our honorable colleagues were snoring conscientiously for two hours, and that Thibault and I were overcome in the end, like the rest. It was probably then that you came in, and that you were able to discover the serious occupations to which we had devoted ourselves. You doubtless didn't take long to make yourself scarce, for which I congratulate you.'

"As I wanted to accumulate proofs, I continued: 'It's certain that no one saw me, especially Poulard, from whom I've promised myself to pluck a few feathers, and soon.'

"'Ah!' said Dulaurier. 'You heard...'

"'No, but I've been told that he used the word *absurdities*?'

"'He didn't go as far as that; he contented himself with the expression *nonsense*.'

"I was convinced. I shook my colleague's hand, telling him that hazard alone had brought me to his door. He saw me out, requesting my silence with regard to his poetical lucubrations, especially with regard to our colleagues. I assured him that he could sleep easy on that score.

"As soon as I got home, I hastened to summon you, in order to give you an account of these marvelous things. I was saving the communication until after dinner. I had nothing really in view then but the interest that would result for us from the exact elation of the strange exaltation of thought, which permits sight through space, time and matter, when the desire you expressed to know what will be happening on Earth in a thousand years abruptly gave birth in my mind to the most audacious project.

"I tell you this solemnly: I have the sincere, profound and absolute conviction that any person who absorbs an infinitesimal fraction of the substance, taken to its superior degree of concentration, will be able to read the future as clearly and I read the past; for there is certainly, between the past, present and future—which are, after all, only ideas of relation—a fatal link of which he will be the master. It will be sufficient to concentrate his thought on the mystery into which he wishes to delve, as soon as the first physiological symptoms make themselves felt."

Fixing his ardent eyes upon his guests, the doctor continued: "Would you like to try the experiment this evening?"

"Certainly," the physicist replied, calmly. "But don't you fear, Antius, that the ingestion of the alkaloid, concentrated to the maximum, might sent us to make conjectures in a better world?"

"Have no fear in that regard; I've taken precautions. This very morning, I experimented on a guinea-pig. Not only did I make it swallow a quantity far superior to the one we shall take, but I even injected a similar quantity into the subcutaneous tissues. It did not seem to be at all inconvenienced. Instead of going, as is its habit, to hide in the darkest corner of my study, it gravely came to sit down on my table. For half an hour it remained pensive. Then, perceiving Bourbouze's new galvanometer,[5] which I purchased last month, it immediately

---

[5] Jean Bourbouze, a laboratory assistant at the Sorbonne, achieved brief notoriety during the siege of Paris in 1870,

got up and went to walk around it, inspecting it with the attention of a connoisseur. This evening, it was still very cheerful, but its gaiety was dignified. It directed glances toward me in which I caught a hint of a rather pronounced ironic sentiment."

"In that case, I see no objection," said the physicist.

"I'm eager to know how our descendants will travel," exclaimed Gédéon, whose imagination was already at work."

"We'll slip away to the laboratory quietly," said Antius, in a low voice. "If Madame Boquet, who is doubtless presently asleep beside her ovens, wakes up, all will be lost."

---

when he suggested that the problem of getting information in and out of Paris might be solved by passing an electric current along the Seine and measuring its modifications at a distance using a galvanometer. According to Henri de Parville, who reported the experiment, he demonstrated that the method could work by transmitting such a message between the Pont d'Iena and the Pont d'Austerlitz. He deposited at least one sealed letter with the Académie in order to register priority in a subsequent invention, but it does not seem ever to have been opened.

VIII. The Proof

The three diners got up silently and went along the corridor, muffling the sound of their footfalls. The doctor, who was marching in the lead, lamp in hand, headed for the pavilion, the door of which he opened.

Terrier and Gédéon, who were following close behind him, stopped. Turning toward them, he said: "Come in carefully; I'll close the door behind you and leave you in darkness momentarily. It's important that I send Madeleine to bed, in order that she doesn't inspect the house from cellar to loft, as is her habit."

The two men went in. The doctor turned the key in the lock as an extra precaution and went to the kitchen.

Madame Boquet, who was sitting on a narrow stool with her head on the entablature of an old dresser, was profoundly asleep, maintained in that awkward position by a kind of unconscious equilibrium.

The doctor went up to the housekeeper and shouted in hr ear: "Madeleine!"

The old lady woke up with a start, rubbed her eyes and exclaimed: "Do you think I'm deaf? For a start, I wasn't asleep, I was just a little drowsy." Looking at an old cuckoo-clock that was ticking dully on the mantelpiece, she said: "Oh my God, is it possible? Midnight already! Do you all want to make yourselves ill. Where are the others? Is it good sense to go out at this hour in this deserted quarter?" She got up. "I'll see them to the door."

"They went home more than an hour ago," said Antius. "I saw them out myself. So go to bed—I won't be long doing likewise."

The worthy woman lit an inch-long candle-stub from the dying flame of the lamp that was flickering over the hearth, blew out the latter, and, having paraded her gaze around the

43

theater of her exploits, went out of the kitchen and went upstairs, ponderously.

The doctor went out into the corridor and waited there, immobile, for a few moments. When Madame Boquet had gone into her room, he went out into the garden that extended in front of the house without a light. Ten steps from the perron he turned round and looked up at a small widow that had just lit up. After five minutes, the window went dark again. Convinced that he was now safe, he went back in, locked the door and headed for the laboratory.

His two companions were standing up, motionless.

"All's well," he said. "Now, no one will disturb us."

Then he shone his lamp over the walls, searching all the corners with his gaze.

"Ah, there he is!" he exclaimed, showing his friends the guinea-pig, stretched out voluptuously on a Ruhmkorff coil.

The animal, surprised by the exclamation, got up on its four feet with dignity, looked at them one after another with a kind of disdainful fixity, and then nonchalantly resumed its original posture.

"It's certain that that insignificant mammal, which is looking at us impertinently, is animated by a singular force," said the physicist.

"And he's marvelously healthy," added Antius. "Sit down, while I get everything ready."

The professor and the young man took their places in two vast leather armchairs next to the experimental table. The doctor opened a cupboard hollowed out in the thickness of the wall and took out a small bottle, which he examined in the light.

"This is the substance," he said.

Gédéon leaned over. "I can't see anything," he said. "Are we going to practice homeopathy?"

Antius poured the contents of the bottle on to a disk of polished glass; five microscopic globules, brown in color, fell on to the surface.

A sudden emotion had gripped the three men.

44

"My friends," the doctor said, gravely, "before hurling ourselves into the unknown, let us fix firmly in our minds the following resolution: as soon as we experience the first symptoms of intellectual overstimulation, let us concentrate all the might of our thoughts on the mystery whose depths we wish to plumb, and above all, let us not lose sight of the fact that an indissoluble link must constantly bind us together."

As he said these words he put two globules back in the bottle, which he locked away. Then he took three graduated glass vessels, into each of which he poured two grams of distilled water. He handed one to the young man, the other to the professor.

Following his example, each of them took a globule and set in on his tongue. Then, drinking the liquid that was to wash it down, each of them swallowed all of it with a vigorous gulp.

The glasses were replaced on the tray. The doctor spoke again. "Now, by the grace of God," he said, solemnly, "let us remain cam and collected, and focus all our thoughts invariably on the subject in hand."

For ten minutes, an absolute silence reigned in the laboratory. Everyone maintained complete immobility.

Suddenly, Gédéon gave some evidence of agitation, and then became as calm as before. Shortly thereafter, the same symptoms were manifest in the two scientists. The silence was still profound and solemn.

After a further quarter of an hour, the young man suddenly closed his eyes, stiffening in his seat. "Uncle, Master, what a strange sensation!" he said, in a halting voice. "I'm being carried through space. My God, how frightful! I'm devouring distance at lightning speed. I'm flying ahead of the Earth in its orbit. Don't leave me!" And his head fell back, inertly, against the back of the armchair.

The two scientists gripped the young man's cold hands in their own.

"Perhaps we were wrong to attempt to fathom the future," said Antius, in a dull voice.

"The die is cast," murmured the physicist. "I too can feel my heart freezing. I'm experiencing a sensation of rapid displacement. Oh, what frightful speed! The Earth is no longer anything but an atom behind us—but you're both close to me." And he slumped backwards, slowly.

The doctor was gripped in his turn by a profound shiver. He pronounced a few unsteady words and, his fists clenched, threw himself backwards.

A few seconds later, the three men, motionless, inert and frozen, seemed to be sleeping the eternal slumber.

Part Two
A THOUSAND YEARS LATER

I. Resurrection

The sun was emerging over the horizon and sprinkling the countryside with golden arrows when Gédéon opened his eyes. All the objects surrounding him appeared at first to be drowned in a kind of iridescent mist, for he was no longer possessed of clarity of vision.

"Uh oh!" he said. "Am I the victim of a case of diplopia?" he sneezed vigorously several times, and added: "If I still have doubts on that score, I'm certain with regard to a cold in the head." He pulled back his hand, which he had extended in front of him, and found it to be wet. "Of course," he said. "That explains it. I'm simply lying in the dew." After further examination he muttered: "My unmentionables are well and truly soaked."

He tried to get up, and, trying to obtain a point of leverage on the ground, put his hand on a muddy boot, which remained inert on that contact.

"That boot is harboring a foot, to which a leg is attached, which belongs to someone, for sure," he added, aloud. "If my sight is troubled, my reasoning is clear, thank God!"

He stood up and, moving his legs apart in order to preserve his balance, encountered an object that caused him to stumble. He bent down, reaching out his arm, and grabbed the toe of a slipper.

"How is it that so many citizens took it into their heads to sleep in the open last night?" he said. "I don't understand."

He rubbed his eyes vigorously, and, after ten minutes of effort, was gradually able to distinguish his surroundings.

"Great God!" he cried. "Uncle! Monsieur Terrier! How can they be here? Here's an adventure, damn it! Let's wake them up—perhaps they'll have the key to the mystery. Oho! If serious men are spending the night away from home..."

As he spoke he shook the two sleepers, gently at first and then with increasing vigor. Eventually, they opened their eyes. Profound amazement was painted on the faces of the two scientists. They were making vain efforts to collect their ideas and appeared to be struggling against the influence of a nightmare.

For a few moments, questions overlapped volubly, but their situation was becoming increasingly inexplicable when Antius summarized it. "We're in an admirable park," he said, "which seems to be maintained with infinite artistry. The region is certainly inhabited, for nature doesn't take as much trouble as that."

A few steps away, a little stream was rippling its crystal waves over a bed of silvery sand.

"That watercourse must go somewhere," said Gédéon. "Let's follow it. At least we'll have something to drink."

This proposal was accepted. The three travelers started walking along the bank.

After a hundred paces, the young man stopped dead, and exclaimed: "Look, a woman!"

"A woman?"

"Don't worry—she's made of stone."

"My word, he's right," said Terrier.

"Let's go interrogate her," said Gédéon.

"Don't laugh—she might give us the key to the enigma."

They advanced rapidly into an open space framed by a circle of majestic trees. A superb white marble statue mounted on a brand new pedestal stood in the center of the circumference.

"What does that beautiful creature represent?" asked Antius.

"In truth, I can't see any name—only a date. The sculptor isn't very good at chronology, mind—read it for yourself."

The doctor came forward and read, engraved in golden letters in the middle of the pedestal, the inscription: MMDCCCLXXX.

"Two thousand eight hundred and eighty!" he exclaimed, slapping his forehead. "My friends, we're all a thousand years older. The enchanted beverage has suspended our existence for ten centuries, and we've woken up today."

"Well, I'm not sorry," said the professor. "I'm eager to know whether physics has kept all its promises."

"Great God, I'm a thousand and twenty-four years old!" exclaimed Gédéon, running to the stream.

"Are you going to drown yourself for that?" asked Terrier.

"No, I'm going to examine my wrinkles and count my hairs, if I still have any."

After five minutes he came back, wearing an expression of evident satisfaction. "Well," he said, "I've got away with it nicely. It even seems to me that I look younger." He suddenly burst out laughing. "That's funny, though!"

"What is?" asked Terrier, anxiously, seeing that he was being examined from top to toe.

"My dear Professor—for I can now address you in familiar terms, since we're both old men—your boots are very elegant, but your top hat is coming apart; my uncle is wearing his Greek skullcap, but only has slippers on his feet. As for myself, I confess that I'm dressed rather extravagantly." The young man added: "I believe, in consequence, that we're going to cut a fine figure in society—but are we really still on the same planet?"

"Yes, of course," the professor replied.

"You've decided very quickly."

"Look at the sun. Doesn't it have the same apparent diameter?"

"Yes. What does that prove?"

"Age must have put a little lead in your head," said the doctor. "If we weren't on Earth we'd be nearer or more distant from the sun, which would appear larger or smaller. Suppose

49

that we were on one of the two plants nearest to the Earth. From Mars, the sun would seem twice as small; from Venus, twice as large—not to mention that in the former case we'd be frozen, and in the latter roasted."

"Good. But if we're on Earth, where are we?"

"We'll soon find out, for, at the far end of that avenue of old elms, I can see a palace," said Terrier, whose gaze had been searching in all directions for a few moments.

"Let's go," said the doctor.

They set off.

A long and broad grassy avenue bordered by gigantic trees extended before them; they went along it.

After twenty paces, Gédéon suddenly stopped. "Look!" he exclaimed, seizing his uncle's arm and extending the other toward the sky.

The two scientists looked up and saw, to their amazement, a long dark object cutting through the air at the speed of a bullet.

"The canon that fired that projectile must be at least as big as a cathedral," said Gédéon.

"Is it really a projectile?" murmured Terrier.

The travelers continued on their way, variously preoccupied.

II. Reciprocal Astonishment

A few minutes later, Antius suddenly halted. "Through the foliage," he said, "a hundred paces away, I can see someone walking in parallel to us, in the opposite direction."

"Let's go toward him."

"By following that pathway, which is perpendicular to our direction, we can catch up with him in two minutes," said the doctor.

They raced forward, and soon found themselves on the same path, a hundred paces behind the early-morning stroller.

The latter was singularly dressed. He wore a sort of burnoose of extremely light white cloth over his shoulders; his broad trousers, fabricated with a vegetable fiber of remarkable delicacy, partly disappeared into pale brown leather boots, the legs of which were dotted with holes that facilitated the circulation of air. His head was coiffed with a hemispherical white leather hat, the summit and base of which presented numerous orifices.

"There's an indigene who, whether or not he knows the scientific theory of the radiation of heat, is applying it intelligently," said the professor.

At the sound of the three men's hurried steps, the walker turned round and came to a sudden stop.

They advanced toward him.

"Monsieur," said the doctor, taking off his hat, "we're travelers who have strayed into this place. Would you be good enough to tell us where we are?"

"Messieurs," the walker replied, "you're in the Luxembourg Park."

"What—we're so close to home!" said Gédéon. "I hope the Rue de Fleurus still exists."

"I don't know of any street of that name in Paris."

"What! But it touches the Luxembourg."

"You've been misinformed, Monsieur. There are only avenues around the Park, which extends as far as the old port."

"As far as the old port?"

"Yes, Monsieur."

"Paris is a sea-port then?"

"It has been one, but isn't any longer—not for four hundred and fifty years. The port no longer had any industrial or commercial value once science had conquered the prodigious means of transport that we have at our disposal today. It's the same with the lake, where several thousand vessels could maneuver with ease, but is no longer anything more than an ornament of the city."

"Monsieur," said the physicist, "we would be very glad to know what we ought to think about the opaque, elongated, almost cylindrical body that we saw passing over our heads with extreme rapidity."

"Just now?"

"Twenty minutes ago,"

"That's the American mail; it arrives at the same time every day."

"People travel through the air now?" exclaimed Antius.

"Yes, of course, Monsieur—for a long time now we haven't employed any other means of transport. Once, aerial transport was reserved for a few rare scientific experiments, but that invention, lost in the night of time, has made such progress and has become so practical, that thousands of machines traverse the seas and continents every day carrying prodigious loads." Having observed the amazement that his replies had provoked in the three men, the stroller continued. "May I, Messieurs, ask for a clarification in my turn, if you would be so kind?"

"Gladly," said the professor.

"To begin with, you're strangers, and have doubtless come a long way."

"What makes you think that?"

"Many indications—first of all, your astonishment at things one sees every day."

"That's fair. But on the other hand, our language indicates that we're French."

"That doesn't prove anything, Messieurs, for all peoples speak the French language as correctly as we do."

"My word—I'm amazed!" said Gédéon, dazedly.

"In addition, Monsieur," the individual said, addressing Terrier, "there's something about your costume that intrigues me greatly."

"What?"

"That black tub you're wearing on your head."

"It's the habitual *coiffure* of my compatriots."

"Really?"

"I assure you."

"Well, we see the inhabitants of all the countries in the world every day, and it's the first time I've found myself in the presence of such an extraordinary head-dress. My attention had also been struck by an object whose purpose I can't deduce."

"What?"

"That metal chain you're wearing over your stomach."

"The chain is only an accessory, Monsieur," said the physicist, taking a magnificent chronometer out of his fob-pocket. "This is the object it maintains."

"A watch! It's a long time since I've seen one of those. That one is very beautiful and very old; you'd get a good price for it at the Museum of Antiques."

"Thank you for the information—if necessary, I'll part with it, as well as the chain, which is equally valuable."

"The chain, Monsieur, has only a feeble value by comparison. It's gold, I believe?"

"Rolled gold, Monsieur."

"Well, gold is modestly priced here."

"Too bad," said Terrier. "But how do you know what time it is?"

"Every house in the city—indeed, every room in every house—has a clock whose hands are moved by a universal electric current, regulated by the Central Observatory."

"Many thanks, Monsieur."

"If you follow the broad avenue that you left just now, you'll reach the lateral avenue of the Museum within ten minutes."

The professor and his companions bowed to the stroller, who returned the gesture and resumed his interrupted walk, murmuring: "Where can those three singular men have come from? And more importantly, how did they get here?"

"So," said the doctor, abruptly, "We're in the Luxembourg, probably at the same place where we went to sleep a thousand years ago! Oh, my friends, what prodigious astonishments are in store for us! Into what sort of world, what sort of society, have we been suddenly hurled? We've crossed the abysm of time. We're going to be, with regard to our descendants, what a Polynesian savage abruptly thrown into the most brilliant center of civilization would previously have been to us."

"No," said the professor, gravely, "for reason and verity are one and indestructible. Between the cannibal and the scientist of the 19th century, there would have been no possible standard of comparison. Between us and our descendants, no matter what their state of scientific perfection, there will only be differences. In the already-ancient epoch in which we devoted ourselves to our endeavors and research, more than twenty centuries separated us from Pythagoras, Euclid and Archimedes. We were already drawing precious crops from the field in which those three giants of ancient science had traced the first furrows. Suppose that, in all the blaze of their genius, they had suddenly been resuscitated in the century of steam and electricity. Their astonishment would certainly have been immense, but, by following the chain of abstract speculations of which they had forged the first links, they would not have taken long to familiarize themselves with the whole of the materials amassed by science in two thousand years. Undoubtedly, marvelous conquests will strike our eyes, but, by means of patient and methodical study, we shall have no difficulty connecting them to the applications of our old epoch, which many people considered to be the Pillars of Hercules of progress."

"If you like," said the young man, "unsupported as I am, like you, by transcendent philosophy, and only guided by gross common sense, I'll tell you what I think."

"Go on."

"I think that in talking to us about a lake in the middle of Paris and air mail from America, that Parisian was telling us bare-faced tall tales, such as I've never heard. Furthermore, on examining your watch-chain, whose title you've so proudly guaranteed and from which we hope, if necessary, to obtain a considerable advantage, our man said: *gold is modestly priced here*. What do you think of him now?"

"It isn't about him that the statement makes me think," said the physicist, "but about us. I admit that the observation frightened me. Perhaps gold really has very little value, and banknotes probably have none at all."

"Yes," Antius added. "I was struck, as you were, by the stroller's opinion. Fortunately, Terrier, you have your chronometer, which might, according to the observations of the obliging city-dweller, get us out of difficulty for a little while. Gédéon also has his watch..."

"Alas," the latter replied, slapping his forehead, "I only have the chain. A month before the famous supper, I took it somewhere."

"That's unfortunate," said the doctor.

"All the more unfortunate that it was to hang it in the nail."

"The nail?"

"Yes—at the *Mont de pieté*,[6] if it's necessary to dot the *i*s. I was advanced a hundred francs, and I had to redeem it

---

[6] An institution originally founded by the Catholic Church as a means of helping the poor, which, by 1880, had become the most significant pawnbroker in Paris, very popular among the young men of the Latin Quarter.

within a year, at ten per cent interest, under penalty of losing that family treasure forever."

"Well, I don't advise you to go and get it back," said Antius.

"Why?"

"Because you'd have ten thousand francs to pay, in simple interest."

"And if you'd borrowed at compound interest," added Terrier, slowly, "it would be necessary to part with a sum compared with which the Earth's weight in solid gold would only be an insignificant fraction."

"Oh!" said Antius, raising his head. The choice of that formidable quantity as a measure of comparison had appeared to him to be a complete perversion of his companion's mathematical faculties. "Has the geometrical regularity of your habitual language giving way to the audacities of hyperbole now?"

"I haven't yet fallen into second childhood, thank God," the professor replied, "although my age must be, in a sense, immeasurable. I can demonstrate the exactitude of my affirmation, in spite of its prodigious character.

"The sum of a hundred francs, deposited at ten per cent compound interest for a thousand years, doubles the hundred twenty-seven times, and produces a capital surpassing seventeen tridecillion francs. Now, a thousand francs occupies a volume of sixteen cubic centimeters. The volume of the specified sum would therefore be at least two hundred and seventy two duodecillion cubic centimeters, or two hundred and seventy-two sextillion cubic myriameters. On the other hand, the volume of the Earth is one billion eighty million and seven hundred and fifty-nine thousand cubic myriameters. The mass of gold in question is, therefore, at least two hundred and fifty thousand billion times greater than our planet." With the tone of a judge at the assizes pronouncing a sentence, the professor declared: "In consequence, Gédéon owes the *Mont de pieté* a sum far superior to the one we have calculated."

"I won't pay, then," cried the young man, astounded as much by the skill of his former teacher as by the size of the debt.

"For the moment," said the doctor, "it's a matter of doing what we can to get us out of difficulty."

They retraced their steps and, having reached the central avenue again, followed it in the direction of the monument that Terrier had initially taken for a palace. The closer they came to it, the appearance of the construction, initially indecisive because of the distance, became gradually clearer, and the qualification of which the professor had made use seemed increasingly merited.

It really was a marvel of architecture. The various stories were set back upon one another and opened on to vast terraces laden with small trees, flowers and verdure. Groups of coupled Corinthian columns, of decreasing thickness, rose up to the next level, framing monumental windows. The effect was simultaneously charming, rich and grandiose.

III. Official Dispatches in 2880

The travelers reached the end of the avenue, which widened out abruptly into a vast semicircle of verdure, framed by giant trees whose dense crowns formed somber clouds against the dazzling sky. Several gushing fountains in white marble were projecting dense liquid sprays, disappearing at times in a compact mist, which expanded a delightful freshness.

The terrace of the park, which extended as far as the eye could see, overlooked a causeway a hundred meters wide, which, on the side opposite the hemicycle was bordered by magnificent buildings along its immense extent.

The three men moved forward, gripped by admiration, and their gazes were able to embrace a magical spectacle.

A quadruple row of trees of precious species, different in appearance but grouped with infinite artistry, divided the avenue into three shady paths. The middle one was covered with clumps of dazzling flowers, jets of water and statues.

Another part of the scene, however, took their astonishment to the limit. As far as the eye could see, the portion of the causeway that was not invaded by verdure presented a uniform surface, as clean and shiny as the deck of a ship. The color of that singular coating was reminiscent of the shade of bistre brown.

The travelers were losing themselves in conjectures regarding the nature of that astonishing pavement when their attention was attracted by a confused noise of speech, which became gradually more distinct.

Soon, a group of people emerged from behind a bush, heading toward the balustrade. At the sight of the three strangers, a rapid expression of astonishment crossed their faces, but they continued their conversation regardless.

"The *Éclair*," said one, "has a much faster speed; it only takes seven hours to fly from Paris to Tawai Pounamou, stopovers included."[7]

"Tawai Pounamou!" repeated the professor, in a low voice.

"Do you know that country?" asked Gédéon.

"Of course—it's in the region where I was nearly put on the spit."

"The exhibition was truly remarkable," the speaker in the group continued. "The electric studios were of a rare perfection, the chemistry collections very abundant and very varied, and the photopainting salon merited the eulogies of all the critics. As for the metal exchange—and I can speak with authority because, in my capacity as a founder, I've visited all those in the world, I can affirm that I've never seen one as grandiose."

"Did you buy anything?" asked the man to his left.

"I bought three hundred tons of platinum," the industrialist replied, modestly.

Terrier pricked up his ears.

"That's a provision that will permit the whole city to renew its saucepans," said his interlocutor, laughing.

"Damn!" murmured the physicist, "I used to pay five hundred francs apiece for my medium-sized capsules."

The doctor, who had not take his eyes off the ground of the avenue, suddenly intervened in the conversation. "Messieurs," he asked, taking off his hat, to the voyager who had mentioned New Zealand with so much enthusiasm, "Would you kindly give us some enlightenment with regard to the magnificent paving of your city."

"Certainly, Monsieur. The covering of the ground, throughout the city, is made of molded wood."

"Molded wood?"

---

[7] Tawai Ponamou, or Te Wai Ponamu, is the Maori name for New Zealand's South Island.

"Of course. You're not unaware that disintegrated wood, bound by certain chemical substances, can take any form when it is still in its pulp state, and that, as soon as it is hardened by heat, it has the solidity of cast steel."

"Of course," Antius replied, with embarrassment.

"Well, Monsieur, Sweden, Norway, Finland and a part of Siberia count among their most flourishing industries that of pulverized wood, which arrives here in bulk, and which we treat on location. As for precious woods from the equatorial regions, they are, as you know, reserved for the fabrication of furniture, which can take the richest and most varied forms at slight expense. The pavement of Paris, as you can see for yourself, is in Northern fir, molded over a layer of asphalt, and it lasts forever."

"The procedure is truly marvelous," exclaimed Antius, who was not generally given to enthusiasm.

"It's certain," affirmed a stroller who had not yet spoken, swelling with pride, "that Paris is better paved than any other city in the world, not even excepting Constantinople."

The travelers bowed to the group and drew away.

"Why did that odd fellow mention Constantinople?" said Antius, suddenly slapping his forehead. "Everyone knows that the streets in the Turkish capital are replaced by mud and dilapidated staircases, and that stray dogs are in sole charge of the city's cleaning. What do you think of this molded wood, Terrier?"

"Very highly. That invention—or, rather, that progress in kind—should not surprise us at all, for you'll certainly recall that the industry of hardened wood was already applied in our day to the manufacture of certain objects of ornamentation. It's evident that the timid trials of our contemporaries have, thanks to the incessant progress of the applied sciences, led to the results that we have before our eyes."

A broad stairway descended to the avenue at a gentle slope. They went down slowly.

"What a magical city!" said Gédéon. "How vast, rich and superb everything is! Only demigods are worthy of living here, that's for sure!"

The foreigners had been walking in silence for some time when the physicist stopped and gripped each of his companions by the arm.

"It's certain," he said, pursuing aloud a train of thought that he had been ruminating privately for some time, "that the extraordinary abundance of platinum, a metal once rare and very precious, corroborates the affirmation of the first citizen we encountered here, with regard to the scant value of gold. Not only should that situation not surprise us, but it was inevitable. Armed with the incomparable force of aerial navigation, seconded by machines of a perfection and a power that we can hardly imagine, the engineers of the 29th century must certainly have extracted from the Earth a notable proportion of the wealth distributed at its surface."

At that moment, a shrill whistle resounded behind the travelers, who turned their heads abruptly.

A vehicle with three wheels, rather singular in form, seemingly moving of its own accord, was bearing down upon them with the rapidity of an arrow. They moved aside swiftly, and the vehicle went past them, with no other sound than a series of multiple crepitations, accompanied by myriads of blue sparks, springing from the tips of a metal brush applied to the axle of the large wheels.

Semi-recumbent in the tricycle, an individual with a placid physiognomy was nonchalantly using his left hand to operate a tiller that controlled the rear wheel.

"That's a very ingenious electrical apparatus," the doctor remarked.

"All the more ingenious," added the physicist, "because it must furnish motive force and light at the same time, for the lens it carries in front is certainly illuminated by a slight deviation of the principal current."

Several locomotives of the same kind appeared successively in the lateral paths without coming into the central causeway, which appeared to be exclusively reserved for pedestrians. The drivers had the skill to meet all challenges, for, on several occasions, two vehicles that appeared to be about to crash into one another, having almost made contact, avoided one another by describing the most graceful curves.

"Well," exclaimed Gédéon, marveling, "if I had been informed that Paris will one day enclose a genuine lake, my imagination as a champion of the Rowing Club would have been singularly delighted. The hypothesis of aerial navigation would only have found me mulish—but anyone who had claimed that carriages would one day move of their own accord would have been strongly suspected of having delved into the old papers of Cyrano de Bergerac."

The travelers reached the central causeway.

Two hundred meters away, the view was partly interrupted by a quadrangular pyramid. Twenty curious individuals seemed to be examining its faces with keen interest.

"Why do all those citizens have their noses in the air?" asked Gédéon. "Are they participating in some religious ceremony practiced at sunrise? Are we looking at a Parsi sect? Oh—that's odd!"

"What is?" said Antius.

"I can see a strange movement in the middle of the face of the pyramid."

The two scientists concentrated their gazes on the monolith, vainly.

"I can't see anything," the professor declared.

"But I, who have the visual acuity of a lynx," replied the young man, "can clearly see a wide pale blue strip, which is gradually extending and has already attained an area a meter square. Now it's stopped moving."

"Let's go closer," said Antius, enthusiastically.

At fifty paces, Gédéon exclaimed: "But the strip has printing on it."

"It's probably some official notice that has just appeared," said the professor.

Moved by curiosity, they increased their pace, and soon found themselves close enough to the pyramid to recognize that the physicist's conjecture was well-founded.

"That's truly prodigious," said Gédéon.

In the meantime, the crowd had dispersed in all directions. They continued forward and stopped in front of a frame about a meter square, which was imprinted from top to bottom in large letters.

Without pausing before offering his services, Gédéon said: "Listen," and with a certain tremor in his voice read aloud: "*Official bulletin, Sunday fifteenth June 2880. Night telegrams, Dover eleven forty-two. The fifth arch of the bridge from Calais to Dover has been severely shaken by the tempest that been raging in the Channel in recent days. Nevertheless, the engineers affirm that traffic ought not to be interrupted, and that a few hours should be sufficient to repair the damage.*"

"A bridge over the Channel!" exclaimed the doctor.

"I foresaw that," said the physicist, tranquilly. "It must be the eighth wonder of the world, having victoriously superseded that frightful tunnel, which, by some strange mental aberration, had won the favor of our contemporaries." To the astonished young man he said: "Go on."

"Gladly. *Panama, six p.m. A portion of the old track established along the Darien Canal, which once linked the two Oceans, has just collapsed because of insufficient repair work. Discussions have begun on the subject in the Society of Engineers of the State of Colombia. A few members have proposed that things be left as they are, considering that the track, and the canal even more so, no longer have any utility, by virtue of atmospheric transportation, but the majority, opposing these conclusions, has taken the view that the central government of the Southern States should make funds available as a matter of urgency for the execution of the repairs necessary to the conservation of that work of great archeological value.*"

"So the isthmus of Panama has finally been pierced?" said the doctor.

"Some time ago," replied Gédéon, "For they're talking about conserving the canal as an antiquity. But what does *track* mean?"

"It means," said Terrier, "that because the canal was not adequate to the abundance of traffic, a railway track was established on one of its banks."

"The reasoning is plausible," said Antius. Feverishly, he bade his nephew: "Continue."

Gideon read: "*Bangkok, fifteenth June, eleven a.m...* are they mad out there? Eleven a.m., when it's only seven o'clock in the morning?"

"Bangkok is ninety-nine degrees east of Paris," the professor replied. "We are, therefore, ninety-nine degrees west of that capital, and our clocks have always been six hours thirty-six minutes behind those of that longitude."

"Since it seems clear to you, I'll go on: *Bangkok, fifteenth June, eleven a.m. In spite of the inferiority of our agricultural exploitation, which still employs steam as a motive force, the rice harvest has been very abundant this year. Everything suggests that the wine harvest will be no less fortunate, the disastrous effects of storms having been partially annulled by the hailshields.*"

"Hailshields?" queried the physicists.

"Yes, it's certainly a barbaric term," the young man. "I'm familiar with lightning-conductors, windbreaks, umbrellas and so on,[8] but I only know two ways of avoiding being damaged by hail: get under cover or have oneself vaccinated. What astonishes me even more is their harvest of wine. I thought they only drank water."

"For myself," Antius said, "nothing surprises me on the part of people who confess, with embarrassment, that agriculture in their country is still reduced to the employment of

---

[8] This passage loses its alliterative symmetry in translation; in the original the term *paragrèle* [hailshield] is contrasted with *paratonnerre* [lightning-conductor], *paravent* [windbreak] and *parapluie* [umbrella].

steam engines. What system do the others employ? What other surprises does this astonishing newssheet still have in reserve for us?"

"I've only read half of it," Gédéon replied.

From two lateral faces of the monolith, which they had not yet been able to examine, seven prolonged and equally-spaced sonorous vibrations sprang forth simultaneously.

The reader continued: "*Tripoli, fifteenth June, five a.m. The anticipations of our meteorological observatory have been fulfilled. The Algerian Sea has been troubled since yesterday evening by a furious tempest, which is attaining its maximum intensity at this moment. All the coastal ports were warned several days ago, and we may hope that no disasters will occur.*"

"The Algerian Sea!" Antius exclaimed. "That's strange."

"Of course," the professor riposted. "It had to happen. Do you recall that all observations had demonstrated that the Sahara is merely a dried-up sea. Have you forgotten the works of Captain Roudaire?[9] Don't you remember that at the very

---

[9] François-Élie Roudaire (1836-1885) was commissioned to map the French colony of Algeria in the late 1860s, employing what were then new surveying methods. Finding a good deal of land below sea level, associated with the inland lakes known as *chotts* he became convinced a huge salty depression extending toward the Gulf of Gabès in eastern Tunisia was the dried-up bed of a sea once described by Herodotus as the Bay of Triton. He proposed that the area be reconnected to the sea by a canal. The idea was taken up by Ferdinand de Lesseps after the completion of his Suez Canal project; a joint-stock company was formed to organize the project. Preliminary surveys were carried out between 1876 and 1878, but the Ministry of Public Works withdrew its support in July 1882. In 1883, while *Dans mille ans* was being serialized, Roudaire and de Lesseps undertook a further survey. The readers of the *Musée des familles* would have been very familiar with the

moment we left the old world, the question of the Tunisian *chotts* was on everyone's mind? I'm convinced that the riches of the old world must be concentrated today on the shores of that sea, created by human hands."

"Yes," Antius added, "those immense extents where dryness, desolation and death once rules, must now by furrowed by thousands of ships, which must cram their holds with the inexhaustible riches of the Sudan and the surrounding countries. Who knows whether the heart of Africa might now be occupied by powerful and civilized nations?" To his nephew, he added: "Go on."

"*Ujiji, fifteenth June, three a.m...*"

"You're right, Antius," said Terrier. "Here we are in the heart of Africa. It's at Ujiji, on the eastern shore of Lake Tanganyika, that the celebrated explorer Stanley, sent by the *New York Herald*, found the great Livingstone."

"*Ujiji, fifteenth June, three a.m. The inauguration of the aerostatic palace has been celebrated by a grand fête. The number of curiosity-seekers hastening from all points of Central Africa has been estimated at five hundred thousand. A gala concert was put on by the government for the members of the conference, and the presidents, vice-presidents and secretaries of the five hundred scientific Societies arrived from all over the continent. The sight of the hall of the Grand Opera was magical. For the next week there are to be free performances in the capital's twenty-two theaters.*"

Gédéon raised his arms into the air. "All these extravagances are making my head spin!" he cried. "Personally, I think that if there's an Opera House out there, one would count more caimans and hippopotamuses in the orchestra stalls than music-lovers. This is the rest of it: *Yesterday, before an illustrious assembly in the great hall of the Museum, Professor Aboko gave a very interesting lecture on the history*

---

idea and the progress of the project, although it subsequently died with Roudaire.

of the discoveries that led to aerial locomotion. Have we been afflicted by some gigantic hallucination?"

"All this is indeed marvelous," said the physicist, who now seemed to be armored against any surprise, "but it's all perfectly rational."

IV. A Useful Monument

At that moment, a rapid shadow ran over their feet. On raising their heads, they perceived another moving object, a hundred meters from the ground, with powerful metallic wings that were cleaving the air with hurricane speed.

Either because they were used to the spectacle in question or because the sight of the three men at whom they were directing astonished gazes interested them more, the strollers passing close by did not deign to look up in the air.

"Another balloon," said Antius, "but this one has moving wings."

"Wings and a tail," added Terrier, "for it's steered by a powerful rudder."

Gédéon, who had gone around the side of the pyramid, suddenly exclaimed: "Here's practical people for you!"

The two scientists went forward and found themselves facing a large white marble plaque, in the center of which was the dial of a monumental clock, indicating the hour, the minute, the second, the day of the month, the day of the week, the phase of the moon, the coordinates of the sun and the equivalent time at the principal points of the globe.

At the top, fixed symmetrically in the corners, there was a pair of thermometers to the left, one graduated in centigrade divisions, the other with a maximum and a minimum indicating the highest and lowest temperatures of the day, and an extremely sensitive aneroid barometer to the right.

In one of the lower corners, an admirable celestial planisphere was painted in dark blue, on which the stars were represented in relative dimensions by exceedingly bright dots. In the other, the gaze was arrested by a complex instrument containing a hygrometer and a udometer, the construction of which intrigued the physicist greatly.

"Have you not been struck," he said, suddenly, "by the extraordinary brightness of those brilliant dots representing the heavenly bodies?" He pointed to the planisphere, presently inundated by sunlight, and added: "They're diamonds."

Gédéon looked at his former teacher in amazement.

"That's true," said Antius, after an attentive examination. "They're probably manufactured today with the same facility as window-glass."

Continuing their inspection of the pyramid, the travelers found that the third face was entirely occupied by a vast and very detailed terrestrial planisphere. The four corners enclosed statistical tables, which seemed extremely complicated at first glance.

The fourth face of the monolith was a reproduction of he second, with the result that the two clocks were visible from two long avenues that intersected the one they had been following at this point. The pyramid was erected at the junction of two causeways.

The sun was now high above the horizon and the sky was shining with a remarkable purity. The large bands of shadow that extended beneath the dense foliage of the quadruple row of trees seemed black. Thousands of birds with bright plumage were hopping from branch to branch, like winged gems. An atmosphere of incomparable calm, restfulness and coolness enveloped the magnificent pathways.

Tormented by a legitimate curiosity, the three men had so far remained almost insensible to the ardor of the sun.

"What frightful heat!" Antius exclaimed, all of a sudden, having been unconsciously sponging his face for some moments, after having pushed his skullcap back to the confines of the occiput. "Let's go sit down under the trees—there are comfortable benches. At any rate, we urgently need to consider our situation. I confess that, for my part, I'm extremely anxious."

They experienced a vivid sensation of wellbeing as they passed beneath the dense crown of foliage, which extended all the way to the horizon and protected the morning coolness against the blaze of the sun. After a few steps, they let themselves fall on to a large bench with an angled back, the intelligent design of which facilitated rest and sleep equally.

"It would be good to live here," said Gédéon, "if one only had an income of thirty-five thousand livres!"

"What you just said is meaningless, at least with regard to income," Antius replied. "Everything we've seen has thrown our ideas on that subject into the deepest confusion."

"Certainly," the physicist added. "We can't yet affirm anything about the relative value of metals. Gold is abundant here, as those massive moldings ornamenting the ridges of the monument testify. In any case, I approve unreservedly of the employment of that metal, which is virtually unalterable by the air. On the other hand, the fabrication of diamonds furnishes our descendants with first-rate pivots and optical lenses of great power."

Since the travelers had sat down on their rustic bench, which, by virtue of the phenomena they had witnessed, threatened to become for them the raft of the *Medusa*, the causeways had become less deserted. Clad in light fabrics, whose usual colors spanned all the shades of the pastel scale extending from dazzling white to bright bistre, groups were gradually emerging from the verdure of the bushes, as if some magician had suddenly animated and multiplied the white marble statues that had previously been the only inhabitants of that luxurious solitude.

The doctor, who had been watching the pedestrians for some time with sustained attention, suddenly turned to his two companions. "I've noticed something odd," he said, "which is entirely to the advantage of the city's inhabitants. You'll notice, if you haven't already made the observation, that the people offer, without exception, manifest signs of strength and health. I conclude directly that today, the education of the body marches in parallel with that of the mind."

"For vigor, health and nobility of attitude, the women lose nothing by comparison with the men," said Terrier, pointing at a group of magnificently-dressed young women, who were examining the bushes filled with bright flowers as they came forward.

When they came abreast of the three men, a slight smile brushed their lips, provoked by the eccentricity of their clothing.

V. A Fortunate Incident

Suddenly, a little girl, who seemed to be about ten years old, emerged from the group of young ladies and ran towards the travelers. She stopped abruptly in front of the physicist.

Her anxious mothers hastened after her. "Lydia," she called, softly, "why are you disturbing these foreigners?"

But the child, her eyes fixed upon the respectable professor's hat, was not listening.

The young woman blushed. "Please excuse her, Monsieur," she said. "The child, barely eight years old, is unaware of her lack of deference."

"The charming little girl is still at the happy age at which speech is only guided by the eyes or by the heart," the scientist replied, "and I cannot blame her for her astonishment. I confess, moreover, that this headgear, which is adopted by almost everyone in my country, must appear strange everywhere else. On the other hand, Madame, if our costume can provoke surprise, and perhaps amusement, among the inhabitants of this admirable city, which we have entered today for the first time, the spectacle of your wealth and civilization has impressed us greatly, and it is not without fear that we find ourselves in absolute isolation here."

"Your anxieties are exaggerated, fortunately," the young woman said, "for all strangers are welcomed benevolently here. All arms and all minds find it easy to be occupied in our society, and, as the ancient fabulist said, work is the resource of which there is no lack.[10] I don't doubt, Messieurs, that by exercising your professions you will soon succeed in winning esteem and prosperity. I am glad that my child's naïve curiosity has given me the opportunity to help you glimpse a better future than the one you seem to fear."

---

[10] The reference is to one of Jean de La Fontaine's aphorisms.

"We thank you, Madame, and are ready to make every effort to make ourselves useful. In the society from which we hail, we had a certain status in the liberal professions, and, in spite of the incontestable superiority of the milieu into which we have been suddenly projected by the most extraordinary events, we hope that, after a profound examination, we might be good for something."

"Monsieur," said Terrier, indicating the doctor, "is a physician, and his scientific works have become classics."

Antius removed his cap.

"Our young friend," the physicist added, indicating the young man, "has not yet made a choice of career."

Gédéon bowed naively.

"For my own count, Madame, I have been a teacher of physics and chemistry for thirty years."

"You are a colleague of my husband," the young woman replied, excitedly, "and that fortunate coincidence gives me a duty to procure you the means of utilizing your talent and put these messieurs in communication with those who might be useful to them. I can't go to the School right now, for I'm taking the child to the baths, but my presence is unnecessary. This is what you need to do. The School governed by my husband is ten minutes' walk from here. As soon as you have rested, go along the avenue as far as the Museum Square, which contains several remarkable monuments, including the Museum of Antiques, which you will recognize easily by its imposing aspect. The School, which is next door to the Museum, bears a very visible inscription in the middle of the fronton, which will guide you. You may go in with confidence and ask for the director, who will welcome you with the frankest cordiality. It will be sufficient to tell him about our conversation for him to be entirely at your disposal."

"Madame," said the doctor, "please accept our profound thanks, for this has been a providential encounter."

"I'm glad to be able to be useful to you. I shall soon see you again at the house, where you will be able to discuss and ripen your future plans, for you will remain our guests."

With a gracious gesture of farewell, the young woman took her little girl away, and they drew away at a run, while the travelers, touched by her generosity and marveling at her grace, remained under the influence of an indescribable emotion.

"It's certain," said Gédéon, in an agitated voice, "that encountering the young lady will bring us good fortune, or Providence would be both blind and deaf. And to think, my dear Master, that it is to your topper that we owe our salvation!"

They got up. Confident and joyful now, they set off at a rapid and steady pace in the direction indicated.

From time to time, the pedestrians looked with astonished eyes at the travelers, who no longer paid any heed to the sensation that their costume provoked.

They had scarcely covered five hundred meters when their gaze was embraced by the full extent of a vast and magnificent circular plaza, bordered by palaces of an incomparable richness. In the center of the immense circle stood a pyramid whose dimensions were at least quadruple those of the previous one. Its decoration was much richer, although it appeared, according to the decoration of the side facing them, to have the same instructive function.

Between the center and the periphery the gaze took in a considerable number of statues, gushing fountains and white marble vases overflowing with rare flowers. All these works of art rested on a thick carpet of grass, which extended to the thresholds of the monuments. The dazzling sunlight was interrupted by a dense crown of foliage produced by several circular rows of gigantic trees. The travelers were about to cross the area that separated them from the square when their attention was caught by a few sonorous and precipitate musical notes apparently produced by the horn of a harmonious brass instrument.

They turned their heads and retreated swiftly to the edge of the pathway.

A gigantic three-tiered vehicle loaded with passengers was heading toward them at high speed. The powerful machine, resting on compressed rubber wheels, was moving in profound silence. Soon, it went past their dazzled eyes like a lightning-bolt. Only a few crepitations accompanied by sparks, escaping from the central axle, reached their ears. Even so, Gédéon was able to read, on an elliptical band that extended along a lateral panel from front to rear, the words *Electric Omnibus* pointed in golden letters a foot high on a blue background.

The various compartments of the monumental vehicle were furnished with pale brown leather divans, on which some passengers were sitting, while others were walking back and forth on the circular balconies surrounding the various tiers.

"It would be very pleasant to travel like that," said the young man, scarcely recovered from the shock, "but I pity distracted people crossing the road!"

"It's a mode of transportation that recommends itself by three essential qualities: speed, elasticity and silence," observed Terrier. "What superiority over the ancient public carriages, so deformed, whose victims, piled up and shaken as if in a sieve, experienced the temperature of Senegal in June and that of Kamchatka in December. Furthermore, if all the vehicles crossing the city are established on an analogous model—as we have every reason to suppose, given the perfect cleanliness of the roadway—there is no reason why the duration of the surface should not be indefinite."

"Undoubtedly," Antius approved.

"I expect that river-dwellers are as favored as road-travelers," continued the professor, a great lover of silence who had never lived in any but macadamized streets and had routinely had it inscribed in his lease that he had the right to decamp on the day he saw a pavement being laid outside his door.

Meanwhile, the animation of the boulevard was increasing continually, and public and private carriages were going in all directions.

Nine o'clock chimed on the flanks of the pyramid that stood in the center of the Museum Square.

"I believe," Gédéon observed, alarmed by the immensity of the plaza, "that it will be difficult for us to locate the hospitable building—but we can ask for directions. There's a fellow coming toward us smoking a panatella, whose blue smoke attests to its quality. I'll ask him."

The pedestrian was no more than three paces away when the young man addressed a profound bow to him, exaggerating the gesture.

The city-dweller stopped and took off his hat.

"Monsieur," said the young man, "could you point out the School building to us? We're going to see the director."

"The School, Monsieur, is on the other side of the plaza, in the direction of the central pyramid."

The travelers advanced rapidly into the middle of the square. Five minutes later, they were beneath the vault of the trees again.

Gédéon, who was marching in the lead, suddenly stopped, mouth agape.

VI. The School

The two scientists were a few steps behind when the young man abruptly turned round and showed them a black marble frame in the idle of which shone, in golden letters, the word *School*.

Facing them, over an extent of two hundred meters, a vast two-story building opened in the shape of a horseshoe around a lawn. The central part of the edifice bore a monumental dome crowned with statues, presenting the most grandiose architecture.

The monument, whose base was raised several meters above the level of the promenade, communicated freely with it by a large and magnificent stairway. The two wings ended twenty meters from a balustrade that overlooked the place by several feet.

To the right of the School, a vast monument of an admirable architecture, the base of which was at exactly the same level as the neighboring establishment, rose up behind luxuriant flower-beds.

They traversed a broad strip of asphalt covered with sparkling mosaics and climbed the staircase.

The door of the central block was open. They followed the semicircular pathway that went around the lawn and son found themselves in front of a huge open door with two battens. They went in.

At the same moment, a lateral door opened and a white-haired old man appeared on the threshold, whose attitude, simultaneously dignified and affable, was not compromised by the presence of an enormous feather duster that he was clutching under his arm.

"The Messieurs have doubtless come to visit the collections," he said, depositing his pacific weapon on an armchair. "I am at their disposal."

"We thank you for our benevolence, Monsieur," Antius hastened to say. "We have come to speak to the director of the establishment."

"Very good, Messieurs. I shall have the honor of taking you to the honorable Monsieur Herber. He will be delighted by your visit, which he was not expecting for several days."

"He's expecting us?" said Gédéon.

"Yes, Monsieur, for you're doubtless members of the Schoolmasters' Conference that is due to open on July first? Each of the eighty schools in the city is to offer hospitality to forty members, and your lodgings are already prepared. You must be very tired after such a long journey, for I judge that you must have taken at least three days to come from your homeland."

"Why do you assume that we're come so far?" asked Terrier.

"Your costume is sufficient indication, Messieurs, for it's very similar to that worn in the Marquis Islands."

Under Antius' severe gaze, Gédéon repressed a burst of laughter.

"We are indeed employed in education," said the physicist, who, by reason of his top hat, appeared to have given specific rise to his interlocutor's hypothesis. "Have I the honor of encountering a colleague in you?"

"A former colleague, yes, Monsieur, for I retired ten years ago, but as inaction wearied me far more than work, the governors, at my request, entrusted the position of curator of the school collections to me, and I am very happy therein. Now, Messieurs, I shall have the honor of taking you to the Master, who has not left the School this morning, for he would have warned me if he had gone out."

The old functionary came down the steps of the perron slowly and took a pathway symmetrically connected to the one the three travelers had followed. They followed him.

On the side of the peristyle, lodged between two enormous Corinthian columns, a marble group attracted the attention of the two scientists. In the middle of the pedestal a seated woman with a majestic and serene head placed her right hand on a terrestrial globe while the left was extended over a stack of folio volumes. That respectable allegorical form did not have the merit of novelty, and the two scientists would have gone straight past if their curiosity had not been provoked by the details of the work. The underpinning and the pedestal were, in fact, ornate instruments whose nature and usage were absolutely unknown to them.

While they lost themselves in conjectures Gédéon had caught up with the old man and was walking beside him. "What strikes me most about your establishment," the young man said, "is its extent."

"What you see here, Monsieur is only a fifth of it."

"A fifth!"

"Yes, Monsieur. Behind the hemicyle there is a court-yard four hundred meters wide and three hundred deep. It has magnificent shade. On the right hand side are the classrooms, on the other, the gymnasium and the theater. It's the disposition generally adopted in our establishments.

"You could accommodate a regiment, then!"

"A regiment? You're employing an old word that has fallen into absolute disuse. It refers to a group of armed men that were known as soldiers."

"That's right. What do you call armed men nowadays?"

"Men of that profession—or, if you prefer, men destined to fight one another—no longer exist in the civilized world."

"My word—that's what Monsieur Terrier predicted one evening at table, a thousand years ago."

"Which proves, Monsieur, that there were men of good sense in the olden days."

"I ought to add that I am of the same opinion."

"Pardon me—you *are* of the same opinion."

"I should say that I was of that opinion, for it was in response to my comment that he uttered that memorable prophecy."

The old man stared at Gédéon. "Is it permissible to make fun of men of my age and profession in your country, young man?" he asked, severely.

"I beg your pardon," said Gédéon, realizing that he had nearly compromised everything. "I'm explaining myself badly. I meant to say that one day, wondering whether the ancients could have foreseen the fraternity that is no longer a vain word today, I consulted books by the greatest minds of the era."

"I understand. But I'm unfamiliar with that philosopher. When did he die?"

"Die!" exclaimed Gédéon. "In fact, I don't know exactly when he died, but I know that he was definitely alive in the year 1880."

"Well, if he didn't die before 1920, we can obtain his complete biography, if you wish, from the Necrological Palace."

At that moment, the two scientists abandoned their examination and hastened their steps in order to catch up.

A few minutes later, the four men went into a large vestibule whose hemispherical ceiling, painted blue and speckled with brilliant dots, represented the sky of Paris, Around the walls were a series of large red-upholstered divans. A modestly-sized oak box with a copper funnel in its center was fixed to the wall. The former teacher went to the instrument and pressed an ivory button. Immediately, a clear, strong and perfectly articulated voice emerged from the metal opening.

"I shall be in the laboratory all morning."

The travelers' astonishment was immense.

"Unless Monsieur is a ventriloquist," the young man murmured, "I don't understand at all." In a louder voice, he asked: "Is Monsieur Herber nearby?"

"He's four hundred meters away at present," said the curator.

"Four hundred meters?"

"Yes—I'll inform him of your arrival."

"But haven't you just informed him electrically?"

"No, Monsieur; I've only switched on the current to hear the words that Monsieur Herber spoke into the phonograph—an hour ago, as the dial indicates."

"The words we've just heard spoken were pronounced an hour ago!" exclaimed Gédéon.

"One hour and eight minutes, Monsieur. The words are conserved indefinitely in the phonograph."

The former master had taken hold of a mobile cornet attached to the wall by a thick silk cord, which had a metallic membrane at its orifice. He put his lips to it and sounded a long whistle.

A few seconds later, a voice whose timbre, accent and intensity were an exact replica of the one that had already spoken through the copper funnel said: "What is it, Monsieur Ravan?"

The latter said, in a loud voice: "Three Oceanian visitors would like to speak to you."

"Offer them my excuses and ask them to be so kind as to wait in my study," the voice replied. "I'll be there in ten minutes."

The venerable curator opened a large lateral door, asked the foreigners to go n, and took his leave of them, saying: "Please forgive me, Messieurs, if I don't remain with you. I have to return to the galleries, for the visitors will soon be flooding in, and even though my presence is not indispensable, the public is accustomed to my explanations, ordinarily capped by a little lecture that is always followed with an interest that I find very flattering."

And he set off back to the school museum.

The doctor was the first to enter the schoolmaster's study.

Scarcely had he crossed the threshold than, swiftly putting his hand to his cap, he bowed profoundly. Terrier and Gédéon were behind him. They shivered. They suddenly found themselves in the presence of the young woman who had given them directions to this hospitable abode. They bowed deeply.

Madame Herber remained motionless and smiling in front of a door made of a single sheet of polished glass, lightly tinted with pale blue and encased in a vast artfully-sculpted gold frame. The threshold was raised about a meter above the floor—a particularity that struck the travelers.

"Madame," said the doctor, "We shall retain an eternal gratitude for the generosity with which you took us under your protection. In a few minutes, we shall be joined here by Monsieur Herber."

"In that sincere expression of our sentiments," added the physicist, "we do not forget the charming little fairy who was the original cause of that fortunate encounter."

Madame Herber, without saying a single word, retained her gracious smile.

"Your presence," Antius continued, "is the most fortunate augury for the conversation that we are about to have with your husband."

The young woman's face still maintained an absolute immobility.

The amazement of the visitors was at its peak when Gédéon laughed and said: "Can't you see that it's a portrait of our benefactress to which you're speaking at present."

Terrier approached the frame and, after a few seconds' hesitation, turned round and said: "I've never seen such perfect work. I'll even add that I don't believe that it was produced by an artist's hand."

"It's a photopainting, Messieurs," said a man, still young, who had just come into the room, lifting up a velvet curtain, and was standing beside them.

VII. The Schoolmaster

Offering them chairs, he added, in a frank and cordial voice: "Welcome, Messieurs. I'm the schoolmaster."

Generosity, intelligence and energy and engraved their triple seal on the newcomer's face. His attitude presented the double character of simplicity and grandeur—appearances that have always seemed mutually exclusive in the sublunar world.

When the foreigners were seated, he went to his arm-chair.

"This morning, Monsieur le Directeur," sais Antius, who took the floor in his quality as the doyen of the party, "the three of us were sitting—or, rather, had collapsed—on a bench in a nearby avenue, and we were envisaging with terror the miserable future that was reserved for us in this admirable city, into which we had been thrown without resources. Despair had already invaded our souls when a pretty little girl, attracted by the singularity of our costumes, ran toward us.

"Her mother, a charming young woman, came to extract her gently from her naïve contemplation, and, seeing our distress, said to us: 'Go to the School, Strangers; you will find aid and protection there. The director is my husband. It will be sufficient to say that I have sent you to him.'

"We came straight here. A venerable man whom we met as we came into the establishment accompanied to the vestibule of your lodgings and withdrew after having introduced us into this room."

"I'm glad, Messieurs," said Herber, "that chance has procured me the satisfaction of being the first to come to your aid. Human beings form one vast family, and it's a sacred duty, in which no one fails, to aid one another mutually. My old friend, the respectable Monsieur Ravan, told me that you had arrived from the islands of Oceania, and although science and civilization reign almost everywhere in the world, it's certain that each people still has its particular mores and genius, and that some of our customs might seem strange to you. One the other hand, Messieurs, it is important that you tell me whether you have come to this country as simple travelers, or whether you have the intention of settling here permanently, in order that I can act accordingly."

"We have come," Terrier relied, after a moment's reflection, "to make a careful study of the civilization, mores and, most important of all, the industrial and scientific condition of your countries. Our sojourn does not, therefore, appear to be limited for the time being. In these conditions, we would be glad to find work appropriate to our faculties, which would permit us to make ourselves sufficiently useful to society not to be a burden to anyone."

"It is in that direction that all my efforts will be expended," said Herber, "but for the moment, it is important above all to ensure your material needs. Until the educational conference opens, you shall stay here. By the time I place the establishment at the disposal of its members, we shall probably have found resources. The conference will only last a fortnight, and in the worst possible case, I shall then have the means to furnish you with a convenient apartment. When the delegates leave, if we have been obliged to separate temporarily, you can come back here to stay indefinitely. As for the nature of the work that is appropriate to you, we shall investigate. For now, the first operation we shall undertake together will offer no difficulty; it is simply a matter of going to table."

The master pressed an ivory button.

Ten seconds later, a middle-aged woman appeared on the threshold of the entrance door.

"Madame Cassan," said Herber, "set three extra places for every meal until further orders. It's ten-seventeen; you still have thirteen minutes in hand."

At that moment, joyful cries resounded in the corridor. The door opened and the little girl who had run toward the strangers an hour earlier hurled herself into her father's arms. A slight noise became audible in the vestibule, and Madame Herber appeared on the threshold, in all the brightness of her grace and beauty. She came to sit down next to the schoolmaster.

Putting her hand on her husband's arm, she said: "Herber, these Messieurs must have explained the circumstances in which my daughter and I met them this morning. I asked them to come to the school, assuring them that they would find help and support here.

"You did well, Jeanne," the schoolmaster replied, simply.

"I ought to add that Monsieur," the young woman continued, indicating Antius, is a renowned physician, and this Monsieur"—she turned to Terrier—"is a professor of physical sciences of the highest merit."

Herber bowed. "Messieurs," he said, "I am glad that chance has brought you under my roof. Your arrival is not only a favor, it is now an honor for me."

The two scientists bowed.

"Jeanne," said the schoolmaster, "it's ten twenty-eight."

"I understand—but nothing is compromised," replied Madame Herber, hurrying out of the room.

As the hand of the clock reached the thirtieth division, a golden bell fixed to the wall emitted a long trill.

"The meal is ready, Messieurs," said Herber. "Permit me to show you the way."

Followed by his three guests, he went out and went to the far end of the vestibule. He then took a lateral corridor lit by high windows, hidden for the moment by screens that interrupted the rays of sunlight. When he reached a glazed door the schoolmaster stopped. The two battens opened of their own accord, and the travelers went into the dining room.

The smiling Madame Herber, standing beside an oval table set with sparkling pure gold cutlery, was waiting for her guests. The abundance and delicacy of the dishes that were covering a tablecloth that shone like silk were worthy of the splendor of the cutlery. The young woman noticed the astonishment and admiration that was suddenly reflected on the strangers' faces. With a gracious gesture, she set the two scientists down to either side of her while Herber amicably placed Gédéon to his right and the child to his left.

The service was carried out dexterously by two young women whose costume, attitude and distinction of manners hardly seemed in keeping with the humility of their functions.

The travelers, put to the proof by the fatigue and emotions of the morning, at with a hearty appetite. A monstrous tuna from the Sahara Sea had the honor of being subjected to two successive assaults.

After that, Antius, who ordinarily analyzed with attention and certainty what was put on his late, found his sagacity in default for the first time before a gilded and perfumed disk that had just been served to him.

"This fillet is certainly delicious," he said, in a voice whose authority in such matters was dogma in the world of gourmets, "but I can't tell to what quadruped it belongs."

"It's bison, doctor," replied Madame Herber.

"I approve," said Gédéon, wiping his lips, "the flattering epithets with which the ancient romancers of the wilderness have gratified the flesh of that monstrous herbivore, although they only ever mentioned its hump, cooked in the Indian manner."

"Today," said the schoolmaster, "the enormous ruminants in question are reared in vast herds, and their highly-esteemed flesh aliments a substantial fraction of Europe."

"Are antiseptic agents or the artificial production of cold employed for the conservation of the meat during the crossing?" asked Terrier.

"No means are employed," said Herber. "Transport is carried out in particular conditions of altitude and speed. The altitude adopted is between three and four thousand meters, and in those regions the temperature is very low. On the other hand, the distance that separates of Far West, the center of exploitation, from the markets of Paris, London, Liverpool, Bordeaux, Lyon and Marseilles is traversed in thirty-six hours, on average."

"A speed of sixty leagues an hour!" exclaimed Antius.

"Yes, Monsieur—and that speed, which seems to surprise you, is nevertheless inferior to that of certain express transports constructed in special conditions and designed for long hauls. It must be added that they are only laden with cargoes considerably inferior to those that the apparatus reserve for industry and provisions carry."

"I imagine," said Gédéon, "that the shepherds of the prairie, to ward off Indian scalpers, must have exchanged the crook for the carbine."

"It has been eight centuries, Monsieur," Herber replied, "since the Indian races disappeared. Rifles and firewater, in turn, prepared and completed their ruination. The last tribes eventually melted into the vast current of civilization. Nevertheless, the type has not completely disappeared, at least for science. In a greatly esteemed work, *Researches on the American Races*, Mr. Fuller of the Baltimore Anthropological Society assures us that it is not difficult to recognize, especially among the members of the most elegant American circle, the Atlantic Club, the authentic descendants of the ancient scalp-hunters.

"The wilderness, of course, no longer exists, and on the soil of virgin forests, town halls academies and theaters now stand. In those relatively new regions the most colossal farms in the entire world are found. Agriculture and the raising of livestock are conducted on the largest scale by the most advanced methods. It is from there that the most remarkable agricultural innovations come. The greater part of the savage inhabitants of the prairie have been reduced to domesticity and subjected to the most expert methods of fattening and growth. In that fashion, a healthy, agreeable and varied alimentary mass has entered in torrents into general circulation. I ought to add that, although one encounters fewer opulent cities in the immense territory of the South Amrican pampas, one finds an equally advanced agriculture there.

"We have come a long way from the epoch when those vast countries only exported a few thousand emaciated bulls, whose flesh was cut into strips and then dried under the ardent tropical sun. Today thanks to regular, continuous and sagely progressive husbandry, the cattle of South America carry off a veritable harvest of laurels at agricultural exhibitions all over the world, and those detestable Chilean sheep that once made the most intrepid stomach recoil now contribute their fleeces to our finest textile manufactures, and aliment the most distinguished tables with their flesh."

The guests had already attacked several pyramids of enormous fruits with an exquisite taste.

"If I were the owner of the fortunate orchard that produced these marvels," said Gédéon, while respectfully slicing a peach as big as a melon, "I would guard it with as much care as the Garden of the Hesperides."

"All of this dessert," said Herber, "was picked in the properties of my friend Guillaume Dryon. That celebrated agronomist, who is both a first-rate scholar and one of the most knowledgeable of bibliophiles, possesses an immense estate on the plateaux of north-west Tanganyika. By means of the most intelligent large-scale cultural methods, he obtains crops sufficient to aliment an entire State. He maintains veritable forests of fruit trees, whose products have won him eulogies from agricultural juries the world over. His fortune is immense, and he makes the most praiseworthy use of it. He is also numbered among the most influential members of the Congress. As he does me the honor of counting me among his friends, he sends me frequent consignments of fruits of every sort. I'll introduce you to him."

"Are we going to set out for Central Africa?" asked the physicist tranquilly.

"No," Herber replied. "The opulent proprietor, who is in the Orient at present, will soon be spending a few days in Paris, where he has an admirable palace. You can count on the most benevolent welcome."

"Master," Gédéon observed, "we owe you all our gratitude for your generosity, but we greatly fear not being sufficiently correctly dressed to be introduced into society, and if our friend is rigorous in matters of etiquette..."

"In his eyes, that will be of no importance," said Herber. "However, it would be appropriate if you were dressed like everyone else. When we leave the table we'll board the atmospheric railway that passes behind the school buildings, and I'll take you to the General Stores, which don't close until five o'clock. As for the insignificant expense that your equipment will necessitate, you have no need to worry about it."

"We thank you from the bottom of our hearts, dear colleague," said Terrier, emotionally, "but we still have some resources. He displayed ten louis, which he had taken from his depths of his fob-pocket.

"Does that money still have value in your country?" asked the schoolmaster.

"Very great value. At home, gold is worth about fifteen times as much as silver. We also have a third kind of money, whose value is much inferior to that of silver. It's an alloy of copper and tin. It serves as payment for the least costly items."

"Here," said Herber, "there is little difference between the value of gold and silver. Nevertheless, by virtue of certain properties unique to it, the price of the former metal sometimes undergoes temporary increases in its value. Thus, by reason of its malleability, and, most of all, it unalterability, gold is particularly employed in our cutlery and for vessels designed to keep liquids hot, for its emissive power is very limited. It's also sought after for the manufacture of objects that need to retain an unalterable gleam.

"The new monetary system that is exclusively employed here, however, differs in every respect from the old one, the usage of which you appear not to have abandoned entirely. It's essentially fiduciary and universal, and thus used throughout the entire world. I beg you to observe how, by virtue of that last character, it is superior to the ancient conventions, applicable respectively and exclusively to limited regions. In order to cross those fictitious boundaries called frontiers, the very different values of disks of gold, silver and bronze that composed it were obliged to submit to the onerous exploitation of the bizarre form of parasitism known as exchange.

"Today, the same banknote, subject to the same subdivisions and applied to all transactions, not only has the same value everywhere, but also sets aside the illogical dualism of two variable currencies, metal and merchandise, which, according to their respective abundance, are subject to incessant and contrary variations capable of upsetting all calculations."

Herber took a sheet of paper out of his pocket, the texture of which seemed very resistant, and handed it to the doctor. "This is our current money," he added.

The physicist and the young man leaned toward their companion and were able to read, framed in very elegant vignette, the value of a hundred francs, in embossed print. At the head was the inscription: *Universal Bank.*

"I see with pride," said Antius, "that the French monetary unit has survived, at least nominally."

"Like the entire decimal metric system," the schoolmaster replied. "No one raised any objections in that regard, for France had the initial honor of that admirable system, decreed by the constitutional Assembly of 1790, and whose elements repose of geodesic measurements incapable of offending any national susceptibility."

VIII. The Telephone and the Phonograph

The meal was nearing its end. Madame Herber put light pressure on an ivory lever set on the table within arm's reach. One of the young women immediately appeared, carrying a massive gold tray surmounted by two vertical stalks supporting an elegant ewer capable of moving backwards and forward on its props. Beneath the curved neck of the vessel was a cylinder with two tightly-sealed compartments. Two slightly-tilted metal capsules were fitted to the lower part of the uprights.

Herber gently detached the edges of a little cloth covering the center of the table and gently moved two almost-invisible switches to the right and the left. Two rods wrapped in green silk thread, which surrounded them throughout their length, then inclined toward the concavity of the capsules, where they found a point of connection at their tips.

A slight crepitation was heard inside the vessel and was soon followed by the shrill characteristic hiss that the first molecules of vapor produced at the bottom of a heated vessel produce as they escape.

The two scientists followed the experiment with interest, almost able to take account of the phenomena.

Gédéon concentrated his gaze on the accessory pieces of the tray, searching in vain for the mysterious source of the hest that was warming the ewer so energetically.

During these investigations, a few threads of vapor were escaping, agitating the metal lid; then the liquid suddenly began to boil violently.

"That particular employment of the electric current is very ingenious," said Antius.

"Yes," said the physicist. "It's probable that it heats up a thin platinum disk soldered to the bottom of the vessel. At that contact, the water heats up rapidly."

The schoolmaster approved this exact explanation of the phenomenon with a nod of the head.

"The theoreticians of past centuries, while admitting the possibility of the industrial application of electrical heat," Terrier continued, "did not in general direct their studies toward that important objective. One can explain that abstention by the necessity of other more immediate research imposed by the resource of the electric current. Others thought that the discovery of the telegraph constituted an ultimate achievement compared with which other applications would be unimportant."

"And telegraphy, which was rightly able to cause our 19th century ancestors to marvel," said Herber, "now occupies a very secondary rank in communications."

"It must, however, have been difficult to replace advantageously an agent capable of traveling a hundred thousand leagues a second," Antius objected.

"The telephone, doctor, functioning, as you know, by electromagnetic action, possesses the same speed, but it employment is much more advantageous, for speech is twenty times as rapid as writing."

"The instrument in question is very widespread, then?" asked the professor.

"Very widespread," the schoolmaster replied. "The schools, in particular, are very generously equipped in that respect by the State. We're in permanent telephonic communication with the five Academies and the Astronomical Circle, the Societies of Mathematics, Physics and Chemistry, the Mineralogical Society and the Association of Prehistoric and Anthropological Studies. All their deliberations are collected on the phonographic printer, and we thus possess the most complete and most authentic archives.

"From the general point of view one can say that every house possesses at least one telephone and one phonograph. When one wants to speak directly to a distant correspondent, it is sufficient to call up the central office of the section, which immediately establishes a connection with the station nearest to the point of arrival. The latter informs the intended recipient, who makes the necessary dispositions at his end. In return for a fee, one can converse for a determined time.

"This system of communications, which has replaced electric telegraphy properly speaking almost everywhere, is even employed by deliberative bodies. The Académie des Sciences, which holds official and public sessions on Thursdays, is in direct communication by means of its apparatus with a large number of scientific bodies, which meet on the same day at the same time. One can say, rigorously, that all those illustrious assemblies for a single whole."

"In spite of the marvelous character of these conversations at an indefinite distance," the physicist objected, "it seems to me that it must give rise to problems when the correspondent is not at home."

"In that case," the Schoolmaster went on, "the arrival station collects the speech, which is silently engraved in a phonograph, the mechanism of which is put in contact with the intended recipient's wire. As soon as is presence is signaled, the post unrolls the drum, and the flying telegram is borne to his ear.

"The phonograph is also much in use in dwellings. It frequently happens that a visitor arrives at the door of a house, pronounced what he has to say into the orifice of an instrument he finds within easy reach and goes away, having accomplished his mission. His speech is collected either immediately, or in the course of the day.

"The telephone plays an even more important role in our interiors. There isn't a single family in the entire city who is not in communication with several theaters every evening. Thus, from that point of view, the instrument is dear to stay-at-home people, who, from their armchair or their bed, can hear everything that is said or sung on the stage as clearly as if they were in the auditorium close to the stage."

"Doesn't any confusion result from all those auditions?" asked Gédéon, whose scientific conceptions were rather obscure.

"Not in the least. Among the thousands of wires that run through the subterranean tubes of the public highway, there is one for every theater, and for a modestly-priced subscription, one can take as many branches as one desires."

"I had an idea just now whose application would be a great success," said the young man.

The doctor and the physicist began to tremble.

"What is it, my young friend?" asked Herber.

"That of extending the wires to the provinces."

"It's a good idea, but it's not new, for the provinces furnish a million subscribers to every stage."

"Are the auditoria absolutely deserted, then?"

"On the contrary, the theaters are very busy, for the splendors of the settings, which procure an absolute illusion, attract many spectators."

"That's very fortunate; I feared that the invention might only leave the pantomime theaters undamaged—if they still exist."

"That kind of spectacle is much in favor," replied the schoolmaster, "especially comic pantomime, which, among our ancestors perverted by the banal trivialities of the operetta and the music hall, only had charms for delicate minds. I hasten to add that comedy, vaudeville and musical drama do not suffer at all from that preference, for the theater, whether it presents depictions of real life or whether it raises us into the serene regions of the ideal, is profoundly integrated into our habits."

While these digressions ran their course, Madame Herber had uncovered the upper part of the two-part cylinder, whose orifice was dotted with holes. Tilting the ewer, she slowly poured out the boiling water. An exquisite aroma of mocha was suddenly manifest, invading the entire dining-room. The cups were filled. The coffee was delicious, and the three strangers, fully restored by an Olympian repast, lavished the most flattering eulogies upon it.

A tray of old liqueurs constituted the apotheosis of the feast.

IX. Paris in 2880

"Messieurs," said Herber, "we shall, if you wish, go into the courtyard and sit down in the shade. We'll smoke a few cigars."

All the guests got up. Lydia was the first to take flight. Madame Herbert remained in the dining room to give instructions, and the three travelers, conducted by the schoolmaster, went into the interior courtyard, an immense park, with grass covering its entire extent, shaded from the sun's rays by enormous trees.

They took their places on seats disposed beneath an elm several hundred years old, and one of the young women soon appeared, holding a tray of cigars of the most magnificent appearance in one hand, and a platinum heater containing ardent coals in the other, from which each of the guests lit his panatellas in turn.

"Master," said the doctor, after a moment, launching a blue spiral toward the sky, "everything in your city is veritably marvelous, but of all the elements constituting its magnificence, the one that has struck us most is certainly its extent. Our gazes are surprised by the majestic proportions of our parks, your gardens and your avenues."

"What is also strange," said Gédéon, "is that we have only found in our path wide causeways full of trees, flowers, fountains and statues. We have not yet seen any *streets*, properly speaking. On the other hand, the gaze is struck by an infinity of strangely-shaped gas-outlets. That last observation, which has escaped these messieurs, constantly at grips with questions of transcendent philosophy, is my own, for, even though I'm not a scientist, I'm rather observant, although I say it myself."

"Gas-outlets, you say, my young friend?" Herber replied. "I don't know what you mean by that."

"I'm referring to public lighting, for I can't believe that a city as brilliant by day is illuminated by candlelight at night."

"We're illuminated by electric light. As for streets, you haven't seen them because they're behind the dwellings, and you haven't been able to go along them because no one walks along them."

"Although your gravity puts you above suspicion, my dear host, I could believe that, in saying that a street is a place that no one sees and where no one walks, you were making a rather original joke."

"The explanation is simple," said Herber. "Throughout the city, the facades of houses overlook thoroughfares as broad and ornate as those you have already walked along. Everyone, in fact, from the richest to the least fortunate, has a magnificent plaza outside his door. At the rear of the gardens—for every house possesses a grassy garden at the rear, planted with trees and similar to the promenades—are the streets, incessantly traveled by rapid trains, which ensure all communications in the most comfortable manner. The track is usually open to the sky; however, by reason of the great extent of certain monuments, they sometimes go underground. An example is not far away. A hundred paces from here, we would find ourselves over a tunnel that passes under the courtyard of the school."

"I did, in fact, hear a kind of subterranean rumble a few moments ago, the nature of which indicates that the track lies at a rather considerable depth," said the physicist.

"The vault, however, is less than three meters below ground—the absence of noise inherent in the rolling of a large mass is due to the perfect construction of the vehicles and the motors."

"Every house being a palace, and every avenue being a veritable park, the city must cover an immense extent," Antius concluded.

"The city, Antius replied, "is limited to the south, the north and the east by old rampart walls, rather well-conserved, which have no other value than their antiquity. To the west, it extends over the hills of Issy, Meudon, Bellevue, Sèvres, Saint-Cloud and Ville-d'Avray. That part is inhabited by the wealthy, because of the lake."

"It exists, then!" exclaimed Gédéon.

"We can even take it as the objective of a walk, on emerging from the clothing warehouse, which is scarcely five hundred meters away. As for the population of the city, it does not exceed fifteen hundred thousand souls."

"It seems to me," Antius observed, "that in a distant epoch, Paris counted as many as two million inhabitants."

"It even counted three and a half million five centuries ago," the schoolmaster replied, "but that monstrous agglomeration of individuals in a restricted area gave rise to all the inconveniences—one might even say, all the disasters—that inevitably result from a concentration so contrary to the simplest principles of social economy. Property rents attained prices so scandalous that all producers—artisans, technologists, writers, artists and scientists—were, in effect, only working to cover the enormous expense of the indispensable element of their lodgings. The most urgent needs could barely receive sufficient satisfaction.

"In spite of everything, Paris continued to be the magnetic pole of all dreams and all ambitions. For two centuries, that abnormal state of affairs, with its procession of miseries, ruinations and calamities, conserved a maximum of intensity of which history furnishes no other example. Finally, that frightful and inextricable situation, which had previously resisted the efforts of all statesmen and all the economists' alarm calls, was abruptly resolved by the sudden development of a force with which science had long enriched humankind and to which industry suddenly gave a formidable impetus.

"Aerial travel, which, by reason of the high cost of transportation, had only so far been used for scientific research and luxury voyages, received a considerable boost in a short time. Powerful companies, supported provisionally and temporarily by the State, and organized with immense capital, created regular daily services throughout the world. The cost of transport was brought within the range of the most indigent.

"On the other hand, supported by the studies and works of engineers, geographers and scientific bodies, publicists showed the proletarian masses the immense deserted regions of Asia, Africa and Central America, where a generous virgin soil was simply waiting for the ploughshare or the miner's pickaxe to yield its riches.

"Emigration then commenced with the intensity common to all reactions. It was not only concentrated in Paris. All the capitals that were choking under the accumulation of population were relieved in a matter of months by those powerful means of release. Armed with improved instruments, able to exploit first-rate mechanical applications based on the expansion of gases suddenly raised to high temperatures, guided by practical, audacious and indefatigable minds, emigrants founded colonies, which, within half a century, arrived at a level of wealth and development such that it was possible to believe that the centers of civilization and industry were going to be displaced. Four centuries of oscillatory movement resulted, whose conclusion marked the definition industrial decadence of the old world.

"In spite of everything, we still conserve the uncontested empire of all the elements that ornament life: letters, sciences and arts. In addition—and the opinion finds no contradiction—Paris is now the most splendid city in the entire world. All circumstances have, moreover, concurred in the most fortunate manner in the development of its magnificence.

"At the time when it had three and a half million inhabitants, the city was a formidable center of production and consumption. In spite of their multiplicity, railways had become insufficient for its alimentation and the distribution of its products. Under the pressure of events, and driven by public opinion, the State concentrated all its means of action in order to make a concept that had previously been considered utopian into a reality.

"The broad and profound canalization of the Seine between Paris and Rouen, and the creation of a vast harbor west
of the city, which was best suited to that gigantic project, were
decreed simultaneously. Capital flowed from all directions,
and, thanks to the already-powerful machines of contemporary
industry, that prodigious task was carried out in less than thirty
years.

"For a century, Paris Seaport,[11] which had periodically
animated the verve of satirical journalists in ancient times,
became a reality, and was the foremost port in the world.
When aerial navigation developed with such sudden an extraordinary intensity, however, it concentrated all means of
transportation in a few years, and instead of hundreds of ships
incessantly furrowing it, the harbor ended up presenting a
bleak and tranquil surface.

"On the other hand, the colossal emigration that had en-
couraged—or, rather, determined—the abundance, rapidity
and low cost of aerial communication had reduced the population of the city to one and a half million inhabitants. It has
scarcely varied since.

"That mass desertion, in a city whose new buildings had
been driven back as far as the ramparts, was a thunderbolt for
those who had been exploiting the ground so mercilessly for
several centuries. Half the houses were empty, and people that
had previously had to pay through the nose to be lodged in a

---

[11] The idea of digging a ship canal between Paris and Rouen—
a frequent feature of French futuristic fiction in the 19th century—had first been mooted in the days of Henri IV, but it was
taken seriously during the post-Napoléonic Restoration, when
work almost began, only to fall victim to the July Revolution
of 1830, after which investment was switched to railways. In
1881 an engineer named Bouquet de la Grye drew up a
scheme for a canal to Le Havre, costing sixty million dollars,
with which the readers of the *Musée des Familles* would have
been familiar, although the Rouen canal always seemed the
likelier prospect.

cramped, sordid, unhealthy and uncomfortable hovel could henceforth obtain for the same price an entire house with its outbuildings. Grass grew thickly and abundantly in streets where circulation had once been difficult and dangerous, and several quarters once reputed as noisy centers of activity presented a spectacle of the most profound calm and the most complete tranquility."

"Will you please tell us, my dear colleague, by virtue of what transformations the city attained this marvelous combination of wealth, grandeur and magnificence?" the professor asked.

"That transformation has lasted three centuries. There is no need to tell you that the human appetite for luxury and wellbeing inevitably increases in the wake of the progress that produces them. The consequences of that incontestable principle imposed themselves with a remarkable intensity in the era when it was necessary to transform a few quarters of the city that had fallen into dilapidation. The authorities, obedient to public opinion, who wanted Paris to gain in splendor what it had lost in population, submitted plans for new constructions and thoroughfares to various competitions, giving free rein to the imagination.

"According to their various competences, artists, architects, engineers and hygienists took part therein, and the sum of their endeavors resulted in the general conception of the design, as it exists today, but which, in the beginning, could only be applied to two or three quarters of the city. As it answered all needs and all satisfactions, it was adopted for the whole city and found few objectors, even in the timid and reactionary circles riveted to tradition.

"The capital had become extraordinarily rich, by virtue of the continual movement of an opulent and numerous floating population. Its artistic industry was powerfully developed; its monuments, its nascent splendor and its pleasures attracted tourists from the entire world. On the other hand, the citizens whom fortune had maltreated set off boldly for the newly-exploited regions in order to become wealthy, while those who had accumulated considerable fortunes in exotic lands, leaving their instruments of labor in the hands of newcomers, returned once and for all to the magical city in order to enjoy the pleasures of life to the full.

"Then again, because the progress of architecture and technology, the employment of new forces of incomparable power, and the rapid transportation of materials by air, reduced the difficulties considerably, the grandiose plans were gradually implemented at various points. Finally, its wealth increasing incessantly, the entire city ended up being transformed, and presented in its entirety the character of sumptuous magnificence that the most audacious imaginations of ancient times would not have dared to conceive."

"The city seems to have been particularly lavish in the construction of its schools," observed the doctor. "You're in a veritable palace here."

"We occupy ten hectares," Herber replied, modestly. "All scholarly monuments are nearly identical in appearance and extent. Each school has between two and three thousand pupils. Today, of course, they're deserted, because it's the day of rest.

"Discipline can't be easy to maintain," said Gédéon, who had once given his teachers a hard time.

"It doesn't cause us any difficulty," the schoolmaster replied, "for a certain level of education is compulsory, and a child, in quitting the paternal home, falls directly and exclusively under our authority. That way, discipline is respected because it's all-powerful. I ought to add that the education of the body preoccupies us no less than that of the mind, and has a sovereign influence over the character. You can see from here, in the left wing of the building at the back of the courtyard, twelve arched doors. They open into the gymnastics hall, which is abundantly provided with all the apparatus necessary to develop strength, dexterity and health.

"You must have noticed, doctor, how admirable the present generation is with regard to muscular strength and beauty of form. That is the result of the physical education to which men and women are subjected from infancy to maturity. I will add that the great majority of citizens continue to practice gymnastic exercises into old age, and that all houses have two special rooms, one of which is devoted that beneficent recreational labor and the other to hydrotherapy, which rounds it off.

"That universal system, which no one dreams of neglecting, is based on public education, uniform everywhere, which inculcates in everyone, from an early age, a set of habits that generally become indispensable needs. Thus, endemic diseases, caused and maintained as much by the absence of the most indispensable cares of hygiene as by the privation of bodily exercise, have disappeared completely. Nothing about us resembles those emaciated generations of bygone ages, weighed down by speculation or twisted by bureaucratic life."

"One cannot approve too highly, in fact, of care devoted to physical culture," Antius agreed. "Not only does it constitute the most solid rampart for health, but its influence also extends in the most fortunate manner to the mental and intellectual faculties."

X. A Model Cellar and Kitchen

At that moment, a man of robust appearance suddenly emerged from a doorway twenty paces away from the guests. The furrows that time had engraved on his calm and reflective face revealed that he was over sixty. His curly white hair, which resembled a mass of snowflakes, his bronzed skin and thick lips, established a very obvious African origin.

The individual appeared to be plunged in grave meditation, which did not prevent him from puffing in perfect cadence on the end of an enormous meerschaum pipe, the color of which attested to long and honorable service.

"Come here, Master Nyera!" Herber called to the silent smoker.

The latter stated walking at a measured pace and, having arrived within four paces, gravely saluted the assembly.

"Messieurs," said the schoolmaster, "you have before you an artist who would have been worthy of the ovens of Apicius. Moreover, Master Nyera is a scholar who has written remarkable commentaries on the Latin poets. After several voyages to France, our excellent maître d'hôtel, who is originally from Timbuktu, decided to settle in Paris, which he declared to be the hearth of fine literature, and I was fortunate enough to make his acquaintance and obtain his services."

"In truth, Monsieur Herber, it is written on high that everyone must live on his trade," the cook replied.

"I am curious to know," said the physicist, "why a literate man like you, Monsieur, has been led to exercise a profession that, although very honorable, appears to be in scant harmony with the qualities of your mind. In antiquity, we see Cincinnatus steering the plough after having led Roman armies, and later the great Linnaeus darning his own socks, but they were glaring exceptions."

"My story," Nyera replied, "is much more modest. In Timbuktu, my father owned the Grand Continental Hotel. As a child, my primary intellectual faculties were exercised in the culinary field, doubtless less brilliant but more fecund and more useful than many others. While giving me a solid education, my father favored that particular disposition, because he anticipated that I would succeed him, and it was important for him to put the future and the reputation of the house into hands that would not let them slip.

"For ten years I balanced literature and cuisine, my intellectual efforts being devoted to each in turn, in the morning to scholarly books, in the evening to the paternal ovens. My name was sometimes cited eulogistically by my professors and with veneration by our guests.

"That association of the spit and the lexicon gave rise to an opusculum entitled *De re coquinaria apud Romanos*,[12] which attracted a certain attention. In sum, everything presaged a settled future for me, honored and full of material and mental wellbeing, when, in the wake of reckless speculations, my father was completely ruined and our magnificent establishment was sold. The old man did not survive the catastrophe; as for me, having shaken the dust of the place that had seen my downfall from my shoes, I came to Paris, with which I was already familiar, and a stroke of luck introduced me to the honorable Monsieur Herber, in whom I found a devoted protector, an sincere friend and, thank God, a great connoisseur."

"Master Nyera's case does not constitute an exception, as you might think," the schoolmaster added. "You will frequently encounter artisans endowed with a remarkable education, for that capital element of our civilization and progress is within the reach of everyone here. Many, like our friend Master Nyera for his research on the ancient culinary arts, have merited the public eulogies of the Institut for their work, a favor that constitutes a superiority before which everyone bows."

---

[12] "On Roman domestic cookery"

"We cannot, at present, fully appreciate your estimable maître d'hôtel from the point of view of his art," said Antius, "but we are sure that he is unrivaled in that regard."

"Messieurs," said the culinary litterateur, forcing himself to maintain an equilibrium between his conscience and his self-esteem, "I can only accept a fraction of the felicitations that you would like to grant me, for they are almost all due by rights to Monsieur Herber, who has put at my disposal a laboratory equipped with the latest improvements, and a cellar incomparable in extent, profundity, temperature and humidity."

The topic of conversation seemed to the doctor to offer a providential opportunity. "We would be very glad, my dear host," he said, "to visit those two rooms with you, so important in a well-run household."

"We are at your disposal, Messieurs," the schoolmaster replied, with a gesture full of courtesy, "and if you will grant us a few minutes we shall direct our steps in that direction."

The five men went back into the building. A few minutes later, they entered a corridor illuminated by high arched windows. After fifty paces, they stopped in front of a massive oak door, which opened silently in response to slight pressure.

In a half-light that the contrast with the dazzling light outdoors rendered almost dark, the travelers perceived the first steps of a broad staircase with a gentle slope, which extended underground. The maître d'hôtel reached out an ivory switch beside the door and pressed it. A dazzling light suddenly filled the corridor and the visitors went down.

Below the thirtieth step they found themselves on a floor of shiny fine sand, confronted by a vast vaulted hall above which shone an electric globe. Several rows of stout barrels, whose shadows were sharply outlined on the walls, were wedged on oak beams. Every label bore a name famous in gastronomic litanies.

The doctor, who was singularly astonished by that catalogue, turned to the maître d'hôtel excitedly. "My dear host," he said in a voice that gave evidence of as much admiration as sympathy, "the transcendent nomenclature that we have before our eyes plunges me into a delight that is not exempt from surprise."

"Those two sentiments are very flattering for our domestic economy," Herber replied, "but I cannot explain them."

"I tell you sincerely," Antius continued, "that my friends and I were convinced that, in spite of the opulence of the house, the excellent wines served at table this morning constituted very flattering exceptions established in our favor, but the examination of your cellar seems to indicate that we have simply been subjected to your habitual regime."

"That's true," said the schoolmaster.

"In that case, I believe that there are few gourmets as richly and as exclusively equipped as you are."

"You're mistaken, my dear guest. All cellars are very similar to this one, at least in terms of quality."

"In certain places, however, the authenticity of *grands crus* is merely a myth, cleverly exploited."

"In my turn, I don't understand."

"I'll explain. I've always thought that every year, a hundred times more fine wines than Burgundy and Médoc can produce are routinely sold under deceptive labels."

"Once, that might have been possible," Herber replied, "but now we transform our wines ourselves in our cellars."

Antius looked at his host in amazement.

"Of course," the schoolmaster continued. "You know that costly wines only owe their preeminence to certain oenanthic ethers, that these substances, with which our ancestors were preoccupied from the viewpoint of analysis, have for a long time been capable of perfect synthesis, and that it is sufficient to pour a few drops of those volatile compounds into a barrel of coarse wine to obtain the corresponding liqueur. Vulgar wines, however, generally represent differences in composition, which assign to each of them in advance the terms of the transformation.

"I should add that the perfection of methods puts the various species of oenanthic ether within the range of every purse, and that everyone has the intelligence to take advantage of modern science."

Paralyzed by astonishment, the travelers remained silent.

Assuming that their curiosity was satisfied on this point, the schoolmaster proposed a visit to the kitchen.

The five men went back upstairs. On the top step, the schoolmaster flicked the switch, and darkness fell behind them.

Ten paces from the door to the cellar they turned into a lateral corridor, which opened into a large square room paved with flagstones, with a profoundly vaulted ceiling sustained by arches, reminiscent of those monumental kitchens depicted by Van Ostade in his marvelous interiors.[13]

A hundred receptacles of every shape and size, suspended symmetrically along the walls, glittered in the daylight that was flooding through high arched windows on both sides. Two middle-aged women dressed with extreme neatness, whose opulent forms would have constituted a very reassuring advertisement for the temples they served, were occupied in restoring a normal luster to the equipment that had been used in preparing and serving the morning meal.

The clink of a fish-kettle on a polished marble table-top caused the physicist to prick up his ears.

"What is that metal?" he asked, unceremoniously.

"An alloy of silver and platinum, of which almost all the equipment is made," Herber replied.

"Platinum was once very expensive," ventured the professor, prudently avoiding plunging more deeply into discussion.

"Yes, but inexhaustible mines were discovered in regions unexplored by our ancestors, and the metal has become as commonplace as iron. You will admit, my dear colleague, that it suits its purpose very well in the present instance."

---

[13] The Dutch master Adriaen van Osttade (1610-1685) became famous for his paintings of rustic indoors scenes of everyday life.

"Undoubtedly, and I know nothing preferable, platinum only melting at two thousand degrees, and only being attackable by a very limited number of chemical substances."

"Here are a few vessels in iridium, a metal that always accompanies native platinum," the schoolmaster added, indicating a series of kettles that appeared to occupy a place of honor.

"I've never seen as many at one time," murmured the professor,

On the left hand side of the vast culinary laboratory stood a long oven in heat-resistant brick, whose top, covered with enameled porcelain, was pierced with a large number of hemispherical, cylindrical and conical cavities.

At the back, several demi-ellipsoids, capped with reflectors and equipped with metallic grilles, were fixed to the wall. Antius looked at these singular items of apparatus curiously.

"What do you think of our ovens, Doctor?" asked Herber, who had drawn nearer to his guest.

"I can't quite grasp the theory," the scientist replied, frankly. "What is the significance of these cavities, especially those niches lined with sheets of solid gold?"

"The hollow molds in forged iridium are designed to accommodate items of cooking equipment, which are adapted to them perfectly. The supports, resting on crowns of quicklime, are brought to red heat by the electric current and transmit their heat to platinum vessels, which heat up rapidly and can maintain a constant heat for an indeterminate time. The shiny furnaces you were examining so attentively are simple rotisseries. The grilles, made of iridium wire, are rapidly brought to red heat by a slight deviation of the current acting on enclosed stones, which also receive a large quantity of radiant heat by reflection."

"What progress!" exclaimed Antius. "What superiority over the murderous ovens of Parisians of the past, in which all substances were gradually covered with a layer of noxious hydrogen products capable of sowing devastation in the most intrepid stomachs."

During this conversation, the physicist examined a series of shaped tubes fitted with taps, on which were engraved the numbers 30, 50, 70, 90 and 100.

"You see, my dear colleague, that we have water heated to all desirable temperatures," said the schoolmaster.

An electric mincer, operated by means of a mercury switch, which began to function under the expert eye of a kitchen-maid, had captured Gédéon's full attention.

The kitchen communicated via a large bay with a parlor cluttered with glazed shelves laden with hermetically sealed vessels, the labels of which advertised condiments collected in all latitudes. After that, a room annexed to the dining-room contained several carved oak dressers filled with vessels of crystal and gold.

Herber received the eulogies of his companions regarding the state of perfection of the two departments they had just visited with modesty, and led his guests back to the central courtyard. It did not take long for an interesting discussion of the radiation of electric heat to begin between the physicist and the schoolmaster. The doctor and his nephew followed a little way behind. The latter suddenly stopped his companion by taking hold of his sleeve.

"I wouldn't be sorry," he said, "to submit a reflection to you."

"A sensible one?"

"I think so."

"Speak."

"This is it: It seems to me that there's a singular disproportion between present-day alimentation and that of yore."

"The reflection is indeed more sensible than I expected, for it had occurred to me too—except that I have resolved the question logically, which you would have been incapable of doing."

Gédéon admitted that, modestly.

"It was sufficient for me," the doctor went on "to compare the resources of our original contemporaries with those of their 17th century ancestors. All the chroniclers who lived under Louis XIV, notably a celebrated bluestocking whose letters, rightly or wrongly, make the people of our epoch swoon,[14] agree in depicting the peasant of the era of the Sun King as a sort of anthropomorphic animal, scantily clad in rags and living on nothing but acorns, plants and roots—a diet highly recommended by the vegetarian school, but which the most wretched of 19th century indigents would have rightly disdained.

"Now, it's unnecessary to be a profound mathematician to establish the following proportion: the alimentation of our descendants relates to ours as ours does to that of our ancestors."

"I understand—but why, if you please?"

"Because, naïve young man, the ultimate result of progress is the mental and material improvement of individuals. If the astronomer Hippalus of Alexandria had not hypothesized the existence of the monsoon,[15] which permitted the organization of the double navigation of the Red Sea and the Indian Sea, Europe would have been deprived for a long time of the riches of the Orient. If Flavio Gioja of Amalfi had not, in 1300, discovered the compass,[16] the American continent might never have been discovered. If Salomon de Caus had not prepared the reign of steam[17] and Galvani that of dynamic elec-

---

[14] Madame de Sévigné (1626-1696).

[15] Hippalus of Alexandria was a fictitious navigator—not an astronomer—who allegedly discovered the monsoon wind system of the Indian Ocean, thus opening up trade with the spice islands. Strabo's *Geography* tentatively gives the credit to Eudoxus of Cyzicus instead, but that story is probably apocryphal too.

[16] Like Hippalus, Flavio Gioja was a fictitious character invented as the hypothetical pioneer of the naval compass, but it was in use long before 1300 and was largely irrelevant to the discovery of the Americas.

[17] Salomon de Caus did publish a description of a steam-driven pump in 1615, but it was not original, and François

tricity, the formidable material development of the 19th century, to which we have been the witnesses, would not have happened.

"In sum, if human genius had been indefinitely struck by inertia, instead of finding ourselves in a marvelous world that the most audacious imaginations would not have dared to conceive, we would be wandering at this moment in the midst of the burrows dug by our ancestors."

Arago's attribution of the invention of the steam engine to him in consequence was grossly exaggerated. Given that the citation completes a hat-trick, it is tempting to think that Calvet might be aware that Antius is talking through his hat, but it is not obvious that his readers would have got the joke, if so.

XI. The Atmospheric Railway and the River

The four men had returned to their departure point.

"It's half past ten, Messieurs," said Herber, after having darted a glance at the vast electric clock-face ornamenting the rear fronton of the school museum, "We're going to go to the nearby station, which is three hundred meters away."

The travelers followed the schoolmaster, who traversed the courtyard. When reached the extremity of the planted area, he went to an immense oak door, ornamented by shiny bans of polished steel. In response to a light pressure exerted on a spring fixed in the wall, the two battened swung majestically on their hinges. They passed under an elegant stone arch, while the monumental door slowly closed behind them.

Herber and his guests went along a path that opened on to a rectangular plaza covered with bushy chestnut-trees arranged in quincunxes. In the distance, fifty Parisians of all ages and both sexes were waiting in the vicinity of an elegant structure disposed as a shelter.

The group was presumably composed of inhabitants of the neighborhood, for they all tipped their hats to the schoolmaster, who replied with an all-round greeting.

Suddenly, the sound of a powerful horn was heard to the right, and a few moments later, a train composed of ten luxurious carriages towed by a powerful machine came to a stop opposite the shelter.

The travelers stepped on to the footplates, and the train moved off again.

A hundred meters away it suddenly plunged into a broad tunnel illuminated by resplendent globes attached to the walls. The train had already resumed its customary speed, and the electric lamps fled backwards like dazzling meteors.

"We're going at least sixty kilometers an hour," said the physicist.

"Seventy," said Herber. "It's the regulation speed."

"The carriages are admirably suspended," observed the doctor. "One doesn't experience the movement of trepidation that shook travelers on ancient railways. I also noticed that the wheels are solid and rather massive, which favors our relative comfort."

"What I find charming," said Gédéon, "is the essentially comfortable disposition of the carriages. There are wide, soft seats for Epicureans, and a balcony surrounding the entire train for those in a peripatetic mood." As the train emerged into the open, he added: "But it seems to me that the track is curved."

"The track is absolutely circular," the schoolmaster replied. "I can explain our intramural circulation to you briefly. A dozen circular tracks, almost equally spaced, divide the city into concentric zones. On the other hand, a great many radii converge toward the center, but without reaching it, for they stop at the fifth zone, establishing numerous connections between the various points of the outer lines. The spaces within the mesh of that gigantic network are served by electric carriages that cross them in all direction, in such a way that there isn't a single point in the city that can't be rapidly reached on leaving one's house.

"You must have observed, when we set off, that no one paid in order to board the train. That singularity will be explained when you know that every inhabitant pays a special tax that constitutes an obligatory subscription. Only pupils in schools and universities, professors and members of scientific societies enjoy complete gratuity, from which their guests benefit. As for foreigners passing through, they pay a price proportional to the duration of their stay—an insignificant expense, which the less fortunate are spared."

"I see with satisfaction, and, I might say, with pride, that members of the educational profession not only enjoy the highest consideration here but some very enviable immunities."

"It can certainly be said that occupy the highest rank in the social scale," replied Herber, "but the position is one of the most difficult to acquire. It is only after ten years of effort, labor, struggle, examinations and competitions that it is possible for a few people to achieve the envied title of schoolmaster. As for that of director of an establishment, it is only conferred on those who have the merit and good fortune to be singled out by some significant discovery."

"You have several masters under your orders, then?" asked Terrier.

"Under my orders is not the proper expression; they are my auxiliaries, for I don't have the right to determine who they teach."

"Their position, without being equal to yours, is doubtless very satisfactory from the material viewpoint?"

"Yes. They're very comfortably lodged in the school buildings. Their salary is twenty thousand francs, and if, in accordance with what you've told me, my ideas are correct regarding monetary comparisons, that corresponds to the situation of someone in your homeland who possesses an annual income of thirty thousand francs."

"The present-day conditions of education, my dear colleague," the professor said, "plunge us into a profound astonishment. In the society that we have just left, the career is full of disappointments. It is the refuge of poverty, often that of misery."

"You surprise me equally," the schoolmaster replied. "Our role is, however, the most important in the entire social estate. It is into our hands that a being is put whose mind, heart, conscience and will are still drifting in the void, and which the hazard of currents might as easily draw toward evil as toward good. It is reserved for us to develop, fortify and direct all the forces of which he is unaware himself.

"Although, in a remote epoch, a frightful moralist dared to write that the executioner is the key to society's vault,[18]

---

[18] Joseph de Maistre (1753-1821): "All grandeur, all power, all subordination to authority rests on the executioner; he is the horror and the bond of human association."

today, Messieurs, everyone is firmly convinced that it is the schoolmaster. As the great Leibniz said: *The man who is the master of education can change the face of the world.*"

For a few minutes, Gédéon had been giving signs of an extraordinary agitation. Suddenly, he lunged toward his companions, exclaiming in a loud voice; "Look, Messieurs—of all the magnificent things we have seen, there is the one that appears to me the most grandiose and the most astonishing." Pointing westwards, he showed the amazed scientists a magnificent bridge six hundred meters long, a colossal construction, presenting five cast iron arches and three hundred feet of opening, admirable crowned with sculpted stone masonry.

At that moment a dull and prolonged rumble indicated that the train was passing over the river, half a kilometer upstream of the monumental bridge. It was as if the train were suspended above the river, which was deployed in all its splendor, flowing with the profound metallic noise that is the prerogative of great masses of moving liquid.

"That's what I call a river!" exclaimed Gédéon, to the astonishment of the passengers. "It could swallow the old Seine three times over without swelling by an inch. What majesty there is in those broad quays, bordered with splendid palaces! What incomparable richness in the prodigious number of works of art!"

This series of passionate interjections was suddenly interrupted by the disappearance of the train between two high walls.

"It's certain," said Terrier, addressing the schoolmaster, "that to bring the Seine to that enormous width, terrible difficulties must have been overcome. In what epoch was the riverbed extended?"

"The works are contemporary with those of the lake," Herber replied.

"But the monuments that were on the banks must have been demolished!" exclaimed Antius.

"You're talking as they did a long time ago, Doctor. When the engineers set to work, serious objections were raised by the Archeological Society, who wished to conserve the ruins of the Louvre, after having succeeded in obtaining respect for those of the ancient cathedral, Notre-Dame de Paris. We have got past that point, and the river has a similar breadth for an extent of thirty kilometers. It is traversed within the city by fifteen bridges, in different styles, but all as magnificent as one another. Ships of large tonnage once went upriver as far as two thousand meters beyond the old ramparts."

"That enterprise must have cost hundreds of millions," Terrier remarked, "for, in addition to the works, properly speaking, fabulous sums must certainly have been paid out for the expropriations."

"The expense was indeed very considerable; however, thanks to the perfection and power of machinery, and especially by reason of the dilapidation of the riverside constructions, both public and private, it had been calculated in advance that the expense would be considerably inferior to what it would have been in other conditions, when the project would rightly have been considered utopian.

"The economic benefits realized surpassed the most optimistic predictions, and the city finally possesses a magnificent river, absolutely necessary to a seaport. The enormous widening of the river bed has reduced the speed of the current, a circumstance favorable to navigation."

"The honorable corporation of Seine boatmen must have undergone a fabulous development," hazarded Gédéon, strongly agitated by the memory of his nautical exploits.

"Of course," Herber replied. "Navigation for pleasure is one of the complementary branches of gymnastics, which is the general basis of corporeal education."

The horn resounded again and some of the passengers got up in order to get off at the next station. The train decelerated rapidly and, after a few seconds, came to a stop beside a new shelter. A hundred passengers launched themselves out of the carriages and were replaced by an almost equal number of newcomers. The signal-horn blared again and the train moved forward.

"We're getting off at the next station," Herber said. "We'll only be fifty paces from the warehouse. I didn't have to bring you so far, for we have one of the twelve shops near the school, but this one is directly on the way to the lake.

"What! There are only twelve shops to clothe all Paris?" the young man exclaimed. "Everyone must employ thousands of hands."

"A few hundred," the schoolmaster replied, "for humans today only have to supervise, command and direct. Humans leave labor largely to a worker of incomparable strength, nourished by fire and chemical agents, who extends a hundred thousand arms, though which life circulates incessantly, relentlessly and untiringly. Thanks to that prodigious strength, the difference between the price of raw materials and that of the finished article is not very great."

The stop signal sounded a few minutes later, and, a hundred meters further on, the train, which had gradually reduced its speed, came to a halt.

The travelers got down, and, guided by their host, they went along a broad shady thoroughfare. A short distance from the station, the suddenly found themselves in front of an immense building ornamented with columns and attributes. On the central fronton a semicircular shield bore the embossed words CLOTHING STORE.

Followed by his guests, Herber climbed the steps of the peristyle and went into a vast hall.

A young man who was walking with a measured step, hands behind his back, seemingly enduring his sentry duty philosophically, turned round when the visitors came in, advanced toward them and bowed.

Herber handed him a card. The employee's face suddenly expressed surprise and deference. "Monsieur," said the schoolmaster, "I have brought these friends to your store. They have come a long way and desire to abandon, at least for a while, the fashions of their own country in order to dress like us."

"We're very honored by your visit, Messieurs," the young man replied. "Someone will take you to the clothing gallery." He pressed a bell-push, and a few seconds later, the two battens of a lateral door opened. A colleague appeared in the doorway, making vain efforts to stifle an expressive yawn, but he very kindly put himself at the disposal of his clients.

Twenty minutes later, the fur visitors, dressed in an almost uniform manner, left the warehouse, not without having darted a glance into the workshops, where several hundred looms were only waiting for a simple electric contact to become animated once again.

XII. The Lake

The profoundly blue sky had not a single cloud, and the sun was pouring torrents of light and heat on to the earth. The caravan set off under the shady vault of tall trees, in the midst of a cheerful and noisy crowd that was going in the same direction.

"Everyone's going to the fête," said Herber.

"I don't really understand the general excitement," hazarded Antius. "When one has a speed of transportation in excess of a hundred and twenty meters an hour available, a thousand meters above ground, it seems to me unimportant to know whether one pleasure-boat can move a little less slowly than another."

"The races on the lake always attract an immense crowd of spectators, for several reasons," the schoolmaster replied. "In the first place, Parisian youth, since the remotest times, has always been passionate about nautical sports, and the ship that the city bears on its coat of arms is a telling symbol. Secondly, rowing is a gymnastic exercise much esteemed by people of all ages. Finally, Parisians are very proud of their lake and seize every opportunity, or every pretext, that can take them to its shores."

The avenue along which they were walking sloped upwards sensibly, and the silvery sheet of the Seine appeared to their gaze occasionally through lateral gaps.

"If I'm not mistaken," the doctor said, "we're going up toward a part of the city once occupied by the eminently peaceful quarter known as Passy."

"Your conjecture is correct," Herber replied. "As soon as we've reached the end of the avenue, we'll see the lake at our feet."

"In which part of the ancient city has it been hollowed out?" asked he physicist.

"The lake has absorbed in total, on the left bank of the river, the part of the city and the suburb that our ancestors once called the plain of Grenelle, and on the right bank, the entire territory of Boulogne. Around its periphery it's delimited by the hills of Issy, Bellevue, Sèvres, Saint-Cloud, Ville-d'Avray and Passy. Those heights, one scantily inhabited, are now covered with palaces and constitute an ensemble of marvels unrivaled in the entire world. All the habitations are preceded by magnificent terraces, from which the gaze embraces an admirable panorama. The lake, at its greatest width, measures more than three thousand meters; its length extends for nearly two leagues."

At that moment, the travelers arrived on the plateau. Guided by Herber, they went into the trees of a vast garden. Wide pathways roofed with verdure ran parallel all the way to a terrace bordered by a stone ramp supported by sculpted columns. Scarcely had they emerged from the park than they instinctively hastened their steps, and a triple cry of admiration escaped them at the same time.

The lake, like an immense gleaming mirror, extended at their feet. Several thousand spectators were sitting on the inclined lawn, whose slope extended into the waves. An innumerable quantity of walkers was strolling along a wide circular boulevard, which made an admirable frame for the liquid expanse. From top to bottom, the hills were covered with luxuriant parks and splendid palaces.

The magical scene, bathed by the ardent effluvia of the sun, presented the most grandiose and gripping sight. The three travelers, mute with admiration, devoured the marvelous spectacle with their eyes, while the number of walkers flowing over the terrace became ever larger. On the lake, several hundred pleasure boats of every shape and size were tracing rapid furrows.

Races were held at the same time in several parts of the basin From time to time, the faint echo of distant applause announced a victory. In response to an invitation from the schoolmaster, the travelers went down a sloping path that led to the foot of the hill. Following the shore of the lake, they took a long walk, discovering further magnificence at every stride.

The sun was sinking toward the horizon when Herber asked his guests to climb back up the bank to go to the nearest station.

As they reached the vast estuary where the river flowed into the lake, Gédéon stopped. "What is that solitary and motionless biped doing, perched on the water's edge on that tree-trunk?" he asked.

"That's an angler," Herber replied.

"An angler! I suspected as much." The sight of the placid fisherman had awakened his memories of the furious arguments in which, in his capacity as a freshwater sailor, he had once engaged with inoffensive citizens of that category. "The last angler will survive the last century," he remarked, in a lyrical tone. "The worlds will fall apart before that impassive being, half-human and half-vegetable, rooted to the bank. It's him to which the words of Horace might apply: *Impavidum ferient ruinae.*"[19]

A judicious observation by the schoolmaster regarding the hour of departure extracted him from his contemplation. They hastened their steps, and, ten minutes later, went into the courtyard of the station, encumbered at that moment by a compact crowd of city-dwellers waiting for the train.

The horn-signal did not take long to sound, and a powerful machine towing a long line of carriages came to a stop beside the shelter. The mass of travelers broke up, and the carriages were taken by storm. The train moved off again and went over a monumental bridge.

Twenty minutes later, the schoolmaster and his guests came into the main courtyard of the school.

Madame Herber and her daughter, running down the steps of the perron, came to meet them. The foreigners bowed

---

[19] Approximately: "The ruination will find him unafraid."

respectfully to the young woman, who asked about their excursion with interest.

Antius was concluding an account full of color, corroborated by the expressive gestures of his companions, when the carillon of an electric bell was heard.

"Dinner is ready," said Madame Herber.

Antius rounded his arm and offered it to his charming hostess. The guests started walking toward the dining-room. A few moments later, they were sitting around a sumptuous table.

The dinner ran its course amid that mild gaiety of which the school of Epicurus has signaled the influence in its feasts.

The long summer twilight, which had been lighting the horizon for some time, was invaded in its turn by the shades of night.

"Messieurs," said Herber, "the weather is mild and invites us to take a walk. I propose that we go down to the river. The quays are nowadays the most animated and most elegant meeting place in the city.

The proposal was greeted with enthusiasm.

"As for us," said Madame Herber, darting a tender glance at her daughter, whose graceful head, invaded by drowsiness, was resting on her bosom, "we'll go back to the apartment."

The guests got up and, after bidding farewell to the mistress of the house, went out into the plaza, resplendent with the blaze of electric light and busy with the bustle of a compact crowd of pedestrians.

XIII. An Old Memory

They traversed the immense square and went into an avenue sparkling with light and animated by a brilliant crowd. A double current bore the pedestrians on one side toward the central plaza, and on the other toward the river.

A large number of city-dwellers were sitting on large benches with inclined backs, covered by the crowns of the trees, while others, of a more emphatic Epicurean humor, had installed themselves in front of cafés, in which gold, mirrors and bright wallpaper were bathed by the ardent effluvia of electric lights.

In a matter of minutes, they reached the river. The immense causeway, throughout its extent, was furrowed by four rows of luminous globes, which illuminated in all its depth the majestic vault of the great trees. The same magical spectacle was faithfully reproduced on the right bank, separated by an expanse of water six hundred meters broad.

The animation was at its maximum here, and the quay appeared to be the favorite promenade of the Parisians.

For an hour, the schoolmaster and his guests walked through an elegant and active host. Continuing their path, it did not take them long to find themselves in a part of the quay that was not as busy, where a relative calm reigned.

Suddenly, Gédéon, who was scanning the river with his gaze, gripped the doctor's arm feverishly.

The latter turned his head in the direction in which his nephew was pointing. "Notre-Dame!" he said, emotionally.

Terrier shivered and drew nearer to his companions. "Let us salute," he said, "the only acquaintance that we have yet encountered in this marvelous world."

And they bowed toward the somber mass of the old basilica, which rose up from the bosom of the waters, isolated and silent.

The two towers stood out sharply against the sky, illuminated by pale moonlight, but the profile of the high wall bore the profound imprint of the erosion of past centuries.

"You're rendering pious homage, Messieurs, to the most ancient of our monuments," said Herber. "For my part, I'm surprised to the highest degree when I think that the marvelous work in question, gigantic for its era, could have been built more than fifteen centuries ago, when, according to all indications, humankind was in a state of incontestable impotence and inferiority."

Herber and his friends continued their walk, along the river bank. Still agitated by the sudden appearance of the old cathedral, the travelers remained silent.

"Do you realize," said Gédéon, coming to a halt, "that we now have an excellent reference-point for superimposing the old map of Paris on the new city?" Without paying any heed to the irritated expressions of his two traveling-companions, who were justly alarmed by the fit of stupidity, he continued: "It's probable—certain, even—that at this moment we're between the Quai des Grand-Augustins and the Boulevard Saint-Germain, opposite the Cité, which has disappeared under the water." With assurance, he added: "The quai on the right bank must be beyond Les Halles."

Herber looked at the young man in surprise. "You appear to know ancient Paris astonishingly well, my young friend," he said, marveling at such precision.

Convinced by that reflection, and by the consternation on the faces of the two scientists, that he had just committed a grave imprudence, Gédéon, trying to get out of the awkward situation in which he found himself, made matters worse. "I confess, my dear Master," he stammered, effortfully, "that few antiquaries know old Paris as well as me." Before the fiery gaze of his uncle, the young man lost his head completely. "I should have said like us," he added, designating the doctor and the physicist, without knowing what he was doing or saying.

"Messieurs," the schoolmaster said, laughing, "I disapprove of your discretion. Why hide the fact that in addition to your professions, distinguished as they are, you have devoted yourselves to the study of ancient times, and in particular, it seems, to that of old Paris?"

"It's true, my dear host," Antius replied, no longer able to beat a retreat, "that we have a fairly precise knowledge of the old Cité, having found ourselves in conditions very favorable for studying it, but we could not suppose that the detail had any interest for you."

"It has a very great interest for me and for everyone," the schoolmaster replied, swiftly. "Everything that concerns the history of the city is full of interest for its inhabitants. For one thing, Doctor, I'm convinced that your investigations and those of your honorable colleague Monsieur Terrier must have been especially devoted to the scientific and industrial state of old French society."

"Yes," said Antius, burning his ships, "my friend and I have studied the 19th century in depth, not only from the intellectual viewpoint, but also its political, social and philosophical aspects."

"I understand all the interest and also all the merit of your archeological labors, and I regret not being able, like you, to imagine old Paris at an interval of ten centuries."

"The vision is not without its melancholy aspects," the physicist thought aloud, emotional at thought of being so close to his old laboratory, now drowned in the river.

"I'm truly amazed," Herber went on, "for in general, we have only vague ideas about the old Ciité and its successive transformation."

The walkers continued to go along the Seine. They soon found themselves level with the old cathedral. Somber and silent in the middle of the stream, isolated on an islet supported by magnificent works of art, the ruined basilica was the sole item of wreckage that survived of the Cité.

The strangers searched in vain upriver for the Île Saint-Louis, but it had disappeared beneath the waters, whose surface, silvered by the moon, extended as far as the eye could see.

"I'm surprised," said Antius, involuntarily emotional, "that the ancient cradle of the capital wasn't saved."

"It's certain, Doctor," Herber replied, "that it was only after having exhausted every possible plan and means capable of protecting it that it was decided to annihilate the ground that bore the first huts of the Lutecians, of whom we conserve a pious memory, but it was necessary to go on. All the public edifices and houses of the quarter were falling into ruin, and the suppression of the two islands, which gave a considerable impetus to the development of the bed of the Seine, demanded by everyone, was accepted. It marked the commencement of the immense endeavors pursued almost simultaneously on the two banks." He addressed himself to Gédéon, to add: "But, my young antiquary, have you conserved an exact memory of all the monuments that once ornamented the Île de la Cité?"

"Yes, my dear Master," said the young man. And he embarked on such a precise and detailed description of that part of the old city that the schoolmaster could not contain his astonishment.

Antius prudently put an end to that prolixity, unnecessary at best, by attacking the right bank in his turn and talking about the Louvre and the Tuileries, with a moderation of which archeologists do not always give proof.

They had been retracing their steps for a few moments when the physicist stopped.

"A hundred meters from here," he exclaimed, pointing to a vague area of the river, "One could contemplate at one time the glided slices of the cupola of the Institut." Bitterly, he added: "The Académie des Sciences has had its day, then?"

"The Académie des Sciences is the honor of the nation," Herber declared, solemnly, "for which the door opens wide its battens. The palace that was constructed a century ago to shelter the five Académies whose ensemble constitutes the Institut de France is the most magnificent in the city. I'm even counting on taking you to next Thursday's grand session, which will be of great interest, because the celebrated mathematician Howey-hu will be revealing a great invention on which he has been working for thirty years in the most profound secrecy, and which, according to rumor, is destined to change the face of the world."

"The scientist's name appears to indicate an Oceanian origin," observed Antius.

"Yes, Ho-wey-hu was born in Honolulu and is the honorary president of the Académie des Sciences of that opulent city. I have the honor of counting him among my best friends, and it is thanks to our acquaintance that I will be able to obtain four seats, for the president, by reason of the solemnity of the occasion, has been besieged by demands signed with the most illustrious names in the five continents. The telegraphic companies have already made arrangements for the record to be printed, posted up and distributed throughout the entire world that same evening. Because of the impenetrable secrecy in which the inventor has carried out his research, all the scientific bodies are waiting impatient for the official transcript of the session."

The stranger testified to their host all the gratitude that this new proof of sympathy inspired in them.

The two scientists were now almost reassured with regard to the consequences of their young companion's untimely reflection. The flattering assumption of the schoolmaster—who, by virtue of the precision and certainty of their descriptions placed them above the most celebrated members of the Society of Antiquaries—had averted all peril for the moment. In addition, the pleasure they had were able to give the generous host who had welcomed them was an immeasurable source of satisfaction for them.

The state of scientific knowledge in the 19th century and the organization of the ancient Institut became the theme of a conversation, and the doctor and the physicist were able, in turn, to excite the schoolmaster's attention to the highest degree.

"Messieurs," he said, suddenly, "I should like to ask you for a favor."

"Master," Antius replied, "to the fullness of our abilities, we are entirely at your disposal, without any hope of ever repaying your kindness toward us."

"The perfect knowledge you have of the old world has amazed me so much and caused me so much pleasure that I would consider it egotistical to be the only one to profit from your erudition."

"What do we need to do. my dear colleague?" asked Terrier.

"I would be very happy if, tomorrow, at our customary Monday meeting, in the school theater, before our regulars and a few intimates of the Institut that I will invite especially, you would each offer a description of the old society from the scientific, industrial, political and social viewpoints. The entire quarter will certainly appreciate as it deserves the honor reserved for the Museum Plaza School."

"We are entirely at your disposal," said the two scientists, in unison.

"Thank you. Tomorrow, you can occupy yourselves entirely in drawing up the program."

The travelers had crossed the entire length of the broad avenue that had led them to he river. The crossed the square in a straight line. Only a few strollers were abroad now.

"In spite of the dazzle the marvels of the city have caused me," said Antius, turning toward his host, "I've made one observation whose negative character intrigues me to the highest degree."

"What's that, Doctor?"

"I haven't yet seen a single agent of the authority."

"I don't know what you mean by that word."

"I'll explain clearly. There is doubtless here, as everywhere, a group of people charged with watching over the security of their fellow citizens."

"Everyone is responsible for that, even though it is a perfect sinecure. You will not observe any disorder or violence here, for our schools strive to make everyone an educated, honest and well brought-up individual. In any case, from the viewpoint of order and security, the law, reduced to simple, brief and precise formulas, only contains one article: *The inhabitants of each section of the public highway are responsible for any illegal act that might be committee there.*

"I repeat, however, that I've never heard mention of any crime whatsoever against persons or property. Independent of the wellbeing spread in torrents by the progress of science, a condition that distances humans from misery, the active and deadly source of evil, moral education puts them on guard against their own passions. A child soon understands that happiness lies in the practice of the duties dictated by conscience, duties summarized in self-respect, the love of one's fellows and gratitude to the supreme power, which, in giving one intelligence, has ornamented one with its own substance."

At this moment, the strollers went into the main courtyard of the school.

"Before leaving you, Messieurs," said the schoolmaster, "I must show you around your new abode." And, preceding the travelers, he guided them to the extremity of the left wing, which was opposite the one inhabited by himself and his family.

XIV. Furniture and Wall-Decorations

The schoolmaster climbed an elegant staircase in pink marble, pushed open a thick door that swung silently on its hinges, and set his hand on an ivory lever designed to complete an electric circuit. Suddenly, several frosted globes lit up simultaneously in the corridor.

Following their host, the travelers climbed a broad staircase that went up at a gentle slope to a landing covered with a thick carpet of vegetable carpet, on to which opened three tall doors lined with green velvet, situated a few paces apart.

Herber headed toward the one facing him.

"This is your room, Doctor," he said to Antius, "And as those of those Messieurs are almost identical, the examination of this one will inform your companions sufficiently."

So saying, he opened both battens at the same time.

The strangers took a step forward, and remained momentarily nailed to the spot by admiration.

Fixed in the middle of a hemispherical vault, painted with infinite artistry and representing a clear sky decorated with a few white clouds that appeared to be raised in relief, a polished globe was emitting a gentle yellow light into a room of incomparable splendor.

At the back, as high as a cathedral porch, stood a sculpted ebony bed, whose spiral columns supported a dome enriched by allegorical figures in relief, from which waves of Havana satin hung down, supported by enormous fringes.

A carpet with a white background decorated with blue and pink flowers extended all the way to the walls. A quilted divan large enough to permit an entire family to rest on it at the same time occupied the left hand side. Various dressers ornamented with bas-reliefs, carved with a rare perfection, were disposed against the other walls, scarcely leaving enough space for half a dozen flared armchairs, the sight of which would have plunged a paralytic into ecstasy.

The glass in the windows, cut by long curtains of bright cloth, was composed of single sheets, and the walls, covered with cast landscapes obtained by photopainting, opened infinite horizons to the startled eye.

Over a green marble fireplace, whose mantelpiece supported an electric clock and a host of art-works, rose a mirror of extraordinary dimensions, the top of which was integrated with the moldings of the ceiling. Opposite, a massive set of bookshelves, whose shelves were protected by sheets of crystal so transparent that one hardly noticed their presence, offered several rows of rare books, whose sumptuous and sparkling bindings seemed to summon the gaze. Fixed between the two windows was a panoply of scientific instruments, in which the expert eye of the physicist was able to recognize, even though their form had changed significantly, a maximum/minimum thermometer, an improved barometer, a hygrometer and an exceedingly complicated table of astronomical phenomena corresponding to each day.

Through the gap in the curtains of a glazed panel in a door that opened at one of the corners of the room, the travelers were able to distinguish a white marvel fountain whose massive gold taps could pour out torrents of water at various temperatures. A porphyry bath was set alongside it.

The excessive character of the splendor that reigned in the place preoccupied Antius to such a degree that his host noticed it.

"Has anything been forgotten or any mistake been made in your installation, Doctor?" he asked, anxiously.

"No, truly, from every point of view we are overwhelmed by wellbeing, but I was reflecting on a subject more wide-raging than that of our enthronement in this marvelous apartment. I was wondering if many citizens could afford the price of sculpted items of furniture similar to those we have before our eyes—a price that is doubtless formidable, for, by virtue of the profusion and perfection of the sculptures, every room must have absorbed the entire existence of a skilled workman."

"My dear guest," the schoolmaster replied, "everything that surrounds us is the conquest of progress rather than that of fortune—and eminently moral conquest, since it works to everyone's advantage.

"It's certain that in the 19th, or even the 20th, century an opulent collector would have been able, strictly speaking, to create a room almost exactly the same as this one, but the great majority of citizens could not, without being accused of madness, dream of the possession of furniture as rich as the items that ornament all houses today—the price of which is very modest, for it is sufficient to throw a few handfuls of wood-pulp into an appropriate mold to obtain admirable panels, which, after a few hours, while preserving a remarkable lightness, have the solidity of tempered steel.

"You will doubtless object that the method would seem to result in uniformity, but you will abandon that argument when you know that the number of models is very considerable, and that it is sufficient to modify a few details in an template to change the character of an item completely.

"The furniture in this room is in molded teak, which grows very abundantly in Indo-China, once very neglected. Thus prepared, teak takes on the rich and severe tint of old oak. The wall-decorations and carpet, which you appear to admire, are obtained very rapidly and cheaply in our electrical workshops, which obtain their raw materials from plantations and silkworm-factories throughout the world. But these furnishings are not here solely to provide ornamentation; they also have to contain a certain amount of linen."

Seizing a handle of polished steel the schoolmaster drew out a batten, which revealed a pile of dazzlingly white perfumed linen, the sight of which would have sent the most ambitious housekeeper to the seventh heaven.

"I believe, mine host," said Antius, "that you have united in this miraculous room all that the most difficult imagination could desire, or even imagine." He smiled, and added: "So I assume that the elegant bell-rope suspended by the bed-head is quite superfluous."

"That instrument, Doctor, is a telephone," Herber replied, surprised by the mistake. It communicates with the nocturnal service-room, where the staff on duty is always ready to receive your orders.

"Now, Messieurs, the time has come to leave you to a repose of which you must be greatly in need, by reason of the great voyage you have made in recent days and the uninterrupted activity of the day, to which I must have contributed in no small measure."

"Master," proclaimed Antius, emotionally, "no language has terms profound enough to express the sentiments of gratitude that your generosity inspires in us. This morning, we were wandering desperately in the middle of the immense city. We could only envisage the future with a somber terror. Suddenly, a charming vision came to take us by the hand and lead us to your hearth, where we are suddenly surrounded by all the conditions of wellbeing, and where, although strangers, we are heaped with benefits. Thank you, Master!"

"That's well said!" exclaimed Gédéon, in a strangled voice, seizing the schoolmaster's hand, while the physicist, emotional for the first time in his life, maintained a silence and immobility that were even more eloquent.

"Goodnight, my friends; sleep well," said Herber, whose self-composure was visibly weakening. He escaped outside.

"If there is ever a procession of good men, that one will carry the banner," said the young man, passing his hand swiftly over his eyes.

"My friends," said the doctor softly, "we're all extremely tired; let's go to bed. Sleep will restore our calm of mind. Tomorrow, perhaps, we shall be able to analyze coolly the strange things that we have seen today, and reflect on the mysterious power that has snatched us from our world to wake us up a thousand years later."

They each retired to their own rooms. The cupboard contained varied collections of all the objects necessary to the most complicated nocturnal toilette.

After serious reflections on the matter of coiffure, the physicist had made the choice of a large yellow headscarf fastened in front of his forehead by a knot of expert symmetry, while the doctor, following the example of the king of Yvetot,[20] pulled the large hem of a magisterial cotton bonnet over his ears.

Gédéon had no fear of exposing his hair—as coarse and bushy as a wolf's—to the ambient air. After having turned his lamp down to a low level with the aid of a few turns of a lever, he plunged his fists under his pillow, saying: "The old world? I've had it up to here!"

---

[20] A character is a French humorous ballad, which has an English version by William Makepeeace Thackeray. The possessors of the seigneurie of Yvetot, a small town near Rouen, were given the title of *roi* in 534 by Clotaire I, so "le roi d'Yvetot" is a person of great pretention but meager means; hence the simple cotton bonnet in which the one in the ballad goes to bed.

XV. The Awakening, the Museum and the Library

Eight o'clock was chiming on the clock of the central building. The vibration of the final chime was still resonating when the physicist, whose existence was as regular as a chronometer, opened his eyes.

A large pool of sunlight covered the foot of the bed. "Fine weather for optical experiments!" he said, and sat up.

The sight of the unfamiliar objects that surrounded him plunged him into profound amazement.

"Am I the victim of a nightmare and have I not woken up?" he exclaimed. "My mind seems to be in a state of stable equilibrium, thank God. Let's be rational, or at least try.

"It's certain that the day before yesterday, Saturday the fourteenth of June 1880, I explained in my classroom the complete theory of the formation of images in mirrors, both concave and convex—a theory crowned by a thorough algebraic discussion. It's no less certain that I lay down in this bed of my own accord, unless some genie or fairy has transported me during my sleep. Now, at no epoch in no country have genies and fairies taken an interest in men of my age and character. Besides which, I vaguely recall having come into this room—which is not mine, for it differs from it in form, size and especially richness—last night.

"Although I occupy a rather distinguished rank in the honorable educational profession, I do not have the means to put fifty thousand francs into the furnishing of my bedroom. I don't know any of my colleagues who has a purse full enough and a head empty enough to permit this Babylonian luxury. *What then, is this mystery*, as I heard sung at the Opéra-Comique one evening when I had the bad idea of going to see a cut-throat musical?"

The professor slapped his forehead, and added: "But Antius is here. Let's go and find him. He alone can provide an explanation of this strange adventure."

135

After twenty minutes, the scientist had concluded his toilette. He went out of his room at a deliberate pace and knocked on the neighboring door.

"Come in," said a clear voice.

Terrier opened the door and, like Lot's wife, stood there petrified with astonishment.

The doctor, clad in a vast floral-patterned dressing-gown and still ornamented by his magnificent head-dress, was looking into a mirror as big as a coaching entrance and plying a razor, on which his gaze was fixed, with a sure hand.

"Did you have a good night, my dear friend?" he said to the physicist, tranquilly, without turning round.

"It's not to bring you news of my health that I've come here, Antius," the professor replied. "I've come to find out what I ought to think about the strange mystery in which we've been enmeshed for twenty-four hours, if my memory serves me right."

"My dear chap," said Antius, "I've been thinking about it longer than you. It's quite certain that we exist, for each of us can, like Descartes, say: *Cogito, ergo sum.* As for the solution of the problem, after a thousand conjectures, I have arrived at this conclusion, which explains nothing, but which it is essential to adopt, for the security of our minds: Let us go along with events, and not think about the past, at least until further developments."

The doctor passed a brush laden with foam over his chin, and continued: "For the moment, I am, as you can see, devoting myself to an important operation, which requires solitude, and, without kicking you out, I invite you to go and wake my nephew, who will certainly not be racking his brains trying to fathom the mystery."

Abashed, Terrier turned on his heel and went to knock on the young man's door.

The latter, abruptly snatched from the early morning slumber of which an ancient poet has sung the praises, cocked an ear with the anxiety that grips a hare surprised in its covert by the baying of a pack.

Those raps brutally struck so early in the morning on a bachelor's door can't augur anything good, he thought. *There's no one in the world but my tailor and my boot-maker, after their money—or, rather mine—who would do such a thing. The Code certainly has a serious lacuna in not decreeing a severe penalty for people who come to wake their fellow citizens at such an hour. I have a great desire to have inscribed on my door the famous phrase of Dante*: Abandon hope all ye who enter here.

A further series of raps cut this internal monologue short.

It's surely the boot-maker, the individual under siege continued. *All the studies that my unlucky star has led me to make of creditors have convinced me superabundantly that, representing the importunity of a tailor as one, one can confidently represent that of a boot-maker as four. What is the reason for that extraordinary proportion?*

Terrier's voice became audible. "Do you intend to sleep until noon?" the professor shouted.

"That intention seems legitimate to me," the young man replied. Having recognized the timbre of his former teacher's voice, however, he propped himself up on his elbow.

All the splendors of the apartment were suddenly revealed to his eyes, and a profound astonishment was painted on his face. Meanwhile, the memory of the previous day's events gradually took form in his mind, and he could only find, to summarize the present situation, one conclusion: "My creditors have been sleeping the eternal sleep for a long time, thank God. May they rest in peace!"

Reassured by this observation, Gédéon got out of bed and, after having put on the magnificent trousers that he owed to the generosity of the schoolmaster, he ran to the door and opened it.

"How are you this morning, my dear Professor?" he asked.

"Like the towers of Notre-Dame," the physician replied, as he came forward, not disdaining hyperbole.

"In that case, I commiserate, for they're exceedingly dilapidated."

"Alas," said Terrier, still preoccupied with the mysterious problem.

"Don't worry—you're not, yet."

"Do you know what your uncle is doing at this moment?"

"I was about to ask you."

"Calmly shaving his beard."

"I don't see anything culpable in that operation—no pun intended.[21] But what does he think about our situation?"

"Nothing."

"Then we should do the same, for, if a commentator of his ability remains mute, it's because there's nothing to discuss."

"He's clad in a superb dressing-gown and coiffed in a cotton bonnet as tall as a bell-tower," the physicist added.

"I recognize that. He's a man who doesn't easily forsake his habits."

"I'll leave you alone; get dressed quickly," said Terrier, who got up and went away with a distracted expression.

Gédéon ran to a marble bowl as big as an altar with a deep and broad excavation in the center. He pressed a lever in the middle of the upper face sat hazard, and a torrent of clear water ran into the basin

The bowl surely serves a dual purpose, he thought, *for it can also serve as a bath.*

After his ablutions, he dressed swiftly and came out of his room just as Antius was coming out of his. Uncle and nephew found themselves face to face.

"How superb you look this morning, Uncle," said the young man.

"I was about to say the same," replied the doctor, looking him up and down.

---

[21] The French *coupable* [culpable] can also be construed as "cuttable," hence the allegedly-unintended pun.

"See what time can do—in the old days, we'd only have met with bitter remarks."

Alerted by this dialogue, Terrier came out to meet them. The three men went down to the main courtyard. On seeing them, the little girl, who was playing on the grass, came to embrace them, each in turn. Then she ran toward the museum, shouting for the curator.

The old man appeared in the main doorway, holding a retort in his right hand and a hygrometer in his left. Having placed his instruments carefully on the entablature of a column, he came to shake hands with the travelers, who advanced to meet him.

"Did you sleep well, Messieurs?" he asked.

"Like logs," Gédéon replied.

"My friend Heber, who is visiting the work-rooms at the moment, will be very glad to wish you good day."

"Have the pupils returned?" asked Terrier.

"Yes, Monsieur, since eight-thirty."

"But we can't hear any noise," said the young man.

"Absolute silence is maintained during classes. That precious habit is the most powerful auxiliary of our instruction. It is also the indispensable basis of go education. Later, a man who has become habituated to silence in his youth instinctively conserves a great respect for language, and generally only says sensible things, for mind and intelligence are primarily formed by meditation. A person who reflects embraces a world of ideas in a few minutes; hence his superiority. An individual who talks loudly is often, and fatally, a fool."

The curator's age maxims were interrupted by the cries of the child, who launched herself away from the group to run to her mother. Madame Herber came toward the strangers, who bowed simultaneously. Antius appointed himself the interpreter of his companions' gratitude.

"Messieurs," said the young woman, "the bell for the morning meal will ring at eleven o'clock precisely; you don't, therefore, have time to venture far from the house, but fortunately, we have means of distraction here capable of occupying your attention for two hours. I invite you to visit our museum; it contains collections worthy of the interest of scientists."

The doctor and the physicist thanked their benefactor's wife profusely, and, followed by Gédéon, who had only welcomed the proposal with a mediocre enthusiasm, they advanced toward the peristyle, preceded by the old master, who was ready to show them found the theater of his operations.

When they arrived at the main door, they rapidly climbed the steps of the monumental stairway. The curator carefully picked up the instruments he had set down and introduced his guests into the vast entrance hall where they had met him for the first time the day before. He headed then toward a large arched door in the middle of the right-hand side wall and opened its two battens.

The travelers stepped through, and could not retain an exclamation of admiration. They found themselves on the threshold of an immense rectangular room whose ceiling, covered with rich allegorical paintings, appeared to be sustained by paired Corinthian columns adjacent to the four walls. On the upper entablature, a triple row of Florentine bronze busts arranged in chronological orders represented al the scientists who, from the remotest antiquity to modern times, had made themselves illustrious by some useful invention.

"We're in the physics hall," said the old master, simply.

The expert eye of the physicist had already succeeded in recognizing, lost in the midst of apparatus that was unknown to him, a whole series of instruments used in the 19th century.

The order and brightness of the collections attested to both the care and competence of the curator. The latter could not repress a smile of legitimate pride on seeing the ecstatic admiration of his guests.

"All our instruments," he said, "are grouped methodically. The left hand side of the hall contains all the apparatus concerned with weight, statics, hydrodynamics and gaseous fluids. To the right are those of heat and electricity, facing us, of optics, and behind us those of acoustics. The museum is of genuine historic importance, for we conserve a host of instruments that are only valuable by virtue of their antiquity, such as steam engines, old electric piles and the ancient apparatus of spectral analysis."

"If circumstances don't take us to the antipodes," exclaimed the physicist, "we shall make frequent visits here."

"You will always be welcome, Messieurs," said the old man. "As you can only cast a rapid glance over the ensemble today, we can, if you wish, go into the technology hall."

The four men traversed the length of the vast room. Having arrived at the far end, the curator opened a large door and they penetrated into an arched gallery so vast that the first room seemed to be its antechamber. There were grouped all the machines of contemporary industry.

They went forward, parading their eyes over all the marvels.

Suddenly, the physicist shuddered and grabbed the doctor's arm. He had perceived, set up in an immense display-cabinet, the models of all the apparatus that human genius had successively created to reach the solution of the capital question of aerial navigation—a problem whose definitive solution had spread wealth throughout the entire world.

The antique hot air balloon was followed by aerostats, inflated in turn by hydrogen and lighting gas, constituting the entire series of apparatus less dense than the atmosphere, the modest role of which had been necessarily limited to ascensions motivated by pure curiosity or to more useful experiments in hygrometry, electricity and atmospheric pressure.

A long file of instruments of every shape and size attested to the number and ingenuity of the seekers who had pursued the problem of aviation. Some had been propelled by the movements of rectilinear generators, others by circular movements. The initial force animated, in turn, planes, springs, helices and metallic elytrons. The later models, laden with miniature goods and travelers busy with all kinds of occupations, testified that the accumulation of effort had finally produced practical results.

Twice over, the curator, astonished by their persistence, had said in a loud voice that time was getting on and that they still had two halls to visit before the library. No one appeared to be listening. By dint of obsession, however, he succeeded in extracting them from their examination and taking them back to the vestibule.

The entrance to the chemistry and mineralogy displays was opposite the door to the physics hall. They went in. The room lost nothing in size or richness to its predecessor. The most precious stones, the rarest minerals, the most perfect crystals and the most delicate preparations abounded there. A heap of diamonds as big as a fist darted fulgurant flashes at their dazzled eyes.

Preceded by their guide, they went into the natural history display, whose extent equaled that of the technology hall, of which it formed a symmetrical reproduction. An enormous quantity of animals of every sort, perfectly conserved, populated that immensity.

"Here," said the old master, "there are several species that have virtually disappeared, notably in the family of ferocious animals, which humans have hunted to their ultimate lairs—thus, we conserve them with a care that is not exempt from anxiety for the future." Monsieur Ravan added: "It's half past ten, Messieurs. We'll go up to the library, where we can wait for the moment to go to table." And he took his delighted visitors to a large marble staircase that led to the first floor.

That part of the edifice was illuminated by an immense rose-window set in delicately-worked stone, the multicolored panes of which flooded the interior of the monument with a slightly pink-tinged light. When they had reached the upper floor, the curator opened the battens of the central door, which opened on to the landing, and went in with his companions.

They moved from one marvel to the next. The grandeur of the room initially struck them with amazement. Throughout its extent, which occupied the total length of the museum, and from floor to ceiling, the gaze embraced an immense array of books of every size, bound with as much taste as sumptuousness.

"Our library is methodically arranged," said Monsieur Ravan. "The right hand side includes all the literary, philosophical, historical and geographical masterpieces of all epochs. To the left, we have grouped, according to their nature, the best scientific works written since remote antiquity. You will find there the astronomical systems of the Hindus, the observations of the Egyptian priests, the geometry of Euclid and a host of rare works."

"It seems to me, my dear Master," said Gédéon, who had never gone into a library in his life, "that, even assisted by the methodical divisions that you have adopted, a visitor searching for a book in this room would have white hair before he found it."

"Nothing is easier and simpler," the curator replied. "To each scientific or literary group, the name of which is printed in capital letters on the corresponding section of the ceiling, is attached a large volume containing the names of all the authors in alphabetical order and, with regard to each name, the title and date of his works."

Antius' eyes lit up. "I'd be very glad," he whispered to Terrier, "to know whether I survived my century."

"Me too," replied the professor, tranquilly.

"While we carry out some brief bibliographical research," Antius said to his nephew, "you can keep our excellent Master company, if that's all right with him."

Monsieur Ravan smiled. "The old man and the young man are already friends," he replied.

The doctor and the physicist marched off, looking upwards, until they encountered, almost simultaneously, the words PHYSIOLOGY and PHYSICS.

On a long table covered in a green velvet cloth were the indicative volumes relative to each science.

Antius feverishly opened the volume concerning his profession, riffled through as far as the syllable ANT and scanned the lines rapidly.

He got as far as the name of DR. ANTROEM without having yet seen his own. He was gripped by a shiver of anxiety. He began again reading from top to bottom with a kind of repressed anger. Suddenly, his muscles relaxed and a smile of satisfaction illuminated his face. His eyes were riveted to two lines: ANTIUS, ANDRÉ-JÉROME, member of the Académie de medicine. *Researches on the Functions of the Brain*, Masson, 1867. *Note. This work stimulated lively controversy on its first appearance.*

"I should think so!" exclaimed the author, proudly, thinking of the battles he had fought so intrepidly.

For his part, the physicist, who had observed his friend's gestures, contented himself with reading aloud: "TERRIER, JEAN-BAPTISTE. *The Mechanical Theory of Heat*, Gauthier-Villars, Paris 1869." The physicist modestly left out the postscript: *Note: This work is one of the important scientific landmarks of the 19th century.*

"Well, Terrier, it appears that we're not entirely dead," said Antius, with a smile that was not exempt from vanity.

"Not in any fashion, fortunately," the professor replied. "I must add, however, that our scientific longevity surprises me as much as our corporeality."

"Why, if you please?" asked the doctor, stiffly.

"Because it's rare for a purely speculative theory on a particular point of experimental science to conserve its authority for more than half a century, and it's generally buried with the memory of its author."

"It's necessary to conclude that ours have been consecrated by the future," replied Antius—who, in matters of self-esteem, always fought every step of the way. Swiftly, however, he added, looking at his interlocutor: "My satisfaction is not yet complete, however. It's necessary for me to assure myself that one of my most solid and cherished convictions is correct."

He took the volume and riffled through it rapidly.

"I thought as much: Poulard has not survived," he said, after having ascertained that the name of his most intimate enemy was missing from the catalogue. "All his nonsense doubtless served only to aliment the manufacture of contemporary paper trumpets." And he took his companion by the arm, leading him back to their departure-point.

The travelers went back down to the courtyard.

"I'll tell you something that will astonish you," Antius said to his nephew.

"Nothing can astonish me now," the latter replied.

"Just now," the doctor went on, "Terrier and I discovered our scientific works, duly catalogued."

"If you think that astonishes me, you must think I'm a fool."

XVI. A Lawsuit in 2880

At that moment, Herber came down the steps of the peristyle in front of his private abode and came toward them.

The travelers went to meet him and shook had effusively.

After having inquired as to whether his guests had slept well, the schoolmaster led them to the dining room. Each guest took the place that he had occupied the previous day.

While doing the honors of the table with her habitual grace, Madame Herber congratulated her guests for their remarkable work they had done on the history of the capital and expressed her pleasure in advance at being able to host a very interesting soirée, to which she had already invited a few of her young female friends, whom she would welcome to her home.

"The program will be printed in an hour and posted throughout the quarter," said the schoolmaster. "I think that the hall will be full to overflowing for the session. You have doubtless determined the topics on which each of you will speak, Messieurs?"

"I don't believe, my dear colleague, that it will be necessary to hold a long discussion on that subject," replied the physicist. "The doctor, who has occupied himself successfully with economic science, will doubtless deal with social life in the 19th century, as well as the state of natural and medical science in the same period." Antius approved with a nod of the head. "As for me, I shall talk about the state of the sciences in general, and will strive to merit a certain attention."

"Very good!" said Herber, with satisfaction. "And our young scholar?"

"Me!" exclaimed Gédéon, throwing himself backwards.

"Of course."

"I believe, my dear Master, that you would be prudent to accept the excuses of my young nephew, who is not accustomed to public speaking," the doctor declared. "He might well stand there open-mouthed before the audience, and might even embarrass us all in the most ridiculous manner."

"Although it pains me to admit it, I think we have just heard the language of wisdom," said Gédéon, frankly.

"I don't share your opinion, Messieurs," said Madame Herber, smiling, "And I formally request our young archeologist to take his turn. I'm convinced that he would interest everyone by specifying the customs and habits of our ancestors, and that he would obtain a great success by offering a picturesque description of the old city."

The strangers seemed very embarrassed in confrontation with such a formal request by the person whose providential intervention has extracted them from distress and despair.

"Messieurs," declared Herber, laughing, "All resistance has become impossible. In any case, our public is essentially benevolent, and will not fail to encourage our young orator."

After a few objections formulated by the three travelers in turn and rejected one by one by Herber and his wife, it was agreed that Gédéon would say a few words at the end of the soirée, after having begged the indulgence of the audience.

During this amicable debate, the meal pursued its course.

The presence of several exotic dishes, for which progressive culture had developed the succulent taste, astonished the travelers. Herber gave an account of each one, as a consummate botanist, and also identified a large number of precious substances whose alimentations had been enriched by science. Some, whose toxic elements had been eliminated, furnished highly-spiced condiments.

When the coffee served by the gracious hostess had crowned a repast as sumptuous as that of the day before, Antius declared that he and his companions planned to take a long walk through the city that afternoon.

The schoolmaster gave them very precise and extensive topographical indications for that purpose. "Now, Messieurs," he added, "you can't set forth without money. I have, therefore, set aside some cash for that purpose, which will suffice for any expenses you might incur." And he handed the doctor an elegant leather wallet with golden fittings.

The schoolmaster seemed surprised by the warm thanks, and especially by the unanimous refusal, that his guests opposed to his generous offer. "Messieurs," he said, "in treating you thus, I'm accomplishing a sacred duty, and you have no more right to prevent its accomplishment than those who attempt to refuse your help in similar circumstances. It's a simple transmission that I'm confiding to you, for, when the time comes, it will pass from your hands to those of your fellows whom you find in need of it."

All opposition became impossible before that noble and elevated speech. Antius silently put the wallet into his pocket.

Twenty minutes later, the strangers set off along the wide thoroughfare that led to the river. Shortly after that, they set foot on the monumental bridge that prolonged the avenue.

The broad river was flowing placidly between two rows of palaces and monuments, the most distant of which were confused with the plane of the horizon. The two nearest bridges were displayed in all their magnificence.

To the right, eight hundred meters away, the old basilica sadly raised up its two towers, ravaged by the centuries.

"How many monuments that were once the pride of the Cité have disappeared!" said Antius, gravely. After a momentary pause to sponge his brow, he added: "If the Pont des Arts had been as long as this one, mind, I know a great many academicians who would often have missed the Institut's sessions."

The travelers reached the right bank. Suddenly, their gazes were attracted by a considerable crowd that was agitating under the centuries-old trees on the quay, facing a monument whose gigantic proportions overshadowed all the neighboring edifices.

"Let's go that way—we'll learn something new," said Gédéon, who had once conscientiously added a precious continent to any assembly of idlers he had encountered in his path.

They veered to the left and advanced to the edge of the crowd. Having penetrated to the middle of the circle, their attention was particularly provoked by a compact group at the center of which three or four people were speaking in turn, animatedly.

The young man elbowed his way through the ranks and, followed by his companions, penetrated the densest part of the crowd. As it seemed to him to be difficult to grasp the object of the discussion, he bowed to the orator who was standing beside him and said: "I beg your pardon, Monsieur, but we are foreigners, and we would be very interested to know what has caused so many honorable citizens to gather here."

Several people raised their hats. "Monsieur, it concerns the famous case of the Mines of Kantara, which is being heard today at the Palais de Justice," replied the person interrogated, pointing at the nearby monument.

"Would you be so kind as to tell us the nature of the case?"

"Gladly, Monsieur," the citizen said. "A joint-stock company was set up for the exploitation of that country's gold mines. After a few years, the results obtained being derisory, the business was abandoned. Twenty years later, a new association of capitalists resumed the project, and, in consequence of works skillfully executed, and even more so of very favorable circumstances, obtained a formidable return of auriferous mineral. When it came to sharing out the dividends, the original shareholders claimed their part, but the later ones argued that, by virtue of the law of the land, the original company had effectively ceased to exist because of the dispersal of the society's funds and the abandonment of the work. The affair is further complicated by virtue of the concession of the territory of the deposits to a rapid railway company employing the electromotive system, made in the interval between the two exploitations by the country's government, which wants to impose taxes on all three groups of shareholders. Hence, there is one suit between the companies and one between the companies and the government. There has been no agreement regarding the choice of arbitrators. The case has been brought before the Tribunal of Paris, which is to settle the question definitively.

"In what country are these mines situated?" asked Terrier.

"In the Mountains of the Moon, Monsieur."

"In the Mountains of the Moon!" exclaimed Gédéon, bursting into laughter. "I thought that heavenly body, excessively perforated by the financiers of all ages, offered nothing but holes."

"The Mountains of the Moon," said the physicist, "are in Africa, on the sixth degree of north latitude."

"The case," the obliging interlocutor continued, "is as extraordinary for its duration as its complication. The definitive judgment will not be pronounced until this evening, and the affair has been before the Tribunal for ten days!"

"Ten days to judge that affair!" exclaimed the former legal clerk. "It seems to me that the case in proceeding with marvelous rapidity. If such a case had been brought before a 19th century court, for example, all the interested parties, even those in swaddling-clothes, would have been dead before the question had been definitively settled." As the number of interested spectators continued to increase, he added: "But what is the ingenious mechanism that permits you to deal with judiciary matters so swiftly?"

"It's quite simple," a neighbor replied. "Those who are contesting the case accumulate in their respective submissions all the arguments that are in their favor. The documents are handed to the judges, chosen from among the most honorable and illustrious citizens, who, after a profound examination, pronounce a definitive verdict."

"Which is clear, rapid and sensible—and gets rid of all the advocates, attorneys and bailiffs."

"What do those words signify?" asked several individuals.

"Messieurs," said Gédéon, solemnly, "if the important tasks that have brought us to this city left us the leisure, I would make it my duty to explain to you the sorry picture of a civil lawsuit in the 19th century—a historical matter of which I have made a special study. Furthermore, I would sketch portraits in turn of each of the members of that trilogy of individuals with whom you have the honor of being unacquainted—but the two scientists who are accompanying me will not permit that lecture at the moment; it would take us out of our way, to the great prejudice of the archeological world, which is feverishly awaiting the results of our investigations."

For some time, in fact, the doctor had been tugging the sleeve of the turbulent orator, who gravely saluted his audience and left the scene, followed by his two companions.

"You'd do better to conserve your loquacity for this evening," Antius said, "and to set aside your old habits as an open-air orator for the time being."

"I don't know that will happen this evening," Gédéon replied, "but just now, I was in full flow, and all those curiosity-seekers are missing out on some fine details of the world of the ancient Palais."

XVII. Two Antiquaries

The walkers stopped, indecisively.

"It's only two o'clock," said Terrier, "and we have plenty of time. I think it would be good to go back and follow the great boulevard level with the bridge we've just crossed."

This proposal was adopted. The three men retraced their steps and turned into the broad avenue that extended on their left. The promenade was more animated. Numerous groups, reduced to immobility by the ardent heat of the sun, were standing in the shade. Others, more intrepid, were walking slowly beneath the vault of large trees. Nothing could be heard but the murmur of fountains and the joyful cries of children playing around the flower-beds.

After walking for a quarter of an hour, the travelers took another thoroughfare that made an obtuse angle with the first and, so far as they could tell, ought to lead them into the area occupied by the great boulevards. Five hundred meters further on, they perceived a large uncultivated space to their left, behind which a number of large buildings were under construction.

Attached to the walls of buildings at various heights, lightweight machines appeared to be functioning under the action of powerful electric currents, lifting up, disposing and sealing carved stones, red bricks and malleable cast iron with a silvery gleam in layers of cement. The components were arranged with an admirable rapidity and regularity. The houses seemed to be growing visibly.

Several stacks of polychrome marble colonnettes, sculpted with marvelous artistry, had been arranged on the roadside. The physicist approached one and started examining it with profound attention.

"What do you think this substance is?" he asked the doctor, suddenly.

"I would willingly believe," the latter replied, after a long enough examination, "That we're in the presence of calcium carbonate, which has been transformed by an exceedingly high temperature into magnificent marble—and I can now explain the profusion and richness of the ornamentation of edifices."

Gédéon looked at his uncle with an astonished expression that lent itself to several different interpretations.

"That opinion appears to surprise you," said the physicist.

"I'd say, rather, that it pains me, for who could possible believe that one can make marble from chalk?"

"Anyone who has the most elementary notion of chemistry," the professor replied, peremptorily. "Fifty times over, with the same rifle-barrel, sealed at both ends and full of pulverized chalk, I've manufactured marble. It's therefore not astonishing that the method is used industrially today, like many others that once appeared bound to remain in the purely scientific domain."

At that moment, a sheet of fluted brick forty meters square rose up like a gigantic curtain before the façade of an almost-completed house; after a few oscillations, it settled to cover a part of the roof already clad in broad planks of fir-wood.

"One might think that artistry has reached its peak," said the doctor, taking some delight with his pun. "That kind of roofing is very graceful, and singularly pleasant to behold, instead of offending the eye with those sinister metallic strips, which damp air does not take long to cover with a dull and dirty layer of zinc hydrocarbonate."

"Astronomy must have a great many devotees here," the physicist observed, pointing out circular kiosks surrounded by green bronze fluted columns, which topped the majority of edifices and whose shiny cupolas were surmounted by lightning-conductors supported by allegorical figures." Almost immediately, as his eyes followed a sparkling balloon supported by steel cables that was rising rapidly beside a high façade, he added: "The ghost of my illustrious colleague Sainte-Claire Deville must be satisfied."[22]

"You think that metallic mass is made of aluminum?" queried the doctor.

"Undoubtedly. It's obvious that a means has been found of producing aluminum cheaply—a substance very resistant to chemical agents but very widespread in nature, since the pure clay is, as you know, nothing but hydrated aluminum silicate, resulting from the decomposition of feldspar, and is not rare anywhere. Moreover, the employment of that light metal, tenacious and inalterable in air, seems to me to be entirely appropriate in the present case. You'll notice, in addition, that the balconies that have been in place for some time have not lost the slightly fatiguing glare of pure aluminum, thanks to a particular burnishing that is done in place and furnishes the softest shades."

Profoundly impressed by the spectacle of the marvels taking place before their dazzled eyes, the travelers slowly continued on their way.

After walking for a few minutes, their gazes plunged into a vast excavation recently hollowed out, in which a great many people, widely distributed, were actively digging.

Several orators were holding forth in the middle of groups that appeared to be lending sustained attention to their words.

"What can all those people by doing?" Antius wondered, highly intrigued.

"There's someone who can tell us," said Gédéon, pointing at a man of respectable appearance who was toiling up the bank toward us, carrying an object wrapped in gray paper under his arm.

When the citizen had completed his ascent, the strangers went to meet him and the doctor, after a profound bow, asked him the reason for the assembly.

---

[22] The chemist Henri-Étienne Sainte-Claire Deville (1818-1881) developed a process for the extraction of aluminium.

"Monsieur," said the pedestrian, raising his hat, "the trench in front of you has been opened on the site of some buildings of old Paris for the establishment of a group of new houses. The discovery of several curious objects, of very ancient origin, has attracted a great number of searchers." Pointing to the mysterious object that he was carrying with such precaution, he added: "For my own part, I am more than a little satisfied with my find."

With the expansiveness characteristic of happy people, the amateur antiquarian, in order to show his treasure to the strangers, began removing the surrounding sheets of paper one by one. Finally, he exposed a singular instrument formed by a curved handle about half a foot long, riveted to a hollow sheet metal disk five or six inches across and badly chipped. The apparatus had only retained half of its lid, represented by a bulbous strip of copper pieced with numerous holes.

"It's obvious," the fellow said, authoritatively, "that half the object is missing. I've dug all around the hole where it was buried in search of the complementary part, but in vain. I've been lost in conjectures for some time to divine what use our ancestors made of it. Moving from one deduction to another, I've been led to the certainty that I'm in the presence of a defensive weapon, of a quite widespread employment in the barbaric epoch when cities were exposed to sieges of various duration. It's probably in this receptacle that the besieged enclosed boiling oil or pitch, which they poured on to the heads of the besiegers from the top of the ramparts. I admit with confusion, however, that I've tried in vain to translate the incomplete inscription that it still retains to this day."

And the amateur showed the strangers a few irregularly-spaced letter on the edge of the lid, engraved on a horizontal stalk.

The doctor fixed his gaze attentively on the remains of the inscription, disposed in the following manner:

B S N IRE B V ÉE S. D. G.

"Monsieur," he said, "suddenly raising his head, the inscription, incomplete as it is, will add, if necessary, further strength to the opinion that I formed of the object at first glance. The object is not, as you imagine, a weapon of war. Its usage is, on the contrary, entirely peaceful, and you will share my opinion when you learn that the inscription, in its entirety, reads: *Bassinoire, brevetée sans garantie du government*—a formula whose last four terms were obligatory from the legal viewpoint."[23]

"Really, Monsieur?" said the amateur, whose self-respect was even more offended by the humility of the functions of his apparatus than the falsification of his own hypothesis.

"There's no possible doubt about it in that regard," agreed the physicist, while Gédéon dared not say a word for fear of bursting out laughing.

"I thank you sincerely, Messieurs," the Parisian said. "I'll write a note this very day to the Society of Independent Antiquaries, to which I belong."

And after exchanging a deep bow with the travelers, he went along the avenue.

The doctor and his companions went down into the excavation and soon found themselves near to a group of curiosity-seekers, in the middle of which a self-important middle-aged gentleman was holding forth.

"You all know, Messieurs," he was saying, "that in a very remote geological era, the Earth was covered with a liquid layer, which various volcanic eruptions gradually drove back into the lower regions of the terrestrial crust. The seas

---

[23] Patents issued for new inventions in 19th century France required the recipients citing them to include the formula in question to emphasize that the granting of a government patent was no guarantee that the device in question would actually fulfill its intended purpose. A *bassinoire* is a warming-pan used to heat up a cold bed. A very similar but rather risqué version of the same joke is used in Alfred Bonnardot's "Archéopolis" (1857; tr. as "Archeopolis"), one of a sequence of classic stories in which future archeologists digging in the ruins of Paris make amusing errors of interpretation.

have no other origin. The presence of a considerable quantity of marine fossils in the orographic system of the globe offers evident proof of that state of general submersion.

"I have, personally, had the good fortune to find, in the same area of ground in which we are presently digging, irrefutable evidence of that geological system, which was only extremely controversial, but which is now considered to be a well-established scientific certainty."

The orator displayed a heap of seashells in his hand, and continued: "The mass of fossils that is at our feet is constituted in large part by the fossils of *Ostraea edulis*, commonly known as the oyster.[24] The agglomeration of this debris in this location by the seas of the geological epoch constitutes a remarkable case. I will add, Messieurs, that I have encountered one particularity here before which all my conjectures remain impotent. You can see here, disseminated without any order, the fossil bones of several fish that nowadays live exclusively in fresh water, the presence of which in the midst of these marine shells constitutes an anomaly that I cannot explain."

At that moment, one of the most attentive auditors, perched on the summit of a mound of earth, who was testifying his admiration by opening a mouth as wide as a well-head, suddenly lost his balance and fell backwards, with increasing velocity down a slope several meters long.

The weight of his body had dislodged from the flank of the mound an avalanche of shards of bottle-glass and crock-

---

[24] This joke too can be found in one of the classic "ruins of Paris" stories, in this case Alfred Franklin's *Les Ruines de Paris en 4875* (1875; tr. as "The Ruins of Paris in 4875", included in *Investigations of the Future*, Black Coat Press, ISBN 978-1-61227-106-4), demonstrating that Calvet was well aware of the literary tradition in which he was working. In Franklin's story the joke is left unexplained, the reader being required to deduce the true nature of all the discovered artifacts on the basis of the clues provided, but Calvet presumably disapproved of that obliquity.

ery, which had doubtless been lying dormant there for several centuries, and contact with which caused a significant grimace to run over the face of the victim. Arrived at the terminus of his fall, the individual, by virtue of his acquired momentum, landed on his hands and showed the crowd a twenty-meter rip that a piece of glass had made in his clothing.

While he was getting to his feet, torn between confusion and pain, Terrier, who had not missed any of the phases of the accident, ran forward, to the great astonishment of the crowd to the place from which the amateur had tumbled. This singular maneuver convinced the idlers that the professor was about to produce a voluntary repetition of the catastrophe, but the physicist, having arrived at the top of the mound, leaned over, sought points of support with both hands, and then came down the slope backwards with such prudence that all the members of the crowd were immediately reassured on his behalf.

Half way down the scientist stopped. As soon as he was sufficiently well-balanced he stretched out his hand and grasped a fragment of porcelain in the form of a quarter-circle, whose soiled surface nevertheless allowed a glimpse of a golden arabesque. He rubbed the face that had caught his attention methodically with a corner of his white burnoose, and made a gesture of surprise whose suddenness almost precipitated him to the bottom of the trench.

"Messieurs," he said, addressing the crowd, which had followed these various maneuvers with keen curiosity, "the fall of the honorable citizen, who has fortunately resumed the assault on the height where you are standing—a fall that I would qualify as providential, if it had not been marked by an accident that was fortunately not serious—has just brought to light an interesting topographical fact.

"A moment ago, while anxiously following the perilous descent of the estimable individual, my eyes were struck by the gleam of a few shiny lines designed on the object I am holding in my hand—and object which, in its integrity, was obviously a porcelain plate. I have taken possession of it, thanks to a tactic whose audacity, to which I am unused, has been amply rewarded.

"As you will be able to assure yourselves momentarily, the fragment that I have before my eyes bears the embossed inscription painted in fine Gothic script, the two words: *Café Anglais*, words even more significant for gourmets than for antiquaries. We are incontestably on the site of that celebrated restaurant, which, in its time, had conquered the clientele of all the ichthyophages in the capital.

"That fact acquires in my eyes a value all the greater because it permits me to explain at the same time to our honorable geologist the anomaly presented to his legitimate scientific convictions by the abnormal proximity of marine and freshwater fossils. The former are, in reality, merely the shells of oysters, and the latter the bones of pike, carp and eels, thrown into the depths of some deserted courtyard by the waiters of that famous establishment."

A formidable outburst of laughter greeted the physicist's explanation.

Only the consternated geologist took no part in the general hilarity. Terrier generously came to his aid. "Monsieur," he said, politely designating the disappointed scientist with his hand, "presented to us jut now some lofty geological conceptions with such precision and authority that his great competence cannot be called in question by an incident that no one could have foreseen. Furthermore, the frankness with which he made us party to the embarrassment caused to him by the simultaneous presence of the debris of marine mollusks and river fish testifies eloquently to the fact that his scientific honorability is no less than the depth of his knowledge."

Having thus placed over the wound he had inflicted a balm of whose efficacy he was well aware, the professor gravely climbed to the top of the bank. Then, following his companions, he went back to the avenue that bordered the pit.

XVIII. The Press in the New World.
The Communal House

"What function can that strangely formed kiosk fulfill?" asked Gédéon, pointing at a elegant booth standing under the crown of an elm several centuries old.

"It's a newsstand," the physicist replied, perceiving a stroller drawing away from the booth unfolding a gigantic sheet of paper whose lower edge was skimming the grass.

"Aren't you curious to know today's news?" asked the young man.

"Certainly," said Antius, handing his nephew a twenty-franc bill. "Go and buy a newspaper."

Gédéon ran to the little edifice. Having arrived before the display, he ran his eyes over various rows of publications, but the inspection left him perplexed, by virtue of the unfamiliarity of the titles.

"Madame," he said to a middle-aged woman who seemed to be fighting drowsiness, lifting her head up repeatedly with the regularity of a pendulum, "I'd like a well-informed paper."

"The *Continent* has just appeared," the lady replied, waking up with a start.

Gédéon took the sheet, handed over his banknote and collected his change. "I should have asked about the opinion of the paper," he muttered, as he drew away. "Anyway, if it's not mine, I'll give it to my uncle. In politics, what exasperates me cheers him up prodigiously, and *vice versa*."

The two scientists were sitting comfortably on one of the avenue's benches. Having arrived before them, Gédéon, without asking for permission, read aloud: "*Political news. It is not without courage that, struggling against the formidable current of innovations, or rather follies, that is drawing the entire world along, the conservatives...*" In a cavalier manner, the reader interrupted himself. "Let's pass on—we know the rest."

He turned over. "*Miscellaneous events*—this, at least one can read with tranquility. *In the semi-barbaric era in which our forefathers buried their dead...*" The young man interrupted himself again, alarmed: "What the devil do they do with theirs? *...their dead, the air of the great cities was saturated with pestilential miasmas given off relentlessly by the immense cemeteries that formed the funereal girdles of cities. The recent excavations made in the northern part of the city have led to the discovery of a prodigious quantity of bones, which explains the terrible epidemics that were rife in those miserable times.*

"*Several tombstones have also been unearthed, which testify to the naïve vanity of our ancestors. A few, by virtue of their bizarre texts offer curious problems to our antiquaries. Take, for example, this one: Here lies Claude Lesturgeon, hatmaker, member of the Board of Arbitration, good husband and loyal national guardsman. What can that last phrase signify?*

"You can reply to that impertinent reporter, Uncle, having once been a model *bizet*."[25]

"The epithet is too flattering," the doctor replied, "for I came before a disciplinary council every three months."

"I'll continue," Gédéon said. "*The most ancient urns in our modern necropolises, which are nevertheless rich in epitaphs, do not contain any of the terms that represent the multiple functions of this individual.* Urns?"

"That clearly signifies," observed the doctor, "that the system of incineration is today universally practiced. I have, for my part, fought in writing and in speech against the opposition raised in certain parts to that procedure, which resolves a grave problem of public hygiene."

"*The day before yesterday*," the young man continued, "*the passengers on the* Astrolabe, *twenty leagues out to sea*

---

[25] The literal meaning of *bizet* refers to a breed of sheep— hence its use in *argot* with reference to Frenchmen doing their obligatory term of national service.

rounding *Cap Palmas, which is situated on the west coast of Africa. At 10° east longitude and 4° north latitude, saw, two hundred meters below the balloon, a sea-monster half a kilometer long, the coils of which were writhing in the ocean.*"

"That one I know," said the doctor, raising his head, it's definitely the *Constitutionnel*'s old sea-serpent."[26]

"Now, here's an article of the highest importance for us: *The arrival in Paris has been announced of Monsieur Guillaume Dryon, the illustrious agronomist, who makes the most intelligent and generous use of his colossal fortune. It is well-known that the illustrious landowner, who is also an intellectual of the first order, exploits an immense territory of thirty thousand hectares in Central Africa, on the shores of Lake Tanganyika, open to all progress and all industrial and agricultural innovations. Monsieur Dryon's library and collections are among the most famous in the entire African continent. The magnificent house he possesses in the Place des États in Paris is one of the marvels of the city.*"

"That is indeed important news for us," said Antius. "We ought to have only one objective: work. Inaction would be more than a privation; it would be a dishonor for us."

The travelers had already covered two hundred meters following the left hand side of the avenue, when their gaze was arrested by an edifice that was distinguished from the neighboring houses as much by its size and general appearances as by the nature of the materials that had been exclusively used in its construction.

All along the extent of the façade, the gaze was unable to encounter any other substances than iron and glass. With those

---

[26] A famous cartoon by Henri Daumier published in *Les Bons Bourgeois* in 1846 has a snatch of dialogue as a caption in which one assures the other that the sea serpent's existence is obviously possible, since its sighting has been reported in the *Constitutionnel* (a famously conservative newspaper). "The *Constitutionnel*'s sea-serpent" thus became mocking shorthand for any improbable news item.

162

two elements, however, an architect of genius had succeeded in forging a work that was as astonishing by virtue of its grandiose character as it was charming by virtue of the exquisite artistry of its ornamentation. Throughout the metal frame, which affected the purest and most graceful forms, panes of glass were enclosed whose azure reflection was infinitely soft. The ground floor opened via large bays on marble staircases, which descended in a gentle slope to the causeway. The incessant movement of the crowd through its doors indicated that it was a much-frequented monument.

"That metallic palace must be the seat of some permanent exhibition," said Terrier. "We could always go in."

His companions having approved this proposal, they headed for the building.

Above the door, a heavily-ornamented shield bore the inscription: COMMUNAL HOUSE.[27]

"It's the district Mairie," said Gédéon, aloud, convinced that he has surely solved the problem.

"You're mistaken, Monsieur," said a pedestrian who was passing by them. "The Mairie of the right bank is a long way from here."

"That way of putting it, Monsieur," said Antius, "seems to indicate that there are only two Mairies in the entire city."

"Yes, Monsieur, that of the right bank and that of the left."

---

[27] Owen Jones, the architect of the Crystal Palace constructed in London's Hyde Park for the Great Exhibition of 1851 and subsequently rebuilt on Sydenham Hill—where it was still standing in 1883—proposed building a similar "people's palace" in Muswell Hill. The idea of such "people's palaces" remained in the air throughout the Victorian Era; although none was built in London one was eventually constructed in Glasgow in the 1890s, although only a part of the building took the form of a huge glazed conservatory. Calvet obviously liked the idea.

"That organization seems to me to be very inconvenient for administrators who live a long way from the center."

"No one complains," the pedestrian replied, "for our means of communication are so multiform and so rapid that one can be transported between any two points in the city in a very short time."

"We're now in considerable difficulty in divining the purpose of this building," Terrier observed.

"Messieurs," the citizen said, in a very courteous tone, "it is a duty for each of us to place himself at the disposal of strangers, and if you would do me the honor of accepting me as your guide, I shall show you the principal parts of the palace."

"A thousand thanks, Monsieur," the physicist replied. "We're profoundly grateful for your kindness."

"Every quarter of Paris possesses a communal house," said the obliging individual, who was now advancing toward the edifice, surrounded by the strangers. "There is even a very praiseworthy competition between citizens to ornament and equip their respective citizens with the largest quantity of amenities. Everyone has the right to enjoy all the advantages that these meeting-places can offer, which, over and above any other function, has that of linking the inhabitants together with bonds of fraternity."

"That's very fine in itself," the doctor approved.

"Furthermore, it frequently happens that one quarters offers a feast to another, and general sympathy can only gain from that indefinite expansion."

"That is certainly the most admirable thing that your city has offered to us," said Terrier, who was normally miserly with superlatives.

"In addition, Messieurs," the citizen continued, "every communal house has a library, a museum, a conference hall, a ballroom and concert hall, several lecture rooms, a free bank, a justice of the peace whose officers are nominated periodically by their fellow citizens, a laboratory of physical and natural sciences, an observatory, a hundred luxurious bathrooms, an extensive gymnasium, a grassy park for the children and a dispatch room bringing the most recent news from all over the world."

The visitors passed under the porch at that moment. A large, rather deserted entrance hall extended before them. Several signs set up at intervals indicated the way to the lecture rooms, the courtroom, the conference halls, the library and the ballroom.

Conducted by their guide, the travelers went into a broad corridor that extended beyond long curtains, at the far end of which were several scientific establishments.

The professor was heading straight for the physics hall when the doctor held him back, saying that time was pressing. They turned round and went up a monumental staircase to the first floor, where they were able to cast a rapid glance over the museum and the collections of physics, chemistry and natural science. The mineralogical display cases, filled with precious stones of extraordinary size, would have given vertigo to people whose faculties had not already received so many rude shocks.

Conducted to the top of the edifice, they advanced to a platform in the middle of which an elevated observatory was constructed, equipped with a host of advanced instruments whose mechanism was unknown to them.

At that height, the panorama was admirable. Their gaze plunged into the mass of verdure that surrounded the capital. At their feet, a swarm of children and young people moved hectically in frantic gymnastic exercises, in the midst of a crowd of spectators, who were following their capers with evident interest.

The visitors, still preceded by their guide, went back down to the avenue.

"I greatly regret, Messieurs," said the latter as he parted from them, "that you have not been able to visit our communal house at the time of its greatest animation—which is to say, in the evening. You would have been able to attend several instructive or amusing sessions in succession, and you would have been welcomed by all the families in the quarter. If, however, these meetings can offer you any pleasure, I would be delighted to have the honor of introducing you to them."

The doctor and his companions, having testified their gratitude to the benevolent citizen who had put himself at the disposal with so much affability, continued on their way.

After walking for twenty minutes, they found themselves at the end of the monumental bridge, and when the three-quarter hour sounded on the clock of the school museum they were climbing the staircase that led to the monument's main courtyard.

At that moment, Madame Herber emerged from a clump of flowering bushes, from which she had gathered an abundant harvest. "Have you had a good walk, Messieurs?" asked the young woman, coming toward them.

"Yes, Madame, a very pleasant, and also very instructive walk," Antius replied.

Herber soon appeared and asked with interest about his guests' itinerary. "I told you, Messieurs," he added, "about the arrival of my friend Guillaume Dryon. I shall have the honor of introducing you to him very shortly. I'll let him know about your visit this evening."

The strangers bowed gratefully.

"Dinner is served," said Madame Herber.

The doctor offered her his arm and went into the vestibule at a processional pace.

The institution of communal houses and its advantages from the viewpoint of sociability provided a topic of conversation for a significant part of the meal.

They were on the point of leaving the table when Antius suddenly broke the silence he had maintained for some time.

"My dear host," he said, with a kind of brusque joviality, I have only been able to testify as yet a small part of my admiration for the happy concord that reigns among the inhabitants of the city—a sentiment of which the cause and effect can equally well be explained by incessant frequentation, but there is one point that remains enigmatic for me."

"What is that, Doctor?"

"The amenity of mores notwithstanding, do your fellow citizens always conserve calmness and reciprocal politeness in political debates?"

"Political debates?" said Herber, astonished. "What do you mean by that expression?"

The strangers looked at one another with amazement.

"I would like to know," Antius said, "whether everyone is in accord with regard to the form of government."

"Of course," said Herber, laughing.

"I must say, my dear Master," Antius added, "the two words you have just pronounced surprise us more than everything we have seen until now."

"Messieurs," the schoolmaster declared, gravely, "I don't know how public affairs are conducted where you come from, and I don't know exactly what you mean by *government*, but here and throughout Europe there is absolute agreement on the matter. Our laws are wise, humane and above all preventative. Everyone bows down before their sovereign authority. Their application is confided to those who offer to take charge of it, and who, to that end, submit themselves periodically to the ballot of their fellow citizens. Everyone appreciates the devotion of those generous individuals, voluntarily undertaking tiresome and monotonous work, which condemns them to a situation that is rather obscure and not much sought-after.

"The unanimity of opinions regarding everything that concerns public life, which appears to surprise you, is the result of the development of the education of the masses. Politics, which is now gathered into the scientific domain, and thus only occupies a very restricted place here, protected, in consequence, from the ever-unreliable suggestions of passions, is under the exclusive jurisdiction of the intellectual domain, and is firmly attached to the fixed laws of reasoning. True ideas no longer have any contradictors, false ones no champions. Hence, general agreement."

167

"If I'm not mistaken," said Antius, "thinkers once declared that the important terminus of social progress in question would never be attained."

"The fundamentals of the problem then being very incomplete," the schoolmaster replied, "the conclusions were necessarily false. What philosopher of the 19th century, for instance, could affirm that science would create a new force, the immediate effect of which would be an extraordinary increase in wealth, and the diffusion of which would overcome the crucial obstacle that paralyzed all economic efforts—the proletariat?"

The schoolmaster became pensive, and added: "However, the conception of that economic equilibrium would have seemed less strange if the speculations had considered the complete analogy that history offered, in terms of the continual elevation of the social level, always in proportion to scientific development. Why, in their ignorance, did they dare to set limits to progress and justice?"

The strangers, absorbed in their own thoughts, remained silent.

The tinkling murmur of the foliage, agitated by the evening breeze, became audible.

Herber invited his guests to go down to the terrace.

Having taken leave of Madame Herber, who had decided to put her daughter to bed in order to spare her the fatigues of a session whose duration it was difficult to foresee, Antius and his companions followed the schoolmaster.

When they arrived at the balustrade overlooking the square, the strangers perceived numerous groups heading for the west wing of the school. A few people following the path circling the plaza greeted Herder and his guests respectfully as soon as they were within range.

When they reached the pilasters that ornamented the base of the great staircase, most of the strollers stopped in order to take cognizance of a printed notice—a fact that excited Gédéon's attention. Curious to know the reason for these multiple pauses, the young man watched the bottom of the stairway indifferently for a while, and then descended rapidly to the causeway. He then saw an immense poster sixed to the wall, on which the following program could be read:

THÉÂTRE DE L'ÉCOLE DE LA PLACE DU MUSEUM
Today, Monday 16 June 2880, 8 p.m.

LECTURESON
THE 19TH CENTURY
by Messieurs
J.-B. TERRIER, PHYSICIST
A.-J. ANTIUS, DOCTOR IN MEDICINE
& GÉDÉON CAHUSAC, ARCHEOLOGY STUDENT

The two scientists will talk about the scientific, industrial, political, social and economic conditions of that remarkable historical period.
The young antiquary, having recalled a few interesting details of the 19th century, will offer a general description of old Paris.

"There are titles that my original contemporaries would have had the ignobility to refuse me," the reader exclaimed. "Now it's a matter of meriting them."

And he rejoined his companions.

While the physicist and the schoolmaster were exchanging impressions regarding the advantages that astronomy had obtained from the progress of optics, Gédéon approached his uncle.

"I've just seen the poster," he said.

"Well?"

"Do you know the titles they've given me?"

"No, I don't."

"They're calling me an archeologist and an antiquary."

"My word," said Antius—that's the first extravagance I've discovered in the new world."

XIX. The Two Scientists' Speeches

Eight o'clock was chiming when Herber and the guests went to the theater in which each of the strangers in term was to present a different description of the old world from which a mysterious force had abruptly separated them, to hurl them into the midst of a new society a thousand years later.

The strangers traversed the right wing of the central building. Scarcely had they set foot in the interior courtyard than the large bays of the cupola, glittering with light, struck their gaze.

As they drew nearer to the monument, the dull and confused sound of conversations that reached them gained in intensity to such an extent that the schoolmaster declared that the hall must already be full.

Because the monumental door reserved for the public opened to the exterior, the access to the edifice from the interior courtyard was almost deserted. Only a few invited intimates of the school could be seen among the quincunxes, walking rapidly toward the hall, going up a marble staircase and disappearing behind the long curtains.

Herber led the strangers toward the most distant part of the theater, and then stopped in front of a door whose two battens were moved by a lever. A short staircase covered with a thick carpet took the four men into a private room behind the stage, where several individuals had already gathered.

The schoolmaster introduced his guests in turn, and then told the travelers the names of his friends, who, with few exceptions, were among the most illustrious in modern science.

Antius and his companions, already identified as antiquaries of an incomparable erudition, were welcomed with respectful sympathy.

The conversation had been going on for a few minutes in the most cordial tone when Herber, who had disappeared momentarily, came back into the room and asked for permission to open the session. The two scientists having declared that they were at the disposal of the audience, the door at the back of the stage was opened wide.

A brightly-lit hall overflowing with spectators met the strangers' eyes. The balconies, occupied in advance by the ladies, dressed in their bright summer clothes, unfolded around the room like brilliant strings of pearls. The entire auditorium was admirable in its architecture. Rows of vast, comfortable and widely-spaced armchairs rose gradually from the parquet and stooped in front of a circular wall of elegant boxes separated by columns of white marble supported by groups of allegorical figures. Above them, two vast sloping balconies permitted every spectator to have a view all parts of the hall. The panels, covered with pink velvet and separated by golden frames of the purest design, caressed the gaze. The ceiling, charged with bright mythological paintings, opened in the center to allow a glimpse of the depths of the sky, bathed with pale twilight. Four powerful electric elements fixed in the friezes and imprisoned in faintly tinted globes poured floods of pale blue light over the spectators.

At the edge of the stage an elegant podium, raised by a few steps, awaited the orators.

At Herber's invitation, the travelers set themselves at the head of the procession and, under the fire of the gazes of the entire audience, went to take possession of the three chairs of honor disposed at the back of the stage, while the schoolmaster's guests headed for a row of seats that extended in a semi-circle on both sides all the way to the front of the stage.

A profound silence suddenly fell. The schoolmaster approached the physicist and, with a gesture full of courtesy, invited him to go up to the podium.

The professor got up and, with the assurance given by frequent public speaking, marched forward. After a profound bow that enveloped the entire auditorium, the scientist began his speech.

"Mesdames et Messieurs," he said, "the magnificence of the civilization and the scientific knowledge of the 29th century, the source of the general wellbeing that surrounds us, ought not to make us forget that our conquests, as much from the speculative as the material point of view, are the result of the endeavors and efforts of past centuries, associated with those that we have been able to furnish ourselves to ensure the fatal and sovereign march of progress.

"Thus, the precise examination of an epoch, in its intellectual, social and economic aspects, offers a keen interest, as much by virtue as the ensemble of comparisons that flow therefrom as the information it includes, if one makes a careful study of the relations linking effects and causes.

"The corresponding period of the 19th century, to which our endeavors have attached us and of which it is permissible for us to trace a rigorous description, will be exposed here in various facets by two men whose entire existence has been consecrated to science and who, thrown suddenly into the life of the great city, for which nothing has prepared them, have been called by a providential hazard to the hearth of a generous man, to whom they are glad to be able to offer at this moment the public expression of their gratitude."

At the last words, pronounced in an emotional voice, all gazes converged on the schoolmaster, in whom surprise appeared to overwhelm any other sentiment.

"Doctor Antius," the physicist continued, "intends to explain the condition of the natural sciences toward the end of the 19th century and cast a general glance over the political, social and demographic aspects of the historical period that we have studied with so much care, and in incomparable conditions of certainty.

"Finally, on the perhaps-imprudent insistence of a young woman whose charm permits no resistance, our young companion with paint a picture of old Paris, which he has searched in every direction, and his narration, in default of any other merit, will certainly have that of an irreproachable exactitude."

The doctor and his nephew were briefly the focus of the assembly's attention, and stood up to that entirely benevolent scrutiny with sufficient self-composure.

"The honor of establishing the state of physical science among our ancestors, from the double viewpoint of theory and applications, has been reserved for me. I shall strive to maintain the conciseness, clarity and method that such subject-matter demands."

After a momentary pause during which his eminently disciplined mind had condensed and organized the elements of his discourse, the professor continued: "All historians have recognized that, if the 17th century fixed the French language definitely, thanks to the literary monuments that illustrated it, the following century, by means of its scientific discoveries, which it only possessed in the condition of seeds, prepared for the enormous industrial development of the 19th century"

Developing the essential elements of that theme, as vast as it was profound, the physicist showed his attentive audience the application of the expansive force of vapors in the experiments of Denis Papin and the conceptions of Salomon de Caus, and excited a profound emotion by describing the heroic efforts of Robert Fulton to endow his contemporaries with steam navigation, which, by mastering the two redoubtable elements of winds and contrary currents, ensured rapid and regular communications with the most distant regions.

On the same subject, he described the progress resulting from the application of the helical propeller to the movement of ships, and recounted the bitter disappointments suffered by its inventor, Sauvage.[28]

The orator then described the resistance that the establishment of the first railways had encountered among the most eminent of men, and painted a magnificent picture of all the

---

[28] Frédéric Sauvage (1786-1857), the inventor of the marine propeller, demonstrated in 1832 that it was more efficient than paddle-wheels as a means of driving steamships, but was cold-shouldered by the French navy and went bankrupt when he tried to develop the invention himself, ending up in a debtor's prison.

riches that the new force, whose conquest had been imposed in spite of all obstacles, had spread through the civilized world.

The network of railways that covered the old continent, the rapid construction of works of art by the employment of iron, the piercing of mountains, which had previously opposed insurmountable barriers to communication, and the establishment of inter-oceanic canals passed in turn before the surprised eyes of the audience.

The application of gases furnished by the distillation of oil, as a source of light, heat and power, was treated with precision, and astonished a large number of spectators, whose ideas of methods they considered as primitive were rather vague.

The misfortunes of Philippe Lebon, forced to trail his invention from door to door all the way to Watt's workshops, where he finally found shelter, excited the sympathy of the audience,[29] and the terror of Parisians, opposed to the laying of pipes in their streets for fear of to sleeping on a volcano, provoked some hilarity.

The examination of various systems of aerial navigation, alternately commended and condemned by experimentation, and the opposed prognostications that divided the scientific world on the immense problem, whose solution was to renew the face of the world, excited attention to the highest degree.

Pursuing the origin of great inventions, the professor described the history of dynamic electricity, from the first mysterious phenomena that had sparked rivalry between Galvani and Volta, to the telegraphic exploitation of currents, which, a hundred years later, incessantly streamed over the surface of the globe and the depths of the seas.

The orator briefly summarized the observational sciences. "Astronomy," he said, "had shone with a vivid glare in the previous century with Laplace, Lalande, Clairaut, Herschel,

---

[29] Philippe le Bon, or Lebon, who industrialized the extraction of lighting gas from wood, fared even worse than Sauvage, being murdered in 1804 in mysterious circumstances.

Cassini, Lacaille, Maupertuis, Bradley and a host of other illustrious names, but the 19th century counts with pride the great Arago: astronomer, physicist and technologist, his genius cast light on previously-unfathomable; illustrious scientist, profound thinker, integral citizen, he had every glory. Solely by the power of his calculations, his colleague Le Verrier divined the presence in the heavens of the planet Neptune and determined its volume, its distance and its orbit. The telescope, in confirming his formula, filled his contemporaries with admiration for the resources of celestial mechanics.

"Delaunay studied the moon to the extent of the depth of its craters. Faye and Jansen sounded the atmosphere of the sun. Chacornac, Laugier, Marié-Davy, Foucault and Puiseux shone among the most illustrious astronomers of the epoch. The observational sciences, seconded by the positive method, took great strides.

"In less than a century, chemistry, rationally founded by Lavoisier, Fourcroy, Berthollet, Scheele, Priestley and Rutherford, gathered such momentum through the work of Davy, Gay-Lussac, Liebig, Dumas, Chevreul, Claude Bernard, Deville and Berthelot, that in less than a hundred years it had attained the level of other sciences, which had been amassing their materials for several centuries.

"The magnificent theories of Ampère in magnetism, Faraday's studies of electromagnetic induction, the research of Helmholtz on acoustics, the works of Arago, Fresnel and Brewster on light, constituted physics.

"That fecund period, on which we ought to look back with gratitude, can also list in the first rank of its conquests the study of the general physics of the globe and the first attempts to organize meteorological science; the discovery of the action of light on silver salts, which was the source of photography; the intimate knowledge of the chemical constitution of organic matter; spectral analysis, which permitted the determination with the aid of the prism of the presence of known and unknown metals in milieux where they only existed in an infinitesimal state, thanks to which physicists and chemists extended their investigations with certainty into the heavens; and finally, the mechanical theory of heat and the transformation of forces, which opened the most elevated horizons to the philosophy of science."

The professor's elegant and precise speech, the precision of facts, places, dates and circumstances, the remembrance of the names of glorious toilers of science, tarnished if not forgotten by ten centuries of events, held the audience in thrall for a long time.

"Such are," he said, in concluding his peroration, "the conquests that illustrated the 19th century. If one compares it to the present era, its gleam would doubtless be considerably lessened, but if one sets it alongside the centuries that preceded it, one recognizes that it overshadows all of them by the prodigious character of its discoveries and the sum of relative wellbeing that it injected into the great current of humanity.

"Among its contemporaries, many regarded it as the highest achievement to which humankind could aspire, but if it had been possible to allow them to glimpse the radiant image of the 29th century, they would have recognized the sovereignty of the fundamental principle of the evolution of the human species: *Every century adds a new stone to the edifice of progress, and progress has no limit*."

The interest and astonishment provoked by the physicist's speech suddenly overflowed in the prolonged applause of the audience.

The orator bowed one last time and slowly descended to the stage. The schoolmaster went to meet him and, while congratulating him warmly, led him back to his chair. As he sat down, the scientist's eyes encountered those of Madame Herber, who testified her satisfaction with a gracious gesture.

In developing the description of events in the midst of which he had still been living two days before and from which ten centuries now separated him, the professor had invoked the specter of the past, which, for the first time, presented itself supported by the oral testimony of a contemporary. The strange sentiment of curiosity that agitated the entire hall was further stimulated by the approach of the doctor, who, led by Herber, advanced toward the podium.

Antius climbed the steps with the same ease that had once caused the members of the Biological Society to marvel, and paraded an assured gaze over this brilliant audience. After having taken a form grip on the podium with his left hand, a gesture that was customary to him, the orator bowed to the assembly.

"Mesdames et Messieurs," he said, in a clear and perfectly-pitched voice that had once won the admiration of all stenographers, "although a faithful description of an epoch from the viewpoint of the physical sciences and their industrial applications establishes an important base, fertile in deductions of every sort, the examination of what it discovered about the mysteries of organic matter offers a considerable interest, as much by virtue of the immensity and variety of the field of investigation as the critique of theories. If we consider as a whole the progress that the 19th century realized in the study of the human organism and its protection, we will find results whose true value the contemporaries did not always appreciate.

"It can be affirmed today that the period in question witnessed, if not the first, at least the most constant efforts of science to subject medicine to the sage methods of observation and detach it from the vague and baseless concepts that had previously opposed an insurmountable barrier to its progressive development. Supported by the other sciences that were growing around it, it began to gain a regular momentum that was to be a guarantee against going astray.

"Already, surgery, ensured by the profound study of human anatomy and powerfully supported by the employment of anesthetics, had acquired an authority and a certainty that had resisted the efforts of the best practitioners of the previous century. For the first time, the science submitted the intimate constitution of tissues to the power of the microscope, and histology was created.

"The 19th century saw the birth of a powerful endeavor that had thus far, by virtue of its immensity, defied all attempts. A man who was perhaps the most erudite and whose genius was affirmed simultaneously in philosophy, history, linguistics and all the observational sciences, Littré, presented to the astonished world a complete history of medicine since antiquity, founded on the authentic documents of all epochs.[30]

"A creator of the positive method, inaccessible to the tendencies that draw the human mind toward regions that it cannot reach, the great thinker said: *Let the human mind reject firmly the vain desires that are not its condition, and, to be recompensed for its resignation, it will see revealed all those agencies that accomplish the work of the world, in the cultivation of the ensemble of the sciences, the precious and powerful intermediary between the thought that contemplates and the hand that acts...*

"The epidemics that had devastated Europe in previous centuries had found a powerful barrier in the developments, even though very restricted, of general hygiene. On the other hand, the magnificent discoveries of Pasteur regarding the inoculation of certain principles in humans and animals had extinguished on location those epidemic agents that had terrified our forefathers and condemned them to an impotent fatalism."

The doctor then displayed to the wonderstuck eyes of the audience the rapid development of physiology, supported by the progress of chemistry, and the genesis of anthropology, which, reaching back through the course of the ages, had

---

[30] Émile Littré's *Reprise du Dictionnarire de medicine, de chirurgie, etc.* (1855) was actually an updating of an earlier work by Pierre-Hubert Nysten, on which Littré collaborated with Charles-Philippe Robin, but he had produced definitive translations on the works of Hippocrates and various other relevant scholars. Littré is now far more famous for his monumental *Dictionnaire de la langue française* (1863-73)

traced the history of the human species back to its appearance on the globe.

Then he described the marvelous resources of paleontology, reconstituting vanished worlds with the aid of a few fragments, and receiving striking confirmation of its deductions in discoveries made in the most distant regions.

The orator paused momentarily, and applause resounded throughout the hall.

"The political condition of France in the 19th century," he said, raising his head again, "is more difficult to assess. Society had suffered all the struggles characteristic of epochs of transition. Erected with difficulty on the ruins of a past whose crumbling had caused a new world to emerge, it was often tossed between two contrary excesses. Sometimes comprised by fear and egotism, sometimes undermined by appetites, the state of society only rarely found equilibrium.

"However, it ought to be recognized that the century counted a great many men of progress, disinterest and devotion to humanity. The great principles of national sovereignty, the abolition of slavery, political equality and individual liberty were proclaimed then.

"Obligatory education, decreed by the peoples who marched at the head of civilization, not only opposed a powerful barrier to moral degradation by ennobling human beings in their own eyes, but also favored the blossoming of all the great intelligences that would have been stifled in a latent state without any profit to society. Although still shackled by the political condition of Europe, the fraternity of peoples was glimpsed by a great many generous minds."

And in a surge of great eloquence, the orator displayed to his audience the inordinate ambitions of rulers, the rivalries of peoples, the bloody wars and, by virtue of that state of affairs, as barbaric as it was paradoxical, the anxiety that gripped everyone as soon as the slightest conflict broke out anywhere on the continent.

"The enormous progress of industry, commerce and navigation consequent on the extraordinary development of the applied sciences," he added, "offers us a less somber and desolate picture. Industrial expansion in all its forms brings endeavor everywhere and expands around it a previously unknown wellbeing. The condition of the disinherited classes is considerably ameliorated and the gradual extinction of poverty delights the philanthropic soul.

"The end of the 19th century no longer saw lamentable hordes clad in rags, corroded by misery and malady, trailing painfully along the public highway. On the other hand, seconded by the facility, safety and rapidity of communications, the authority of old Europe overflowed into the remotest regions. Rich colonies were founded and gradually raised to the level of the motherland. Bold pioneers, the majority of whom were to swell the martyrologies of science, had already ventured into the mysterious depths of the African continent that now occupies such a high rank in the scale of civilization."

The orator then described the history of each of the great European nations, fixing with rigorous figures its extent, population, military and naval power, industry and commerce.

Narrowing his frame, he concentrated on old Paris, and before his audience, whose attention had suddenly intensified, he commenced an extensive nomenclature of its monuments, the greater number of which had disappeared, its schools, its museums, its libraries and its scientific societies, a strict critique of which permitted him to launch an attack on the homeopaths.

Subsequently delving into family life with the independence of a bachelor, Antius introduced hi audience to the hearths of their ancestors. He took the child from the cradle through all the phases of life, extending himself particularly on the education of youth in the old world, coming to grips with all the errors that had their principal points of support in routine and ignorance.

Recalling the benefits of physical culture and artistic education, once greatly neglected, he congratulated the modern maters who afforded them such an important role.

By establishing with marvelous precision the description of 19th century society and pursuing it, in turn, through political life and social life to the domestic hearth, with an incomparable surety in the whole and in the details, the doctor had excited the imagination of his audience to the highest degree. After a few general considerations of the splendors of the present time and the progress of contemporary society from the viewpoint of morality, education, health and universal fraternity, the orator quit the podium.

The enthusiasm that he had excited and maintained with an unparalleled artistry provoked frantic applause. He had to return to the edge of the stage twice to salute the public, and when he went back to his armchair, accompanied by noisy testimony of general satisfaction, he could not prevent himself from saying to the physicist in a low voice: "This evening, for the first time in my life, I've spoken without kicking up a storm."

XX. A Humorous Lecture

The first two parts of the program had been a great success. While congratulating themselves for having been able, in some measure, to testify their gratitude for the generous hospitality they had received, the scientists retained grave anxieties regarding the denouement. Although their young companion was singularly endowed with imagination and had often given proof of an inexhaustible verve, they feared that he might suffer the intellectual perturbations that always accompany the fatal moment when an orator sees the terrifying gazes of the public focused on him for the first time.

At that moment, a fortunate diversion occurred, which postponed the moment of peril.

The schoolmaster had advanced to the edge of the stage and announced to the audience that, by reason of the importance of the speeches they had just heard and the attention they had provoked, the session would be interrupted by an interval of a few minutes during which all those who had been kind enough to come to the soirée were expressly invited by Madame Herber to do honor to the refreshments that were about to be distributed in the hall.

Scarcely had these words been pronounced that twenty servants of both sexes, the majority of whom had been supplied by the school's neighbors, emerged from all directions, offering the guests vast trays laden with ice-creams and sorbets.

The cordiality that appeared to reign in the new world was affirmed, in the eyes of the strangers, as much by the frank acquiescence of the spectators as by the amicable simplicity of the invitation. In the meantime, Herber introduced the travelers and the individuals occupying the stage into the next room, where an abundantly-laden table awaited the guests.

The two scientists, surrounded by the schoolmaster's friends, received congratulations with a modesty that, in default of their temperament, the consciousness of the scant effort they had been obliged to make in order to retrace past times made into a duty.

The schoolmaster, after a few words of encouragement, had just left Gédéon when the physicist and the doctor approached the young man.

The latter, absorbed by reflections in which dread and self-confidence appeared to alternate their dominance, was standing with his eyes fixed on the depths of a cup made from a single turquoise, which he had emptied with particular care. "Sublime or idiotic," he suddenly murmured, without noticing his two companions, who were standing beside him looking at him with manifest anxiety.

"What are you thinking about?" asked Terrier, generously.

"My speech—and I've arrived at the bizarre but certain conclusion that I shall either be stunning or inept."

"Alas," said the doctor, who seemed to be having difficulty admitting the first term.

Meanwhile, Herber had already darted two or three glances at the public when, after a final inspection, he turned round swiftly and announced to his guests that the second part of the program could begin.

Opening the door, he stood aside to let his guests through, and they went back to their respective seats. The strangers followed them, Gédéon in the lead, thanking an important member of the Institut, who had already given him a few premature eulogies, with a pale smile.

Herber seized the young man in passing at took him to the podium.

Instantly enveloped by the attentive gazes of two thousand individuals, Gédéon climbed the steps with a lack of urgency of someone mounting the scaffold. A false step, which nearly precipitated him to the bottom of the steps, did more to help him than any advice or encouragement could have done.

Conscious of the ridicule that he had just escaped, he steeled himself with a supreme energy, and, his face pale and his muscles contracted, suddenly found himself face to face with his audience. A providential hazard dictated that his first glance encountered the charming visage of Madame Herber, who sent him a smile of encouragement from the edge of her box. The sight of the graceful enchantress, who had picked up the strangers at the moment of their distress, appeared to him to be a manifest sign of divine protection and calmed his mind as if by magic.

He bowed with sufficient distinction, and then, in a voiced whose sonority was altered by a slight tremor, he began his exordium.

"Mesdames et Messieurs, it is not appropriate either to my age or my slight experience to grasp the past in its scientific, industrial, philosophical, social and economic aspects, as the two illustrious scientists have just done, of whom I have the honor of being the most assiduous and devoted pupil..."

At this insidious preamble the physicist's face lit up with a rather caustic smile, while the doctor's took on a much more significant expression.

"...But I believe that, even in a modest sphere, it is always possible to educate one's peers."

"His peers are damnably in need of it," Antius said to the physicist.

"In the world in which we live, in which progress seems to be overflowing in every form," the orator continued, his voice having gradually recovered its normal tone, "the remembrance of a few details relevant to the period we are studying, would perhaps find them as incredulous as censors, if we had not taken the sage precaution of guaranteeing its accuracy with all the authority of which its contemporaries could have disposed.

"To begin with, the spectacle of a lawsuit that was being heard this very morning at the tribunal has furnished us, with regard to the important question of arbitration between citizens, terms of comparison that are entirely characteristic.

"Marveling at the rapidity, clarity and integrity of today's judiciary operations, we heartily congratulated a group of honest citizens who were surrounding us, for not having lived in the epoch when disputes of that sort were gripped by formidably complicate gear, and by a trilogy of individuals who attempted to impede the mechanism even further.

"To the questions that were addressed to us from all directions—What are advocates, attorneys and bailiffs?—we were, to our great regret, unable to respond because of the urgent tasks that have brought us to the capital. We can take them up now with calm, precision ad impartiality."

Gédéon, who had been a legal clerk for six months and in whom the military magistracy had always inspired an aversion of which he made no secret, continued as flows: "An advocate, Mesdames et Messieurs, was a citizen whom the exigency of circumstances condemned to live, during the best years of his life, in the insipid commerce of a host of dotards like Ulpien, Justinian, Tribonius, etc.

"As soon as he thought himself nourished by assiduous study of Roman Law and the Civil Code, he presented himself, clad in a sack of black wool and coiffed in a comical hat, before a group of peevish old men, and made them a speech peppered with barbaric words, the meaning of which, fortunately for him, he did not understand.

"If hazard determined that somnolence sometimes replaced ill humor in the venerable jury, the candidate was saved, for, on awakening, the judges would suddenly pronounce the *dignus est intrare*.[31] From then on, he entitled himself the defender of widows and orphans. In reality, his role condemned him henceforth to substituting himself— temporarily, of course—for individuals of greater or lesser importance, from whom the courts sometimes demanded money, and sometimes liberty. His talent then consisted of casting a shadow over everything injurious to his case and

---

[31] "He is worthy to enter."

185

lighting up everything favorable to it. Many could be seen passing off as white what was black, and vice versa.

"In spite of everything, they rendered veritable services in lending the support of their erudition, their eloquence and, above all, their aplomb to a number of timid individuals who often remained mute before the majesty of the court. Some of the cleverest turned their backs on the court to climb to the podium, and sometimes thus arrived in high positions of State, which they often filled with honor.

"Now, the picture will darken somewhat, and, in spite of my respect for the truth, I fear the agitation I might now cause to sensitive hearts, in sketching portraits of the other two individuals.

"The attorney was once the turnkey opening all civil lawsuits. He was the one holding the tiller and disposing, activating and animating the discussions I don't suppose for an instant that you can believed that he did it solely for love of the art. Furthermore, if you adopt as true the proposition consecrated by experience that where there was profit is a lawsuit, that profit went to the attorney, you will be absolutely correct.

"You will then understand that, the more obscure, tortuous and envenomed a case was, the more right the attorney has to applaud his windfall, for it was almost certain that, in the end, when the two parties left the tribunal, shorn, bruised and lacerated to the quick by expenses of every sort, the origins of which sometimes go back to Philippe le Bel, he alone would see his purse significantly rounded.

"The bastion where he set up his batteries was a huge square room whose breadth caused moralists to shiver and philanthropists to groan. There, the gaze came fearfully to rest on four walls of green cardboard whose ensemble constituted, for imprudent risks, a necropolis of incomparable security.

"In those frightful surroundings, half a dozen young people with wandering eyes, some sitting opposite the others, bent over sheets of paper filled with barbaric formulas, delving into all the most obscure corners of the quarrel.

"Well, Messieurs, when the god of that Inferno had taken off his spectacles, untied his cravat and put away his black coat, he suddenly become an amiable, gallant, bustling man, full of distinction."

Intoxicated by the applause, mingled with frank bursts of laughter, that greeted the beginning of his improvisation, and retaining after ten centuries a dull rancor for the misadventures he owed to the solicitude of the ministerial officer he had described, the young man let his imagination off the bridle entirely.

"With the third term of that paper-shuffling assembly, we enter into drama," he said, in a somber voice. "The bailiff, Mesdames et Messieurs, was a carnivore of the most redoubtable species. That bloodthirsty animal was especially skilled in hunting men, an exercise that he carried out with as much cunning as ferocity. One did not go near him without being bloodily bitten. Better open the door to plague or cholera than that dismal and impassive biped, who only entered to sow terror and ruin.

"Messieurs, a rapid and impartial account of a true story, which I have extracted with the utmost care from the annals of the 19th century, will show you, more clearly than the most energetic aphorisms, the individual in all his horror.

"A young man, the chronicle says, in whom all the qualities of the heart and mind were combined with bodily grace, had more imagination and appetite than money. One day, when the time came to settle a bill, he found himself short—a situation with which he was quite familiar. The creditor, convinced of the immediate impossibility of obtaining his due, succeeded by a diabolical artifice in extorting the unfortunate fellow's signature—who, in signing a promise of payment whose due term seem to him to be half a century away, was committing one of those stupidities for which the recidivist merits internment in a madhouse.

"When one is due to receive money, time crawls; when one owes it, it flies. One fine day, or, to be perfectly accurate, one evil day, our man was snatched from the sweetness of

187

morning sleep by raps brutally struck on his door. Now, at that moment he was plunged into delightful dreams. Sitting at a baccarat table, playing for high stakes in honor of his epoch, he had paid for a hand with his last fifty-centime piece. By an extraordinary stroke of luck he had drawn nine twenty-five times on the trot, and at each stroke his bank had doubled its value.

"Without being a transcendent force at mathematics, the player was not astonished by the height and diameter of the pile of gold and banknotes that the miraculous progression had amassed in front of him. Around the table, the cleaned-out players were offering a picture of consternation. Anyone can propose a *banco*, the fortunate banker thought, prudently, but not many capitalists can clear it, and he prudently ended the session. All the victims decamped in unison.

"Left alone, for he had sent the casino lackeys in search of a sturdy cart to take away his treasure, the new Croesus was wondering seriously whether, to utilize his capital, he ought not to finance the building of a submarine tunnel of which there as much talk at the time or, realizing his most cherished dream, he ought to found an empire in the Pampas, from which men of law, poets, musicians and etchers would be strictly banned. It was that the precise moment when he was weighing these serious questions that he as abruptly awakened.

"'Is the cart big enough?' he cried, pursuing his dream. But the sudden sight of the familiar objects that appeared successively around him tipped him out of the empyrean. 'I'll give whoever has just crushed my illusions a good ticking off,' he said, as he ran to the door.

"He opened it abruptly and found himself face to face with a surly mug lodged between a black bicorn and a Bluebeard jacket. 'Monsieur le Commissaire!' cried the young man, losing his head, I swear it wasn't me who unhooked the notary's signboard in the Rue de l'Odéon and hung it on the shutter of his next-door neighbor, the bric-à-brac seller.

"'I'm not the Commissaire,' said the astonished visitor.

"'Who are you, then? If you're looking for the funeral director, you're on the wrong floor.'

"'I'm a bank employee,' and I've brought you a bill for sixty francs.'

"'It's good of the bank to send me money,' the young man replied, who believed it an unaccustomed gallantry of that organization. 'I'll drop in on the manager tomorrow.'

"'I've come to collect sixty francs from you, in accordance with your promissory note,' said the bicorn, who seemed quite flabbergasted.

"'Then the bank will be disappointed, for I have no money,' replied the imprudent signatory, suddenly enlightened.

"'Very well, sad the man, in a detached tone. And, putting a little piece of white paper in the hands of the debtor, he went away shaking his head.

"'Well, said the astounded young man, putting the piece of paper—which he assumed to be a receipt—in his pocket, 'it's easy to do business with that company; I'll go there more often.' And he went back to bed.

"Twenty-four hours later, his porter gave him a sheet of paper covered in communicatory formulas and demanding final payment of sixty-seven francs fifty centimes, signed Barnabé Cornefer, bailiff, usher etc.

"*This Cornefer is mad!* he thought. *I can't pay sixty francs and he wants to force me to pay sixty-seven!* He examined the piece of paper carefully, to see whether it bore the postmark of Bicêtre or Charenton.

"A week later, a new summons couched in the same style. 'If they expect to wear me down with their correspondence,' the debtor said, 'they're mistaken.'

"Some time later, at about eleven o'clock in the morning, as he was putting the final touches to his toilette, and individual of criminal appearance suddenly presented himself to him, saying that he had come to seize him.

"Quick as lightning, the young man leapt upon and old buckler hanging on the wall, and shouted: 'If you come near me, I'll split your skull, which will give me a fair shot at this year's Prix Montyon.'

"The malefactor recoiled, but suddenly straightened up. 'My name is Nicolas-Barnabé Cornefer,' he said, emphatically, 'and I've come in my official capacity to seize your furniture, in response to a debt of sixty francs, represented by an unpaid promissory note, which I have already served three times, and whose expenses currently amount to thirty-seven francs sixty, double penalty included.' And, turning around, he examined the room, including its darkest corners; then, sitting down without being invited, he started to write. Five minutes later, he got up and handed a piece of paper to a young man, addressing him by the title of 'custodian of the seizure.'

"The latter, thinking that it was a practical joke, abused the bird of prey roundly with all the wealth of his vocabulary. At the nineteenth epithet, the dazed bailiff left, exclaiming: 'Confronted by the debtor's refusal, we're going to effect a garnishee.'

"The young man, who had been living in a nightmare for some time, had the good idea of going to obtain advice from Maître Desiflard, a respectable lawyer and friend of the family, who, on this occasion, manifested a grandeur of soul that one very rarely observed in those days in notaries."

"What audacity, to recount his own adventures thus before two thousand people," said Antius to the physicist, in a low voice concentrated by anger.

"After having gratified his client with a long series of reproaches, recommendations and maxims," Gédéon went on, "he put in his hands a sum more than sufficient to extract him from the merciless claws of all the carnivores by whom he had been attacked. The imprudent signatory ran to the bailiff's lair and, with a brutality for which he will long applaud himself, snatched his papers, the nominal value of which had become insignificant by comparison with the expenses—or, to put it another way, judiciary extortions—with which they had been loaded.

"From all that, he learned a lesson: that of knowing that in a country that pretended to be civilized, the mot insignificant debt could, thanks to the artifices of a vampire now fortunately extinct, take on colossal proportions."

Although relying on ideas, incidents and principles very distant from the contemporary morality reigning in the new world, the general meaning of that burlesque story of times past had been grasped perfectly by the audience. Thus, Gédéon's improvisation, already frequently interrupted by bursts of laughter fired in all parts of the hall like sonorous rockets, determined at that moment such a fit of general hilarity that he was obliged to suspend his speech temporarily.

When calm had gradually been restored, he picked up the threat of his discourse.

"I have had the honor," he said, "of introducing a few characteristic types, whose existence our forefathers, in their error, thought to be absolutely necessary to the happiness of humankind. I will not say anything more about the ensemble of individuals and institutions, which presented the same paradoxical character, for the exhaustion of that subject would take the youngest members of this assembly to the limits of old age. After having painted an epoch from the viewpoint of its prejudices, it seems reasonable to trace the scenery in which they struggled."

And, the splendors of new Paris stimulating his imagination, he launched into a parallel comparison, in which fancy occasionally took the place of exactitude.

"I shall not surprise anyone," he said, "by affirming that, from the viewpoint of general appearance, old Paris cannot by any means be compared to our present-day Paris. It is, however, necessary not to lose sight, if one wants to do it justice, of the fact that the Parisians of the 19th century arrived at the same conclusions when they compared their city, whose progressive embellishments they were continuing, with the old city of the Middle Ages, which, drowning in filth, was stifling within its walls. That observation reminds us that in this world, everything is relative—a principle that history makes evident perennially.

"One can even add that the first of the profound transformations that gradually led the capital to the state of magnificence that it enjoys today, took place in the precise period that is the subject of this series of lectures.

"Of course, we find ourselves facing a singular contradiction in observing that the activity of contemporary administrators was particularly devoted to the periphery of the city, while, on the other hand, the central part conserved its ancient appearance almost entirely.

"Where those magnificent avenues as broad as rivers, covered with verdure, works of art and majestic trees now extend, narrow and noisy streets crawled, bordered with tall houses in which the unfortunate citizens, cloistered in cells and deprived of breathable air, rivaled one another in etiolation.

"The public highways of central Paris were incessantly furrowed by a feverish crowd, cleaved with difficulty by strangely-shaped public carriages known as omnibuses. These primitive contraptions were governed by two men, one of whom stationed at the rear, piled up the victims, while the other, perched on a high, narrow and isolated seat, directed the horses and required prodigies of skill not to crush a hundred people on every journey.

"The catalogue of heavy and crude vehicles that made the pavement resonate unremittingly with the most horrible racket would be of no interest to the audience. Of all the revolutions that has transformed the old world, Mesdames et Messieurs, perhaps the most marvelous is the one that has developed the river in such proportions that contemporaries would never have dared to imagine. How astonished the Parisians of the Iron Age would be if they could dart a single glance over that magnificent expanse of water, on those majestic bridges, and most of all that admirable lake, about which the majority of them would not even have dare to make a joke.

"Many people would refuse to admit as real a scene representing that river two hundred meters wide, encumbered by deformed boats and encased by gray and monotonous walls. However, in those miserable conditions, nautical sport developed with an intensity and perfection that the young people of today, under penalty of ingratitude to their ancestors, ought to rate highly.

"We shall abandon to them all superiorities regarding the splendor of their schools and the sum of pleasures that a more advanced civilization has reserved for them. We shall not even attempt a description of our ancient colleges, which were equally reminiscent of prisons, a monasteries and barracks, especially of the harsh life that young people led there between the ages of ten and twenty. We shall take a young man at the expiration of his punishment and already launched into that legendary region known as the Latin Quarter, whose ruins are beneath our feet at this moment.

"Historians who have studied that strange land must have run into contradictions at every step. General life presents itself there, in fact, in totally different aspects as one descends the social scale. At the top are students of the Romantic school, bizarrely dressed but ardent in their convictions with regard to art, literature and politics. At the bottom are their pale successors who have gradually moved down to the rungs that confine the most bourgeois prosaicism.

"In spite of everything, the highest regions are almost recruited from the heterogeneous milieu, which offers the singular spectacle of a group of convicts, drowned in the midst of a more numerous legion of fantasists, capable of losing their way twenty times over if, by chance, they ever wanted to go to the Faculty.

"Latin society generally cuts its capers in a famous establishment in which choreography, deserting academic principles, has no other guides than the imagination or psychological state of its disciples. Thus, the sight of a ballroom fly on the boil initially produces the fantastic impressions of a nightmare.

"One might, on that subject, wonder what the pleasures of the mass of Parisians were. If we set aside the examination of the rather restricted category of citizens then designated by the name of the privileged class, who believed themselves to be obliged to make a tour every day of a pond pompously called a lake, and to remain nailed down every night around a green baize table, many others were gladly engulfed in narrow, uncomfortable and overheated rooms in which an orchestral travesty served to season plays whose plots implored the greatest indulgence.

"Beneath that was the unceremonious genre of the music hall, which had a deadlier influence on the brains of our ancestors than all political and social complications.

"Now, what pleasures were in store for those naïve citizens' days of rest? Did they allow themselves to be borne away like us to distant shores through the pure regions of the atmosphere? Alas, they only had before them two equally false tracks. One led to the racecourse, where an honorable corporation of mobile bankers known by the fallacious name of bookmakers emptied the purses of the public with the regularity and precision of a vacuum pump; the other led to suburban restaurants, whose frequentation was tantamount to suicide.

"The conclusion of this little chat, Mesdames et Messieurs, is imposing itself strongly. I have tried to recall a few salient and characteristic points of the life of our ancestors. If nobility of conception and philosophical amplitude have been lacking in my discourse, truth and impartiality, the safeguard of which I invoked in stepping up to this podium, have been scrupulously respected.

"Finally, if I have abused the sympathetic attention that has been testified to me, the memory of which I shall retain eternally, it is only necessary to condemn my sincere desire to establish an exact comparison between present and past time."

The sonorous and sustained applause that greeted the orator's peroration reassured him fully with regard to the effect produced by the originality of his language, the unexpectedness of his reflections and the infectious gaiety that he had spread.

He descended to the stage with assurance, and received the compliments of Herber and his friends with satisfaction. His two companions seemed equally satisfied with the unexpected result of an attempt whose consequences they had redoubted.

Meanwhile, the crowd was gradually trickling way through the vast bays of the edifice, and when Herber's friends, gathered in the drawing room, had taken leave of the schoolmaster and his guests, the hall was empty.

Preceded by the schoolmaster, the strangers went down into the central courtyard and headed toward the main building.

As they went into the main courtyard they saw Madame Herber bidding farewell to a few lady friends who had been fortunate enough to witness the soirée from her box. The travelers headed toward the young woman in order to greet her, and were obliged to accept her congratulations for the interesting evening that they had procured for the inhabitants of the neighborhood.

"All Paris will be talking about it tomorrow," she added, with a very evident sentiment of satisfaction.

"Undoubtedly, Messieurs," Herber agreed, having noticed the astonishment that the last opinion had produced in his friends. "Your speeches were recorded by stenographers from the *Siècle*, the *Continent*, the *Globe* and the *Nouveau-Monde*. In consequence, they will appear tomorrow morning in the four most important newspapers in the capital.

"My word," Antius declared. "We didn't expect such an honor."

"I will add that the majority of the other papers will at least include a summary, and that they'll appear *in extenso* in the most important magazines," said the schoolmaster.

After having shaken their host's hand and thanked Madame Herber for the honor and encouragement that her presence at the soirée had lent them, the strangers headed for the main building.

"We've become celebrities," said Gédéon.

"Yes," Antius replied, "but let's hope that our success stops there; we might not be sure of keeping our heads."

"I agree," said Terrier.

One o'clock was chiming when the travelers went into their apartment.

XXI. The Museum of Antiquities

The sun was already high over the horizon when Antius, suddenly woken up by a flood of light that invaded his room, gravely got out of bed and deposited his magnificent headdress on the pillow.

Faithful to his habits, the doctor arranged the implements necessary to the care of his beard symmetrically—an operation to which he delivered himself incontinently.

Twenty minutes later, fresh and disposed, he emerged, tightening the blue silk girdle of his dressing gown in a cavalier fashion. He knocked on the physicist's door. Terrier, who had just finished dressing, came to open it.

After exchanging a few words about the events of the previous day, the two scientists headed for Gédéon's door and knocked.

The young man, who had, with sybaritic foresight, lowered his window-blinds completely the night before, woke up in profound darkness. "Who can be knocking sat this hour?" he said, ill-humoredly.

"Get up," said Antius, in a firm voice.

"What fly's stung you, coming to wake a placid citizen at two o'clock in the morning?"

"Are you mad?" asked the physicist. "It's at least eight o'clock."

"There's one astronomer who has a mania for committing errors with regard to the march of the sun," muttered Gédéon. "And to think that he's one of the bigwigs at the Observatory!"

Antius, whose bad mood had already been expressed in energetic terms, rattled the door vigorously.

The young man ran to the blind and opened it vigorously. He closed his eyes against the radiant sunlight that struck him full in the face. "I'll catch up with you," he said.

The two scientists drew away. Antius went back into his own room, rapidly concluded his toilette and rejoined the physicist, who as waiting on the terrace. Ten minutes letter, Gédéon found them there.

"My friends," said the doctor, "we'll soon be introduced to one of the mot important people in the city, in whose establishment, according to the schoolmaster, we might find work. God grant that it be so, for we can't continue to abuse the sumptuous hospitality of our host for much longer."

"For myself," observed Gédéon, "I'm not at all sure how I could be usefully employed." Swiftly, he added: "In any case, I don't think it will be permissible for me to apply for a job cleaning the city's streets."

"Why not?" said Antius, simply.

"There's the reason," said the young man, pointing toward the square.

The two scientists watched with astonishment as the immense square was gradually covered with a compact mist emitted by a large number of gushing fountains situated at ground level, obedient to an invisible hand.

"Before the morning meal, shall we visit the Museum of Antiquities?" said Gédéon.

"Good idea," said the professor.

"I agree," said Antius.

The travelers went into the square. Five minutes later, they went into the main courtyard of the Museum.

To the great astonishment, they did not see any warden or hear any noise in the monument. An inscription placed above the entrance door enlightened them with regard to the absolute isolation in which they found themselves; Gédéon read it aloud: "*These collections are placed under the safeguard of the citizens.*"

The travelers climbed the steps of a monumental staircase that rose up in the middle of the edifice and went into a semicircular vestibule, in which two vast sculpted oak doors opened on the opposite sides. The one on the right bore the following words painted on its upper half in golden letters:

WEAPONS OF WAR, AGRICULTURE.

The one on the left said:

SCIENCE, INDUSTRY, EVERYDAY INSTRUMENTS.

"Let's go into this one," said Antius, heading for the former, whose batten he pushed.

The three men advanced in line into a large rectangular hall in which was disposed, in perfect order, the largest collection of murderous engines imaginable.

Every type, from the most ancient to the most recent, the most monstrous to the tiniest, the most primitive to the most advanced, was gathered there. From the ballista and catapult to 20th century continuous-fire machine-guns, from the twenty-five ton cannon to the beech-loading revolver, from the Malay kris, the Indian tomahawk, the Australian boomerang, and the poisoned arrow of the equatorial African to the hunting-rifle with an automatic compensator, all models were represented.

Each of them bore a frame of variable size containing the most extensive documentation of its origin and usage.

The visitors stopped in front of an enormous artillery piece, which had probably lain dormant there for centuries, inoffensively, mouth agape.

"What do the people of today think of this monstrous engine?" the professor wondered.

Gédéon picked up a caption attached to the sight and read the following text: "*Instrument of long-range fire, founded on the principle of expansive gas. In his dictionary of Industrial Antiquities, a book full of errors and now devoid of authority, Bauer calls this war-machine 'the upper portion of a drainage tube.'*"

Without pausing, the travelers passed along a compact hedge of rifles, the series of which commenced with a gigantic arquebus of the 15th century.

Then they cast a distracted glance over several hundred swords of every sort, which, from the famous blades of Damascus to the vulgar cabbage-chopper, represented the principal genres of the great family of blank weapons. At the front, an immense display-screen of red velvet was constellated with daggers of every shape and size.

"Curse these imbeciles!" cried the doctor, angrily.

"What's the matter?"

"Can't you see that they've put the surgical scalpel in the middle of these homicidal weapons!"

"Oh well," said Gédéon, turning round.

Antius shrugged his shoulders without saying another word.

As he turned round the young man nearly staved in an old rusty drum, which rolled over the parquet, making a terrible racket. "Damn," he said, anxiously. "I didn't see that rolling drum—no pun intended." He raced after the instrument. "The commentaries are engraved on the drum-skin," he added, as he picked it up. Here's the opinion of the antiquaries: *'Noisy apparatus that regulated the march of soldiers. Small scale models of the instrument were manufactured, which rendered a house uninhabitable.* Bauer's Dictionary: *No precise opinion has been formed regarding this object. Some believe it to be special hygrometer that rendered different sounds according to the quantity of water dispersed in the atmosphere. Others affirm that it was a commonplace instrument of dialysis.'* Dialysis! What's that novelty?"

"The mixture of liquids through a membrane isn't a novelty," said the physicist. "Even so, the opinion is singular."

Gédéon replaced the drum and picked up a fireman's helmet; there was a piece of parchment attached to its neckchain and he read the following: *Apparatus designed to protect the head of elite soldiers known as sapper-firemen. These strong, agile and courageous men had the mission of extinguishing fires. They maneuvered very primitive machines that threw a great quantity of water over the burning fire, with the result that, if the neighbors escaped the fire, they did not escape the flood. It is evident that these primitive instruments could not render the service of the advanced pumps of our era, which project masses of liquid carbon dioxide, the sudden evaporation of which reduces the disaster in a matter of minutes."*

The left hand section of the hall was occupied by naval engines of war, and the gaze could follow the parallel progression of conical heaps of cannonballs and the thickness of armor plating.

The travelers paused briefly in front of a monstrous torpedo. The caption said: *Machine designed to blow up ships. That opinion was contested for a long time by a large number of archeologists, who did not want to admit that the ancients could have been so insane as to exaggerate the perils of the sea, against which their means of defense were already so limited.*

The central part of the wall was pierced by an arched bay; the travelers went through. They found themselves in a room no less vast than the first, which was reserved for agriculture.

Alongside ancient instruments with which they were familiar, the most advanced of which relied on the employment of steam power, the two scientists noticed with interest a large number of new machines powered by electromotive force. The most powerful of these machines bore the title of "ground-clearing instruments," and must have been used in distant exploitations.

At the back of the hall, a vast picture contained abundant detailed explanations of each machine. Special items established the prodigious agricultural development of the Orient, the two Americas and, most of all, Central Africa, since the invention of aerial navigation, which had thrown the idle hands of the old world into those immense territories.

XXII. Eccentric Antiquities

The three travelers retraced their steps and went back to the vestibule.

"Lets go in here," said the physicist, heading for the door opposite, which gave access to the scientific and industrial museum. "I imagine that surprises will be in store for us there."

His companions followed him and penetrated with him into an immense gallery, as vast as the one they had just traversed.

The left-hand wall was occupied in part by a formidable display of kitchenware, in which all systems of culinary apparatus, from the cauldron to the pressure-cooker, were represented. A series of turnspits, the largest of which would have accommodated a wild boar and the smallest a hummingbird, were symmetrically arranged on the wall-panels.

"How do they do their cooking, then, if these respectable instruments have been put on the index?" Gédéon asked the two scientists, who were examining with interest a switch-mechanism controlled by an electromagnet, probably designed to regulate a rotisserie.

"I don't know," said Antius, "but the art certainly hasn't degenerated."

"I agree."

A considerable collection of shovels, tongs and bellows was simply labeled *Old utensils*.

They went past a collection of candlesticks, lamps and chandeliers of every shape and size, arranged in a frame bearing the label: *Ancient lighting apparatus*.

Under the rubric *Primitive heating*, the visitors recognized almost all models of stoves and fireplaces, which scarcely rendered a tenth of the heat received in the best conditions.

Gédéon picked up a rolling-pin, designated under the disrespectful name of *Skittle*, to which a note added: *Game popu-*

lar among our ancestors. Beside it was a modest candle-snuffer, conscientiously labeled: *Usage unknown.*

The presence of a scissor-action candle-snuffer intrigued the visitors, and the physicist, having picked it up, read aloud: *"Many archeologists have sought to identify the purpose of this bizarre instrument in vain. Some have thought that the mysterious devices was designed to trap insects that laid waste to habitations, others that it served to compress objects of small volume; in his book, Bauer attributes the most extravagant functions to it."*

Their gaze was then attracted by an old hat, of which time had respected neither the form nor the fabric.

"Is that your topper, brought here the day before yesterday?" the young man asked the physicist.

"Mine was new, retorted the physicist, huffily, "And that one is exactly the same as the one caricaturists attribute to Robert Macaire."

"Let's see what it says," said Gédéon, and read aloud the caption: *"Apparatus with which the ancient coiffed the straw mannequins they set up in fields to frighten birds."* The reader burst out laughing. "Perfect!" he said, "I would be sorry, either, to know what the antiquaries say about that black coat hanging beside it." And having seized the garment he turned it round. In the middle of the back he was able to read the singular statement: *"Exceedingly unsightly vestment in obligatory usage at funeral ceremonies."*

Further on, an assortment of instruments of dentistry was labeled: *Instruments of torture.*

"In truth, they're right about that," said Terrier, gaily.

However, the designation of a group consisting of a dynamometer, a Nicholson aerometer, a vacuum pump, a prism, a Galilean telescope and a mercury eudiometer as *Children's toys* troubled him deeply.

"Look—a clarinet!" exclaimed Gédéon. "There are no more blind people! It's certainly the usage of that annoying instrument that once populated the Quinze-Vingts.[32] This is what it says about it: *Woodwind instrument introduced into dramatic music by the famous composer Gluck.*"

Indicating a piano whose yellowed keys had been inoffensive for several centuries, the young man added: "Of course, I'm not sorry to see this homicidal instrument relegated to this place. It's thus defined: *Instrument once very widespread in Paris, to the detriment of the healthy part of the population. It succeeded the harpsichord, which had the advantage of being less noisy. It was Bartholomeo Cristafulli of Pauda, in 1711, who brought about the substitution, the need for which no one felt, and which resulted in a significant increase in cases of rabies.* You said it!"

"The author is not mistaken about this object," said Terrier, pointing out an old compass. "He rightly attributes the discovery to the Neapolitan Flavio Gioja at the beginning of the 14th century, and refrains from citing the widespread but unjustified opinion that Marco Polo had brought once back from China in 1260, where, according to the Chinese, it had been known more than ten centuries before Christ."

The physicist was interrupted by Antius, who read another caption: "*Known in the remotest antiquity.*"

"What was?" asked his nephew.

"The gnomon."

"What's that?"

"I'm talking about the sundial before my eyes. The Chaldeans made use of the first, as the caption rightly recognizes."

---

[32] The *Centre Hospitalier National d'Ophtalmologie des Quinze-Vingts* is the principal institution for the study of ophthalmology in Paris, descendant from a hospital for the blind; it was in the process of transition in the 1880s. Even Gédeon cannot possibly believe the old wives' tale that shrill sounds can induce blindness, and is merely using it to express his (and presumably Calvert's) distaste for music.

To one side, the biretta of an assize-court judge, mounted on a stalk, was designated under the label *Indoor headgear*.

"Look," said Terrier. "A clock of our era, perhaps the only one in the city—and the explanation given of it is very detailed. Here it is:

"This badly damaged apparatus once served to measure time. The first clock to appear in France had been sent to Pepin le Bref in 760 by Pope Paul I. Caliph Haroun al-Rashid, in 807, sent another to Charlemagne, along with an organ, a musical instrument then unknown to Occidentals. Chiming clocks appeared in the middle of the 14th century. In 1647 Huygens added the pendulum, discovered by Galileo. It is only from that epoch that the division of the hour into sixty minutes, and the minute into sixty seconds, date."

The sagacity of the commentator appeared to have been misled, however, by a cylindrical object equipped with a thick layer of bristles, which bore a card reading: *Unknown object.*

"What is that?" asked Antius.

"It's a hairbrush of the latest model, by which the head of the patient is labored with extreme rapidity," said Gédéon. "But here, of course, is an object that's not unfamiliar to you." He held up a large pair of spectacles mounted on a vertical axis.

"I'm only on my eighth pair, thank God" declared the doctor. "What does it say about them?"

"It says," replied the young man, leaning over the instrument, "that their invention goes back to the 12th century, if one attributes it to Roger Bacon. It adds that magnifying lenses are due to the Dutchman Jacques Metius or, according to others, his compatriot Zacharius Jansen. Galileo, the note adds, constructed the telescope shortly afterwards, which permitted numerous scientific discoveries, and in the 17th century, Rheita fabricated the first binocular telescope. Is that true."

"Quite true," said Antius.

"O vanity of vanities!" exclaimed the physicist, who had just plunged his gaze into a large display-case. "We find here, relegated to the rank of antiques, the apparatus of which the

19th century was justly proud." His companions drew closer to him, and he continued. "Here are the various telegraphic systems that replaced one another successively over a period of thirty years by reason of their relative improvement. There's the old dial telegraph, improved by Bréguet, which was almost exclusively reserved in our time for service on the railway, but excited great admiration at first. Here's the Morse system, which constituted a great advance in the speed, ease and reliability of translation of dispatches. This next one is the Hughes apparatus, which was operated like a piano and printed telegrams with great rapidity. Finally, in that corner, you can see the instrument invented by Caselli, which reproduced the sender's message with absolute fidelity. Let's see what the contemporary opinion is."

And the scientist read aloud: *"Primitive instruments of electric telegraphy, How different they are from our apparatus, founded on the triple effect of the current, the telephone and the phonograph, which permit continuous conversation over a distance of five hundred leagues."*

"Ho ho!" said Gédéon. "Isn't it a descendant of Monsieur de Crac who wrote that caption?"[33]

"It is not permitted to anyone to set limits to the progress of applications of electricity," replied the physicist, peremptorily.

"What's the significance of this hood?" Gédéon asked, pointing to a kind of gutta-percha burnoose of bizarre form. Having drawn nearer to the singular object, he cried "Oh, marvelous! I'll read: *Twentieth-century umbrella. This comfortable apparatus was carried coiled around the waist. By pressing a switch on the right hand side, the envelope was suddenly extended, and the traveler found himself sheltered beneath and impermeable tent."* The reader concluded: "Which was rather ingenious."

---

[33] Monsieur (or Baron) de Crac is a character featured in several French comic operas, based on the character of Baron Münchhausen, as popularized by Rudolf Eric Raspe.

His gaze went to the wall. "But here's a violin with its bow," he continued. "One could, without compromising oneself, hang it alongside the dentist's pincers and label it the same way. It's interesting to know the opinion of today's melomaniacs regarding that instrument, which renders the operator so pretentious and the listener so peevish." And, standing up on tiptoe, he read—with some difficulty, because of the distance, the following commentary:

"*Musical instrument, which inflicted considerable damage on the youth of ancient times. Maneuvered by a skilful hand, it was merely annoying; tortured by a mediocre performer, it could provoke attacks of epilepsy in the most phlegmatic. The instrument, like several others that were equally dangerous, is founded on the vibration of strings.*" The young man added: "The curator of the museum has employed a certain method in the arrangement of objects. I can see another apparatus beside the violin that's equally annoying."

"Damn!" said the doctor, who had considerable pretensions with regard to the article in question. "You're very disrespectful of the game of chess."

"I agree with Gédéon," said Terrier. "I would even add that the chessboard, which absorbs all the intellectual efforts of its fanatics, offers very great dangers. I don't mean for you, Antius, who have only ever been a mediocre player."

"Mediocre," he doctor replied, dryly, "is not the word I'd use."

"Great God!" cried Gédéon, suddenly, raising his arms to the heavens and giving signs of extreme agitation. "It's her!"

"Have you lost your mind? Is it necessary to administer a shower with this instrument?" asked Antius severely, pointing to an old watering-can hung on the wall and elevated to the rank of "artistic curio."

"It's her, I tell you!" the young man cried, insistently, leaning over a large display case.

"Who's *her*?" asked the physicist, very intrigued.

"The one who left me so often, in spite of the chain that bound her to my heart, who was my plank of salvation on bad days, who made the journey to the Rue des Blancs-Manteaux thirteen times over, for whose absence all three of us wept on the day when we set foot in the new world—it's my old Toledo watch!" The young man was laughing and weeping at the same time.

"I observe that you have a good heart," Terrier remarked, "but you're doubtless the victim of a hallucination.

"Oh," Gédéon replied, in an elegiac one, "if your chronometer had rendered you as much service, you'd recognize it after a separation of ten thousand years."

"He's right, damn it," said the doctor, who had leaned over the object. "I recognize that old crock, permanently deprived of a minute hand, which periodically made the journey to the Mont-de-Piété."

The young man, in whom joy was always manifest by some extravagance, started whirling on his heels like a dervish, but came to a sudden stop uttering a cry of pain, accompanied by a sequence of curses. In his rotation he had bumped into a gas-jet that rose up sadly in front of the wall, which bore a label on its stem on which two words were legible: *Old lamp*.

"Moderate your delirium, or you'll bump your head," the professor advised, mildly.

"Now he tells me—thanks!" the victim riposted.

"As for your watch," Antius observed, "it now enjoys a very well-deserved repose, and you ought to be more than a little proud to be contributing to the education of present generations, in the form of that old cheap clockwork."

By this time the travelers had made a circuit of the immense room and had been able to ascertain that it contained varied specimens of the majority of scientific, industrial and domestic instruments of the ancient world—instruments now abandoned, either because the civilization of the present had adopted more advanced ones, or because the arts that they facilitated had undergone complete transformation.

"I believe," said Antius, for whom exactitude was a fundamental virtue, "that we would do well to return to the school. Our visit has been so interesting that the hours have flown by without our noticing."

The travelers left the gallery and went through the vestibule. As they passed through the entrance door, eleven successive chimes sounded overhead.

The three men went across the courtyard.

Suddenly, the professor, stopping his companions, pointed out an old Crampton Engine,[34] which was standing in a corner and was only drawn to the attention of visitors by the two words: *Rare specimen.*

"Are they making fun of us?" Gédéon asked.

"How's that?" asked Terrier.

"Yesterday, I believe, as I was pronouncing a funeral oration for men of law worthy of figuring in collections of contemporary moral exemplars, there was a lawsuit concerning railways in progress at the Palais de Justice."

"Yes," the professor replied, "but the machines of the Central African railways us an electromotive system. It's as if you'd said: I had a watch, whose sand still exists."

Stunned by the argument, the young man remained silent.

As they went into the courtyard of the school, the strangers ran into the schoolmaster coming to find them.

"Messieurs," he said, "I'm bringing you an invitation to dinner tomorrow evening, at Monsieur Dryon's house."

The travelers thanked their generous host.

"The illustrious agronomist, who's coming back for the conference," Herber continued, "called me this morning. He'll only be in Paris for forty-eight hours. The day after tomorrow,

---

[34] A kind of steam locomotive patented by Thomas Crampton in 1846 and widely employed during the subsequent railway boom; they were particularly popular in France, where *"prendre le Crampton"* came to mean catching an express train. One specimen is still preserved in the Cité du Train, the French Railway Museum at Mulhouse—perhaps the same one that the time-travelers find in 2880.

his aerial transport, the *Arago*, will launch forth into the air again."

The parlor bell rang.

The four men headed for the dining room, where Madame Herber was waiting for them, giving her final instructions.

After greeting the young woman, the guests sat down at the table.

The visit to the museum of antiquities became the topic of conversation. The subject was treated prudently by the two scientists, and Gédéon, carefully monitored by his uncle, did not commit any stupidity.

"Messieurs," Herber said, "you have been able to observe how defective our ancestors' inventions were, especially with regard to travel, as that old steam engine in the front courtyard testifies. What inferiority, by comparison with our balloons, some of which, like the *Arago*, devour twenty leagues an hour. At the end of the 20th century, it took a fortnight to reach the heart of Africa, but today, Monsieur Dryon can set foot on the shore of Lake Tanganyika after a twenty-four hour journey."

"The opulent landowner has doubtless come to spent the fine season in his magnificent Palais in the Place des États?" queried Madame Herber.

"No, Jeanne," the schoolmaster replied. "In spite of the fatigues of the Congress, Monsieur Dryon intends to leave on Friday for his estates."

"You say, my dear Master," Antius put in, "that your illustrious friend has come for a Congress."

"Yes, Doctor."

"Is that a political Congress?"

"Yes, the great Congress of the United States of Europe."

"Where is it held?" Antius asked.

"In Constantinople," Herber replied, surprised by the question.

"In Constantinople!" the doctor exclaimed.

"Yes, Messieurs—the General Congress has been held in that city every year for five centuries. Every State has its own individual Congress, in which local issues are considered, approximately a month before the great Congress, but all governmental questions are dealt with in the capital of the old continent."

The doctor and the physicist, mute with astonishment, dared not ask about the political commotions that had transformed Europe in the course of ten centuries."

The young man came to their aid, rather cleverly. "My dear Master," he said to Herber, "I'd be very glad to know the circumstances that led the European nations to an understanding that could not have been foreseen in ancient times. I confess that, on many historical points, I only possess rather vague notions, and that my education requires completion in that respect."

"I can briefly remind you of the general causes of the major events, my young friend. You know that, by the end of the 20th century, ballistics had made such progress, and the apparatus of extermination had become so murderous, that governments could only envisage the frightful responsibilities of war with terror. In that epoch, a few international differences put to arbitration having produced excellent results, the idea of disarmament gradually took hold.

"The ground was thus prepared when a providential circumstance permitted the permanent assurance of general peace. Turkey, which had been the firebrand of European discord for two centuries, had just been neutralized. Suddenly, a simple idea of absolute efficacy became clear. It was understood that no political agitation would be possible in Europe if the nations had an army and a fleet equipped at common expense at Constantinople, in the most favorable strategic position in the world, ready to descend like lightning on anyone who attempted to disturb the peace.

"Radical as it seemed to our ancestors, the measure, it must be said in their honor, encountered few adversaries, who eventually ended up accepting the general opinion. After five years of deliberation, they set to work. Two years later, a formidable European army occupied Turkey, charged with policing the old continent.

"The result was admirable. General disarmament was carried out in a matter of months. For thirty years, the harmony was so perfect that, with a common accord, the federal army was reduced by half. After a further period of absolute tranquility, it was further diminished in the same proportion, and so on, with the result that, by the end of the 22nd century, the police force changed with maintaining the security of Europe consisted of a few hundred mariners and soldiers, whose maneuvers were reduced to the fanatical practice of angling on the shores of the Bosphorus. As no one gave any thought to filling the gaps that old age or illness produced in that venerable troop, it gradually faded away without anyone noticing its disappearance.

"All international questions continued to be settled by independent tribunals, and it became unthinkable that the interested parties, even in the epoch when no threat hung over their heads, might seek to defy the decision of the arbitrators. People eventually got into the habit of regarding Constantinople as the true capital of Europe, and an annual Congress designed to tighten the bonds of amity that already united all its peoples was instituted there, which still function today. That, Messieurs, is how the United States of Europe were founded.

"Profound harmony, unshakable peace and the reciprocal esteem and sympathy of nations, were not the only benefits that resulted from that great peaceful revolution. Five million men were returned to agriculture, industry, maritime commerce, the arts and science. Labor increased in a formidable proportion, and a considerable overflow of wellbeing expanded through the western world. Taxes were reduced everywhere, in spite of the extraordinary development of major projects of public utility and the enormous momentum given to public education.

"Libraries, laboratories, museums and schools multiplied infinitely, and there was soon no township in the remotest corners of Europe that was not proud of its local academy, in which all scientific, literary, economic and industrial questions were treated in turn. Such are, my young friend, the opinions of the contemporary historical school of the principal events that prepared and determined the United States of Europe."

XXIII. The Pont Neuf. Meteorological Questions.
The Gulf Stream

A few minutes later, the diners left the table. Herber, re-tained by his duties, wished his friends well and left, heading for the interior buildings. After having bid farewell to their gracious hostess, Antius and his companions went out in their turn.

Five minutes later, the travelers, gathered at the foot of the school's monumental staircase, conferred to determine which way to go.

"Let's go down to the river," Gédéon proposed. "We'll be nearly in the center of the city, and it will be easy to make a decision from there."

"You reason like Pythagoras," said Terrier.

Antius nodded his head, and the three men set off on the lawn of the plaza, which they crossed in a straight line.

They had taken a hundred paces when a gigantic shadow, advancing toward them with lightning rapidity, made them recoil instinctively.

"It's only a balloon," said the young man, calmly, point-ing at an aerostat that was cleaving the air above their heads, whose projected shadow was now running over the crowns of the trees. "By the way," he added, addressing the physicist, "I wouldn't be sorry to be able to put one over on the scientists of old."

"In what way?" asked the professor, for whom that prop-osition, in view of the scientific abilities of its author, seemed the height of extravagance."

"I believe, having heard you say so, that a thousand years ago, only bodies lighter than air could be maintained in the atmosphere."

"I've never affirmed such an absurdity," the professor declared.

"In that case, I must have been dreaming," admitted the young man, philosophically, who willingly gave in on questions of that sort.

"Or, rather, you're lending an absurd meaning to the enunciation of a principle that no one had ever contested."

"What's that, if you please?"

"This: a body suspended in a fluid is only at equilibrium when its weight is equal to that of the fluid displaced."

"If the weights are equal," Gédéon riposted, with a certain assurance, "they're not different."

"I said a body at rest, not a moving body. In the latter case, I can convince you by an argument so banal that it will be within your range."

"Thank you very much."

"An eagle weights four or five kilograms, but only displaces ten grams of air. Now, at all times, I think, eagles have been able to fly."

"Obscure, but true," Gédéon concluded.

At that moment the travelers went into the avenue leading to the river. Ten minutes later, the majestic sheet of water unfurled before them.

They had been walking for some time, following the magnificent pathway that bordered the left bank of the Seine in the direction of the current, when their eyes progressively made out a sparkling line traversing the river eight hundred meters downstream. Soon, as their gaze plunged obliquely across the river, they were able to count fifteen supporting arches, beneath which the sheet of water was flowing slowly.

"It's the sight of that bridge, which one might believe to be constructed out of a single diamond, that has rendered our young man epileptic," said Terrier.

"What do you think of that bridge of ice, in midsummer?" exclaimed Gédéon, who was ten paces ahead.

"Ice? You mean glass, I think," said Antius.

"That's evident enough," said the physicist.

Curious to see the astonishing work that was resplendently displayed before them at close range, the travelers increased their pace. They had not gone a hundred meters when the crystal bridge, to their great astonishment, suddenly lost its transparency and took on the scarlet tint of rubies.

"What do you think of that change of décor?" the young man asked his companions.

"Nothing yet," Antius replied, while the silent physicist sought an explanation for the phenomenon.

Soon afterwards, the bridge threw off a last gleam of red and suddenly glittered with the green fires of emerald.

"My word—one might think that a rainbow were gradually unfolding its girth over the river," said Gédéon.

"I've finally solved the puzzle," said Terrier, coming to a halt. "We're in the presence of a mass of iridescent glass, which takes on different hues as one's viewpoint shifts. That curious phenomenon was observed for the first time toward the end of the 19th century, and was due to certain perturbations accidentally produced in a molten flow. Today, they make use of that remarkable property."

The three men resumed their march and saw all the colors of the solar spectrum gleam before them in turn. Ten minutes later, they found themselves at the end of the bridge and were able to admire all its details.

The causeway was covered with a thick layer of rubber, and their tread suddenly became soft and elastic.

The architectural marvel presented, in its entirety, a particular character of simplicity, heightened by lines of irreproachable elegance. The parapets seemed to have been cast in a single piece, for no juncture could be seen from one bank to the other.

In the middle of the bridge, a man who was placidly watching the water flow told them that they were on the Pont Neuf, a monument cast on the spot, which still retained its name even though it was already two hundred years old.

"It was proposed to cast glass houses," he added, "but we're not yet in the fortunate era when the well-behaved can brave all gazes."

"That's the first misanthrope we've encountered in this world," said Gédéon, in a low voice.

The marveling travelers passed on to the right bank and went back along the river. The heat was overwhelming. The effluvia of the hot air were visible along the course of the avenue, and a bleak silence reigned over the motionless foliage.

Antius suggested to his companions that they rest momentarily. The three men let themselves fall on to a bench on the promenade.

A few electric carriages rolling silently along the causeway, laden with panting passengers, were the only things moving in that torrid panorama.

After a pause of half an hour, the strangers, continuing on their way, came into an unfamiliar quarter. They had been walking for an hour amid incessantly renewed magnificence, when Antius, sponging his forehead, leaned back against a gigantic chestnut tree.

"We're a long way from the school," he said. "Besides which, under this burning sky, we'll be forced to walk slowly, so we ought to retrace our steps."

"My throat's damnably dry," said Terrier. "How about you, Gédéon?"

"I feel as if my chest is full of hot coals," the young man replied. "My God, I'd like to run across a licorice-water seller!"

"It seems to me," said Antius, "that I can see a café on the left hand side of that boulevard, and, although we ought to exercise an extreme moderation in using the money confided to us, we ought not to hesitate to take some refreshment."

The proposal was adopted. Ten minutes later, the three travelers were sitting at a table in the shade in front of a luxurious establishment whose terrace was ornamented by a triple row of exotic plants. The presence of a few palm trees, imprisoned in rectangular boxes full of vegetable earth, had suggested to the café-owner the simple and logical idea for his sign, on which the words PALM TREE CAFÉ could be read in flamboyant letters.

A customer who had preceded the travelers by a few minutes and had taken a place some distance away pressed an electric button fixed to the side of the table in front of him. A young woman appeared n the threshold. At a signal from the client she went back inside and came back with a laden tray.

"That's extraordinary," said Gédéon "Waiters are girls now."

"What shall we have?" asked Antius. "We mustn't ask for things that no longer exist and make ourselves seem ridiculous."

"The simplest thing is to ask for information," Terrier suggested.

"Without seeming to do so," Gédéon added. We don't want to give a posthumous performance of *La Cagnotte* at the Théâtre du Palais-Royal."[35]

"Mademoiselle," Antius said to the young woman, who came over, carrying an ornate cotton napkin. "What beverages are the most popular in this heat?"

"At present, Messieurs, there's a strong demand for iced lemon syrup with essence of vanilla."

"Serve us some, if you please."

The young woman came back with a tray containing three large goblets hollowed out from enormous rubies.

"It wouldn't be prudent to break a glass here," observed the professor.

"This stone is doubtless manufactured artificially today," Antius remarked.

Gédéon raised the beverage to his lips.

"I warn you that there's a good fluxion of the breast at the bottom of that glass," said the doctor, stopping him.

After a few minutes' rest, the travelers began to imbibe the delicious liqueur slowly.

A group of customers, streaming like the gods of the sea, came to sit down nearby. "What a crushing temperature!" one

---

[35] Eugène Labiche's vaudeville *La Cagnotte* [The Kitty—as in a card game] was premiered at the theater in question in 1864

of them exclaimed, while his neighbor orders a beverage identical to the one the strangers had.

"Yes, but we're finally going to have a cool spell," said another. "The Académie des Sciences has made arrangements for us to have rain within twenty-four hours."

Gédéon started. The two scientists pricked up their ears.

"Do the members of that scientific body now perform incantations like negro sorcerers?" asked the young man.

"Shut up and listen," said the doctor brusquely, in a low voice.

"It's been decided that twenty aerostats will go up into the higher regions this evening, and each furnish fifty formidable explosions of nitroglycerine in the middle of the vapors, which won't take long to resolve into rain. The effect ought to extend over a circle of at least thirty square myriameters."

"This time last year," a fourth recounted, "they determined torrential rain that lasted for two days."

"Meteorological conditions have been considerably modified here," the first resumed. "Once, it seems, before the deviation of the Gulf Stream. Paris was covered in snow in winter."

The physicist started, and attracted the attention of the customers. "Monsieur," he asked, taking off his hat to the person who had just spoken, "can you tell me what the average temperature is in this region?"

"Sixteen point eight degrees, Monsieur," his interlocutor replied, bowing.

"So it's gone up six degrees in a few centuries?"

"Yes, Monsieur, since the change in the direction of the Gulf Stream, which now bathes the coasts of France and permits warm sea-baths to be taken in the month of January."

"Thank you," said Terrier. Pensively, he murmured: "So nature has also had its revolutions?"

A few moments later, a young man of intelligent and alert appearance came to sit down beside them. While unfolding a newspaper as big as a coaching-entrance, the newcomer ordered iced sherry from a second young woman, who had just appeared in the doorway.

"Monsieur," Antius suddenly asked the young city-dweller, who was already scanning the first page, "is service in public establishments habitually provided by young women?"

"Yes, Monsieur," the young man replied, nodding his head. "All labor that does not require a measure of physical strength is generally confided to the fair sex."

"One more question, if you please?"

"I'm at your disposal," said the young man politely, putting down his paper.

"We're strangers, and, wishing to conform to the customs of the land we're visiting—a principle that ought to be the first rule of conduct for a voyager—we'd like to know whether it's usual to give service staff a tip."

"I don't understand what you're doing me the honor of asking, Monsieur," said the young man, seemingly astonished.

"Isn't it customary to give a small gratification to people who serve you?"

"That procedure would extremely hurtful, Monsieur, and I advise you not to employ it anywhere on the continent. Everyone here rightly considers themselves to be equal to everyone else, and would blush to be paid twice for a service."

"Thank you, Monsieur."

The young man resumed his reading, then, short afterwards, threw the price of his beverage on the table, bowed to the strangers and left.

"It's time to go," said Antius, hearing five o'clock chime on a large electric clock set above the entrance door.

Gédéon pressed the ivory button and the young woman appeared. The doctor rummaged in his pocket and, after a few nervous twitches, suddenly seemed extremely embarrassed.

"We'll be in a pretty pickle if you've lost the purse," said the young man.

Obliged to devote himself to a maneuver familiar to distracted individuals, the scientist began to empty his pockets.

He brought out, in succession, a handkerchief, a portfolio, an agenda, a spectacle-case, two pamphlets and a catalogue."

"It isn't with those antediluvian items that you're expecting to pay the bill?" exclaimed his nephew, anxiously.

"Monsieur," said the young woman, in a most amiable tone, "don't worry about having forgotten your money; you can settle your bill next time you come this way. In addition, if you have need of any funds to continue your walk, the establishment's till is at your disposal."

"Thank you, my child, and I'm very obliged to you," the doctor replied, warmly, and then added: "But I'm now out of difficulty"—and he exhumed the wallet, one of whose metal fitments had become attached to the inside of his pocket.

The bill having been easily settled, the travelers set off toward the boulevard gain. With the aid of a few directions given to them by passers-by with perfect urbanity, they set off for the school.

They went across the river again.

Six o'clock was chiming on the main building as they set foot in the courtyard. Herber came to meet them and accompany them to the dining room, where his wife was giving her final instructions. The afternoon's excursion served as the topic of conversation at dinner.

The schoolmaster gave them some very interesting details regarding the crystal bridge.

"From the viewpoint of solidity," he said, "that work of art is superior to all the others of the same kind, because it really is formed from a single homogeneous piece. In consequence, the methods of the 27th century engineers who constructed it have been conserved in their integrity to the present day. As the blocks of glass are brought together, the faces that are to be juxtaposed are only separates by fine platinum mesh, which the passage of a electric current brings to white heat in a matter of seconds. The glass melts superficially, the metallic fabric is removed, and the two planes in the fluid state are in contact. The conjuncture is thus absolute.

"That employment of glass renders immense services, because it permits indestructible bridges to be built over gulfs that had previously defied all the efforts of human genius."

At the request of his guests, the schoolmaster then explained the variation of the Gulf Stream, the warm and vivifying current that runs obliquely across the Atlantic. Its direction had been gradually tilted eastwards, and had significantly raised the temperature of Western Europe.

"The sea, always warm on the coasts of France, bathes over an extent of three hundred leagues a brilliant chain of villas drowned in perpetual verdure. Winter, which is no longer anything but an astronomical expression, has fled conclusively before a mild and luminous spring. On Sundays, several convoys of balloons, loaded with passengers, depart for all parts of the coast, which has become a true suburb of Paris.

"Why hasn't this miraculous city been chosen as the capital of the world?" asked Gédéon, whose imagination was stimulated to the highest degree by all these marvelous stories.

"Paris, my young friend, is still the capital of the nation—or, if you prefer, of France," Herber replied. "It could even have obtained for us the honor of which you speak, but, obedient to the highest considerations of order from the general point of view, we proposed Constantinople ourselves as the seat of central government, and that generosity won us the sympathy of all peoples, who compete in proclaiming our intellectual superiority, without hesitation. We are still the primary representatives of the Latin races that, with regard to the abstraction and expansion of ideas, have thus far been the soul of humankind."

The strangers, absorbed by the reflections engendered in their minds by these political upheavals, remained silent.

The harmonious voice of Madame Herber extracted them from their meditations. "Messieurs," the young woman said, displaying a basket full of enormous clusters of muscat grapes that she had just brought to the table, here are a few specimens of the vines of the high plateaux of the Sudan. They were bought this morning at the fruit-market—but these Messieurs haven't visited the Market yet."

"I can put myself at their disposal to take them there tomorrow morning, if they're curious to visit our great gastronomical warehouse," the schoolmaster proposed.

The voyagers accepted the offer gladly.

After the meal, the visitors went down on to the lawn of the main courtyard. The conversation, which lasted for a long time, was interrupted by a courier from Guillaume Dryon, who brought Herber and his guests an invitation for Thursday evening.

"We'll go straight there when we come out of the session at the Institut," the schoolmaster said.

Having arranged the departure for the excursion to the Market for nine a.m., Herber bid his guests goodnight, and they returned to their apartment.

XXIV. The Market

The next morning, as nine o'clock was chiming on the clock of the school museum, the strangers, refreshed and in god spirits, gathered at the balustrade overlooking the square saw their host walking toward them at a rapid pace.

They went to meet him. Herber offered them his hand.

"We'll have fine weather for out stroll," the schoolmaster said, pointing at the sky, whose dazzling blue was uninterrupted by any cloud.

The four men went down the monumental staircase and were soon on the lawn.

To escape the fiery torrents that the sun was pouring in to their heads, the travelers walked beneath the shady crowns of the giant trees forming the Museum plaza.

Myriads of brightly-plumaged birds were stirring in the branches, sometimes descending to perch in a familiar fashion on the benches of the promenade, in spite of the presence of a large number of citizens reading the morning papers.

"The *Globe* won't keep my custom for long," said one of them as the travelers were passing by.

"Is it ill-informed on some matter?" asked his neighbor.

"I don't accuse it of anything as serious as that, but this morning it's giving me yesterday's news, which everyone knows."

"Today's readers are less tolerant than those of old," observed Gédéon, in a low voice.

"I congratulate them," Antius replied, in the same tone.

Herber and his guests turned into an avenue that made a rather wide angle with the one by which they had arrived three days before.

A few moments later, one of the gigantic public carriages they had seen on the first day came toward them at top speed. At a signal from the schoolmaster, the driver cut off the current and the six wheels, suddenly imprisoned by metal brakes, skidded along the highway.

Herber and his guests went to the back of the vehicle and climbed up on to the platform via a footstep covered in a thick layer of gutta-percha. Silently, the machine moved off again.

Preceding his friends, the schoolmaster showed them, one after another, the dispositions of the first two floors, principally reserved for women, children and old people. After having walked around the circular galleries of those sections, almost deserted for the moment, they went up to the top platform, sheltered by a large awning of striped fabric, under which a few passengers were installed. The travelers went to sit down on benches covered with thick cushions of padded leather.

Turning their backs to the central causeway, which reigned over all the sumptuous thoroughfares, they had a fine collective view of the magnificent habitations that bordered the avenue.

For a few moments Gédéon had been exhibiting manifest symptoms of astonishment, which did not escape the schoolmaster.

"I believe, my young friend," he said, "that something unusual has caught your eye."

"You said it, my dear Master," the young man replied, "and this is what astonishes me. Without missing shops, and most of all shopkeepers, I must admit that I'm very surprised not to have yet seen any department stories on these magnificent highways. Perhaps we're a long way from the commercial center."

"Not at all, my dear friend. From the viewpoint in question, Paris is much the same from one end to the other. Everyone buys what he needs from the warehouses, where the choice is immense and the prices of all kind of merchandise are set fairly. It's a long time now since we parted company with the multiple devouring parasitism thanks to which raw materials and manufactured goods only reached the consumer after having passed through eight or nine unnecessary hands, each of which took a profit. That has resulted in a lowering of the prices of all items.

"You will not even perceive any workshops on our route, because, by reason of the convenience of transportation, those establishments all function some distance away from the city, where they find all the elements desirable for installation."

At that moment, the carriage went past the last house in the avenue, a rapidly as a projectile, and he marvelous panorama of the river and its banks was offered to their gaze. Soon they found themselves on the bridge and could see the whole of the majestic expanse of water.

The carriage, continuing at the same pace, launched itself into another boulevard, which formed the final branch of a triple avenue meeting at the end of the bridge. After a journey of a few minutes, it stopped in front of a lawn on the far side of which stood a kind of cyclopean construction.

"That's the Market, Messieurs," said Herber, pointing at the monument.

The immense Market formed a square extending for eight hundred meters on each side. In the center of the façade, a broad and elevated gallery traversed the monument all the way through. The fronton of the arch, raised up several meters and ornamented with mythological reliefs, was dominated by an enormous statue of Agriculture.

Crowning the edifice, an octagonal tower of pink marble surrounded by porphyry columns supported a gigantic group representing the four parts of the world, supporting the terrestrial globe.

The entire framework of the edifice was made of malleable cast iron, sparkling like polished steel. The cladding was established in brick and polychromatic marble.

The visitors headed for the gallery.

As they went under the arch, the schoolmaster proposed that they visit, in succession, the markets in fruit, fish, poultry and butchery.

"By what means do all these provisions, which I assume to be very considerable, arrive?" Antius asked.

"Via cylindrical subterranean tubes, which collect them two leagues from the city at the general docks," Herber replied. "It's there that balloons arriving from all over the world are unloaded. Scarcely has it arrived in the cellars of the market than the merchandise is raised up by electromotive machines, which distribute them to their respective places.

"On the other hand, the suburban market-gardeners, whose proverbial cleverness is stimulated by strong competition, are served by a special electric haulage system, which reaches the market via tunnels established under the public highway. That exclusion is necessitated by the requirements of the extreme cleanliness of the city."

The strollers had passed through the archway and were in the midst of a bustling crowd.

Herber drew his companions to the right; in a few steps they crossed the threshold of an immense room, in which the most magnificent, rarest and tastiest fruits were disposed in tall, dense and closely-packed pyramids. It was scarcely possible to see he merchants who were enthroned with dignity in the midst of that vegetal plethora, without harassing customers and, more especially, without engaging in the legendary debates of their equivalents of another era, more remarkable for their color than their amenity.

The moderate level of the prices, established in advance, initially astonished the strangers.

"Nothing is more logical," said Herber. "The entire world is cultivated today, and aerial navigation, extending to all places in accordance with the needs and richness of the soil, maintains both the stability and cheapness of prices."

Exotic fruits, transported through the cool layers of the atmosphere with prodigious speed, arrived at the market with all their succulence and freshness. Many had been picked the previous day and presented the humid velvet quality of fruit on the tree.

The stroll through the hall was an enchantment.

Pyramids of coconuts full of delicious milk and fresh pineapples rose up several meters. Heaps of peaches, grapes, figs, pomegranates, organs and lemons, cultivated in the great plantations of Central Africa, where the precocious harvest precedes that in the temperate regions by several months, rose up on all sides, dividing the attention of the buyers with the equally abundant products of the colossal farms of the South American pampas.

The travelers went into the fish market.

In that new enclosure the entire ichthyological world was represented, either living and imprisoned in marble basins full of fresh water and crystal aquaria filled with sea water, or in a state of dead nature, lying on damp beds of aquatic weeds.

Tuna from the Saharan Sea with shiny scales, extended in long lines, enormous salmon from Lapland, eels from the watercourses of Central Asia and lampreys from southern Spain, still breathing, were particularly sought-after by the purchasers.

The most various conchyological varieties formed veritable walls, cemented by wet grass, which loomed over the customers' heads.

A delightful freshness reigned over that part of the market, and the noise of the crowd was covered by the intense noise of an infinity of gushing fountains, which alimented the reservoirs.

The four areas that the schoolmaster had listed were separated by two wide galleries cutting through the center of the edifice at right angles. The junction was ornamented with a monumental basin covered with steaming cascades, the waters of which, fringed with foam, half-drowned a varied cortege of naiads, gods and sea-monsters, which projected thick liquid sprays in all directions. The basin was surrounded by a crown of bright green grass, round which as disposed a chain of benches with slanting backs, on which several groups of clients of the gigantic gastronomical museum were currently lounging.

Herber and his companions crossed the alleyway separating them from the poultry hall.

Here, the slight and tinkling sound of waterfalls was replaced by the deafening cries of several thousand birds, indigenous or exotic, transported alive and continuing to peck around in cages lined up to infinity. The farms, woods and forests of the entire world had sent their tribute to the sovereign city of the Occident. Mountains of crates of fresh quail, arriving from the high Asiatic plateaux, and flocks of partridges from the Cape, arranged in tight rows, so long that the items in the center seemed cramped for hummingbirds, particularly attracted the doctor's attention.

"Aerial navigation," said Herber, "brings substances within our range every day that once only arrived at determined times. Game is as abundant here during the summer as in winter, for it comes to us directly from austral countries of the world that are under snow while we are under the most ardent blaze of summer."

The travelers, while walking beneath an endless ceiling of hares and woodcock were going along a wall of fattened geese originating from the farms of Patagonia, the sight of which would have delighted Gargantua's maître d'hôtel.

On quitting that extraordinary tunnel, Herber and his guests went into the butchery hall.

As well as the finest specimens of indigenous husbandry, they perceived hecatombs of bison, roe deer, antelopes and a host of once-wild but now domesticated animals, which ingenious methods of fattening had brought to a state of incomparable perfection.

The visitors had been walking for an hour and a half, and had only seen a small part of the immense warehouse to which the entire city came to obtain provisions.

The extreme facility of communications, by suppressing distance, had led progressively to these concentrations of produce, which, by putting the consumers in direct relation to the producers, had done more to ease economic problems than all the books written on the subject in six hundred years.

Eleven o'clock was chiming when Herber took his guests back to the avenue. The four men got on to the first vehicle that came along. Twenty minutes later, all the guests were gathered around the schoolmaster's hospitable table.

XXV. The Necropolis

After the meal, Herber, retained by his functions, wished his friends good day and went back to the interior buildings of the school. The travelers, having taken their leave of their charming hostess, went down to the square. They had been deliberating for some time as to which way they ought to go when Gédéon said: "I've got an idea."

"You do surprise me," said Antius.

"I might even have said a good idea," the young man went on, undisconcerted. ""Of course, I fear that it might not be welcomed by my uncle with all the enthusiasm that it merits."

"Keep it to yourself, then," replied the doctor, in a surly tone.

"That would be impossible, as it's so original."

"What is it?" asked the physicist, intrigued by all these oratory precautions.

"On the other side of the plaza," Gédéon said, "there's a monument that you've already gone past without paying any heed to it, and which bears as a sign the eloquent word *Necropolis*."

"Let's go visit it!" exclaimed the doctor, promptly setting off in the indicated direction.

"What!" said his nephew, trotting behind him, "you have no hesitation about going to inspect a colony to whose development your exploits have made such a considerable contribution?"

"You're like all those who speak ill of medicine," replied Antius, continuing in his stride. "As soon as you have a cold in the head, they gladly summon the entire Faculty."

The physicist, who had caught them up, smiled incredulously, but, sensing that any reflection would only add fuel to fire, he contented himself with saying: "After all, it will be

231

interesting to know how our descendants treat the residues of their ancestors."

The vast square was filed with a delightful coolness, and a large number of city-dwellers were leaning back on the comfortable seats, chatting to one another or reading the newspapers. The air was full of the murmur of gushing fountains, momentarily drowned out by the joyful cries of birds hidden in the foliage.

The travelers traversed the lawn and went back under the shady vault of the centuries-of trees that surrounded the museum plaza. Having taken a hundred strides, they saw before them a superb portico whose tall columns produced an impressive effect. As they advanced, the façade of the edifice unfurled progressively, and they were soon able to appreciate the grandiose and majestic ensemble.

Four sets of paired Corinthian columns, arranged from the base to the summit of the edifice in order of decreasing size, decorated the monument throughout its extent. Vast arched bays, framed with artistically-carved sculptures opened between the columns, traversed by bright draperies of pink silk, which partly intercepted the light of day.

On the fronton of the portico, the word NECROPOLIS stood out in huge golden letters against a background of black marble. The monument, isolated from the neighboring palaces, was surrounded by a thick girdle of magnificent trees, which sheltered an ocean of flowers.

The three men were mute with admiration.

The physicist broke the silence. "What strikes me even more than the magnificence of this gigantic tomb," he said, "is the absence of any characteristic that could awaken funereal ideas in the imagination of the living."

"In truth," said Gédéon, "it makes death seem an attractive proposition."

"Let's go in," said Antius.

"First we need to know whether that's permitted," Terrier objected.

At that moment, joyful cries and youthful bursts of child-ish laughter resounded from the depths of the portico.

"Oh!" exclaimed the young man, taking a step back. "Have today's inventors found a way of cheering up the dead?"

"Poltroon!" replied the doctor. "Can't you guess that it's children playing games inside the mausoleum?" And he went toward the door at a deliberate pace.

The three men went into a vast vestibule decorated with unusual richness. The joyful racket was reaching a crescendo.

"It's truly an inverted world," said Gédéon. "This is the only place in the city that's a little noisy."

A few paces further on, the doctor, who was in the lead, suddenly stopped. "Look!" he said, extending his hand.

The professor and the young man came forward. A curi-ous spectacle met their eyes.

In a vast interior courtyard, covered with a thick carpet of green grass, twenty children were capering around before the attentive eyes of a few young women. The latter were chatting gaily, sitting around an admirable blue marble foun-tain, which occasionally disappeared in a compact mist.

The travelers went into the courtyard without their pres-ence appearing to provoke the slightest attention among its joyful inhabitants.

"Our descendants have given death a different image from their ancestors," said the doctor. "Notice how cheerful the admirable architecture of this interior courtyard is, down to the smallest detail. This abode is veritably enchanting, at least externally. We can now visit the galleries, which are the most interesting aspect for us."

They went back into the vestibule. A large stairway of unpolished marble with a gentle slope led up to the first floor. They went up and soon found themselves on an immense landing filed with paintings and works of art. The window that illuminated it opened on to a balcony, the balustrade of which was supported by a long row of white stone colonnettes.

Opposite the stairway, a high arched doorway bore on its fronton, engraved in golden letters, the dates 2700-2800.

"What does that signify?" asked the young man.

"It's doubtless the gallery reserved for the dead of the 28th century," Antius replied, heading for the entrance.

His two companions followed him.

The doctor opened the door with a confident hand, and the three men went into a room measuring at least two hundred meters in length and thirty broad. The ceiling, slightly vaulted and painted as a luminous sky, presented an appearance of infinite depth.

The four walls disappeared entirely beneath a layer of golden urns about a foot tall. On the floor, a triple row of pyramids with multiple faces were laden from base to summit with similar vessels. Each funerary vase bore a blue enamel plate in its central part, on which the name of the deceased was inscribed, the dates of his birth and death, his profession, the services he had been able to render to society by his works, and the actions by which he had distinguished himself.

"You can appreciate," said the doctor, suddenly, "what immense progress cremation has represented, from the triple viewpoint of public health, piety toward the dead and historical verity. This immense palace, which exceeds in extent and magnificence all the marvels that we have admired, can sumptuously lodge the remains of five million individuals. Enclosed in precious vases, incorruptible in their essence, these remains might last for centuries. Anyone can come to bow down here before his ancestors and follow with his gaze the ascending scale of his own genealogy. The historian surely finds material proofs for his works, and the living are no longer threatened at every moment by the pestilential vapors that cemeteries saturated with cadavers exhale without interruption.

"Of all the arguments put forward by the adversaries of incineration, the most singular, indubitably, is the one based on the impossibility of being able to carry out ulterior research is cases of poisoning. That idea was as absurd from the scientific viewpoint as the social. In the first place, the condition of the residues of combustion is, in the great majority of cases, eminently favorable to chemical analysis, and, in the second place, one cannot admit that cases of violent death are sufficiently frequent to justify endangering public health."

The travelers, who had been standing still thus far, advanced, grave and contemplative, and arrived at the far end of the gallery. To their left another room opened, equally vast and populous as the first. It bore the same dates.

"A lot of people died in the 28th century, then?" Gédéon queried.

"These two galleries," said Antius, "can only contain a quarter of the remains bequeathed by a century. "In our epoch, at least fourteen thousand people died in Paris every year, which is four million per century. We haven't yet seen a million funerary urns."

The travelers continued walking and went through three further halls as crowded as the first. They had covered three wings of the building and found themselves back at their departure point. The funeral procession of the previous century was entirely exhausted. The gallery they had just quit had even been invaded by the dead of the early years of the 29th century.

Slightly fatigued, the two scientists sank down on a divan backed up against the banisters.

"While you rest," said the young man, "I'll cast an eye over the upper parts of the edifice. I want to know whether all the floors are inhabited."

A few minutes later he came down again like an avalanche.

"It's packed to the rafters," he said, "and the higher you go, the more remote the epochs become." Slowly, he added: "I've found urns from the 20th century." He waited to see what effect his discovery had on the two scientists.

"That doesn't interest us directly," said Antius, simply.

"Yes, but it interests me—or might," Gédéon replied.

"Do you believe that your own ashes are up there, under the roof?" asked Terrier.

"Why not? We've seen stranger things. I'll come back."

"If the ashes of generations that immediately followed ours are enclosed on vases of precious metal," the doctor observed, "it's probable that they were put there subsequently, for gold was surely still very rare in the 20th century."

"The uniformity of the models," the physicist added, "is sufficient indication that expenses of that nature are met by the State."

"We can go downstairs if you want," Antius proposed. "We can have a look around the lower floor."

"I wouldn't be sorry to see the combustion apparatus," the physicist declared.

"For my part, I don't want much to," said Gédéon. "It would make my blood run cold."

The visitors went down to the ground floor. The interior courtyard was still as noisy as before.

In the vestibule, a man sitting on a marble bench was reading his newspaper attentively, savoring and enormous cigar. At the sight of the strangers, the smoker got up and headed toward them.

"I'm one of the wardens of the building, Monsieur," he said. "I greatly regret being absent when you arrived. I would have had the honor of accompanying you and giving you any directions that might have been useful to you."

"We thank you, Monsieur," Antius replied to the obliging individual. "We've gone around the whole first floor, and we're quite satisfied with our visit—but we'd be very grateful if you would tell us what the lower floors of the building contain."

"Messieurs," said the warden, "the left wing of the monument is divided into three large rooms intended for the urns of the present century. The first two are full and the third is ready to receive its guests. To the right is the library and the archive hall; the latter is specifically designed for historical research. Facing us is the hall of records of the inhabitants of Paris, including genealogies drawn up with great care. A few go back to the beginning of the 20th century."

"The incineration apparatus isn't here, then?" asked the physicist.

"No, Monsieur, the crematoria are ten leagues from the city. Bodies are transported there by balloon, and as soon as they have been reduced to ashes they are put in urns that are immediately sealed. We receive them once a week, and they're definitively placed and catalogued. I hope, Messieurs, that you will do me the honor of casting an eye over the records hall, which is my special responsibility."

"We accept with gratitude, Monsieur," said the doctor.

The warden advanced to the door that was facing them and opened its two battens, standing aside to let his guests through.

The travelers went into a richly ornamented room whose sides were hidden by four walls of richly-bound folio volumes. Every shelf bore an indicative letter that facilitated research. A vast table covered with a thick green velvet cloth and surrounded by armchairs was at the disposal of those who wanted to consult the precious documents.

The doctor could not help congratulating the warden on the admirable order that reigned in the splendid room. The functionary received the compliments with a modesty mingled with satisfaction.

The travelers made a tour of the room.

A few moments later, they thanked their cicerone and left the Necropolis, marveling at what they had seen.

XXVI. Insurance Tax

At six o'clock precisely, the strangers entered the school's main courtyard. Herber was waiting for them, sitting in the shade with a pamphlet in his hand. As usual, the schoolmaster asked about his guests' promenade.

The two scientists recounted all the details of the strange visit they had just made, and each expressed his admiration for the pious care that the living rendered to the dead.

"Incineration, Messieurs, as practiced today," said the schoolmaster, "connects all the links of the chain of the ages intimately. By its grace, no individual is forgotten absolutely; it creates a kind of historical immortality for the humblest as well as the most illustrious. Everyone can draw inspiration from the virtues or merits of his ancestors, however obscure they might have been.

"In spite of the evident superiority of the system—or, to be more respectful, the institution—it only became general in the 22nd century. Today it is adopted exclusively by all peoples and has entered so intimately into mores that those who are not familiar with history refused to admit that even in the distant past people could have consented to abandoning bodies to corruption by burying them in the soil.

"Respect for the dead in our epoch is such that there is no city in the entire world where the dwelling of those who are no more is not more magnificent than those of the living."

The parlor bell rang, and the four men headed for the dining room, where Madame Herber welcomed them with her charming smile.

During the meal, the sky became gradually cloudier, and as the diners were about to leave the table, a few precipitate flashes of lightning were illuminating the horizon. Soon, large drops of water began to fall on the terrace.

"Here's the rain at last," said Herber, with evident satisfaction, "and doubtless a cooler temperature."

"Is this atmospheric perturbation the result of disturbances determined last night in the upper atmosphere?" asked Antius.

"Undoubtedly," the schoolmaster replied, "and it rarely takes as long for the result to be produced."

The sky was becoming darker by the minute. Suddenly, the rain began to fall violently.

"This abrupt change in the weather, in the absence of any appreciable atmospheric current and any lowering of pressure must indeed by effected by local causes," declared the physicist.

The dry weather that has persisted for two months in our regions had worried the cultivators greatly," said Herber, and the decision was made by the Académie des Sciences' Meteorological Committee was not unconnected with those apprehensions."

"The government ought never to lose sight of such questions," remarked Antius, "for when the harvest is bad, tax returns inevitably fall."

"Tax returns?" said Herber.

"Of course. Doesn't everyone contribute to the expenses of State?"

"You mean insurance?"

"I don't know what you mean by that."

"Insurance covers all expenses of a general order," the schoolmaster replied. "It's obvious that the public Treasury, which flows out incessantly through two main arteries—education and public works—has to be alimented by the mass of citizens. That universal outflow is made up by means of variable premiums, paid regularly. In return, the State guarantees everyone not only efficacious protection and the rigorous maintenance of his rights, but also, in case of disaster occasioned by causes independent of his will, indemnifies the insured individual against any losses he might make and damages he might sustain.

"Each citizen's capital is therefore immovable—and by capital in this instance I mean all the forces of production. A scientist, for example, holds in his brain a capital as important as that of the millionaire, so his insurance premium is rather high. If old age, illness or some accident interrupts his work, the State immediately ensures his wealth. By means of that system, the artisan is sheltered from poverty, the capitalist from ruin.

"When he reaches old age, the worker no longer sees the phantom of poverty looming up ahead of him, for, from the day when the instrument of his labor becomes to heavy for him to bear, his insurance premium guarantees him an abundant existence of ease, honored until the end of his days.

"I beg you to observe how superior our economic system is to those which preceded it. It is honorable, because it constitutes an essential contract with society—a contract that begins with life and only concludes with death. It is equitable, for it is proportional to the interests engaged. Finally, it is based on a simple and true principle, for it is universally approved."

While concluding this speech Herber had advanced to the window and had darted a glance at the sky, the diluvian aspect of which was still becoming darker, in spite of the torrents of water that were falling relentlessly.

"Messieurs," he said, "We shall have rain until tomorrow. For this evening, to my great regret, we shall be forced to renounce those long twilight conversations that I find so pleasant and interesting."

A few minutes later the strangers, after having shaken hands with their host, went back to their apartment. They met in the doctor's room and discussed the following day's program.

At eleven o'clock Antius gave his companions to understand that the time had arrived to go to bed, giving the signal for retreat by picking up his majestic head-dress from his pillow. Considering this gesture as an injunction, Terrier and Gédéon immediately retired.

XXVII. A Model School

The next morning, the physicist, on opening his eyes, was surprised by the brightness of the sunlight playing upon his curtains.

"Bad weather doesn't last long here," he said, with satisfaction "Although the need for water makes itself keenly felt, my colleagues have sagely measured the dose. One is sometimes pleased to see rain arrive, but one always sees it disappear without regret."

With that aphorism, he got up without difficulty and immediately preceded with his toilette. As soon as he was ready he went to the doctor's room. He was about to knock lightly when the clock struck eight.

"If I'm not mistaken," he observed, my friend will just be getting up. Let's give him time to ply his razor." And he began a circular stroll around the vestibule.

At quarter past eight, he set a straight course for Antius' door and knocked.

The doctor came to open it, still sponging his face. "Bonjour, Terrier," he said. "I'm sure the same thoughts have been agitating us since we woke up."

"If you mean the two important events—the session of the Académie and our introduction to the Central African nabob—you're right," the professor replied.

"That's exactly what I was thinking about," declared Antus. "In the former case, we shall be playing the roles, you of the alchemist Basilius Valentinus[36] and me of Paracelsus,

---

[36] The numerous books attributed to the fifteenth-century alchemist Basilius Valentinus are almost certainly apocryphal, the earliest ones actually dating from the early seventeenth century. They include a volume on chemical experiments, one on antimony, one on azote (nitrogen) and one on metallurgical medicine.

witnessing an academic session at the end of the 19th century."

"Undoubtedly," the physicist replied, "but we've already seen so many astonishing things that we can now hear anything without peril.

"As for the second question, it's necessary to recognize that it's very grave, for, in spite of—or, rather, because of—the splendor of the hospitality we're receiving, we can't stay here for much longer."

Terrier nodded approvingly.

"But there's one considerable obstacle to success."

"What?"

"The impoverished personality of my nephew," said the doctor, gripping his interlocutor's arm. "What can be done with him?"

"Don't worry so much about me, if you please," answered a clear voice from the corridor—and the young man came in.

"We were just talking about you," said Antius.

"I know—but when you want to award me a qualification in your fashion, put a little more mystery into it. It's not necessary, in such cases, to let the entire neighborhood into your confidence."

"In any case, there'll be time to think about it if and when difficulties arise," Terrier remarked, whose character as a peacemaker was always manifest in such circumstances.

The travelers went downstairs.

As they set foot in the courtyard Herber, emerging from the opposite wing, came toward them at a rapid pace.

"Messieurs," said the schoolmaster, extending his hands toward the strangers, "I've just received our tickets for the solemn session of the Académie des Sciences."

The travelers thanked their host warmly.

"If I weren't retained by a few tasks that can't be put off," the schoolmaster continued, "I'd gladly accompany you in the stroll that you habitually take before breakfast, but we'll meet up again at table."

"I believe that the best use we could make of the two hours we have before us," Antius proposed, "is to devote them to a visit to the school buildings—if that wouldn't cause you any inconvenience, my dear Master."

"You're completely at home," said Herber. "I'll give you a guide."

"We thank you sincerely for the offer, but it's unnecessary. With your permission, we'll conduct the inspection alone, which will have all the charm of the unexpected."

"You're right, Doctor," Herber replied, smiling, and drew away.

The travelers headed for the central block, and went through it. Having gone up a short staircase they went through a large gallery and found themselves in the interior courtyard.

Shielded from the ardent rays of the sun by the ancient trees, they advanced toward the main building, whose grandiose architecture unfurled progressively before their eyes.

A profound silence reigned in the school.

"The Necropolis is far more animated," Gédéon murmured.

The arched bays of the gymnastics hall caught the young man's gaze, and he drew his companions toward the entrance door.

They went into an immense hall, in which the most varied and most ingenious items of apparatus were disposed in perfect order. At the back was the entrance to a hydrotherapy room.

When they left the gymnasium the travelers went into the central building, the ground floor of which was occupied by laboratories of physics, chemistry and the natural sciences, presently deserted. The abundance and quality of the instruments struck the physicist with admiration.

The travelers went up to the first floor and into a long gallery reserved for scientific collections. A few young people, occupied in drawing up catalogues or arranging displaycases, surprised by the arrival of the strangers, stopped work, bowed respectfully and maintained a perfect immobility while the visitors passed through.

When they left the edifice, Antius drew his companions toward the school library, a large room with a hemispherical vault, walled from top to bottom with technical works and cluttered with elliptical tables laden with atlases, relief maps and terrestrial and celestial globes of colossal dimensions.

Gédéon was attracted by an apparatus operated by a clockwork mechanism, which reproduced with the greatest accuracy the general movement of the planetary system, and stood their absorbed in its contemplation. In the meantime, the two scientists went around the room, inspecting the shelves.

Suddenly, the physicist reached out for a treatise on optics, and started reading it feverishly.

The doctor had discovered a dictionary of physiology, and, carried away by emotion, read the most interesting passages aloud.

The clock in the room, chiming half past ten, tore the young man away from his examination of the satellites of Jupiter. He hastened to warn his companions, who seemed to be equally absorbed in their research.

Regretfully, the two scientists left the room, where they could have reconstituted the chain of scientific progress, so abruptly broken off, year by year.

Five minutes later, they were back in the main building. As they set foot in the main courtyard they found themselves face to face with Herber, who was coming to meet them. While expressing their admiration for the size, the magnificence and the richness of the establishment they had just visited, the school's guests headed for the dining room with their host.

XXVII. The Académie des Sciences

At one o'clock in the afternoon, the travelers, accompanied by the schoolmaster, took their leave from the mistress of the house for the remainder of the day.

The schoolmaster, invited along with his friends by Guillaume Dryon, to whose home they would go on leaving the session of the Académie des Sciences, had warned Madame Herbert that they would not be returning to the school before midnight.

Charged with the most sympathetic good wishes, the four men went down to the Museum plaza and headed for the avenue that led to the Seine.

The torrid heat of the preceding days had diminished under the previous night's torrential rain and he air, mild and lukewarm, was embalmed by the emanations of flowers that had recovered all their freshness and brightness.

After walking for a quarter of an hour, the school's guests reached the bank of the river, whose waters were sparkling in the sunlight.

An electric carriage of colossal proportions came rapidly along the quay toward the travelers. It stopped abruptly at the end of the bridge and let off a few passengers. Before the driver had started the machine moving again, Herber and his companions had climbed the stairway to the upper deck and installed themselves comfortably there.

The vehicle pursuit its rapid course beneath the dense vault of the chestnut trees.

At times, the waters of the river glistened through gaps in the foliage.

An unusual crowd was moving downriver, and the name of the scientist Ho-wey-hu reached the ears of the travelers several times.

Gédéon, lulled by the gentle and flexible movement of the vehicle and gradually invaded by the penetrating perfume of the flowers, became drowsy.

"Today's session," said Herber, "will attract half of Paris into the vicinity of the session hall, for, in addition to the interest provoked in the public by scientific matters, there has been discussion for a month of the discovery of the president of the Honolulu Academy of Sciences. The curious, although they know that they will be unable to get into the building, will be enthusiastic to collect the results first hand."

"Can you not venture some hypothesis regarding the secret that your savant friend will reveal, my dear colleague?"

"No, for Ho-wey-hu, in fear of being troubled, either by criticisms or advice, has kept the nature of his work absolutely secret. However, as he is occupied with astronomy, physics and transcendent mechanics, it's probably to one of those three branches that we ought to attribute the invention that he's going to submit to us."

"Where in the city is the Institut situated?" the doctor asked, suddenly.

"At the end of the Pont des Arts, of course!" Gédéon replied, yawning with his eyes closed. "It was at the book-dealer's opposite that I set the Collardon story a few days ago that went so badly awry."

A furious kick from Antius recalled the sleeper to reality.

"What's up?" exclaimed Gédéon, jumping sideways. "Have we been derailed?"

"You're dreaming, my friend," said Antius, in a perfectly tranquil voice, while looking at his nephew with an irritated expression.

"I beg your pardon," said the young man, prudently drawing away from his guardian. Suddenly, he added: "I was, indeed, dreaming, for there's the crystal bridge." He pointed to a brilliant line cutting the horizon.

"The Institut, Doctor, is five hundred meters from the bridge and overlooks the Seine estuary," said the schoolmaster, attributing the young man's rambling to the incoherence of ideas that sometimes accompanies awakening.

A few minutes later they passed over the glass bridge, busy at that moment with a large number of citizens, the majority of whom were heading for the left bank.

A few minutes later, the electric vehicle arrived at its terminus. The wheels, suddenly imprisoned by their brakes, skidded for a few meters and the machine came to an abrupt stop.

The travelers got down. A few paces further on they left the shady pathway and a magical spectacle was suddenly offered to their gaze.

In front of them, surrounded by the high hills of the west, which formed a grandiose frame for it, streaming with verdure, gold and marble, the lake, as resplendent as a mass of molten silver, unfurled in its full extent.

To the left, behind a vast semicircle of grass, stood a palace of striking grandeur and magnificence.

"That's the Institut, Messieurs," said Herber.

In saying three days before that the palace of the five academies was the most magnificent in the city, the schoolmaster had been voicing an opinion whose exactitude was glaringly obvious. Established on a platform, the palace, constructed in white marble, adopted the form of the arc of a circle and presented, over an extent of several hundred meters, an advanced entablature, sustained by a file of Corinthian columns of admirable effect. The fronton of the monument, sculpted in relief along its entire extent, bore at its center a magnificent statue of Science, surrounded by allegorical symbols.

An innumerable quantity of busts representing the illustrious individuals whose work had contributed to general wellbeing stood out over the façade. The cupola, high and superb, covered with bronzed aluminum with gleams of azure, was constellated with thick moldings of pure gold representing scientific attributes.

A compact crowd was going up the steps of a monumental staircase that extended to the main door.

Herber snatched his companions from their contemplation and headed toward the building with them. The four men joined the stream of the elect and went into a vast vestibule, at the back of which the door to the session hall opened.

The schoolmaster presented the tickets to an usher, who, abandoning the people surrounding him, bowed respectfully and invited the visitors to follow him.

When they reached the landing, the guide headed for a circular corridor, the door to which, carefully closed, he opened. At the end of the corridor, the usher lifted the curtain of a reserved box and stood aside, inviting Herber and his guests to take possession of it.

On going into the enclosure, already overflowing with spectators, the travelers were struck with admiration by the majestic aspect of the hall.

The part reserved for the public, semi-circular in shape, was ornamented with marvelous artistry and organized with a perfect intelligence of the laws of acoustics.

The stage was presently occupied by the entire academic body. Seated on a kind of elevated throne, his hand resting on a table covered with drapes, the president of the Académie des Sciences, an old man full of majesty, overlooked a rich and elegant podium reserved for speakers.

As two o'clock chimed on the palace clock, the president struck a golden bell and a solemn silence was suddenly imposed on the entire assembly. A secretary climbed up to the chair and deposited a few documents in front of the august individual who was in charge of the session. The latter, after a rapid inspection, stood up and, addressing the titular members whose gazes converged upon him, began speaking.

"Messieurs," he said, "because of the important discovery that the illustrious president of the Academy of Science of the Sandwich Islands is to submit to us, we have been obliged to postpone until a later session a few reports that have been lodged in recent days. However, we ought to mention the magnetic observations that have been made this month at the North Pole station."

The physicist and the doctor looked at one another in amazement.

"It is well-known that the observatory established for hundred years ago at the extremity of the terrestrial axis has rendered great services to the general physics of the globe and to astronomical observation. Our forefathers, convinced of the importance of the conquest of the pole, but only able to dispose of primitive means of locomotion, tried in vain to cross the inviolable barrier of eternal ice, and the bones of many martyrs of science whitened in the ice-fields of the boreal world. Let us conserve a pious memory of them.

"For four months, the observers at the polar station have seen the sun describing circles parallel to the horizon without interruption. That confused light constitutes for some a sufficiently wearisome anomaly for them to anticipate impatiently the long six-month night that will commence for them with the autumnal equinox.

"The temperature of the interior sea, the existence of which stimulated so much controversy at the beginning of the modern era, is about ten degrees; that of the atmosphere has reached fourteen. I will add that, in accordance with the wishes of some scientific bodies, the material establishment of the origin of the meridians over an extent of two hundred meters is now an accomplished fact.

"I cannot leave in the shade the remarkable work that the South American Academy of Science has undertaken in the immense plain of the Pampas. The idea of establishing powerful luminous sources on the surface of the ground, disposed in geometrical shapes, in order to provoke the attention of observers on Mars and Venus and to convince them that the Earth is inhabited by intelligent beings, goes back to the 19th century, but only provoked irony in that obscure era, which invariably attempted to stifle all great inventions at their outset.[37] The following centuries, however, more enlightened, opposed a deadlier weapon to it: indifference.

"Today, that audacious conception has been realized. Immense electric beams, departing from a territory of three thousand six hundred square myriameters, is in the process of construction, and the scale of signals has been carefully elaborated. We shall be informed of the precise timetable of experiments, the results of which will be awaited with excitement by the entire world.

"I must now give the floor to our honored colleague Howey-hu. That scientist is ready to reveal to you the famous endeavor which, by reason of its mysterious character and the high renown of the inventor, has attracted everyone's attention for some time."

At these words, a tremor ran through the assembly. At a sign from the president, a rich curtain covering the back wall of the hemicycle was drawn by two ushers, and an old man whose imposing visage bore the sublime imprint of genius advanced slowly toward the stage.

A double salvo of applause greeted his entrance.

At the invitation of the president, the illustrious scientist climbed the steps to the podium. Having arrived in front of the public, the inventor bowed profoundly and began to speak.

"Messieurs," he said, "the principle of scientific conquest, which I have pursued almost exclusively during the most active period of my existence, and the results of which I am permitted to submit to you today, goes back to the period of alchemy, that strange science devoid of method or foundation, which was born of vague scientific conceptions brought back from the Orient on the return from the crusades.

---

[37] Charles Cros first outline this scheme in a lecture delivered at Camille Flammarion's salon in May 1869; the paper was subsequently published in the periodical *Cosmos*, and then as a pamphlet. It is frequently featured in 19th century French futuristic fiction.

"For three or four hundred years, the secrets of alchemy were the province of a few audacious minds wandering in the absurd, whose disordered researches nevertheless rendered great services to the methodical and rational chemistry that flourished at the end of the 18th century. Above all, the alchemists pursued, under the name of the Great Work, a particular instance of the transformation of matter. They were defeated by that redoubtable problem. It is a problem of which today's science is the master."

A formidable salvo of prolonged applause greeted these words.

"Messieurs," the orator continued, "I would not have undertaken my endeavors if, from the start, I had not been able to take as a point of support a discovery that illuminated the end of the 19th century: *radiant matter*.

"We are all familiar with the celebrated discovery of Monsieur Crookes, whose efforts were particularly devoted to the study of the mysterious forces that govern matter. The physicist in question, whose work sometimes brought into evidence seemingly contradictory phenomena, the source of ardent controversy, succeeded in establishing that gases, reduced to a state of almost absolute rarefaction and submitted to the influence of negative electricity, suddenly became endowed with an intense activity and produced extraordinary luminous and calorific effects.[38]

---

[38] William Crookes' "Crookes tube," first developed in 1869, was an electric discharge tube in which "cathode rays"—subsequently revealed to be streams of electrons—were produced. The phenomenon of fluorescence had already been produced in "Geissler tubes" in 1857, which were only partially evacuated, and in which an electric current flowing through the tube caused various gases to glow (as in a neon light); they were mass-produced in the 1880s as playthings. Calvet had no way of knowing that the term "radiant matter" would acquire a new meaning in the late 1890s with the discovery of radioactivity by Henri Becquerel. He would presumably have men-

"The matter thus dissociated was subsequently identified with the *cosmic*, or *primordial* state of elementary matter. All substances being formed of a unique, simple and identical matter—a verity suspected since the 19th century—and the return to the cosmic state having become possible, a capital problem arose: the reconstitution of substances according to the laws presiding over their formation. That is the research that has absorbed me for thirty years, and I can affirm today that with the exclusive source of nitrogen, returned to the state of radiant matter at a pressure of one hundred and twentieth of an atmosphere, I have been able to create all the simple substances known to this day."

A frenetic thunder of applause responded to this declaration by the illustrious physicist.

At the same time, for laboratory assistants came into the hemicircle and deposited on a long elliptical table set up in front the academicians a long series of bottles full of gas, pulverized matter and sparkling crystals.

The products, after being submitted successively to the president of the assembly and the academic body, were passed from hand to hand by the public.

Ho-wey-hu had climbed up to sit down in the place of honor reserved for him to the right of the president, and modestly received the congratulations that his colleagues came in turn to offer him.

At the end of the memorable session, the Académie des Sciences unanimously adopted the following resolutions:

Item One. The illustrious scientist Ho-wey-hu, President of the Academy of Sciences of Honolulu, is a great credit to humankind.

Item Two. The Institut de France considers as an honor the first communication of the great discovery of the transformation of matter.

---

tioned Abel Niepce Saint-Victor's "pre-discovery" of that phenomenon in 1857 had he known about it, but hardly anyone did.

Item Three. The Académie des Sciences confers the title of honorary member on the inventor.

Item Four. A special committee will be set up immediately to examine the endeavor.

XXIX. The Palace of Opulence

Four o'clock was chiming as Herber and his guests came down the monumental stairway of the Institut. Having extracted themselves, with some difficulty, from the immense crowd that extended from the threshold of the edifice al the way to the quay, the travelers, guided by the schoolmaster, went into the avenue that overlooked the lake and followed its shore.

"It's time, Messieurs, to go to Guillaume Dryon's palace, which is situated a few hundred meters from here," said the schoolmaster. "I told him that we would arrive at half past four."

After walking along the shore for five minutes, the strangers and their guide turned into a vast avenue lined by a quadruple row of enormous trees, whose branches overlapped ten meters above the ground and formed a vault impenetrable to the sun's rays. An artificial stream, swiftly flowing and as clear as crystal, ran alongside the entire extent of the pathway, of an incomparable charm and splendor.

The travelers were wonderstruck. For five minutes Gédéon had been reeling off an exceedingly pompous dithyramb about the beauty of the landscape, when he was interrupted by the schoolmaster, who said: "Messieurs, we have arrived."

He turned right; his companions followed him. Twenty paces further on he stopped and, with evident satisfaction, displayed a magnificent palace, which stood beyond a gently-sloping flower bed decorated with infinite artistry. He continued walking, escorting his guests to the threshold of the edifice.

A man of grave and dignified appearance, who appeared to be waiting for the visitors, suddenly emerged from the vestibule and came to bow to them respectfully.

"Monsieur Dryon is in the park at present, waiting for these Messieurs," the individual aid. "I shall have the honor of taking them to him."

"Thank you for your benevolent offer, Master Steward, but we can easily find the master of the house ourselves," Herber replied.

The steward bowed. The four men went through the vestibule. At the back of the entrance hall, a cyclopean stairway of unpolished marble leaden with sculptures and vases overflowing with rare flowers led up to the first floor. The schoolmaster and the strangers went into a broad lateral corridor whose depth seemed infinite.

After twenty paces the visitors turned left and found themselves in a doorway as high and wide as a cathedral porch.

A magical scene unfolded before their eyes.

An immense park, in which all the marvels of nature and art were accumulated, extended before them. The rarest plants of the tropical zone formed entire thickets there. In the background, a large sheet of water, falling like a compact mass from a height of thirty feet, flowed into the garden in two sinuous streams, resplendent in the rays of the setting sun. A ring of giant trees, originally from the highlands of Central Africa, formed a majestic frame for the marvelous scene.

After a few moments of mute contemplation, the strangers, preceded by the schoolmaster, went down on to the lawn that extended before them, and, after having crossed a white marble bridge, advanced along the central pathway.

At the sound of their footsteps, a tall man of imposing aspect sitting on a grassy bank with his back against a giant cedar slowly rose to his feet and came toward them.

"Here's our host," said Herber, in a low voice.

On recognizing the schoolmaster, Guillaume Dryon's noble face lit up with a smile. He greeted the strangers benevolently.

"Messieurs," he said to them, "I'm both gladdened and honored by your visit, and I'm enormously grateful to my dear friend Herber for the idea of putting me in touch with you."

"These Messieurs," the schoolmaster replied, "are originally from Oceania. Paying a first visit to our country, of which they have studied the scientific progress and social condition for a long time, they were initially lost on arriving in Paris. A fortuitous incident brought them to my abode. Every day I have been able to appreciate the elevation of their character and the depth of their knowledge. As the pursuit of their mission seems constantly to preoccupy their minds, I thought that they would find in your vast collections and library the elements they require. They would be glad, at the same time, to repay your generosity by collaborating with your scientific endeavors."

"Your friends are mine," replied Guillaume Dryon, extending his hand to the strangers. "I've read with great interest the magnificent lectures they gave on the 19th century and would be honored to count men of such profound erudition among the dearest guests of my house. I will ask them right now, as an enormous favor, to undertake the temporary direction of the African museums I have recently built, from which my work increasingly takes me away."

Antius took the floor and, in terms that were both warm and elevated, he expressed his gratitude and that of his friends.

Guillaume Dryon led his guests to a belvedere elevated by a few meters, from which the gaze could embrace the entire extent of the marvelous Eden that surrounded them. Several armchairs were distributed in the shade. In response to the invitation of the master of the house, everyone sat down.

The conversation turned to politics. At the doctor's request, the Parisian delegate to the Estates General gave a summary account of the latest session of the European parliament. In detailing one by one the various questions that had been considered, Dryon showed that he possessed an indisputable authority on all the relevant matters.

The orator then established an eloquent comparison between the political institutions of old Europe and those of the African federal states. He was able to demonstrate to his listeners that the men designated by their fellow citizens for the regulation of public affairs had only one objective: incessant progress, from both the double viewpoint of the material and the moral.

The conversation was interrupted by the solemn approach of a majordomo, who announced that several guests had already arrived.

Guillaume Dryon got up and headed for the palace, followed by his guests. He took them into a vast summer room hung with colorful fabrics and furnished with exquisite taste. A dozen people were already gathered there. Among them, four young ladies dressed with extreme elegance were plying their fans with consummate artistry.

The host went to present his respects to them first. Having then offered his hand to each of the illustrious individuals who surrounded him, he introduced the strangers as guests of the palace.

At that moment a tapestry curtain was raised, and a dazzling vision struck every gaze.

A young woman of sovereign beauty, bearing in her visage the imprint of grace, generosity and intelligence, advanced toward the visitors and bowed to them gracefully.

"My Daughter Éva," said Guillaume Dryon to the travelers, not without a hint of parental pride.

Then he introduced the strangers to the young woman. Mademoiselle Dryon greeted them with a charming smile.

Gédéon seemed momentarily petrified by admiration. Suddenly, he gripped Terrier's arm. "That divine creature's large phosphorescent eyes have struck me like a thunderbolt," he whispered.

The professor who had only ever gazed tenderly at his scientific instruments, shrugged his shoulders.

At the request of the master of the house, the doctor and the physicist came to offer their arms, the former to Mademoiselle Éva and the latter to one of the young ladies in front of him, and the guests set off for the dining room. The two scientists marched at the head of the column with an entirely academic dignity.

The table, decked with rare flowers, sparkled with the glitter of crystal and gold.

The splendor of the feast could not tear the young man away from the thoughts that were agitating him. Seated next to his uncle, he could not take his eyes off the charming young woman. Nevertheless, the meal continued in the midst of a general animation and gaiety.

When all the culinary marvels had disappeared in their turn from the sumptuous table of the modern Lucullus, a magnificent dessert, in which the most admirable fruits of the five continents were grouped in pyramids, was set out before the guests.

A few moments later, in response to the host's invitation, he guests went into a vast and magnificent drawing-room, whose high windows opened on to a terrace from which the gaze embraced the marvelous panorama of the garden.

The young woman served everyone a damascened platinum cup full of exquisite coffee.

"Would the ladies like to hear a little music?" asked Dryon, amicably.

"Certainly," the young women replied, in unison. "For a week, no one in Paris has been talking about anything except the marvelous instrument you've had constructed."

The other guests approved the proposal.

Terrier pulled a face. The sincere antipathy that they experienced for music bound the professor and his former pupil together; they retired to the furthest corner of the room.

At a signal from Éva, a rectangular box of medium dimensions was placed on the table.

"A simple spinet," said Gédéon to the physicist. "It's more annoying than injurious. I'm astonished, by the way, that you, who have such a highly-developed observational temperament, haven't been struck by a very apparent singularity."

"What do you mean?"

"You observed the doubtless insincere delight with which the guests welcomed our host's artful proposition. Well, look at them now. They've all prudently drawn as far away from the instrument as possible. They're all lined up along the wall; none of them has remained in the middle of the room to swallow the pill requested with so much enthusiasm."

Eva approached the box, applied a slight pressure to an ivory disk, and returned to sit down with the young ladies.

All gazes turned toward the mysterious apparatus.

Suddenly, a long and profound chord, such as might result from the simultaneous vibration of thirty sonorous harps, filled the room. Soon, an imposing group of violins and cellos came to participate in the symphony, embroidering a suave melody over the bass accompaniment.

Gradually, all the brass, woodwind and percussion instruments of the orchestra irrupted into the concert, and in the midst of a magisterial forte, everyone experienced precisely the impression that an orchestra of a hundred musicians might make, functioning with an irreproachable regularity and mastery.

Admiration was painted on all faces, and when the principal melody had been drawn energetically into a triumphant scherzo, all hands clapped frantically.

"That," said the physicist, "is the cleverest thing I've ever heard, in this world and the next."

"As we're alone," Gédéon added, "you can say the most extraordinary and the most admirable."

"I agree—but what movements can be engendering such vibrations?" The professor became pensive.

Several guests got up and came to surround Dryon, asking him for an explanation of the marvelous instrument.

"Messieurs," the host said, in a loud voice, "I'd already seen an instrument similar to that, although much less complete, at Ujiji. I had the idea of seeking a few distractions in the construction of an apparatus that would produce the maximum sonority in the minimum volume. After a few days of

259

study I gave a skillful technologist a detailed plan, which was executed with the greatest perfection."

"As a generator, I adopted electricity. Some of the strings are moved by plucking, activated by electromagnets, others by short bows, solid wires acting at the same time on tightly-packed rows of the same pitch. The woodwind and brass instruments owe their vibration to the expansion of compressed air contained in receptacles of various caliber. Finally, the percussion instruments are controlled by clockwork. The whole functions under the direction of a cylinder rotating about its axis, on which the music is engraved in metallic studs that regulate the action of the current."

Everyone congratulated the inventor, and the compliments of the three strangers were as enthusiastic as they were sincere.

Darkness was beginning to fall. Mademoiselle Dryon got up and went to the central table. After parting the cloth slightly she pressed an ivory button controlling a metallic contact. Suddenly, six luminous globes in the ceiling lit up.

By popular demand, the electric organ played a second symphony, which had the same success as the first.

A few moments later, two young women came into the drawing room carrying large gilded trays laden with perfumed ices.

Gédéon, intoxicated for the first time by music, had fallen back under the empire of his reverie and had his head in the clouds again. He went out on the terrace.

The scene he had before his eyes was striking. At the back of the park, the cascade was unrolling a sheet of molten silver. In the midst of warm vapors the moon was rising slowly over the horizon. The evening breeze was gently agitating the foliage.

The young man's thoughts, stimulated by the magnificence of nature, underwent an abrupt explosion. "My God, how beautiful she is!" he exclaimed, raising his arms toward the heavens.

Antius, who had noticed his absence, had set out to look for him and had soon caught up with him. At that moment he was standing still behind his nephew. Surprised by the exclamation he had just heard, he looked upwards and, fixing his eyes on the moon, replied: "That's not my opinion—I think she looks rather shabby."

"Shabby! Do you hear that, heavens?"

"Yes, she's rather dull."

"Dull! O sacrilege!"

Is he mad? Antius though, anxiously *Does the night star really have a pernicious influence on sick minds?* "Are you in love?" he asked, ironically.

"Yes, I love her! I can no longer keep within my heart the secret that's stifling it."

"Oh, you fool!" said the doctor, putting his hands over his eyes.

"Yes, I love her, and I'm dying of it. You're the only one who can save my life."

"What can I do, my poor child?" asked the scientist, emotionally.

"Ask for her hand on my behalf," said the young man, in an oppressed voice, without ceasing to stare at the sky.

"My God, have pity on us! But to who am I to address a request for her hand?"

"To her father, who is so good, so great and so generous."

"What, you triple idiot!" exclaimed Antius seizing his nephew by the arm angrily. "You want me to make a marriage request to the father of the moon for you?"

"Who mentioned the moon, you gutless individual? It's a matter of the adorable and the adored Éva."

"In that case, my lad," the doctor replied, coldly, "you're even madder than I thought." And he went back into the drawing room.

XXX. Fatal Resolutions. A Thunderbolt

An hour later, after having bid farewell to their host, the guests left the sumptuous dwelling. As the strangers were leaving, the agronomist had asked them to come back the following morning to sit down at his table, for, the departure being imminent, he needed to make a few urgent arrangements with them.

Herber took his friends back to the school. During the return journey the doctor was somber and pensive. Gédéon was walking like a body devoid of a soul. Only the schoolmaster and the physicist exchanged a few reflections regarding the future.

As the clocks were striking midnight, they arrived in the main courtyard. The schoolmaster shook the strangers' hands emotionally, wished them good night and headed for his apartment.

Scarcely had the door closed on their generous host than the doctor, his arms folded, planted himself in front of the physicist. "Do you know, Terrier, what terrible danger threatens us just as we're about to come into harbor?" he said, dully.

"No," said the professor, anxiously.

You shall. This evening, I surprised this great imbecile gazing at the sky and moaning as if he were being led to the scaffold."

"Was he ill?"

"I wish to God he were! I'd a thousand times rather see him prey to all the maladies catalogued in a textbook of pathology, ancient as well as modern, than have to observe the frightful case of aberration in which he finds himself. In a word, he's presently under the influence of the infection that's not only the most stupid and the most inadmissible, but the most dangerous for him and for us. He's in love."

"Uh oh, my former pupil," said the professor, in a tone of profound commiseration, looking his disciple up and down.

"And who do you think has turned his poor head? I could give you ten years to guess it, but I prefer to tell you right away: Mademoiselle Dryon!"

"Antius," the physicist replied, with imperturbable calm, "I wouldn't have taken ten years to guess that. And in truth, she is charming."

"You're supporting him?" exclaimed the exasperated doctor. "Are you going to be his accomplice. Or has the young woman turned your head upside down as well?"

"If such a dementia ever took possession of me," Terriier replied, "the principal cataract of Niagara Falls wouldn't be an adequate shower to treat my madness. I could say the same of you, Antius, and *a fortiori*, for you're older than me. But I think you're wrong to be alarmed. Without being an expert in such matters, I'd gladly believe that our young man will be the first to laugh at this nonsense tomorrow. Let's go to bed."

Gédéon follow them mechanically.

Half an hour later, the two scientists were sleeping the sleep of the just, while the young man, lying on a divan, was devoting himself to the laborious construction of castles in Spain. Gradually, however, his head became heavy and he ended up falling asleep.

His slumber was continually agitated by a sequence of visions, sometimes delightful and sometimes terrible.

At one moment, he saw himself, after overcoming a thousand difficulties, leading young Éva to the church, holding her respectfully by the hand. The future spouses were followed by an imposing cortege, formed of members of the Institut and delegates to the European parliament, invited in their entirety by his father-in-law.

Fifty paces in front of them, the electric organ, carried by a compressed-air-driven locomotive, was playing a triumphal march.

Suddenly, a monstrous crocodile, which was somehow reminiscent of his uncle, precipitated itself between the bride and groom, and everything vanished into thin air.

Bathed in a cold sweat, the young man sat up on his elbow. His features expressed suffering and despair.

He remained motionless and pensive for a long time.

Suddenly, he raised his head sharply. "If I have to continue to live like yesterday and sleep like last night," he said, aloud, "I'd rather put an end to it."

After a moment's reflection, he continued: "That's decided. I have to cut the thread of my days myself. Why hesitate? Have I not lived long enough? There are only two men in the world who will have had a longer life than mine, and I'll occupy a very honorable rank in Deparcieux's tables.[39] Alas, if only I'd had the foresight to invest my wealth in an annuity way back when, I could have ruined thirty insurance companies—which would be rather meritorious.

"As for my funeral oration, I'm tranquil. Monsieur Terrier is here, and I know, for having seen him at work, how good he is at expanding on the real or imaginary virtues of deceased individuals.

"Of course, for the last day of my life, I need a certain method. I'll go to the Necropolis to choose my place. I don't want to be eternally lodged between a poet and a man of law. As for the cause of death, I'm spoiled for choice."

Proud of his determination and comparing himself to Brutus, he went to the window and activated a spring that caused the shutters to fly open. It was broad daylight. At that moment, the clock struck five. The weather was magnificent.

"The first time I salute the dawn, the situation lacks gaiety," he said, in a bitter tone. And he reflected for a quarter of an hour, his eyes lost in space.

---

[39] The mathematician Antoine Deparcieux published a classic *Essai sur les probabilités de la durée de la vie humaine*, calculating life expectancies on the basis of empirical data, in 1746, and an augmented version in 1760. His data was subsequently used by others for the calculation of annuities in the insurance industry.

"No hesitation!" he exclaimed, suddenly, straightening up. "I shan't walk, I shall run toward death."

He went to the door, put his hand on the knob, and stopped. *It would be extremely impolite*, he thought, *to make the final voyage without leaving my companions a few well-chosen words.*

And he marched straight to an encrusted ebony writing-desk, took out two large sheets of paper ornamented with academic symbols, and, after reflecting momentarily, filled them both, one after the other, with letters half an inch high.

He went out into the corridor quietly and, with the aid of two golden pins, fixed one to the physicist's door and the other to the doctor's.

The first read:

Adieu, my dear professor. I am departing for a better world. If you say a few words over my coffin, don't forget to mention that I once won a silver medal in the boat races at Le Havre.

The second bore the following sentence in a feverish hand:

Uncle, it's you who have cast me into the tomb, or rather the urn. I bequeath you eternal remorse. If ghost is anything but a vain word, I'll save you a few nights, on which you can give me news.

Having cast a final glance of satisfaction over the manuscripts, he went down to the courtyard and into the square.

The immense plaza was absolutely deserted. The silence was only troubled by the murmur of fountains and morning bird-song.

"How beautiful nature is!" he said, with a sigh.

Fearing that his resolve might be weakened by the spectacle that he had before him, he hastened his step. Having arrived in front of the palace of death he shivered.

That happens to the bravest, he thought.

In the vestibule he was surprised by the profound silence that reigned in the edifice.

Suddenly, he slapped her forehead. "I swore to visit the uppermost floor, in order to see whether I could find any acquaintances there," he said. And he started climbing the great staircase at a measured pace.

Having arrived at the very top, he found himself facing a door above which the words *20th century* were painted in gold letters.

"This is it!" he murmured, and went in.

Following the order of the dates with his gaze, he went slowly along the gallery, reading the inscriptions.

Suddenly, he uttered a loud cry, and nearly fell over. Before his eyes, on the enamel of an urn set at shoulder height, shone the two words: GÉDÉON CAHUSAC.

"O Providence," he said, "You've reserved a spectacle for me that no other mortal has ever been able to enjoy. I may shed a few tears over my mortal remains." And his eyelids became moist.

He drew nearer to the vase.

"It's made of gold like all the rest," he said. "That's a consolation. Great God, what's this? A Notice!"

And he read avidly, on the pedestal of the urn, the following information: *Genealogy of the Cahusacs. Hall of Records, Section K2, page 1237.*

Gédéon turned round, shot through the gallery like an arrow and ran downstairs, taking the steps four at a time. He crossed the vestibule in two bounds, violently shoved back the door to the hall that he had visited the previous day with the two scientists, and, marching hesitantly, ran his eyes over the indications engraved on the spines of the enormous registers.

"There it is!" he cried, and launched himself toward a folio marked with a magisterial K.

The book, snatched out violently, fell heavily into his arms, nearly knocking him over. The young man ran to the table, deposited his treasure thereon, and turned the pages rapidly.

When he arrived at page 1237 he read, dazedly, the name:

NICOLAS PLATEAU, *Maître des requêtes au Conseil d'État.*

"They're mistaken," he said, in a pained tone. "And to think that I wept over the ashes of a jurisconsultant. Oh, bureaucracy!"

And he pushed the enormous volume away angrily.

The closed folio displayed to his eye the number 1, an inch high, which he had not noticed in his haste.

A ray of hope illuminated his face, and he launched himself toward the wall again. "Finally, I have it!" he cried, coming back carrying another register—and he consulted the book, feverishly.

When the indicated page was displayed before his eyes, he shuddered as he read his own name, framed within a cartouche ornamented by elegant vignettes.

Below it was written, in a fine slanted and rounded hand, the following genealogy:

ACHILLE-GÉDÉON CAHHUSAC, *son of* PIERRE-ANDRÉ CAHUSAC *and* JULIE-ANTOINETTE ANTIUS, *honorable notary, born 22 September 1856, died 25 October 1928.*

"Notary!" he exclaimed, fearfully. "That's a good one! Let's go on, I might as well have a good laugh before I die."

Husband of ALEXANDRINE-DOROTHÉE DESI-FLARD.

"Oh! They want to prevent my suicide by making me choke with laughter," he said, beating the table with his fists and abandoning himself to a fit of joy that lasted for five minutes and must have astonished the severe echoes of the funereal hall he was in. "Dorothée! The only daughter of our neighbor and friend the notary Desiflard," he went on. "Dorothée, who was always revealing to me mother my most ingenious methods of playing truant, and whose ears I boxed, in revenge, when I found her on her own! Dorothée, who, ten years later, permitted herself to talk about me in front of a schoolfriend in the following terms: 'That great imbecile has already squandered three quarters of his fortune!' My God, give me the strength to go on to the end."

When he was relatively calm again he continued reading, aloud:

SYLVAIN-THÉODORE CAHUSAC, *son of* ACHILLE-GÉDÉON CAHUSAC *and* ALEXANDRINE-DOROTHÉE DESIFLARD.

"Dorothée! Théodore!" he thought, aloud. "In Greek, that means the same thing; it's a logical choice of name."

Celebrated geographer and explorer, to whom is owed the first accurate map of the upper reaches of the Congo.

"An explorer, that's what I'd have liked to be," he murmured. "As for the title of geographer, the Academy that conferred that on me would have been giving proof of great benevolence."

While the young man continued the minute study, his face sometimes darkened and sometimes lit up; once, he clapped his hands in joy when his eyes fell upon one of his descendants described thus:

JÉROME-ANDRÉ CAHUSAC, *celebrated mariner of the 23rd century. Forced the north-west passage with three ships of heavy tonnage.*

"That's rather juicy," said Gédéon. "There's only one shadow—the name Jérome, which I don't like, primarily because it belongs to my uncle. Still, the name Cahusac wipes that out. All in all, it's a worthy conclusion to the series. What's this footnote?

"The captain of the vessel Cahusac having only left a daughter, the direct descendancy changes its name. Similar transformations occurred in the 17th, 21st, 25th and 29th generations.

"All those people don't matter to me—let's skip to the last family," the reader declared, turning the page.

On reading the name that was at the foot of the column, he uttered a terrible cry and fell backwards, in a faint. One the penultimate line, in large letters, was the name and titles of:

CONSTANTIN-GUILLAUME DRYON, *member of the Institut, celebrated agronomist, opulent proprietor of the central plateau of equatorial Africa, member of the European parliament, founder and honorary president in perpetuity of the Universal Expositions of Ujiji, Zanzibar, Magdala, Kazeh and Timbuktu, administrator of the circular railways of Tanganyika and Bangouelo, creator of the Continental African Bank, etc.*

And below it:

AURORE-ÉVA DRYON, *daughter of* CONSTANTIN-GUILLAUME DRYON and LAURE-HENRIETTE BONHEUR.

XXXI. Expansive Testimonies

The young man, whose unconsciousness had lasted for twenty minutes, was recalled to life by a particularly disagreeable sensation.

He opened his eyes and abruptly closed them again—but he had had time to recognize that he had been carried into the courtyard of the mausoleum, and set down near the monumental fountain. There, the curator of the Archives was supporting him with one hand and emptying a carafe of cold water over his face with the other.

As the benevolent functionary reached out to fill his receptacle from the basin again, the patient leapt to his feet.

"One ration is sufficient for me, thank you very much," he said. "How did I get here?"

"Monsieur," the hydropath replied, softly, "I found you in my office, fainted, and I carried you here in order to bring you round. Nothing is as efficacious in such cases as cold water."

"I agree." said the resuscitated individual. "But...hang on..." He put his hand to his forehead, and, suddenly recovering his memory, he set off toward the plaza at a run.

"There's a fellow who's very ill, and whom we'll soon be bringing back," murmured the curator, shaking his head.

To the great amazement of the strollers, Gédéon increased his speed with every stride. When he arrived at the central pyramid he was out of breath. Seven o'clock was chiming at that moment on the side of the monolith.

He stopped.

"Let's moderate our pace a little," he said, "for two reasons. Firstly, I have plenty of time to get there before my two companions get up, whose existence is regulated like a compensating pendulum, and who will get out of bed today, as on every other day, at eight o'clock precisely. Secondly, and more importantly, things have changed henceforth. I'm incontestably the great-grandparent on Éva's great-grandparents, and the gambols of a hind in the woods are scarcely appropriate to that unexpected dignity. From now on, the graces of the suitor must give way to the gravity of the arch-ancestor."

And he resumed walking at a measured pace.

Having arrived at the school, he thought he ought to climb the great staircase at a heavy and weary pace. He went alone the balustrade, leaning on it, in order to conform to the attitude that was now appropriate to him. Before the steps that led to the apartment of the two scientists, however, the old man recovered his strength, and hurtled up to the upper floor at top speed.

Scarcely had he reached the corridor than he stretched out his arms and swiftly detached the two testamentary formulas. He folded them in four and slipped them into his pocket. Then, launching himself toward the physicist's door, he started knocking furiously.

"Monsieur Terrier!" he shouted. "Come and open up! I have something prodigious to tell you. If you don't want to fall over, gather up your self-composure."

The professor, rudely snatched from his slumber, sat up on his elbow and, recognizing the voice of his former pupil, murmured: "What's the meaning of all this racket? Has Antius' prognosis been realized?"

Meanwhile, the doctor, woken up with a start, said, for his part: "That's it. I'll have to ask Herber where the nearest sanitarium is." Leaping out of bed, he put on his slippers, threw his dressing-gown over his shoulders, and headed for the door, which he flung open.

At the sight of his uncle, coiffed in his sumptuous cotton bonnet, which had already attracted the physicist's admiration, the young man, gripped by a bizarre idea, leapt upon the respectable scientist and, seizing him in his arms, forced him to participate, reluctantly, in a most extraordinary choreographical exercise.

Antius, dragged away in a rapid whirl, uttered loud cries, in which anger and terror alternated their dominance.

"Terrier!" he shouted. "Come and get me out of this madman's hands! He's doubtless trying to kill me. Arm yourself with whatever comes to hand."

The physicist suddenly appeared, in his shirt-sleeves, waving an enormous water-jug in a threatening manner

At the sight of that, Gédéon stopped, propping his uncle up against the wall. "Thanks," he said, "But I've already had one rather energetic shower this morning—that's sufficient for me.

"What are you shaking me like that for, savage?" the doctor complained.

"Savage? Moderate your expressions, if you please. Do you know who you're talking to?"

"This is too much!" cried Antius. "He's completely mad, and I'll get him a padded cell of exceptional solidity."

"Uncle," the young man riposted, coldly, "you and your colleagues would gladly lock up half the human race. I tell you that I'm not mad, and that, if I've cut a few capers in your company—which, after all, has nothing condemnable about it—it's because, this very day, I've made a discovery that might well cause you to lose your reason yourself when I reveal it to you. But let's all go back into your room, in order that we can talk calmly, if you please."

"If you come into my room," Antius declared, "I'll slice your jugular with one of my razors."

"Let's go into Monsieur Terrier's, then."

"Thanks," said the physicist. "I received my room in good condition, and I want to return it the same way."

"Messieurs," said Gédéon, with an earnest expression, "I have something extremely serious to tell you. Since you don't want to receive me, come into my room for ten minutes—and after receiving my confidences, you'll cover me with blessings."

And he opened the door.

This objurgation had been uttered with such solemnity that the two scientists looked at one another indecisively for a moment.

Terrier made up his mind first and followed the young man. Antius advanced in his turn, with precaution. The professor threw himself into an armchair. The doctor took up a position at the foot of the divan, near the door, in case he needed to beat a rapid retreat. Then, without saying a word, he directed his nephew to the most distant chair.

Without raising any opposition, the latter obeyed, and, after a few seconds' reflection, started to speak.

"Messieurs, I shall begin at the beginning."

Terrier approved with a nod of the head.

"This morning, I had resolved to reach the somber limits, and here's the proof," said the orator, taking out his pieces of paper and handing each one to the person to whom it was addressed.

After reading his, the professor smiled. Antius shrugged his shoulders.

"But before dying," the young man went on, moving his chair two meters closer, "I wanted, for private reasons, to visit in advance the place where my ashes would be placed. While you were asleep, I traced that last adieu to each of you, and, after having attached the two documents to your doors, I went down to the courtyard. From there I went into the square, which I crossed without hesitation, heading for the Necropolis. I ought to ad that throughout the funereal drama, the stoic courage of Regulus did not abandon me for a single instant.

"As I expected, the building was empty. Having arrived in the vestibule, I don't know what bizarre idea took hold of me to visit the dead of the 20th century, to find out whether I might find myself in the company of some former comrade.

"So, I go up to the fourth floor, with the familiarity of a sitting tenant. I go into the hall, and after five minutes of attentive examination I suddenly perceive my own name on a massive gold urn. I'm bowled over—metaphorically, of course— but I nearly fall over literally when I see a note on my vessel, which says: *The genealogy of the Cahusacs is in the Archives, some register or other, page 1237.*

"I start running, come down the stairs like an avalanche and go into the office we visited together yesterday afternoon. I snatch the volume, find page 1237 and I see...what? A Plateau."

The doctor slowly got to his feet, looking at Terrier.

Convinced, rightly, that his uncle suspected once again that he had lost his mind, Gédéon resumed, calmly: "I mean to say that in my rightful place I find a certain Nicolas Plateau, jurisconsultant. I throw away the register angrily, which fortunately shows me its back. I was mistaken; I needed K2!" The narrator came to his feet abruptly.

"Wretch!" cried Antius, thinking it a further fit and tightening the cord of his dressing-gown as if preparing for a fight.

"My God, Uncle, what a bad mood you're in," the young man continued, without getting excited. "In the presence of a dozen listeners like you, the most phlegmatic lecturer would certainly become rabid. Since it's necessary, for you, to dot the *i*s, I'll tell you that K2 signifies volume 2 of register K. That was how the volume was described by the inscription. If you still don't understand, though..."

"Go on," the physicist interjected.

"I leap on the veritable folio and I set it before me. I start riffling through it with a feverish hand, and I finally find page 1237.

"O miracle! My name occupies the place of honor. The genealogist has even framed me with a certain artistry.

"Now, what will seem prodigious to you is that I was designated under the rubric *former notary*. And to think that the history of nations that we teach to schoolchildren might be no more authentic than mine! But you'll writhe with laughter when you hear that—according to my historiographer, of course—I was the son-in-law of Maître Desiflard, our family notary."

The narrator's prognostication was not realized in the slightest, for the doctor remained pensive and the physicist contented himself with replying: "That hangs together well enough."

"You mean it hangs me by the neck well enough," the young man riposted. "In spite of everything, I didn't fail to bless Providence, which had given me a quarter of an hour of mad gaiety before quitting the earth for a second time.

"I carried on reading, and found myself the father of a certain Sylvain-Théodore Cahusac, famous geographer, who discovered the sources of the Congo. It wasn't an occasion to say *talis pater, talis filius*,[40] for I have no idea myself whether the river in question is in Cochin-China or Andalusia.

"I scanned the innumerable list of my descendants. There were, among others, a rich collection of notaries, two consuls, a judge, for rentiers, an aeronaut and—alas!—two shopkeepers, an orchestra conductor and an inspector of weights and measures.

"At the fourteenth generation, the name of Cahusac fell definitively into oblivion with the most glorious of the troop, a ship's captain who forced the north-west passage, said the note, admiringly. I agree, although, to tell the truth, I have no idea what it means. Until the end, nothing remarkable—but on reading the last name, I received a shock that nearly advanced the hour of my death."

The young man's voice intensified. "Guess," he said, "whose ancestor I am."

The two scientists looked at one another anxiously.

"Of *Guillame Dryon!*" said Gédéon, in a low voice, emphasizing every syllable of their protector's name.

"That's truly marvelous," Antius added, reluctantly impressed.

"And now, Uncle, can you understand the reason for the waltz that I just made you execute against your will?"

"I understand it, without approving of it," the doctor retorted. "But it's important for us to make sure that your story, which exceeds all plausibility, is true."

"Thank you for your confidence. Go and look."

---

[40] "Like father, like son."

"That's what we'll do," Terrier concluded. "In the meantime, you get some rest. Do you agree, Antius?"

"Certainly. Let's get dressed. We'll be back in an hour."

As soon as his companions had left, the young man threw himself on his bed and, exhausted by fatigue and emotion, fell into a profound slumber.

He was soon visited by a gigantic dream.

His descendancy multiplied infinitely. The father of several flourishing nations, he saw his own statue in solid gold in the plazas of great cities.

Every year, on his birthday, he received visits from all sorts of societies, who came in a body to salute his image. He was forced to hear cantatas composed in his honor and executed by formidable choirs. A contest of floral games had been instituted for that memorable day, and he listened with satisfaction to academic speeches in which his virtues and merits were praised.

Finally, just as a temperance society was claiming him as its true founder, the young man was woken up by Terrier's voice, saying: "For myself I only left two descendants, properly bound in calfskin, which, it appears, ornament public libraries."

The young men leapt out of bed and ran to the door.

"Well?" he said.

"Everything you said is scrupulously accurate," declared Antius, "And we can accept the benefits of your descendant without scruple. Of, course, it will be necessary not to claim your title of parentage in his presence."

"Don't worry—I've already had enough cold showers."

"Now, my friends," said the doctor, "we ought to go and thank the generous schoolmaster for the benefits that he has heaped upon us."

XXXII. In a Balloon

A quarter of an hour later, the Herber family, gathered in the drawing room, received the grateful thanks of the strangers. The latter had to promise formally to return to the school every time they came back to Paris, their place being eternally reserved at their friend's hearth.

The schoolmaster accompanied them as far as the palace, and did not leave them until the arrival of the master of the house, who held out his hands to them and tried in vain to retain Herber at his table. The latter objected that he had work to do, and left after bidding his guests a last adieu.

A majordomo came to announce that the meal was served, and the guests went into the dining room.

Éva, who was supervising the final preparations, smiled graciously at the guests. They all took their places at the table, which was as sumptuously served as the day before.

Gédéon, whose paternal instincts were stimulated by the presence of his multi-great-grandchildren, was visibly emotional. He had struck a grave and majestic attitude, and only spoke in sentences, while his companions maintained their freedom of intellect and their habitual calm.

The two scientists ate with a hearty appetite, but the young man, fearful of gastritis for the first time in his life, by reason of his great age, officiated with extreme prudence.

As the cups were being filled with an exquisitely perfumed coffee, Guillaume Dryon took the floor. "Messieurs," he said, "We're leaving in two hours in one of my airships, the *Arago*. We'll arrive at eight o'clock this evening in the city of Livingstone, which is the most animated and most elegant seaside resort on the Algerian Sea. Tomorrow morning, we'll set forth across the African continent, and the day after, we'll set foot on my estates on the banks of the Tanganyika. If you have any preparations to make for the voyage, my people are at your disposal."

The doctor replied that, like the ancient philosophers, they carried all they possessed about their persons, and that they were at the orders of their generous host.

Dryon summoned his steward and gave him precise orders for the departure. Éva, who ran the house with consummate expertise, supervised all the preparations personally.

An hour later, a squadron of porters laden with baggage set off for the embarkation-point.

At one-thirty the agronomist, giving his arm to his daughter and followed by his guests, traversed the garden in a straight line. Behind them marched all the permanently-resident personnel of the palace. On the far side of the park, the majordomo ran forward and opened both battens of a huge door, which gave direct access to a station of the circular railway. The guests of the palace went down on to the lawn, escorted by the sincere good wishes of all the servants.

After a few minutes' wait, they were rapidly conveyed to the aerostatic palace. At the fourth station, Dryon and his new friends got down. The travelers traversed a shady square, almost deserted, and soon found themselves facing a grassy bank twenty meters high.

A man in the prime of life, presently sitting at the foot of a large marble staircase that went up to the summit of the mound, rose to his feet abruptly when he saw them and came to meet them.

"Monsieur Humphrey, our skillful engineer," said Guillaume Dryon, extending his hand to the newcomer.

The engineer and the strangers bowed simultaneously.

"Is everything ready?" the agronomist asked.

"Yes, Monsieur; we're departing in a quarter of an hour, unless you say otherwise."

"Very good."

The passengers climbed a hundred and twenty steps and went across the crown of the esplanade. A singular spectacle was suddenly offered to their eyes.

A hundred rails, as shiny as steel rods in ardent sunlight, ran in parallel from one extremity to the other of a vast inclined rectangle measuring at least six hundred meters in length. Several ellipsoids striped horizontally by curves of polished steel, some measuring as much as a thousand cubic meters, rested on the tracks.

A monument of great magnificence rose up from the inferior base of the quadrilateral, extending as far as the lateral sides.

A few rare pedestrians, braving the torrid afternoon heat, were walking back and forth on the departure platform.

The two scientists were prey to a keen excitement.

"I don't understand your agitation," said the young man. "I can only see a station, more beautiful than the others, with widely-separated rails and carriages that have no wheels." Pointing at twenty empty demi-ellipsoids with horizontal axes, fixed at the extremity of each track, he added: "There are some sentry-boxes of a rather original model."

The engineer headed toward the far end of the platform and pulled a lever fixed to the wall.

Two men came out of the building and advanced toward him. He said a few words to them. The two employees immediately went back in, and the visitors saw, with astonishment, one of the machines slowly descend along the track and slot precisely into the corresponding cavity.

"Messieurs," said Guillaume Dryon, "our transport is ready. We have only to embark."

"How calmly he said that!" murmured Gédéon. "He's obviously a Cahusac. For myself, I confess that I'm beginning to feel rather nervous, and if, in order to make the journey, I were given the choice between a vulgar choo-choo and that gigantic shell, I don't think I'd hesitate for a moment. It's not very courageous, I admit, but at my age, it's permissible to be prudent."

"I believe I have an exact idea of the manner in which the departure will be affected," whispered the physicist, addressing the doctor. "It's obvious that the apparatus, moved by some force, slides over the inclined rails at an increasing speed, and that five hundred meters from the departure point it leaves the ground and launches into the air with the acquired momentum, which doubtless attains four meters per second. But what happens after that?"

The passengers reached the aerial vehicle. Terrier was able to observe that it slid on four runners framed in longitudinal grooves of polished steel. The shiny curves they had noticed on the flanks of the apparatus were due to the gleam of powerful wings of tempered steel, which were presently resting inert on the sides of the vessel. They were articulated with the mass of the apparatus by thick metallic stalks resistant to any proof.

At the rear end, a large parabolic windbreak, mobile in all directions, which formed the rudder, fell back along the dorsal part of the machine. At the front, a slight metallic bulge formed a prow of remarkable delicacy.

"It really is an iron bird with eight wings," said the professor, "but where is the motive force generated?"

The engineer pressed a switch. A door opened in the corresponding partition and a stairway of six steps, covered by a rich Oriental carpet, unfurled to the ground.

Éva ran up it as lightly as a bird and disappeared into the balloon. The doctor, who followed the young woman, shivered as he set foot on the first rung, but gravely climbed the other five. The physicist, who would have coolly taken notes on the rim of an erupting volcano, mounted the stairway calmly and unhurriedly. The young man hesitated momentarily, but, on seeing the gaze of his multi-great-grandson fixed upon him with a certain astonishment, he slapped his sides, uttered an interior *sursum corda* and scaled the six steps as if he was mounting an assault. Guillaume Dryon and the engineer brought up the rear, one after the other, entering the machine in a familiar manner that testified to frequent exercise.

The door closed abruptly under the pressure of an interior spring that the agronomist had activated.

The passengers then found themselves in an elliptical saloon, ornamented magnificently. A thick carpet covered the floor; wide soft divans were fitted along the walls.

A sculpted ebony bookcase was attached to one of the walls, loaded with handsomely-bound books, the majority of which dealt with great voyages and discoveries. A general geography of the globe, in forty quarto volumes, occupied the bottom shelf. On the opposite side a vast planisphere was suspended, surrounded by detailed maps of continents and less extensive regions. At the back, a precision clock separated a barometer and a thermometer, constructed with infinite artistry. At the front there were two compasses, one of declination and the other inclination, indicating the trajectory of the balloon at every moment. In the middle of the ceiling, an electric globe, which could be illuminated by a simple push of a finger, was framed with admirable allegorical paintings.

Four oval windows pierced symmetrically in the walls, at a convenient height, permitted an outside view.

The engineer lifted a heavy curtain at the back of the saloon and disappeared. Shortly afterwards, a slight continuous noise became audible; the vehicle slid along the rails. The passengers sat down on the divans. Gédéon instinctively gripped the top of an ebony box that was close by.

The movement became increasingly rapid, and a few seconds later the young man, having darted a glance out of the window behind him, pulled his head back urgently.

"We're going like the wind," he said to the physicist, who, focused on his hypotheses, did not hear him.

The whistling became extremely shrill, then ceased entirely.

"We've stopped," said Gédéon, "And I can't say I'm sorry." And he looked out again.

The first glance seemed to confirm his opinion, for he could not see anything in front of him, but when he stood up in order to see where they were, he uttered a cry of alarm.

"We're more than a thousand meters from the ground!" he exclaimed. "The houses look like dominoes. Are we going to go up much further?"

"No, my young friend," the agronomist replied, "We're at five hundred meters, the average height we maintain in summer, in order to have a little coolness."

The temperature had, indeed, dropped sensibly.

The two scientists, tormented by a legitimate curiosity, were burning to discover the theory of the machine that was carrying them through the air. Even so, still guided by prudence, they dared not interrogate their host and did not give any evidence of astonishment.

The engineer came back into the room.

"Everything in order?" asked Guillaume Dryon.

"Yes, Monsieur. The water level is perfectly horizontal. We're only traveling at a modest speed, of course, of sixty leagues an hour, because the right wings are a trifle fatigued, and it would be imprudent to force the pace.

"Do we have enough power to reach Tanganyika without renewing our supply at Livingstone?"

"Undoubtedly. We still have more than a cubic meter of liquid hydrogen."

The doctor and the physicist exchanged a rapid glance.

Reassured by the engineer's words, the agronomist came over to the two scientists and began to list for them the series of operations that they were to direct.

The engineer after having made sure that the apparatus was functioning perfectly, remained in the saloon, his gaze sometimes going to the compass, sometimes to the barometer, frequently checking the progress of the aerial vessel.

Éva was attentively reading a book of voyages.

"The composure with which these people travel five hundred feet above the ground is beginning to infect me," murmured Gédéon, who had been motionless since the departure. He leaned toward the window.

The countryside, inundated by sunlight, was fleeing rapidly beneath the airship.

"That's curious, mind," he said, in a low voice. "At the moment we're passing over an immense excavation. That's at odds with my knowledge of the physical geography of the globe. The Earth can't be spherical, as is—or rather was—affirmed. Did the error of the astronomers and geographers stem from the impossibility of the studying the ground from a point as favorable as this one? I must make discreet enquiries about that subject, for, in my new situation as a librarian"—he swelled up with pride—"it's not permissible for me make blunders, and especially not to spread tales.

"That's definitely the Seine, which is snaking away as far as the eye can see, as of old. Its course hasn't been changed, and that's good; of course, from here it lacks majesty. It's a mere stream, and the lake that is about to disappear from view is as big as a vat, at the most. In spite of the paltry figure it cuts at this height, I salute the Marne, which we're just crossing. It reminds me that in 1874 I was unanimously voted the presidency of the regatta. It puts a lump in my throat to contemplate the theater of my old nautical exploits.

"The environs of Paris are rather well-to-do, as those innumerable little palaces surrounded by parks attest. Now I ought to set to work filling in the on-board journal that I've decided to write. When we arrive sat our destination, I'll be sure to extract a picturesque narrative of our voyage, with which my descendants will, I think, be rather satisfied. Of course, as I intend to confide my intimate reflections to it, and don't want to make the acquaintance of the lunatic asylums of Africa, I'll keep the original under wraps."

He left the window and sat down in a large armchair.

He took an elegant album with damascened platinum fittings, which the schoolmaster had given him when they left, from the inside pocket of his embroidered burnoose, and wrote on the first page, in letters half an inch high, the following title:

Voyage of the Airship Arago *from Paris to Lake Tanganyika, On-board Journal kept by Achille-Gédéon Cahusac, assistant librarian of the palaces of the illustrious Guillaume Dryon, member of the European Congress, President of the Circles of the Great African Lakes, Protector, etc.*

On the opposite page he wrote the names and titles of the six passengers.

Surprised by these calligraphic operations, the doctor came over to him.

Gédéon help up his album confidently and announced in a loud voice that he was asking for permission to record his impressions of the voyage for the palace library, reserving the privilege of only communicating the work once it had been relieved of the embarrassments of improvisation.

Dryon and his daughter thanked the young man and put themselves at his disposal for any information he might require.

The agronomist resumed his conversation with the two scientists, while Éva plunged back into her reading.

The historiographer raised his head to the anterior porthole again but pulled it away swiftly.

Antius and the physicist interrogated him with their gaze.

"A second balloon is traveling parallel to ours, at lightning speed," he said, nervously. "It's waving a flag."

"We'll reply to it," said the owner of the *Arago*, tranquilly, reaching out a hand to press an ivory disk. Something rolled audibly over the flank of the airship.

Gédéon looked through the window again and perceived a long strip of yellow cloth covered in large letters, which had unfurled on the side of the vessel.

The agronomist picked up a pair of binoculars and followed the flight of the balloon with his gaze.

"That's the *Orient*, Messieurs, coming from Calcutta to Paris with a cargo of spices," he said, setting down the binoculars on the table.

After one final signal of greeting, the cloth rolled up, and a similar action was effected on the *Arago*. "The crew of the *Orient* is now as well-informed on our account as we are on theirs," added Dryon, sitting down.

"Are these exchanges of signals frequent?" asked Antius.

"They're gestures of courtesy that no one would want to refuse. It's sufficient to establish a simple electric contact for the summary identification of a vessel to unfurl on its flank."

Everyone resumed their positions.

"Now I'm perplexed," Gédéon murmured. "What if, in spite of the map before my eyes, I commit some error regarding the names of the cities we're passing over, and confuse, for example, Yssengeaux with Lyon and Carpentras with Marseilles?"

As if she had divined the young man's anxiety, Éva came to his aid. "Monsieur Cahusac," she said, in her beautiful golden voice, holding him a notebook bound in pink leather, "here's a little book that will save you the trouble of following the map step by step. It indicates the exact time of our passing over each large city. As we're traveling in a straight line with a constant speed of sixty leagues an hour, it will be sufficient for you to consult the dial of the clock."

Gédéon accepted gladly and thanked the young woman from the bottom of his heart.

"That charming child has got her ancestor out of a terrible difficulty," he murmured. "Now let's establish our calculations. We left at two o'clock precisely, and it will be easy to figure out where we are."

He opened the notebook. The first line read: *14 minutes, Mélun, 150,000 inhabitants.*

"That means, I suppose, that fourteen minutes after departure, we pass over that city, which has only ever been famous for its eels. It's time to make an observation, for it's two twenty-three."

Running to the porthole he perceived, a long way behind, an aggregation of microscopic houses fleeing rapidly. To the left and forwards, it was possible to follow the course of the Seine, and that of the Yonne, as far as the eye could see. An almost-imperceptible steam was flowing tranquilly below, which, after mature reflection, he recognized as the Loir.

The hands of the clock marked two-thirty when a second airship passed six hundred meters from the *Arago*. Éva, who had picked up the binoculars and hoisted the flag, identified it as the *Lavoisier*, laden with ivory, arriving from Southern Africa and bound for Paris.

On reading the name of Guillaume Dryon, the cargo vessel multiplied its signals of greeting.

"The elephant-hunting has been productive," Antius remarked.

"Elephants are no longer hunted, Doctor," said the agronomist. "That powerful pachyderm is domesticated in numerous herds, and the *Lavoisier* is loaded with the current year's harvest, gathered from all parts of the continent. The entire ivory industry is centralized in Paris, which manufactures objects in marvelous taste, sometimes of great artistic value."

At two forty-five the Loire, like a sparkling ribbon, appeared on the right, and the *Arago* crossed he extremity of the hills of Nivernais. Although maintaining a perfectly horizontal course, the airship, by reason of the altitude of the region, seemed to be much closer to the ground.

At three o'clock, the young man consigned Nevers to his album and the crossing of the Loire, whose upper reaches were now definitively to the left.

The historiographer's gaze had been attached to the mountains of the Auvergne, which rudely interrupted the circle of the horizon to the south-west, for a few moments when Dryon, after having consulted the clock, declared that they ought to be nearing Lyon. The passengers went to the windows on the left and were able to see a large aggregation of buildings to the east, which covered the junction of two beautiful rivers.

"Lyon has twelve hundred thousand inhabitants," said the agronomist. "Its situation on the Rhône and the Saône has made it a very flourishing city."

A few minutes later, Saint-Étienne was in view.

"I expected to find a city bristling with factory chimneys, but can't see a trace of smoke," said Gédéon, aloud.

"Saint-Étienne is still a first-rate industrial city, but all the factories are powered by electricity," observed Guillaume Dryon. "The city supplies North Africa with is most advanced agricultural equipment."

At four-thirty, the Cévennes were crossed, and the travelers were able to admire the long line of the Rhône, sparkling in the sunlight from north to south. At that moment the balloon was saluted by a party of tourists from Madagascar, who were going to spend a few days on the banks of the Seine.

The physicist, who had not quit the eastward-facing window for some time, had just announced Avignon when the writer, who had been scrupulously keeping his notes, accompanied by a few intimate reflections, looked out of the porthole.

Instead of looking at Nîmes, Avignon and Montpellier, which were almost directly beneath his feet, his attention was captured by a bright line cutting the extreme limit of the southern horizon, gradually extending. Discreetly appealing to his uncle, he asked him in a whisper what the vast watercourse was whose breadth as expanding so rapidly.

"That's the Mediterranean, O expert geographer," said the scientist. "Don't go changing its name and mistaking it for the Channel."

"Don't worry. But neither you nor I have previously seen the sea from this height and at such a distance. It is, therefore, permissible to be mistaken. Isn't that Marseilles down there to the south-west?"

"Yes. You're making progress."

Meanwhile, the balloon was traveling rapidly southwards. The Mediterranean was progressively revealed. They were still a few leagues from the coast when the immense liquid plain embraced a third of the horizon.

A quarter of an hour later, they were directly over the sea, and the shore was fleeing rapidly northwards. Soon, solid ground no longer presented anything but a narrow gray strip, which did not take long to disappear.

The blue waters of the immense lake extending between Europe and Africa appeared to be in a state of absolute immobility, and presented the aspect of a vat polished mirror in which the image of the balloon was reflected with perfect clarity.

To the west, two symmetrical suns were placidly following their course, gradually inclining toward the surface of the water.

The magnificent spectacle of the sea, seen from a height of five hundred meters, had drawn the travelers to the windows.

Gédéon appeared to be prey to a strange fascination. Suddenly, he raised his head. "One can, strictly speaking, take account of the phenomena on land," he murmured, "but in the open sea it defies all interpretation. Either I'm seeing things or the Mediterranean's surface is hollow. I'll clarify the matter."

He headed toward the physicist, who was leaning on the window-sill, parading his attentive gaze over the horizon. The young man took up a position beside the scientist and remained silent for a moment. "I'll wager I can divine the cause of your astonishment," he said, raising his head.

"I'm not experiencing any astonishment," Terrier replied, in a tranquil voice.

"Personally, I'm gripped by the majesty of the spectacle, but I'm more astonished than delighted."

"Why?"

"I ask you to answer me in all sincerity."

"Speak."

"You didn't suspect that the surface of the water is concave?"

"No."

"Me neither."

"I should hope not."

"However, it's necessary to yield to the evidence."

The professor looked at his former pupil with amazement.

"In that case," said the latter, crestfallen, "There's something amiss with my organs of vision, which might be very serious, by reason of my future functions. Since our departure, it's seemed to me that we've been flying over an immense crater."

The physicist burst out laughing. "You seriously believe that it's an infirmity?"

"I admit it."

"Well, my dear friend, it's in your brain, not in your eyes. You're the victim of an illusion common to many of those who go up in a balloon."

"Why is that?" asked Gédéon, now reassured.

"Because the edges of the horizon, usually very distant, appear to us continuously from the height of an aerial trajectory, and we also have an exaggerated notion of the vertical depth—a double appearance that gives rise to the aberration you've just identified."

"Thank you—I'll make a note of the observation."

At six-thirty, the coasts of Corsica, which had been extending for some time to the east of the *Arago*'s course, disappeared entirely, and those of Sardinia began to appear like a vague dark line in the south-east.

Twenty minutes later, the voyagers could see the whole of the island, which extended over the ocean like a vast quadrilateral.

As the balloon cleared the south-west of the island, several cargo-vessels were cleaving the air with extreme rapidity. The *Arago* was only able to salute the *Lincoln*, arriving from Rio de Janeiro and heading for Constantinople.

At seven o'clock the ship caught up with the *Neptune*, a large vessel loaded with passengers who were going to spend the bathing season on the elegant beaches of Livingstone. Without accelerating its pace, the *Arago* went on ahead.

"We'll arrive before the *Neptune*, which is traveling at fifty leagues an hour," declared Monsieur Humphrey, who came into the saloon at that moment.

Suddenly, Guillaume Dryon, who had been aiming his binoculars in a southerly direction for a few moments, exclaimed: "Messieurs, the land of Africa!" And he handed the instrument to the doctor, who discovered a long yellow-tinted strip that was widening rapidly.

Terrier, having recognized the African coast in his turn, handed his telescope to the young man, who thanked him but assured him that he had no need of any artificial aid. His lynx-like vision, which could have competed without any disadvantage with that of the astronomer Struve—who could see tenth-magnitude stars with the naked eye—had already recognized the exactitude of his multi-great-grandson's affirmation.

The airship continued to devour space with the same rapidity, and the continent gradually unfurled under the gaze of the passengers.

When solid ground occupied half the horizon, the voyagers flew over a large city whose domes were sparkling in the blaze of the setting sun.

"We're over Bône," said the engineer, from whom the historiographer, not knowing quite how to continue his journal, had asked advice. "If we were a few hundred meters higher we'd be able to see Bougie to the west, and further away Algiers, the capital of Northern Africa. In an easterly direction, our binoculars would permit us to see as far as Tunis, which is occupied during the winter by a numerous colony of foreigners from northern Europe."

Gédéon hastened to consign this information to his album, but, forgetting the engineer's hypothesis, he ornamented his account with a few lines about the enchanting view that the ancient capitals of Tunisia and French Africa presented.

A few minutes later, the *Arago* was flying over high hills parallel to the shore, and the rock of Constantine became visible in the south-west.

At eight o'clock, the passengers found themselves confronted by the eastern reaches of the Atlas mountain chain, which appeared to be hurtling toward the balloon. The height of the aerial vessel was raised by five hundred meters.

The temperature, which had been regularly maintained until then between twenty and twenty-one degrees Centigrade, fell abruptly to sixteen.

The travelers' gazes were following the high crests of the mountains traversing the north of the continent when Mademoiselle Dryon called their attention to the Algerian Lake, which, like an immense mirror, was growing rapidly to the south. All optical instruments were aimed in the direction of the interior sea. A magnificent scene unfolded before the delighted eyes of the strangers.

Framed throughout its extent by hills covered with luxuriant vegetation, the lake was resplendent beneath the burning rays of the African sun. Several flourishing cities extended along its shores.

Suddenly, the movement of the powerful elytrons sustaining the apparatus appeared to slow down, and the balloon gradually descended toward the surface of the waters.

They were now a few hundred meters above a superb city, covered with splendid palaces and surrounded by magnificent parks. A fairly high plateau overlooked the north of the city. The balloon, maintained at three hundred meters from the ground, was advancing slowly toward the mound in question.

Five minutes later, it descended to the ground and touched the rails of the landing-platform without any jolt.

A few men, who had been watching the maneuvers of the aerial vessel, ran toward the voyagers.

The engineer came back into the saloon and pressed a switch in the wall. The door opened slowly, while the mobile staircase unfolded to the ground.

"Messieurs, we have arrived in Livingstone," said Guillaume Dryon. "We'll go to my villa while our engineer makes arrangements for our departure tomorrow morning."

Monsieur Humphrey bowed, and the passengers stepped down to the ground.

XXXIII. The City of Livingstone

The caravan took a grassy path, which descended at a gentle slope to a large semicircular plaza, from which the gaze could embrace the vast liquid expanse of the Algerian Lake.

In this part of the city the animation was very great. A large number of bathers of all ages and both sexes were strolling in the shade, without getting far away from a large orchestra that occupied the center of the plaza and periodically performing powerful symphonies.

On the sandy shores of the lake, several hundred multicolored tents, symmetrically arranged, produced the most picturesque effect. Elegant boats were furrowing the surface of the waters in all directions.

The agronomist explained to his guests that the city, founded three hundred years ago, had been able to develop enormously, thanks to the mildness of its climate and the beauty of its surroundings.

"It seems to me that the name of Livingstone, who was the first to make southern Africa and the regions in the vicinity of the equator known, would have been more judiciously adopted in the south," Antius commented.

"There are four large cities in Africa that bear the name of the celebrated explorer," Guillaume Dryon replied. "They are distinguished from one another by their geographical situation, and if it had not been for fear of confusion, there would have been more than a hundred, for it is the most venerated name on the continent."

Guided by the agronomist, the passengers went along the quay. Two hundred meters from the plaza their host stopped and showed his friends a magnificent shady garden whose terrace, crowned by a long balustrade of white marble, overlooked the lake.

"Messieurs," he said, "we are home."

He advanced toward the door, which was wide open, and signaled his arrival by pressing an electric button fixed to one of the stone columns that ornamented the entrance to the house.

An old servant came out and bowed to the visitors.

A broad pathway that plunged beneath a somber vault of verdure led to the villa. The voyagers started walking along it and arrived in few minutes at a marble staircase that preceded the vestibule.

The staff of the house, arranged in military order, were waiting for the master and his guests. Two young women hastened to meet Éva, and escorted her to her apartment.

An hour later, all the travelers were gathered in an elegant summer-house on the terrace, around a sumptuous table. A magnificent panorama unfurled before their eyes.

A double row of elegant country houses framed the blue waters of the Algerian Sea, which extended as far as the eye could see. A flotilla of boats of every form and method of propulsion were furrowing the edges of the lake.

"I imagine that this enchanting abode attracts the elegant society of the five continents," said Antius, impressed by the splendor of the spectacle.

"And the French must be proud of counting among their 19th century ancestors the valiant Captain Roudaire, the indefatigable promoter of Algerian lakes," added the physicist.

"We are, indeed, proud," replied Guillaume Dryon. "I speak thus because I'm of French origin, as the genealogy of my family testifies, established with great care all the way back to my venerable ancestor Gédéon Cahusac."

On hearing these words, Gédéon nearly choked. He threw his head sharply backwards.

"Have you swallowed a fish-bone, my young friend," asked his host, with concern.

"Yes, Monsieur, and a big one—but so much the worse for the bone!" replied the young man, who had lost his head.

The two scientists hastened to change the topic of conversation, which was full of perils.

"The desert we shall be crossing tomorrow," said Antius, "no longer opposes the insurmountable barrier that separated Central Africa from Europe for more than fifty centuries?"

"Desert?" queried the agronomist.

"Of course. I mean the immense plains of sand, strewn with oases, that extend from the Nile to Cap Bojador and from Ghadamès to Timbuktu, covering more than fifty degrees from east to west and more than twenty from north to south."

"You mean the old Sahara, Doctor."

"Yes," Antius replied, fearing that he had gone too far.

"That desert no longer exists," said Guillaume Dryon. "The shifting sands that engulfed so many caravans repose in tranquility beneath ten meters of limpid water, and the majority of the oases are fertile and flourishing islands. You're not unaware that the Sahara was a dried-up ancient sea. It's nearly four centuries since human genius restored it to its original state, and it's to the marvelous transformation of the *chotts* that the initiation of that gigantic task was due."

At the request of the strangers, the agronomist gave a rapid description of the political, scientific, industrial and commercial situation of the African continent. He cited statistics to establish that the interior seas were the most fecund centers of activity in the entire world.

For some time, the shades of night had been invading the surface of the Algerian Lake, and the waves were scintillating like brilliant scales in the pale moonlight.

Dryon gave the signal to retire, and an hour later, the *Arago*'s passengers, having retreated to the sumptuous apartments of the villa, were sound asleep.

XXXIV. Across Africa

At sunrise, everyone was on their feet.

The agronomist had several baskets of food taken to the airship, the size and weight of which reassured all minds from the viewpoint of nourishment.

In spite of the early hour, a substantial breakfast was served in the dining room, and each of the passengers took on a sufficient quantity of ballast to brave the journey without reinforcement.

At seven o'clock Dryon and his guests went into the departure hall. Five minutes later the balloon launched forth into the air again.

"Messieurs," said the agronomist to the passengers gathered in the saloon, the distance that separates us from the northern extremity of the Tanganyika is exactly twelve hundred leagues away as the bird flies. Maintaining the speed that we adopted yesterday, the journey would take twenty hours, but I believe that for the sake of our guests, who are unfamiliar with Central Africa, we ought not to stick rigorously to a straight line. First we'll head toward the region of the great tributaries of the Nile. On the other hand, as we'd miss a great many very interesting sights by traveling at night, I propose to stay overnight in Khartoum, which overlooks the sixth cataract. That city is eight hundred and twenty-five leagues away, and we'll reach it in less than fourteen hours."

Antius and his companions, moved by this new evidence of interest, formulated with so much benevolence and delicacy, uttered confused thanks.

"I promise my multi-great-grandson's library a narrative of that flamboyant voyage," said Gédéon, clutching his album feverishly. "What men these Cahusacs are! This one's condemning himself to make a detour of three hundred leagues in order to enable us to admire the sources of the Nile! When one thinks that, in the good old days, the most hospitable landowner would have preferred to see his guests break their arms and legs rather than lend them his horse to make a journey of ten kilometers!"

He tore himself away from these misanthropic reflections to cast an eye over the landscape.

The Algerian lake was fleeing rapidly behind, and the Gulf of Gabès, illuminated by the blaze of the rising run, was shining on the eastern horizon.

Gédéon moved his armchair to the porthole that opened in front of the aerostat and slightly to the left—a position that permitted him to embrace a very extensive horizon.

"To the left," he said, "we see a series of high hills that have been running from north to south for some while, and are now turning at a right angle toward the east. Let's consult the notebook."

The little book was mute on this point.

An omission, he thought.

It was nine-fifteen when the balloon skimmed the summit of a mountain whose name he sought in vain.

"Uh oh!" he said. "Are we going to cross the whole of Africa without having a word to say? That would be disastrous for contemporary geography." He slapped his forehead. "Idiot!" he exclaimed. Éva's notebook is designed for the straight line, not for the route we're now following. I ought to have realized that, for I was about to commit a series of blunders capable of making Messieurs Levasseur, Cortambert and Élysée Reclus spin in their graves."

To the physicist, who had drawn nearer quietly, surprised by his behavior, he said: "Now I'm in a pretty pickle. What am I going to do, my dear Master, to figure out where I am between here and Khartoum?"

"What have you been doing thus far?"

"I confess that I had a *donkey's guide*."

"And it can't guide you any longer?"

"No," the amateur historiographer replied, simply. And he listed for Terrier all the services that the timetable had rendered him.

"I can get you out of difficulty," said the scientist, who went to fetch a map of the African continent from the table. Having unfolded it, he traced in pencil a straight line from Livingstone to Khartoum and divided it into thirteen equal parts corresponding to the thirteen hours of the journey, reserving a fraction for the extra forty-five minutes. "You calculations will now be reduced to frequent consultation of the clock," he added, handing the sheet of paper to the young man—and he went to sit down next to the agronomist.

During this dialogue, the *Arago* passed over a chain of mountains, which separated the tormented region of the Tripolitaine from the plains of Fezzan.

With the aid of binoculars, the passengers were able to observe that the entire country was planted with crops. Numerous trains pulled by electromotive engines were running through the fields.

At one o'clock the balloon was over the plain again and passed within ten leagues of a verdant lake that extended over the territory once occupied by the oasis of Koufarah.

A few moments later, the southern horizon was entirely invaded by a vast dark blue lake, which covered the ancient Libyan desert with ten feet of water.

The airship soon went directly over Kebbah, which had become a first-rate industrial city, connected to the Mediterranean by means of canals as broad as arms of the sea.

At two o'clock the *Arago* had lost sight of the shore. At that moment, the agronomist, who had just consulted the clock, announced that it was time to sit down at table in earnest, because they would not reach Khartoum until eight forty-five in the evening. The proposition was favorably welcomed by al the passengers.

"Now, Messieurs," he added, "we'll have to serve ourselves. Let each of us work to the profit of all."

Everyone set to work.

While Éva set out the solid gold cutlery with which the balloon was equipped, Dryon brought out a portable cellar full of vintage wines, Antius delved into an enormous basket from

297

which he pulled out cold meats—primarily tins of quail and partridge—which he handed to the physicist, and the historiographer abandoned his important functions to grind the coffee.

"The ghost of Van Ostade must be quivering with joy before this interior scene," he murmured.

Ten minutes later the passengers were gathered around the table and delivering an assault upon the dinner with an appetite sharpened by a journey of five hundred and twenty leagues fifteen hundred feet above the ground.

The perfumed mocha won Gédéon compliments, which he modestly passed on to the family grinder. The conversation then took the most amiable and cheerful tone.

At three o'clock the engineer, who had left the table to check on the progress of the balloon, spotted several cargo vessels heading northwards and was able to exchange signals with one of them. The editor of the on-board journal was able to inscribe in his columns the *Equator*, carrying a scientific mission that was returning from the Antarctic Ocean.

In four hours *terra firma* reappeared. Half an hour later, the airship was devouring space over the plains of ancient Nubia, now exploited by an army of agriculturalists.

At six o'clock, the agronomist pointed out a narrow glittering line at the extreme edge of the horizon. "There's the Nile, Messieurs," he said.

The strangers went to the windows and attached their gazes for some time to the mysterious river that had been the cradle of the old Egyptian civilization.

Seven o'clock was chiming when the balloon flew over the high hills that overlooked the ancient desert of Bahiouda. Dusk was beginning to fall, and the balloon switched on all its lights.

At eight o'clock, all the binoculars were focused on Khartoum, whose electric lights were illuminating the southeastern horizon.

Forty minutes later, the *Arago*, under the skillful direction of the engineer Humphrey, descended gently on to the landing-stage at Khartoum, resplendent with light.

They voyagers disembarked and headed for the entrance to the aerostatic palace. When they left the central part of the edifice they found themselves on a broad circular promenade which overlooked the city from a height of two hundred feet. Leaning on a red marble balustrade, they witnessed a magical spectacle.

The city of Khartoum extended before them, streaked in all directions by magnificent avenues, which divided the eastern pat of the city into several districts.

A large number of walkers were moving toward the two quays that bordered the Blue Nile and the White Nile.

Several monumental bridges linked the city to the surrounding country, covered with villas whose roofs were bristling with clumps of tropical plants.

Upstream, the two rivers drew apart at an acute angle, forming two glittering lines running southwards.

In a northerly direction, the mass of the waters, now combined, rolled its foaming waters in a vast cataract, the dull noise of which covered the entire city.

Guillaume Dryon extracted the strangers from the ecstatic state into which the sight of that superb panorama had plunged them

The Arago's passengers went down a vast staircase opposite which the sign of the Hôtel du Nil was blazing—an immense and superb edifice, which, by means of a notice attached to the entrance door, informed travelers that the establishment put at their disposal apartments, a restaurant, a café, a library, bathrooms, reading rooms, gymnasia, conference rooms and concert halls.

At the head of the caravan, the agronomist went into the vestibule and handed his card to a majordomo, who bowed profoundly.

Twenty minutes later, the passengers, who had taken possession of several apartments, went into a dining room as big as a hall and ornamented with as much taste as luxury.

Several groups of travelers, recently arrived and disseminated about the huge hall, were finishing their meals. From the shreds of conversations that reached them, the voyagers were able to understand that a number of engineers and chemists were among the Hôtel du Nil's guests.

The Arago's passengers soon found themselves alone in the dining room and were chatting happily enough about the end of the voyage. At ten o'clock they left the table.

Desirous, after fourteen hours in the air, of treading the ground feely, they left behind an elegant electric calèche that the majordomo had booked in advance for their use. Following a broad avenue of palm trees, they went down to the central part of the city and took a boulevard that led to the Blue Nile.

"I'm truly surprised," Gédéon murmured, "not to have yet seen a genuine negro." Tormented by this apparent anomaly he moved closer to the doctor and submitted the question to him. Antius turned his back on him.

The young man went to the physicist, who, while studying a star map of the latitude, was walking with his eyes turned toward the firmament, and asked the scientist to enlighten him.

"Ask your uncle," replied the professor, without taking his eyes off the constellations shining at the zenith. As an anthropologist, he'll be better able to enlighten you than I am."

"Thanks, but I've tried that. He greeted me, as usual, with the grace of a wild boar."

Then the physicist, descending to earth again, explained at length to his former pupil how, with the passing of time, the characteristic traits of races tended to melt into one another and, in consequence, to disappear. He added that, by virtue of a sage law of nature, they types were gradually drawing nearer to the most perfect, without the metamorphosis having been a lamentable catastrophe.

Adding an example to the precept, he reminded him that in the majority of the guests surrounding them in the hotel dining room, a trained eye could easily recognize the African type. The complexion was generally warm and brown, the hair black, the frame muscular—but one would search in vain, he added, for the flat nose, the curly hair and the characteristic facial angle that had once distinguished the disinherited children of the old African continent.

The listener declared himself satisfied and promised to add to his journal a few philosophical reflections that the subject had inspired in him.

After a fairly long walk on the quay of the left bank of the Blue Nile, swarming with an elegant crowd that became increasingly compact, Dryon and his traveling companions returned to the hotel.

The *Arago*'s passengers exchanged a few goodnights and returned to their respective apartments. The departure for Tanganyika had been fixed for eight a.m.

XXXV. The Heart of Africa

The bed-sitting rooms that the management of the great African hotel had put at the disposal of its guests were over-flowing with all the objects of interior services that the most meticulous, demanding and sybaritic rentier could have desired in his own home, and differed singularly in that respect from the cells of our modern caravanserais, in which the traveler, surrounded by bleak bare walls, experiences such a painful impression of emptiness and abandonment.

The slumber of the *Arago*'s passengers, lulled by the murmurous sound of the cataract, was calm and profound.

At seven o'clock, everyone was up and about.

On the advice of Guillaume Dryon, who had gathered all his guests in the vestibule, the travelers went into the dining room, where a hot light breakfast was served.

At a quarter to eight, the agronomist and his friends, having arrived at the top of the stairway that gave access to the landing-ground, darted a last glance at the marvelous panorama of Khartoum and its surroundings.

Ten minutes later, one by one, the six aeronauts were crossing the mobile staircase by which the landing was connected horizontally to the departure hall.

As eight o'clock chimed on the aerostatic palace clock the metallic hull slid on its runners and drove the aerial vessel forward. Less than twenty seconds had passed when the *Arago*, following a slightly oblique line, launched southwards.

Gédéon had resumed his post and added a few observations to his manuscript that seemed to him to be of great importance. For an hour, the balloon followed approximately the same course as the White Nile as it extended toward its source, and the travelers, leaning on the window-sills, were able to observe that the countryside was subject to the intensive cultivation that habitually torments the soil in the vicinity of large cities.

302

At ten o'clock, the agronomist pointed out the mountains of the Amarha to the west, which broke the circular line of the horizon. The White Nile was now following a sinuous path ten leagues to the east.

At eleven o'clock the aerial vessel crossed the river at the point where two large rivers flowed into it. One, which descended from the north-west had bathed the plains of Darfur in its upper course; the other came directly from the east. The latter, fifty leagues upriver, curved abruptly southwards, separated from a direct confluence into the Indian Ocean by the mountains of the land of Kaffa and the mountains of Gallas.

On the western side the region was bathed by a rich network of important rivers, and appeared to be the seat of a great agricultural and industrial movement.

At midday, the *Arago* crossed the White Nile again and left it definitely to port. The ground rose up gradually toward the high plateaux, and the trajectory of the balloon was slightly deviated upwards, a direction that permitted it to maintain its progress in parallel with the sun.

At one o'clock in the afternoon, the agronomist pointed out Gondokoro in the east, a dot almost imperceptible to the naked eye but which powerful binoculars were able to recognize as an aggregation of large buildings.

The doctor spoke with a certain emotion about the history of that country, which had been the terminus of explorers of the sources of the Nile for mortar than a century, and had become the tomb of the most intrepid.

"When admiring now that magnificent network of railways and those long trains loaded with foodstuffs and industrial products, pulled by rapid and powerful electromotive engines," he added, "one can scarcely cast one's mind back ten centuries and glimpse bare and savage country in which ferocious peoples tore one another apart or treacherously welcomed scientific missions only to murder them in their sleep.

"We are now going into the ancient land of the Niam-Niams, cannibal hordes about whom the ancient geographers had established the most extraordinary legends, and to whom some of them attributed a tail similar to the one that ornaments a certain variety of monkeys, which those indigenes scarcely surpassed from the intellectual viewpoint."

The aerial vessel did indeed see unfolding before it the vast plains whose bloody history the doctor had just recalled.

At two o'clock, the horizon to the let was broken by the chain of the Blue Mountains, which ran from north-east to south-west for a hundred leagues.

At the request of Guillaume Dryon, the balloon was taken up to an altitude of two thousand meters within a few minutes, and the passengers were able to see emerging twenty leagues to the west the sparkling surface of Albert-Nyanza, the discovery of which, in spite of the activity of explorers, had only been firmly established in the second half of the 19th century.

"There, Messieurs," he said, "is the great interior lake through which the mysterious river flows whose geographical conquest, as Doctor Antius was telling us a little while ago, has cost so many disasters. Ten leagues from its northern extremity the lake receives the upper course of the Nile, which, twenty leagues to the east, curves abruptly southwards and extends back to the mountains that separate Uganda from Bunyoro."

At three o'clock the airship crossed the south-eastern tip of Albert-Nyanza and the great lake, sixty leagues long with an average width of fifteen, was displayed in all its splendor three thousand feet above sea-level.

Thanks to the height of two thousand meters that the engineer had maintained, the *Arago*'s passengers were able to see in the distance the vague contours of Lake Victoria, which, speckled with verdant islands, covers a territory of sixty thousand square kilometers.

For an hour, the two great lakes remained within sight of the aerial vessel.

At four o'clock, the agronomist signaled in advance Alexandra-Nyanza, which forms an evident ellipse with closely-associated foci, with a mean diameter of ten leagues.

The *Arago*, which had been flying over the crests of the Blue Mountains for an hour found itself at that moment above the inferior plateaux, and its altitude was returned to five hundred meters. The temperature climbed abruptly to twenty-five degrees centigrade.

At half past four, the balloon passed within a league of Lake Alexandra. A few minutes later, Guillaume Dryon, who had been interrogating the horizon for some time with his binoculars, cried joyfully: "Messieurs, the Tanganyika!"

Swiftly, the travelers drew closer to their hosts, and, with the aid of optical instruments, each of them was able to perceive a slight blue patch in the south, which represented the northern extremity of the famous central lake.

The airship continued to devour space, and at five o'clock the passengers embraced with their gaze an immense expanse of water, whose waves formed brilliant mobile scales, resplendent in the blaze of the setting sun.

The panorama was magical.

The view extended simultaneously over the eastern and eastern shores of the inland sea, which had excited so much controversy ten centuries previously and on the shore of which the voyager Stanley, after four months of the most difficult and perilous travel, had found the great Livingstone, ill and devoid of resources. Numerous watercourses emptied into the lake: a circumstance that led the celebrated explorer to search for the necessary outflow, through which the waters had to run away—a problem whose solution, vainly pursued, would have been the glorious crown of an entire existence dedicated to science and humanity.

Magnificent cities now rose up on those once-deserted shores, whose silence had only been troubled by the war-cries of enemy hordes rushing at one another, spears in hand.

At five o'clock, the *Arago* sped like an arrow over the outskirts of Uvira, a superb city whose magnificent port rivaled that of Ujiji, the great city of equatorial Africa, in its extent and importance.

Twenty minutes later, Éva uttered a cry of joy as she pointed out to her father an amphitheater of high kills, covered with forests, which broke the circle of the horizon to the south.

The balloon was now traveling at six hundred feet above the ground, and the strangers, armed with binoculars, were soon able to perceive the profile of an immense palace of white marble standing on the summit of a verdant hill, sheltered from the torrid equatorial winds by a high mountain covered with woods, whose contour the balloon followed.

"In fifteen minutes, Messieurs, we shall be on the landing-stage of the palace," said the agronomist, pointing to a platform on top of the edifice, dominated by a semaphore on which a flag was fluttering.

As the aerial vessel approached its destination, the travelers discovered an admirable country in which Nature seemed to have spread all her riches. Farms as large as villages, established on the banks of artificial rivers, whose pure waves flowed in the mist of fields covered with flocks, displayed their pink brick roofs in clearing in the foliage of the giant trees of Central Africa.

The magnificence of the palace unfurled progressively before the dazzled eyes of the strangers.

The movements of the semaphore must have signaled the arrival of the masters of the house, for numerous servants of both sexes were covering the terrace of the palace, following the rapid flight of the balloon attentively.

A thousand meters from the aerostatic station, the aerial vessel gradually moderated its speed and, moving horizontally, came to settle twenty seconds later on the rails of the landing-stage.

The service crew raced forwards toward the footstep, and the *Arago*'s passengers stepped down to the ground.

The greetings and felicitations full of frankness and sympathy that welcomes Guillaume Dryon and his daughter impressed the strangers tenderly. At the extremity of the path a broad grassy causeway opened, which led to the dwelling.

The agronomist and his new guests started walking toward the palace and descended on to the terrace, where the masters of the house had to receive further testimonies of devotion.

Guillaume Dryon introduced Antius and his companions, nobly, as permanent guests of the palace, and instructed his steward to have an exceedingly comfortable apartment prepared for them immediately, near the library.

The strangers were then able to admire the edifice at close range, which presented to the east, in the direction of the Tanganyika, a front of six hundred layered porphyry columns supporting sculpted marble balconies.

The sight of an observatory raised twenty meters above the roof plunged the physicist into a rapture of delight.

In front of the terrace, a road twenty meters wide, bordered y trees of precious species, descended the slope of the hill, and joined the high banks of the Tanganyika three thousand meters away.

The splendor of the landscape made a vivid impression of Gédéon.

"After the pen, the brush," he said, clutching his album convulsively, forgetting that his artistic development had not surpassed the limit at which the debutant ought prudently to place an explanatory caption at the foot of his picture, if he wants anyone to know what it was that he was trying to paint.

A few minutes later, the strangers took possession of their apartments, in which a provident hand had accumulated everything that might be agreeable without prejudice to that which might be useful.

Seven o'clock was chiming when the passengers met up again around a table as sumptuous as that in the Place des États.

After a meal brightened by a conversation full of charm, gaiety and sympathy, all the guests went down to sit on the terrace, under the silvery rays of the full moon.

At nine o'clock, the groups separated.

Antius and his companions went back to their wing.

As he went into his bedroom, the doctor could not help a cry of grateful admiration on seeing a superb nightcap lying on his pillow, worthy of coiffing a king of Babylon.

Before mounting an assault on a bed as large as an Egyptian mausoleum, Terrier wondered anxiously: "How are we going to get on with our scientific work?"

For his part, Gédéon, casting a final glance over the landscape bathed in the soft light of the night-star, wondered aloud: "Which should it be—conventional or impressionist?"

An hour later, the god of sleep covered all the inhabitants of the African palace with his mantle.

XXIV. Conclusion

The inhabitants of the Montparnasse quarter will certainly not forget the events that marked the morning of 15 June 1880 for a long time.

That day, at half past seven in the morning, a respectable lady surrounded by sympathy and general consideration, Madame Madeleine Boquet, housekeeper for twenty-five years of the celebrated physician Doctor Antius, one of the leading lights of the arrondissement, had hurtled out of her master's house uttering loud screams and run toward the crossroads at the Observatoire.

It is recognized that the first witness of this event, already extraordinary, was the doctor's nearest neighbor, the grocer Collardot, a self-important and dogmatic man, who was, at that moment, standing on the threshold of his shop with his arms folded, waiting for customers.

At the sight of the old lady running as far as her old legs could carry her and uttering inarticulate cries, the estimable shopkeeper could not help remarking to his three assistants, who were lined up behind him: "Something's happened at the Doctor's, for sure."

Fifteen paces further on, Monsieur Camuzet, manufacturer of leather goods and member of the Arbitration Council, standing in the middle of the road with his nose in the air, in order to determine whether the weather was favorable for a long-debated family trip to the countryside, had almost been knocked over by the aged housekeeper, who had, moreover, not even said sorry.

A third witness, the manufacturer of funerary ornaments Balochard, whose name was perhaps unsuited to his profession[41] but was superabundantly justified by the joviality of his

---

[41] Balochard is an argot term applied to a cheerfully simple-minded individual lacking in practicality.

character, had been unable to keep his impressions to himself, and had gone to join the two abovementioned businessmen, who were already delivering themselves to all sorts of conjectures.

A few of the grocer's clients, having arrived at that moment, joined in the conversation, and, in spite of the habitual tranquility of the quarter, as passers-by began to stop, one after another, a considerable crowd had soon formed in the middle of the street.

As always happens in such cases, all kinds of suppositions, from the simplest to the most extravagant, had not taken long to be voiced.

Contrary to the aphorism claiming that truth emerges from discussion, a quarter of an hour later, the original cause of the assembly, drowned in hypotheses and successive affirmations, had been entirely forgotten.

An expert ear, which might have been able to grasp all the conversations agitating seven or eight separate groups, would have heard a curious specimen of the kind of lucubration that emerges every day in the crowds on the public highway.

"Have the murderers at least been arrested?" asked a timid little rentier who was on his way to take his habitual stroll beneath the chestnut-trees of the Luxembourg.

"Four have been arrested," was the confident reply of a local barber, who, razor in hand, had casually abandoned a client soaped up to the eyebrows.

"It's said that there were forty in the gang," said a third.

"Has there been a crime?" asked a new arrival.

"I'm afraid so," formulated a butcher's boy.

"The smoke could be seen from here," observed someone in the next group.

"Two firemen have already been injured," added his interlocutor.

"As plain as I'm seeing you, Monsieur," said an art student, "I saw the horse going into the shop."

"No one knows who started it, you say? That will make things difficult for the commissaire."

"There's only one things to do—have all those who've been bitten put down," proposed a man who did not beat about the bush.

When the commentaries were exhausted, the crowd gradually dispersed, and twenty minutes later all that remained were have a dozen idlers who had turned the conversation to the ministry.

On the other side of the road, the wreath-merchant, who had remained on sentry duty at the grocer's door, summoned the latter—who, with his pen behind his ear, hastened to come running.

"I've just seen Mère Boquet going past with Doctor Dulaurier," said Balochard.

"You know him, then?" asked the other.

"Do I know him! A man who 's so good for my business!"

Their neighbor Camuzet, who was interrogating the sky again, was hailed by his two friends, and, after a brief conference, the three businessmen declared unanimously that not merely neighborliness and solidarity, but also the profound esteem that they professed for Doctor Antius' household, made it their duty to go and make direct enquiries about the events that had thrown the entire quarter into turmoil.

In consequence, they headed for the doctor's house, followed at a distance by the group of idlers.

Having arrived at the door, which was ajar, the grocer bravely went into the garden and as followed by the leather-worker, who hesitated momentarily but was carried forward by a vigorous push from the maker of funerary emblems. Scarcely had the latter crossed the threshold than he slammed the door in the faces of the rearguard.

The three men, having arrived at the end of the path, went into the house, which seemed to be deserted. Having remained momentarily indecisive, they were suddenly orientated by the sound of Madame Boquet's voice. They went along the corridor and into the interior courtyard.

The three shopkeepers then perceived Doctor Dulaurier, who, hoisting himself up on his stork-like legs, was plunging an attentive gaze into the celebrated physician's laboratory.

On hearing the newcomers, the housekeeper had turned round, and, just as the grocer was about to explain his presence and that of his companions with a few well-chosen words, she sobbed: "Oh, my good neighbors, if you knew what misfortune has just struck our quarter! My poor master and his two friends died last night. All three of them are locked in the laboratory. And to think that I only found out this morning when I went to wake Monsieur...I found the bedroom empty, and..."

"Madame Boquet," Dulaurier interjected, "we need to get in, although the door's locked from the inside. We don't have time to go and look for a locksmith. Perhaps there's still time to save them. I'm going to break a pane and open the window. One of these gentlemen can climb in and open the door. Which of you would like to undertake the mission?"

"Me," cried the brave Balochard. "It's the least I can do for the physician."

On that assurance, the doctor used his key to break the window-pane, which shattered. Then, putting his hand inside, he unfastened the catch and pushed the frame. The window opened abruptly.

The physician leaned forward and, having broadly dilated his monumental nose, which plunged into the room, he said, calmly: "There's no harmful gas in there."

Balochard, whose head scarcely reached the window-ledge, was vigorously hoisted up on to the sill. Scarcely had he darted a glance inside the laboratory, however, than he nearly fell backwards because of the sudden emotion caused by the spectacle that met his eyes.

Three deathly pale men, immobile, their features violently contracted, where lying back in large armchairs. Next to them, a large copper lamp, doubtless lit a long time before, was on the point of going out, casting a yellow glow over the funereal scene.

After a moment's hesitation, the tradesman leapt courageously down to the flag-stones and ran to open the door to his companions.

Camuzet and Collardot hazarded a glance and recoil in alarm.

Dulaurier, who had seen many others, hastened toward the three victims, whom he examined in turn.

"God be praised!" he cried. "Our friends are in good health."

Although it seemed to them to be exaggerated, this opinion caused an immoderate joy to all the onlookers.

Old Madeleine threw herself to her knees, thanking Providence, while the wreath-maker sketched a dance-step.

Reassured by the doctor's exclamation, the grocer and the leather-merchant had entered in their turn.

"Now it's necessary to bring them round," declared the physician.

"If it's a matter of an operation, I'll go, for it's sure to make me feel ill," admitted Camuzet, ingenuously.

"It's sufficient to moisten their heads forcefully and continuously," said Dulaurier. "All three of them are under the influence of a long-lasting congestion, which might have had a fatal result." And he sent the housekeeper to fetch cloths and cold water.

What the Devil could they have drunk to put themselves in that state? the doctor wondered. *Even the liveliest only has a pulse-rate of sixty. Why are they holding hands? There's a mystery in this that intrigues me to the highest degree.*

Madame Boquet came back with three napkins and two jugs full of water.

Dulaurier assigned everyone a post. On his orders, Collardot covered Antius' head with the cloth, previously soaked in cold water. Camuzet and Balochard applied the same treatment, the former to the physicist and the latter to Gédéon.

The housekeeper handed full glasses to the three operators in turn, who had soon conscientiously instituted a triple cascade.

After a quarter of a hour, the hands relaxed—a phenomenon that appeared to the doctor to be a good augury. Half an hour later, Gédéon uttered a profound sigh and opened his eyes slightly, then immediately closed them again, murmuring something unintelligible. The young man turned over on to his side, and appeared to fall profoundly asleep.

A short time afterwards, Terrier and Antius presented exactly the same symptoms.

The practitioner suspended the douches and was able to observe the pulse-rates of the three patients had regained the normal level.

"They're sleeping peacefully," he said. "In half an hour or so, I think they can be woken up without risk."

The tradesmen stood back and went to sit down at the laboratory table. There, they were able to exchange in whispers the reflections suggested to them by the extraordinary event that had unfolded before their eyes.

Madame Boquet, choked by emotion, kept a close watch on the three diners of the previous evening.

Twenty minutes had scarcely gone by when Gédéon stretched his legs, opened his eyes abruptly and, under the influence of a singular hallucination, launched himself toward a jar full of copper sulfate, which he picked up and clutched to his bosom, crying: "Éva, my child, we'll never be separated again!"

Without saying a word, Dulaurier went to seize the young man's arm. The latter put up no resistance, and meekly allowed himself to be led to his armchair, into which he fell back, without letting go of his bottle.

Shortly afterwards, to the increasing amazement of the three worthy bourgeois, who had already been astonished by the previous scene, Antius stood up and shouted, angrily: "Is that imbecile going to send his entire life making plates of spinach on canvas?" And he fell backwards into his seat.

"What the devil is the third one going to say?" said Balochard.

They did not have long to wait for an answer.

After passing his hand slowly over his forehead, the physicist moved his lips gently. "How much force can liquefied hydrogen deliver?" he murmured.

"Don't worry, Messieurs," the doctor said to the obliging neighbors. "This is the end of some formidable nightmare. There's no longer anything to fear with regard to the condition of these gentlemen; in half an hour, at the latest, they'll be on their feet. It only remains for us to thank you sincerely for your kind assistance."

The estimable tradesmen only withdrew after a formal promise had been made to recall them in case of any problems, and they promised the physician to maintain absolute silence as to what they had seen.

The secret was so well kept that within a radius of five hundred meters, that same evening, from the porters' lodges to the mansards, there was no talk of anything but the accident, with all the variations of all the usual commentaries.

Two hours later, Dulaurier, Antius, Terrier and Gédéon, sitting at table in the dining room, launched an assault on a marvelous feast that Madame Boquet had prepared to celebrate the resurrection.

Epilogue

The rapid voyage that they had just made in the future world impressed the three heroes of this story variously.

That same day, the physicist, under the influence of a profound preoccupation, went back to his laboratory and covered large sheets of Bristol paper with technical formulas. The following day, seconded by young Rastoin, his assistant, he set up a powerful apparatus designed for the liquefaction of hydrogen. It was eight o'clock when he came out of his study. Ten paces from his door he stopped abruptly in the middle of the street and slapped his forehead.

"The solution to the problem of aerial navigation is there!" he exclaimed.

The following Thursday, Antius, frequently interrupted by applause, read a very remarkable paper to the Académie, which dealt with the particular action of certain vegetal alkaloids on the nervous centers.

The next day, he received a visit from Gédéon, who came toward him with a grave and compassed step.

"Uncle," said the young man, "the sojourn we've just made in a world in which everyone is honest, good, hardworking and educated has led me to a sincere resolution. I want to become a serious man."

The doctor, convinced that his nephew was planning an assault on his wallet by means of a new kind of skirmish, contented himself with smiling.

"In November," the young man went on, coolly, "I shall enroll in the Faculty of Law."

Antius raised his head.

"And tomorrow, I start work as Maître Desiflard's clerk."

The doctor's eyebrows furrowed. *He must need a large sum*, he thought. "Well, my lad, what can I do for you?"

"Accompany me to your notary's office and act as guarantor of my conduct."

The young man's serious tone made an impression on the scientist. "I'll take you at your word," he said. "In any case, it's necessary to strike while the iron is hot."

They went out.

Two hours later, Maître Desiflard, convinced in his turn, arranged for his new clerk to start the next day.

Eight o'clock was chiming at the École des Mines when Gédéon came to take his place at his desk. He gravely put on a pair of lustrine sleeves and flexed the nib of his pen twice with the nail of his index finger.

After a fortnight, the head clerk said, in an oracular tone: "Monsieur Cahusac will make a first-rate notary."

The certainty of this flattering prediction increased by the day, by virtue of the chronometric exactitude and indefatigable zeal that the future lawyer brought to his new functions. His fantastic wardrobe, which had previously had the privilege of causing the yapping voices of the clothes-merchants who passed beneath his window to increase their pitch by an octave, had been philanthropically taken to the nearby night-shelter. Severely dressed in black from head to toe, the model clerk had adopted without difficulty the gravity of bearing and language that constitutes the essential ornament of the notariat.

While passing through the various stages of his study at regular intervals, he rigorously followed the course at the School of Law, and the professors counted him among the most meritorious of the cohort, as honorable as it was restricted, of hard workers.

He had just won the first prize in Roman Law when Maître Desiflard confided the difficult position of Head Clerk to him.

Our hero was at the top of his profession. The remarkable aptitude for business that developed so miraculously within him preserved the capital of his clients on many an occasion from ambushes of every species with which the world of speculation is bristling.

317

He had become the oracle of the quarter.

Chosen as arbiter in several important affairs, his sagacity, his impartiality and his conciliatory spirit had always made peace between the adversarial parties, who thus found themselves spared the murderous gears of court procedure and perilous contact with the three men of law whose portraits he had once sketched with so much verve and comical humor.

A year later, Gédéon came down the steps of the School of Law, laden with the congratulations of his professors, who had just conferred his degree upon him.

Antius, marveling, did not know what cause to attribute to the profound revolution that had occurred within the young man's life. One day, however, having reflected on the subject for some time, he exclaimed: "I've got it! My nephew really has aged a thousand years."

On the other hand, Mademoiselle Dorothée Desiflard, a young woman endowed with all the charms and all the qualities, had already flatly refused four successive suitors in the space of a year, and was being written off as a very finicky heiress, when an incident clarified a double mystery that no one had suspected.

In the course of a brilliant soirée given by the notary, the young woman, having observed that Gédéon was dancing for the fourth time with a middle-aged widow, was seized by a violent crisis, which was attributed to the heat of the apartment. The young advocate immediately gave such signs of anxiety that Maître Desiflard, while running to his daughter, who was carried out of the room, could not help murmuring, with satisfaction: "I'll soon be able to rest easy, then; the office will be in good hands."

The young woman rapidly recovered her senses.

"This little indisposition caused our excellent head clerk a singular alarm," her father said to her, abruptly.

"It's very kind of him to be concerned about me," the young demoiselle replied, dryly.

"The parties are perfectly in accord!" exclaimed the notary, laughing. "I'll get busy with the contract."

A month later, a brilliant crowd attended the young couple's wedding ball.

For that solemn occasion, Antius had donned the brilliant commander's cravat that he had received from the Minister of Public Education, and Terrier had added to his signature the title of Member of the Académie des Sciences.

"Well, my lad," the doctor asked the newly-married man, "what are you going to make of my first grand-nephew—a doctor or a notary?"

"Or a physicist?" added the professor.

"No, Messieurs," replied Maître Gédéon Cahusac, "a geographer...*it's written!*"

SF & FANTASY

Henri Allorge. *The Great Cataclysm*

Guy d'Armen. *Doc Ardan: The City of Gold and Lepers*

G.-J. Arnaud. *The Ice Company*

Charles Asselineau. *The Double Life*

Cyprien Bérard. *The Vampire Lord Ruthwen*

Aloysius Bertrand. *Gaspard de la Nuit*

Richard Bessière. *The Gardens of the Apocalypse*

Albert Bleunard. *Ever Smaller*

Félix Bodin. *The Novel of the Future*

Louis Boussenard. *Monsieur Synthesis*

Alphonse Brown. *City of Glass; The Conquest of the Air*

Emile Calvet. *In a Thousand Years*

André Caroff. *The Terror of Madame Atomos; Miss Atomos; The Return of Madame Atomos; The Mistake of Madame Atomos; The Monsters of Madame Atomos; The Revenge of Madame Atomos; The Resurrection of Madame Atomos*

Félicien Champsaur. *The Human Arrow; Ouha, King of the Apes; Pharaoh's Wife*

Didier de Chousy. *Ignis*

Michel Corday. *The Eternal Flame*

Captain Danrit. *Undersea Odyssey*

C. I. Defontenay. *Star (Psi Cassiopeia)*

Charles Derennes. *The People of the Pole*

Georges Dodds (anthologist). *The Missing Link*

Harry Dickson. *The Heir of Dracula*

Jules Dornay. *Lord Ruthven Begins*

Alfred Driou. *The Adventures of a Parisian Aeronaut*

Sâr Dubnotal *vs. Jack the Ripper*

Alexandre Dumas. *The Return of Lord Ruthven*

Renée Dunan. *Baal*

J.-C. Dunyach. *The Night Orchid; The Thieves of Silence*

Henri Duvernois. *The Man Who Found Himself*

Achille Eyraud. *Voyage to Venus*

Henri Falk. *The Age of Lead*

Paul Féval. *Anne of the Isles; Knightshade; Revenants; Vampire City; The Vampire Countess; The Wandering Jew's Daughter*

Paul Féval, *fils. Felifax, the Tiger-Man*

Charles de Fieux. *Lamékis*

Arnould Galopin. *Doctor Omega; Doctor Omega and the Shadowmen* (anthology)

Judith Gautier. *Isoline and the Serpent-Flower*

Léon Gozlan. *The Vampire of the Val-de-Grâce*

G.L. Gick. *Harry Dickson and the Werewolf of Rutherford Grange*

Edmond Haraucourt. *Illusions of Immortality*

Nathalie Henneberg. *The Green Gods*

V. Hugo, P. Foucher & P. Meurice. *The Hunchback of Notre-Dame*

Romain d'Huissier. *Hexagon: Dark Matter*

Michel Jeury. *Chronolysis*

Gustave Kahn. *The Tale of Gold and Silence*

Gérard Klein. *The Mote in Time's Eye*

Fernand Kolney. *Love in 5000 Years*

Louis-Guillaume de La Follie. *The Unpretentious Philosopher*

Jean de La Hire. *Enter the Nyctalope; The Nyctalope on Mars; The Nyctalope vs. Lucifer; The Nyctalope Steps In; Night of the Nyctalope*

Etienne-Léon de Lamothe-Langon. *The Virgin Vampire*

André Laurie. *Spiridon*

Gabriel de Lautrec. *The Vengeance of the Oval Portrait*

Alain le Drimeur. *The Future City*

Georges Le Faure & Henri de Graffigny. *The Extraordinary Adventures of a Russian Scientist Across the Solar System* (2 vols.)

Gustave Le Rouge. *The Vampires of Mars; The Dominion of the World* (w/Gustave Guitton) (4 vols.)

Jules Lermina. *Mysteryville; Panic in Paris; To-Ho and the Gold Destroyers; The Secret of Zippelius*

André Lichtenberger. *The Centaurs*

Jean-Marc & Randy Lofficier. *Edgar Allan Poe on Mars; The Katrina Protocol; Pacifica; Robonocchio; Tales of the Shadowmen 1-9*

Xavier Mauméjean. *The League of Heroes*

Joseph Méry. *The Tower of Destiny*

Hippolyte Mettais. *The Year 5865*

Louise Michel. *The Human Microbes; The New World*

Tony Moilin. *Paris in the Year 2000*

José Moselli. *Illa's End*

John-Antoine Nau. *Enemy Force*

Marie Nizet. *Captain Vampire*

C. Nodier, A. Beraud & Toussaint-Merle. *Frankenstein*

Henri de Parville. *An Inhabitant of the Planet Mars*

Gaston de Pawlowski. *Journey to the Land of the 4th Dimension*

Georges Pellerin. *The World in 2000 Years*

Ernest Pérochon. *The Frenetic People*

Pierre Pelot. *The Child Who Walked on the Sky*

J. Polidori, C. Nodier, E. Scribe. *Lord Ruthven the Vampire*

P.-A. Ponson du Terrail. *The Vampire and the Devil's Son; The Immortal Woman*

Henri de Régnier. *A Surfeit of Mirrors*

Maurice Renard. *The Blue Peril; Doctor Lerne; The Doctored Man; A Man Among the Microbes; The Master of Light*

Jean Richepin. *The Wing; The Crazy Corner*

Albert Robida. *The Adventures of Saturnin Farandoul; The Clock of the Centuries; Chalet in the Sky; The Electric Life*

J.-H. Rosny Aîné. *Helgvor of the Blue River; The Givreuse Enigma; The Mysterious Force; The Navigators of Space; Vamireh; The World of the Variants; The Young Vampire*

Marcel Rouff. *Journey to the Inverted World*

Han Ryner. *The Superhumans*

Brian Stableford. *The New Faust at the Tragicomique;The Empire of the Necromancers (The Shadow of Frankenstein; Frankenstein and the Vampire Countess; Frankenstein in London); Sherlock Holmes & The Vampires of Eternity; The Stones of Camelot; The Wayward Muse.* (anthologist) *The Germans on Venus; News from the Moon; The Supreme Progress; The World Above the World; Nemoville; Investigations of the Future*

Jacques Spitz. *The Eye of Purgatory*

Kurt Steiner. *Ortog*

Eugène Thébault. *Radio-Terror*

C.-F. Tiphaigne de La Roche. *Amilec*

Théo Varlet. *The Golden Rock. The Xenobiotic Invasion; The Castaways of Eros; Timeslip Troopers* (w/André Blandin); *The Martian Epic* (w/Octave Joncquel)

Paul Vibert. *The Mysterious Fluid*

Villiers de l'Isle-Adam. *The Scaffold; The Vampire Soul*

Philippe Ward. *Artahe*

Philippe Ward & Sylvie Miller. *The Song of Montségur*

MYSTERIES & THRILLERS

M. Allain & P. Souvestre. *The Daughter of Fantômas*

A. Anicet-Bourgeois, Lucien Dabril. *Rocambole*

A. Bernède. *Belphegor; Judex* (w/Louis Feuillade); *The Return of Judex* (w/Louis Feuillade); *The Shadow of Judex*

A. Bisson & G. Livet. *Nick Carter vs. Fantômas*
V. Darlay & H. de Gorsse. *Arsène Lupin vs. Sherlock Holmes: The Stage Play*
Séamas Duffy. *Sherlock Holmes in Paris*
Paul Féval. *Gentlemen of the Night; John Devil; The Black Coats ('Salem Street; The Invisible Weapon; The Parisian Jungle; The Companions of the Treasure; Heart of Steel; The Cadet Gang; The Sword-Swallower)*
Emile Gaboriau. *Monsieur Lecoq*
Goron & Emile Gautier. *Spawn of the Penitentiary*
Steve Leadley. *Sherlock Holmes: The Circle of Blood*
Maurice Leblanc. *Arsène Lupin vs. Countess Cagliostro; Arsène Lupin vs. Sherlock Holmes (The Blonde Phantom; The Hollow Needle); The Many Faces of Arsène Lupin*
Gaston Leroux. *Chéri-Bibi; The Phantom of the Opera; Rouletabille & the Mystery of the Yellow Room; Rouletabille at Krupp's*
Richard Marsh. *The Complete Adventures of Judith Lee*
William Patrick Maynard. *The Terror of Fu Manchu; The Destiny of Fu Manchu*
Frank J. Morlock. *Sherlock Holmes: The Grand Horizontals; Sherlock Holmes vs Jack the Ripper*
Antonin Reschal. *The Adventures of Miss Boston*
P. de Wattyne & Y. Walter. *Sherlock Holmes vs. Fantômas*
David White. *Fantômas in America*
Pierre Yrondy. *The Adventures of Thérèse Arnaud*

SCREENPLAYS

Mike Baron. *The Iron Triangle*
Emma Bull & Will Shetterly. *Nightspeeder; War for the Oaks*
Gerry Conway & Roy Thomas. *Doc Dynamo*
Steve Englehart. *Majorca*
James Hudnall. *The Devastator*
Jean-Marc & Randy Lofficier. *Royal Flush*
J.-M. & R. Lofficier & Marc Agapit. *Despair*
J.-M. & R. Lofficier & Joël Houssin. *City*
Andrew Paquette. *Peripheral Vision*
Robert L. Robinson, Jr. *Judex*
R. Thomas, J. Hendler & L. Sprague de Camp. *Rivers of Time*